THE NOVEL AS AMERICAN SOCIAL HISTORY

RICHARD LOWITT, GENERAL EDITOR

JIMMIE HIGGINS

books, *Dragon's Teeth* (1942), received the Pulitzer prize, the only important award Sinclair ever received.

Sinclair was an ardent Socialist propagandist and a frequent candidate for public office. He wrote often for Socialist newspapers and magazines; indeed, before its publication as a book *The Jungle* appeared serially in *The Appeal to Reason,* a Socialist weekly newspaper of Girard, Kansas, with a circulation of over 500,000. In 1905 Sinclair was the prime mover in the founding of the Intercollegiate Socialist Society—Jack London was its first president—which quite successfully introduced socialist ideas to college students and older intellectuals. The following year Sinclair, with royalties earned from *The Jungle,* bought a former private school on the Palisades near Englewood, New Jersey, and there established a rather austere socialist commune of writers and artists. Sinclair Lewis, then a temporary dropout from Yale, was a member of the colony. A disastrous fire ended the experiment after only a few months.

The Socialist party before World War I had room in it for almost all varieties of Marxist and Marx-influenced beliefs. Although Sinclair was often pictured in the popular press as a wild and violent revolutionist, he was actually one of the party's moderates. His vision was a cooperative commonwealth in the United States, and he believed such a goal could be accomplished only gradually and through accepted democratic electoral processes. Consequently, he ran for public office on the Socialist ticket several times—for the House of Representatives in New Jersey in 1906 and again in 1920 in California, for the Senate in California in 1922, and for governor of California in 1926 and 1930.

Sinclair's most spectacular political campaign, however, came after he left the Socialist party. He joined the Democratic party of California in late 1933, leaving the Socialist party forever, and the following spring announced his candidacy for the Democratic gubernatorial nomination on a program he called EPIC (End Poverty in California). EPIC proposed a pension of $50 a month for poor people over sixty years old and a system of "production for use" workshops for the unemployed which would be partly producer co-ops and partly state socialist enterprises. The idea caught fire in the Great Depression's atmosphere of social discontent, and Sinclair won the primary. The general election campaign was exceptionally dirty. The Republican candidate received the support of wealthy Hollywood celebrities and of the influential *Los Angeles Times,* which asserted that if Sinclair was elected he would sovietize the state, introduce free love, and nationalize children. Even so, Sinclair ran well. If he had received all the votes of the third-party candidates he would have won.

As readers of *Jimmie Higgins* will readily see, Sinclair's attitude toward World War I was complex, ambivalent, vacillating, and often confused. Opposed to war and militarism in principle, he was appalled by the outbreak of war in 1914, especially by the fact that most European Socialists supported the war, and was strongly for American neutrality. In time, however, he came to regard a victory by the militarist German state as a worse alternative than American participation. When a Socialist party national convention in April 1917 adopted an antiwar position, which a majority of the membership later supported in a referendum, Sinclair left the organization he had been a part of for fifteen years. Lacking a Socialist outlet for his writings, he started his own magazine, calling it *Upton Sinclair's.* The magazine attained a circulation of 10,000 before he decided in December 1918 to abandon it after ten issues and to write again for Socialist journals.

Sinclair in time came to regret his support of the war, and historians and critics have interpreted *Jimmie Higgins* as his repudiation of it. But this is too simple an explanation.

As late as March 1919, when the novel appeared in book form, Sinclair had no regrets about his support of the American military effort in France. Indeed, his hero single-handedly turned the tide of battle against the Germans at Chateau Thierry and Belleau Wood! But the Allied expedition to Archangel, in which American troops participated (including, of course, Jimmie Higgins), was something else. Here the enemy was not German militarism but Russian Bolshevism. In September 1918, American troops joined the Allied expedition force at Archangel, and a practical state of war existed with the Bolshevik government. After the armistice Britain and the United States were reluctant to take military action against the Russians, as the French wished them to, but they did not withdraw from northern Russia entirely until October 1919. Sinclair was bitterly critical of the anti-Bolshevik military campaign. Like his character Jimmie, Sinclair was for the war in the West but against it in the East, "battered back and forth, like a tennis-ball between the two forces of Militarism and Revolution." Thinking the Bolsheviks were simply the Russian version of American Socialists, Sinclair at first was strongly for the Russian Revolution. As he learned more about the Bolsheviks he rejected the communist ideology completely, although some of his books were popular in the Soviet Union, where they were widely published in translation.

Sinclair wrote and published *Jimmie Higgins* in a most unusual maner. The novel appeared first in serial form in at least three periodicals: first, in his own magazine; then in his magazine and a Canadian newspaper simultaneously; and then in *The New Appeal,* a successor to the popular *Appeal to Reason* published by E. Haldeman-Julius, a radical journalist, to be sure, but also a slippery and opportunistic publisher who for a generation got out the immensely popular Little Blue Book series. A review of the dates of serial publication and the Sinclair correspondence in the Lilly Library of Indiana University reveals that the author actually published the first chapters of the novel before he had written the last ones, even indeed before the real events described in the last chapters had happened. The first chapters appeared in *Upton Sinclair's* in early September 1918, just as the news of the American expedition to Archangel was in the daily press. Sinclair apparently did not finish the last chapters until early 1919. Haldeman-Julius wrote Sinclair on January 19, 1919, only a matter of weeks before the story appeared in book form, expressing concern about getting enough *Jimmie Higgins* copy to keep the novel appearing continuously in his weekly newspaper.

Even the book publication was irregular. Soon after the armistice Sinclair sent a printed circular to the subscribers of the about-to-be-discontinued *Upton Sinclair's* announcing that he was himself publishing *Jimmie Higgins* in book form at the end of March 1919. He asked for prepublication purchases—"so that we may know how many to print, and so that delay may be avoided"—at a price of $1.70 for a single copy downward on a sliding scale to $.96 each for 100 copies "if you wish to get up a club of purchasers." He expected to reach only Socialists and other radicals with his edition but thought it important to reach the regular book market "so that non-Socialists may hear [Jimmie Higgins'] story. Accordingly I have arranged with a firm of publishers in New York to handle the book for the trade." Boni & Liveright brought out the trade edition (at $1.60 a copy) at about the same time Sinclair sent out his own edition, which was printed for him by the Western Printing & Lithographing Company of Racine, Wisconsin.

A close reading of *Jimmie Higgins*, with special attention to the details of the background elements, reveals a great deal to a student of the history of American radicalism. The portrayal of the spirit, the composition, and the day-to-day activities of a Socialist local is especially good. Sinclair knew Socialist party life at first hand and wrote about it accurately and sympathetically. Sinclair's choice of name for his central character reveals that he wanted the character to be symbolic of the Socialist common man, for the term Jimmie Higgins had long been used for the dedicated rank-and-filer who worked hard and without recognition. Eugene V. Debs, obviously the Candidate in the first chapter, wrote Sinclair in September 1918, after he had read the first serial installment, to thank him for the "generous and sympathetic treatment" of the Candidate and to commend him for focussing on Jimmie Higgins, "the chap who is always on the job; who does all the needed work that no one else will do; who never grumbles, never finds fault and is never discouraged. . . . The pure joy it gives him to serve the cause is his only reward."

Sinclair's novel is also especially useful for the validity with which it reveals American radicals' confusion about the war. Overwhelmed by the force of world events over which they had no control, events which did not precisely fit their ideology, American radicals were terribly torn about whether or not to support the war, especially after the Bolshevik revolution, the subsequent German campaign in Russia, the Treaty of Brest-Litovsk, and Wilson's announcement of American war aims. Even Debs, one of the most stalwart opponents of the war, wavered briefly in the spring of 1918 and called for a reexamination of the party's anti-war position. Only a fiction writer suffering such anxiety and pain in his soul could adequately describe the radical individual's crisis of conscience, and Sinclair, for all his artlessness, did it well.

Jimmie Higgins, like Sinclair's other works, is artless.

Sinclair sacrificed artistic quality for fast writing and topical timeliness. The sensitive reader will be annoyed by the author's repetition (for example, the too-frequent misunderstandings of Jimmie's wife's name as Eleeza Betooser); will blink with incredulity at some of the twists of plot, as when Lacey Granitch appears as a stretcher bearer in France; will smile at Sinclair's digression, in the book's final climactic paragraphs, into a brief lecture on his cranky diet ideas; and, in this day when novelists frequently use four-letter words, will be surprised by the prim propriety of speech of these working-class characters. Nevertheless, *Jimmie Higgins* has real power. It is powerful because it deals with important personal and social problems and is honestly and passionately written.

It is not possible to estimate accurately the number of readers *Jimmie Higgins* had because the commercial publisher's and Sinclair's sales records are not available. Apparently Boni & Liveright did not find it to be a sustained strong seller, for the firm reassigned the copyright to Sinclair in January 1921, less than two years after publication. But considering the circulations of the periodicals that published it serially in addition to the unknown number of book sales, it must have had upwards of 20,000 readers.

Its critical reception was generally favorable. Radical journals praised it, not surprisingly, and some conservative ones condemned it. A *New York Times* reviewer called *Jimmie Higgins* "propaganda," a criticism which Sinclair answered in a letter to the editor. The *Catholic World* said the book was filled with despicable "class hatred, irreligion and immorality." Critics who were not moved by political considerations were kind. English reviewers particularly were generous, the *Times Literary Supplement* calling it "an excellent piece of narrative work" and a reviewer for the *Athenaeum* describing it as "a readable story with several absorbing episodes." Several writers wrote Sinclair to compliment him on the book, among them Romain Rolland, Gertrude Atherton, George Sylvester Viereck, and George Sterling.

Despite the favorable reviews, *Jimmie Higgins* clearly is no literary masterpiece that will live through the ages. But it is a novel that illuminates an aspect of the nation's history that has been too much ignored, and is an important source for those who would understand the radical past.

JIMMIE HIGGINS

CHAPTER I

JIMMIE HIGGINS MEETS THE CANDIDATE

I

JIMMIE," said Lizzie, "couldn't we go see the pictures?"

And Jimmie set down the saucer of hot coffee which he was in the act of adjusting to his mouth, and stared at his wife. He did not say anything; in three years and a half as a married man he had learned that one does not always say everything that comes into one's mind. But he meditated on the abysses that lie between the masculine and feminine intellects. That it should be possible for any one to wish to see a movie idol leaping into second-story windows, or being pulled from beneath flying express-trains, on this day of destiny, this greatest crisis in history!

"You know, Lizzie," he said, patiently, "I've got to help at the Opera-house."

"But you've got all morning!"

"I know; but it'll take all day."

And Lizzie fell silent; for she too had learned much in three years and a half of married life. She had learned that workingmen's wives seldom get all they would like in this world; also that to have a propagandist for a husband is not the worst fate that may befall. After all, he might have been giving his time and money to drink, or to other women; he might have been dying of a cough, like the man next door. If one could not have a bit of pleasure on a Sunday afternoon—well, one might sigh, but not too loud.

Jimmie began telling all the things that had to be done that Sunday morning and afternoon. They seemed to Lizzie exactly like the things that were done on other occasions before meetings. To be sure, this was bigger—it was in the Opera-house, and all the stores had cards in the windows, with a picture of the Candidate who was to be the orator of the occasion. But it was hard for Lizzie to understand the difference between this Candidate and other candidates—none of whom ever got elected! Lizzie would truly rather have stayed at home, for she did not understand English very well when it was shouted from a platform, and with a lot of long words; but she knew that Jimmie was trying to educate her, and being a woman, she was educated to this extent—she knew the way to hold onto her man.

Jimmie had just discovered a new solution of the problem of getting the babies to meetings; and Lizzie knew that he was tremendously proud of this discovery. So long as there had been only one baby, Jimmie had carried it. When there had come a second, Lizzie had helped. But now there were three, the total weight of them something over sixty pounds; and the street-car line was some distance away, and also it hurt Jimmie in his class-consciousness to pay twenty cents to a predatory corporation. They had tried the plan of paying something to a neighbour to stay with the babies; but the first they tried was a young girl who got tired and went away, leaving the little ones to howl their heads off; and the second was a Polish lady whom they found in a drunken stupor on their return.

But Jimmie was determined to go to meetings, and determined that Lizzie should go along. It was one of the curses of the system, he said, that it deprived working-class women of all chance for self-improvement. So he had paid a visit to the "Industrial Store," a junk-shop maintained by the Salvation Army, and for fifteen cents he had obtained a marvellous broad baby-carriage for twins, all finished in shiny black enamel. One side of it was busted, but Jimmie had fixed that with some wire, and by careful packing had shown that it was possible to stow the youngsters in it—Jimmie Junior and Pete side by side, and the new baby at the foot.

The one trouble was that Jimmie Junior couldn't keep his feet still. He could never keep any part of him still, the little jack-in-the-box. Here he was now, tearing about the kitchen, pursuing the ever-receding tail of the newest addition to the family, a half-starved cur who had followed Jimmie in from the street, and had been fed into a semblance of reality. From this treasure a bare, round tail hung out behind in tantalising fashion; Jimmie Junior, always imagining he could catch it, was toddling round and round and round the kitchen-table, clutching out in front of him, laughing so that after a while he sat down from sheer exhaustion.

And Jimmie Senior watched enraptured. Say, but he was a buster! Did you ever see a twenty-seven months old kid that could get over the ground like that? Or make a louder noise? This last because Jimmie Junior had tried to take a short cut through the kitchen range and failed. Lizzie swooped down, clasping him to her broad bosom, and pouring out words of comfort in Bohemian. As Jimmie Senior did not understand any of these words, he took advantage of the confusion to get his coat and cap and hustle off to the Opera-house, full of fresh determination. For, you see, whenever a Socialist looks at his son, or even thinks of his son, he is hotter for his job of propagandist. Let the world be changed soon, so that the little fellows may be spared those sufferings and humiliations which have fallen to the lot of their parents!

II

"Comrade Higgins, have you got a hammer?" It was Comrade Schneider who spoke, and he did not take the trouble to come down from the ladder, where he was holding up a streamer of bunting, but waited comfortably for the hammer to be fetched to him. And scarcely had the fetcher started to climb before there came the voice of a woman from across the stage: "Comrade Higgins, has the Ypsel banner come?" And from the rear part of the hall came the rotund voice of fat Comrade Rapinsky: "Comrade Higgins, will you bring up an extra table for the literature?" And from the second tier box Comrade Mary Allen spoke: "While you're downstairs, Comrade Higgins, would you mind telephoning and making sure the Reception Committee knows about the change in the train-time?"

So it went; and Jimmie ran about the big hall with his face red and perspiring; for this was mid-summer, and no breeze came through the windows of the Leesville Opera-house, and when you got high up on the walls to tie the streamers of red bunting, you felt as if you were being baked. But the streamers had to be tied, and likewise the big red flag over the stage, and the banner of the Karl Marx Verein, and the banner of the Ypsels, or Young People's Socialist League of Leesville, and the banner of the Machinists' Union, Local 4717, and of the Carpenters' Union, District 529, and of the Workers' Co-operative Society. And because Comrade Higgins never questioned anybody's right to give him orders, and always did everything with a cheerful grin, people had got into the habit of regarding him as the proper person for tedious and disagreeable tasks.

He had all the more on his hands at present, because the members of this usually efficient local were half-distracted, like a nest of ants that have been dug out with a shovel. The most faithful ones showed a tendency to forget what they were doing, and to gather in knots to talk about the news which had come over the cables and had been published in that morning's paper. Jimmie Higgins would have liked to hear what the rest had to say; but somebody had to keep at work, for the local was in the hole nearly three hundred dollars for to-night's affair, and it must succeed, even though half the civilised world had gone suddenly insane. So Jimmie continued to climb step-ladders and tie bunting.

When it came to lunch-time, and the members of the Decorations Committee were going out, it suddenly occurred to one of them that the drayman who was to bring the literature might arrive while there was nobody to receive it. So Comrade Higgins was allowed to wait during the lunch hour. There was a plausible excuse—he was on the Literature Committee; indeed, he was on every committee where hard work was involved—the committee to distribute leaflets announcing the meeting, the committee to interview the labour unions and urge them to sell tickets, the committee to take up a collection at the meeting. He was not on those committees which involved honour and edification, such as, for example, the committee to meet the Candidate at the depot and escort him to the Opera-house. But then it would never have occurred to Jimmie that he had any place on such a committee; for he was just an ignorant fellow, a machinist, undersized and undernourished, with bad teeth and roughened hands, and no gifts or graces of any sort to recommend him; while on the Reception Committee were a lawyer and a prosperous doctor and the secretary of the Carpet-weavers' Union, all people who wore good clothes and had education, and knew how to talk to a Candidate.

So Jimmie waited; and when the drayman came, he opened up the packages of books and pamphlets and laid them out in neat piles on the literature tables, and hung several of the more attractive ones on the walls behind the tables; so, of course, Comrade Mabel Smith, who was chairman of the Literature Committee, was greatly pleased when she came back from lunch. And then came the members of the German Liederkranz, to rehearse the programme they were to give; and Comrade Higgins would have liked first rate to sit and listen, but somebody discovered the need of glue, and he chased out to find a drug-store that was open on Sunday.

Later on there was a lull, and Jimmie realised that he was hungry. He examined the contents of his pockets and found that he had seventeen cents. It was a long way to his home, so he would step around the corner and have a cup of coffee and a couple of "sinkers" at "Tom's." He first conscientiously asked if anybody needed anything, and Comrade Mabel Smith told him to hurry back to help her put out the leaflets on the seats, and Comrade Meissner would need help in arranging the chairs on the stage.

III

When you went from the Leesville Opera-house and turned West on Main Street, you passed Heinz's Café, which was a "swell" eating-place, and not for Jimmie; and then the "Bijou Nickelodeon," with a mechanical piano in the entrance; and the "Bon Marché Shoe Store," which was always having a fire-sale or a removal sale or a bankruptcy clearing-out; and then Lipsky's "Picture Palace," with a brown and yellow cowboy galloping away with a red and yellow maiden in his arms; then Harrod's "Fancy Grocery" on the corner. And in each of these places there was a show-card in the window, with a picture of the Candidate, and the announcement that on Sunday evening, at eight o'clock, he would speak at the Leesville Opera-house on "War, the Reason and the Remedy." Jimmie Higgins looked at the cards, and a dignified yet joyful pride stirred in his bosom; for all of them were there because he, Jimmie, had interviewed the proprietors and obtained their more or less reluctant consent.

Jimmie knew that on this same Sunday, in cities all over Germany, Austria, Belgium, France and England, the workers were gathering by millions and tens of millions, to protest against the red horror of war being let loose over their heads. And in America too—a call would go from the new world to the old, that the workers should rise and carry out their pledge to prevent this crime against mankind. He, Jimmie Higgins, had no voice that anybody would heed; but he had helped to bring the people of his city to hear a man who had a voice, and who would show the meaning of this world-crisis to the working-people.

It was the party's Candidate for President. At this time only congressional elections were pending, but this man had been Candidate for President so often that every one thought of him in that rôle. You might say that each of his campaigns lasted four years; he travelled from one end of the land to the other, and counted by the millions those who heard his burning, bitter message. It had chanced that the day which the War-lords and Money-lords of Europe had chosen to drive their slaves to slaughter was the day on which the Candidate had been scheduled to speak in the Leesville Opera-house. No wonder the Socialists of the little inland city were stirred!

Jimmie Higgins turned into "Tom's Buffeteria," and greeted the proprietor, and seated himself on a stool in front of the counter, and called for coffee, and helped himself to "sinkers"—which might have been called "life-preservers," they were blown so full of air. He filled his mouth, at the same time looking up to make sure that Tom had not removed the card announcing the meeting; for Tom was a Catholic, and one of the reasons that Jimmie went to his place was to involve him and his patrons in arguments over exploitation, unearned increment and surplus value.

But before a discussion could be started, it chanced that Jimmie glanced about. In the back part of the room were four little tables, covered with oil-cloth, where "short orders" were served; and at one of those tables a man was seated. Jimmie took a glance at him, and started so that he almost spilled his coffee. Impossible; and yet—surely—who could mistake that face? The face of a mediæval churchman, lean, ascetic, but with a modern touch of kindliness, and a bald dome on top like a moon rising over the prairie. Jimmie started, then stared at the picture of the Candidate which crowned the shelf of pies. He turned to the man again; and the man glanced up, and his eyes met Jimmie's, with their expression of amazement and awe. The whole story was there, not to be misread—especially by a Candidate who travels about the country making speeches, and being recognised every hour or so from his pictures which have preceded him. A smile came to his face, and Jimmie set down the coffee-cup from one trembling hand and the "sinker" from the other, and rose from his stool.

IV

Jimmie would not have had the courage to advance, save for the other man's smile—a smile that was weary, but candid and welcoming. "Howdy do, Comrade?" said the man. He held out his hand, and the moment of this clasp was the nearest to heaven that Jimmie Higgins had ever known.

When he was able to find his voice, it was only to exclaim, "You wasn't due till five-forty-two!"

As if the Candidate had not known that! He explained that he had missed his sleep the night before, and had come on ahead so as to snatch a bit during the day. "I see," said Jimmie; and then, "I knowed you by your picture."

"Yes?" said the other, patiently.

And Jimmie groped round in his addled head for something really worth while. "You'll want to see the Committee?"

"No," said the other, "I want to finish this first." And he took a sip from a glass of milk, and a bite out of a sandwich, and chewed.

So utterly rattled was Jimmie he sat there like a numb-skull, unable to find a word, while the man finished his repast. When it was over, Jimmie said again—he could do no better—"You want to see the Committee?"

"No," was the reply, "I want to sit here—and perhaps talk to you, Comrade—Comrade—?"

"Higgins," said Jimmie.

"Comrade Higgins—that is, if you have time."

"Oh, sure!" exclaimed Jimmie. "I got all the time there is. But the Committee——"

"Never mind the Committee, Comrade. Do you know how many Committees I have met on this trip?"

Jimmie did not know; nor did he have the courage to ask.

"Probably you never thought how it is to be a Candidate," continued the other. "You go from place to place, and make the same speech every night, and it seems as if you slept in the same hotel every night, and almost as if you met the same Committee. But you have to remember that your speech is new to each audience, and you have to make it as if you had never made it before; also you have to remember that the Committee is made up of devoted comrades who are giving everything for the cause, so you don't tell them that they are just like every other committee, or that you are tired to death, or maybe have a headache——"

Jimmie sat, gazing in awe-stricken silence. Not being a man of reading, he had never heard of "the head that wears a crown." This was his first glimpse into the soul of greatness.

The Candidate went on: "And then, too, Comrade, there's the news from Europe. I want a little time. I can't bring myself to face it!"

His voice had grown sombre, and to Jimmie, gazing at him, it seemed that all the sorrows of the world were in his tired grey eyes. "Perhaps I'd better go," said Jimmie.

"No, no," replied the other, with quick self-recovery. He looked and saw that Jimmie had forgotten his meal. "Bring your things over here," he said; and the other fetched his cup and saucer and plate, and gulped the rest of his "sinkers" under the Candidate's eyes.

"I oughtn't to talk," said the latter. "You see how hoarse I am. But you talk. Tell me about the local, and how things are going here."

So Jimmie summoned his courage. It was the one thing he could really talk about, the thing of which his mind and soul were full. Leesville was a typical small manufacturing city, with a glass bottle works, a brewery, a carpet-factory, and the big Empire Machine Shops, at which Jimmie himself spent sixty-three hours of his life each week. The workers were asleep, of course; but still, you couldn't complain, the movement was growing. The local boasted of a hundred and twenty members, though of course only about thirty of them could be counted on for real work. That was the case everywhere, the Candidate put in—it was always a few who made the sacrifice and kept things alive.

Then Jimmie went on to tell about to-night's meeting, the preparations they had made, the troubles they had had. The police had suddenly decided to enforce the law against delivering circulars from house to house; though they allowed Isaac's "Emporium" to use this method of announcement. The Leesville "Herald" and "Evening Courier" were enthusiastic for the police action; if you couldn't give out circulars, obviously you would have to advertise in these papers. The Candidate smiled—he knew about American police officials, and also about American journalism.

Jimmie had been laid off for a couple of days at the shop, and he told how he had put this time to good use, getting announcements of the meeting into the stores. There was an old Scotchman in a real estate office just across the way. "Git oot!" he said. "So I thought I'd better git oot!" said Jimmie. And then, taking his life into his hands, he had gone into the First National Bank. There was a gentleman walking across the floor, and Jimmie went up to him and held out one of the placards with the picture of the Candidate. "Would you be so good as to put this in your window?" he inquired; and the other looked at it coldly. Then he smiled—he was a good sport, apparently. "I don't think my customers would patronise your business," he said; but Jimmie went at him to take some tickets and learn about Socialism—and would you believe it, he had actually shelled out a dollar! "I found out afterwards that it was Ashton Chalmers, the president of the bank!" said Jimmie. "I'd a' been scared, if I'd a' known."

He had not meant to talk about himself; he was just trying to entertain a tired Candidate, to keep him from brooding over a world going to war. But the Candidate, listening, found tears trying to steal into his eyes. He watched the figure before him—a bowed, undernourished little man, with one shoulder lower than the other, a straggly brown moustache stained with coffee, and stumpy black teeth, and gnarled hands into which the dirt and grease were ground so deeply that washing them would obviously be a waste of time. His clothes were worn and shapeless, his celluloid collar was cracked and his necktie was almost a rag. You would never have looked at such a man twice on the street—and yet the Candidate saw in him one of those obscure heroes who are making a movement which is to transform the world.

V

"Comrade Higgins," said the Candidate, after a bit, "let's you and me run away."

Jimmie looked startled. "How?"

"I mean from the Committee, and from the meeting, and from everything." And then, seeing the dismay in the other's face: "I mean, let's take a walk in the country."

"Oh!" said Jimmie.

"I see it through the windows of the railroad-cars, but I don't set foot on it for months at a time. And I was brought up in the country. Were you?"

"I was brought up everywhere," said the little machinist.

They got up, and paid each their ten cents to the proprietor of the "Buffeteria." Jimmie could not resist the temptation to introduce his hero, and show a pious Catholic that a Socialist Candidate had neither hoofs nor horns. The Candidate was used to being introduced for that purpose, and had certain spontaneous and cordial words which he had said not less than ten thousand times before; with the result that the pious Catholic gave his promise to come to the meeting that night.

They went out; and because some member of the Committee might be passing on Main Street, Jimmie took his hero by an alley into a back street; and they walked past the glass-factory, which to the outsider was a long board fence, and across the Atlantic Western railroad tracks, and past the carpet-factory, a huge four-story box made of bricks; after which the rows of wooden shacks began to thin out, and there were vacant lots and ash-heaps, and at last the beginning of farms.

The Candidate's legs were long, and Jimmie's, alas, were short, so he had almost to run. The sun blazed down on them, and sweat, starting from the Candidate's bald head, stole under the band of his straw hat and down to his wilting collar; so he took off his coat and hung it over his arm, and went on, faster than ever. Jimmie raced beside him, afraid to speak, for he divined that the Candidate was brooding over the world-calamity, the millions of young men marching out to slaughter. On the placards which Jimmie had been distributing in Leesville, there were two lines about the Candidate, written by America's favourite poet:

> As warm heart as ever beat
> Betwixt here and judgment seat.

So they went on for perhaps an hour, by which time they were really in the country. They came to a bridge which crossed the river Lee, and there the Candidate suddenly stopped, and stood looking at the water sliding below him, and at the vista through which it wound, an avenue of green trees with stretches of pasture and cattle grazing. "That looks fine," he said. "Let's go down." So they climbed a fence, and made their way along the river for a distance, until a turn of the stream took them out of sight of the road.

There they sat on a shelving bank, and mopped the perspiration from their foreheads and necks, and gazed into the rippling current. You couldn't exactly say it was crystal clear, for when there is a town every ten miles or so along a stream, with factories pouring various kinds of chemicals into it, the job becomes too much for the restoring forces of Mother Nature. But it would take a dirty stream indeed not to look inviting in midsummer after a four mile walk. So presently the Candidate turned to Jimmie, with a mischievous look upon his face. "Comrade Higgins, were you ever in a swimmin' hole?"

"Sure I was!" said Jimmie.

"Where?"

"Everywhere. I was on the road off an' on ten years—till I got married."

"Well," said the Candidate, still smiling, "what do you say?"

"I say sure!" replied Jimmie.

He was almost beside himself with awe, at this unbelievable strange fortune, this real comradeship with the hero of his dreams. To Jimmie this man had been a disembodied intelligence, a dispenser of proletarian inspiration, a supernatural being who went about the country standing upon platforms and swaying the souls of multitudes. It had never occurred to Jimmie that he might have a bare body, and might enjoy splashing about in cool water like a boy playing "hookey" from school. The saying is that familiarity breeds contempt, but for Jimmie it bred rapture.

VI

They walked home again, more slowly. The Candidate asked Jimmie about his life, and Jimmie told the story of a Socialist—not one of the leaders, the "intellectuals," but of the "rank and file." Jimmie's father was a workingman out of a job, who had left his family before Jimmie had joined it; Jimmie's mother had died three years later, so he did not remember her, nor could he recall a word of the foreign language he had spoken at home, nor did he even know what the language was. He had been taken in charge by the city, and farmed out to a negro woman, who had eight miserable starvelings under her care, feeding them on gruel and water, and not even giving them a blanket in winter. You might not think that possible—

"I know America," put in the Candidate.

Jimmie went on. At nine he had been boarded with a woodsaw man, who worked him sixteen hours a day and beat him in addition; so Jimmie had skipped out, and for ten years had lived the life of a street waif in the cities and a hobo on the road. He had learned a bit about machinery, helping in a garage, and then, in a rush-time, he had got a job in the Empire Machine Shops. He had stayed in Leesville, because he had got married; he had met his wife in a brothel, and she had wanted to quit the life, and they had taken a chance together.

"I don't tell that to everybody," said Jimmie. "You know—they mightn't unnerstand. But I don't mind you knowin'."

"Thank you," replied the Candidate, and put his hand on Jimmie's shoulder. "Tell me how you became a Socialist."

There was nothing special about that, was the answer. There had been a fellow in the shop who was always "chewing the rag"; Jimmie had laughed at him—for his life had made him suspicious of everybody, and if there was any sort of politician, it was just another scheme of somebody to wear a white collar and live off the workers. But the fellow had kept pegging away; and once Jimmie had been laid off for a couple of months, and the family had near starved, and that had given him time to think, and also the inclination. The fellow had come along with some papers, and Jimmie had read them, and it dawned upon him that here was a movement of his fellow-workers to put an end to their torments.

"How long ago was that?" asked the Candidate, and Jimmie

answered three years. "And you haven't lost your enthusiasm?" This with an intensity that surprised Jimmie. No, he answered, he was not that kind. Whatever happened, he would keep pegging away at the task of freeing labour. He would not see the New Day, perhaps, but his children would see it; and a fellow would work like the devil to save his children.

So they came to the city; and the Candidate pressed Jimmie's arm. "Comrade," he said, "I want to tell you how much good this little trip has done me. I owe you a debt of gratitude."

"Me?" exclaimed Jimmie.

"You have given me fresh hope and courage, and at a time when I felt beaten. I got into town this morning, and I'd had no sleep, and I tried to get some in the hotel and couldn't, because of the horror that's happening. I wrote a dozen telegrams and sent them off, and then I was afraid to go back to the hotel-room, because I knew I'd only lie awake all afternoon. But now—I remember that our movement is rooted in the hearts of the people!"

Jimmie was trembling. But all he could say was: "I wisht I could do it every Sunday."

"So do I," said the Candidate.

VII

They walked down Main Street, and some ways ahead they saw a crowd gathered, filling the side-walk beyond the curb. "What is that?" asked the Candidate, and Jimmie answered that it was the office of the "Herald." There must be some news.

The other hastened his steps; and Jimmie, striding alongside, fell silent again, knowing that the gigantic burden and woe of the world was falling upon his hero's shoulders once more. They came to the edge of the crowd, and saw a bulletin in front of the newspaper office. But it was too far away for them to read. "What is it?" they asked.

"It says the Germans are going to march into Belgium. And they've shot a lot of Socialists in Germany."

"What?" And the Candidate's hand clutched Jimmie's arm.

"That's what it says."

"My God!" exclaimed the man. And he began pushing his

way into the crowd, with Jimmie in his wake. They got to the bulletin, and stood reading the type-written words—a bare announcement that more than a hundred leading German Socialists had been executed for efforts to prevent mobilisation. They continued staring, until people pushing behind them caused them to draw back. Outside the throng they stood, the Candidate gazing into space, and Jimmie gazing at the Candidate, both of them dumb. It was a fact that they could not have been more shocked if the news had referred to the members of Local Leesville of the Socialist Party of America.

The pain in the Candidate's face was so evident that Jimmie groped about in his head for something comforting to say. "At least they done what they could," he whispered.

The other suddenly burst forth: "They are heroes! They have made the name Socialist sacred forever!" He rushed on, as if he were making a speech—so strong becomes a life-time habit. "They have written their names at the very top of humanity's roll of honour! It doesn't make any difference what happens after this, Comrade—the movement has vindicated itself! All the future will be changed because of this event!"

He began to walk down the street, talking more to himself than to Jimmie. He was borne away on the wings of his vision; and his companion was so thrilled that he honestly did not know where he was. Afterwards, when he looked back upon this scene, it remained the most wonderful event of his life; he told the story, sooner or later, to every Socialist he met.

Presently the Candidate stopped. "Comrade," he said, "I must go to the hotel. I want to write some telegrams. You explain to the Committee—I'd rather not see any one till time for the meeting. I'll find the way myself."

CHAPTER II

JIMMIE HIGGINS HEARS A SPEECH

I

IN the Opera-house were gathered Comrade Mabel Smith and Comrade Meissner and Comrade Goldstein, the secretary of the Ypsels, and the three members of the Reception Committee —Comrade Norwood, the rising young lawyer, Comrade Dr. Service, and Comrade Schultze of the Carpet-weavers' Union. To them rushed the breathless Jimmie. "Have you heard the news?"

"What is it?"

"A hundred Socialist leaders shot in Germany!"

"Herr Gott!" cried Comrade Schultze, in horror; and every one turned instinctively, for they knew how this came home to him—he had a brother who was a Socialist editor in Leipzig, and who was liable for the mobilisation.

"Where did you see it?" cried Schultze; and Jimmie told what he knew. And then what a clamour broke forth! Others were called from the back part of the hall, and came running, and there were questions and cries of dismay. Here, too, it was as if the crime had been committed against Local Leesville —so completely did they feel themselves one with the victims. In a town where there was a brewery, needless to say there were German workers a-plenty; but even had this not been so, the feeling would have been the same, for the Socialists of the world were one, the soul of the movement was its internationalism. The Candidate, discovering that Jimmie was a Socialist, had asked and received no further introduction, but had been instantly his friend; and so it would have been with a comrade from Germany, Japan, or the heart of Africa—he might not have known another word of English, the word "Socialist" would have sufficed.

It was a long time before they thought of any other matter; but finally some one referred to the trouble which had fallen upon the local—the Candidate had not showed up. And Jimmie exclaimed, "Why, he's here!" And instantly all turned upon him. Where? When? How?

"He came this morning."

"And why didn't you let us know?" It was Comrade Dr. Service of the Reception Committee who spoke, and with a decided sharpness in his tone.

"He didn't want anybody to know," said Jimmie.

"Did he want us to go to the train and think he had failed us?"

Sure enough, it was after train-time! Jimmie had entirely forgotten both the train and the committee, and now he had not the grace to hide his offence. All he could do was to tell his story—how he had spent the afternoon walking in the country with the Candidate, and how they had gone in swimming, and how they had got the news from the bulletin-board, and how the Candidate had acted and what he had said. Poor Jimmie never doubted but that his own thrill was shared by all the others; and at the next regular meeting of the local, when Comrade Dr. Service sat down hard on some proposition which Jimmie had ventured to make, the little machinist had not the least idea what he had done to deserve the snub. He was lacking in worldly sense, he did not understand that a prosperous physician, who comes into the movement out of pure humanitarianism, contributing his prestige and his wealth to the certain detriment of his social and business interests, is entitled to a certain deference from the Jimmie Higginses, and even from a Candidate!

II

You might have thought that Jimmie would be tired; but this was a day on which the flesh had no claims. First he helped Comrade Mabel in depositing upon every seat a leaflet containing a letter from the local candidate for Congress; then he rushed away to catch a street-car, and spent his last nickel to get to his home and keep his engagement with Lizzie. He would not make with her the mistake he had made with the Committee, you bet!

He found that Lizzie had faithfully carried out her part of the bargain. The three babies were done up in bright-coloured calico dresses; she had spent the morning in washing and ironing these garments—also her own dress, which was half red and half green, and of generous, almost crinoline proportions. Lizzie herself was built on that scale, with broad hips and bosom, big brown eyes and heavy dark hair. She was a fine strong woman when she had shed her bedraggled house gown, and Jimmie was proud of his capability as a chooser of wives. It was no small feat to find a good woman, and to recognise her, where Jimmie had found Lizzie. She was five years older than he, a Bohemian, having been brought to America when she was a baby. Her former name—you could hardly call it her "maiden" name, considering the circumstances—was Elizabeth Huszar, which she pronounced so that for a long time Jimmie had understood it to be Eleeza Betooser.

Jimmie snatched a bite of bread and drank a cup of metallic tasting tea, and packed the family into the baby-carriage, and trudged the mile and a half to the centre of the city. When they arrived, Lizzie took the biggest child, and Jimmie the other two, and so they trudged into the Opera-house. On this hot night it was like holding three stoves in your arms, and if the babies woke up and began to cry, the parents would have the painful choice of missing something, or else facing the disgusted looks of every one about them. In Belgium, at the "People's House," the Socialists maintained a *creche,* but the American movement had not yet discovered that useful institution.

Already the hall was half full, and a stream of people pouring in. Jimmie got himself and family seated, and then turned his eager eyes proudly to survey the scene. The would-be-congressman's circulars which he had placed in the seats were now being read by the sitters; the banners he had so laboriously hung were resplendent on the walls; there was a pitcher of ice water on the speaker's table, and a bouquet of flowers and a gavel for the chairman; the seats in the rear of the platform for the Liederkranz were neatly ranged, most of them already occupied by solid German figures topped by rosy German faces: to each detail of which achievements Jimmie had lent a hand. He had a pride of possession in this great buzzing throng, and in the debt they owed to him. They had no idea of it, of course;

the boobs, they thought that a meeting like this just grew out of nothing! They paid their ten cents—twenty-five cents for reserved seats—and imagined that covered everything, with perhaps even a rake-off for somebody! They would grumble, wondering why the Socialists persisted in charging admission for their meetings—why they could not let people in free as the Democrats and Republicans did. They would go to Democratic and Republican meetings, and enjoy the brass-band and the fireworks, pyrotechnical and oratorical—never dreaming it was all a snare paid for by their exploiters!

Well, they would learn about it to-night! Jimmie thought of the Candidate, and how he would impress this man and that. For Jimmie knew scores who had got tickets, and he peered about after this one and that, and gave them a happy nod from behind his barricade of babies. Then, craning his neck to look behind him, suddenly Jimmie gave a start. Coming down the aisle was Ashton Chalmers, president of the First National Bank of Leesville; and with him—could it be possible?—old man Granitch, owner of the huge Empire Machine Shops where Jimmie worked! The little machinist found himself shaking with excitement as these two tall forms strode past him down the aisle. He gave Lizzie a nudge with his elbow and whispered into her ear; and all around was a buzz of whispers—for, of course, everybody knew these two mighty men, the heads of the "invisible government" of Leesville. They had come to find out what their subjects were thinking! Well, they would get it straight!

III

The big hall was full, and the aisles began to jam, and then the police closed the doors—something which Jimmie took as part of the universal capitalist conspiracy. The audience began to chafe; until at last the chairman walked out upon the stage, followed by several important persons who took front seats. The singers stood up, and the leader waved his wand, and forth came the Marseillaise: a French revolutionary hymn, sung in English by a German organisation—there was Internationalism for you! With full realisation of the solemnity of this world-crisis, they sang as if they hoped to be heard in Europe.

And then rose the Chairman—Comrade Dr. Service. He was

a fine, big figure of a man, with grey moustache and beard trimmed to a point; his swelling chest was covered by clean white linen and tight-fitting broad-cloth, and he made a most imposing chairman, reflecting credit on the movement. He cleared his throat, and told them that they had come that evening to listen to one of America's greatest orators, and that therefore he, the Chairman, would not make a speech; after which he proceeded to make a speech. He told them what a grave hour this was, and how the orator would tell them its meaning; after which he proceeded to tell most of the things which the orator would tell. This was a weakness of Comrade Dr. Service —but one hesitated to point it out to him, because of his black broad-cloth suit and his imposing appearance, and the money he had put up to pay for the hall.

At last, however, he called on the Liederkranz again, and a quartette sang a German song and then an encore. And then came Comrade Gerrity, the hustling young insurance-agent who was organiser for the local, and whose task it was to make a "collection speech." He had humorous ways of extracting money—"Here I am again!" he began, and everybody smiled, knowing his bag of tricks. While he was telling his newest funny story, Jimmie was unloading the littlest infant into Lizzie's spare arm, and laying the other on the seat with its head against her knee, and getting himself out into the aisle, hat in hand and ready for business; and as soon as the organiser ceased and the Liederkranz resumed, Jimmie set to work gathering the coin. His territory was the reserved-seat section up in front, where sat the two mighty magnates. Jimmie's knees went weak, but he did his duty, and was tickled to see each of the pair drop a coin into the hat, to be used in overthrowing their power in Leesville!

IV

The hats were taken to the box-office and emptied, and the collection-takers and the Liederkranz singers resumed their seats. An expectant hush fell—and then at last there strode out on the stage the Candidate. What a storm broke out! Men cheered and clapped and shouted. He took his seat modestly; but as the noise continued, he was justified in assuming that it was meant for him, and he rose and bowed; as it still continued.

he bowed again, and then again. It had been the expectation of Comrade Dr. Service to come forward and say that, of course, it was not necessary for any one to introduce the speaker of the evening; but the audience, as if it had read the worthy doctor's intention, kept on applauding, until the Candidate himself advanced, and raised his hand, and began his speech.

He did not stop for any oratorical preliminaries. This, he said—and his voice trembled with emotion—was the solemnest hour that men had ever faced on earth. That day on the bulletin-board of their local newspaper he had read tidings which had moved him as he had never before been moved in his life, which had almost deprived him of the power to walk upon a stage and address an audience. Perhaps they had not heard the news; he told it to them, and there sprang from the audience a cry of indignation.

Yes, they might well protest, said the speaker; nowhere on all the bloody pages of history could you find a crime more revolting than this! The masters of Europe had gone mad in their lust for power; they had called down the vengeance of mankind upon their crowned and coronetted heads. Here tonight he would tell them—and the speaker's hoarse and raucous voice mounted to a shout of rage—he would tell them that in signing the death-warrant of those heroic martyrs, they had sealed the doom of their own order, they had torn out the foundation-stones from the structure of capitalist society! The speaker's voice seemed to lift the audience from its seats, and the last words of the sentence were drowned in a tumult of applause.

Silence fell again, and the man went on. He had peculiar mannerisms on the platform. His lanky form was never still for an instant. He hurried from one end of the stage to the other; he would crouch and bend as if he were going to spring upon the audience, a long, skinny finger would be shaken before their faces, or pointed as if to drive his words into their hearts. His speech was a torrent of epigram, sarcasm, invective. He was bitter; if you knew nothing about the man or his cause, you would find this repellent and shocking. You had to know what his life had been—an unceasing conflict with oppression; he had got his Socialist education in jail, where he had been sent for trying to organise the wage-slaves of a gigantic corporation. His rage was the rage of a tender-hearted poet, a lover of children and of Nature, driven mad by the sight of torment wantonly inflicted. And if ever he had seemed to you an extremist, too angry to be excused, here to-night he had his vindication, here to-night you saw him as a prophet. For now the master-class had torn the mask from its face, and revealed to the whole world what were its moral standards! At last men saw their rulers face to face!

They had plunged mankind into a pit of lunacy. "They call it war," cried the speaker; "but I call it murder." And he went on to picture to them what was happening in Europe at that hour—he brought the awful nightmare before their eyes, he showed them homes blown to pieces, cities given to the flames, the bodies of men pierced by bullets or torn to fragments by shells. He pictured a bayonet plunged into the abdomen of a man; he made you see the ghastly deed, and feel its shuddering wickedness. Men and women and children sat spell-bound; and for once no man could say aloud or feel in his heart that the pictures of a Socialist agitator were overdrawn—no, not even Ashton Chalmers, president of the First National Bank of Leesville, or old Abel Granitch, proprietor of the Empire Machine Shops!

V

And what was the cause of this blackest of calamities? The speaker went on to show that the determining motive was not racial jealousy, but commercial greed. The fountain-head of the war was world-capitalism, clamouring for markets, seeking to get rid of its surplus products, to keep busy its hordes of wage-slaves at home. He analysed the various factors; and now, with the shadow of the European storm over their heads—now at last men and women would listen, they would realise that the matter concerned them. He warned them—let them not think that they were safe from the hoofs of this war-monster, just because they were three thousand miles away! Capitalism was a world phenomenon, and all the forces of parasitism and exploitation which had swept Europe into this tragedy were active here in America. The money-masters, the profit-seekers, would leap to take advantage of the collapse over the seas; there would be jealousies, disputes—let the audience understand, once for all, that if world-capitalism did not make this a world-war, it would be only because the workers of America took warning, and made their preparations to frustrate the conspiracy.

This was what he had come for, this was the heart of his message. Many of those who listened were refugees from the old world, having fled its oppressions and enslavements. He pleaded with them now, as a man whose heart was torn by more suffering than he could bear—let there be one part of the fair garden of earth into which the demons of destruction might not break their way! Let them take warning in time, let them organise and establish their own machinery of information and propaganda—so that when the crisis came, when the money-masters of America sounded the war-drums, there might be—not the destruction and desolation which these masters willed, but the joy and freedom of the Co-operative Commonwealth!

"How many years we Socialists have warned you!" he cried. "But you have doubted us, you have believed what your exploiters have told you! And now, in this hour of crisis, you look at Europe and discover who are the real friends of humanity, of civilisation. What voice comes over the seas, protesting against war? The Socialist voice, and the Socialist voice alone! And to-night, once more, you hear it in this hall! You men and women of America, and you exiles from all corners of the world—make this pledge with me—make it now, before it is too late, and stand by it when the hour of crisis comes! Swear it by the blood of our martyred heroes, those slaughtered German Socialists—swear that come what will, and when and how it will, that no power on earth or in hell beneath the earth shall draw you into this fratricidal war! Make this resolution, send this message to all the nations of the earth—that the men of all nations and all races are your brothers, and that never will you consent to shed their blood. If the money-masters and the exploiters want war, let them have it, but let it be among themselves! Let them take the bombs and shells they have made and go out against one another! Let them blow their own class to pieces—but let them not seek to lure the working-people into their quarrels!"

Again and again, in answer to such exhortations, the audience broke out into shouts of applause. Men raised their hands in solemn pledge; and the Socialists among them went home from the meeting with a new gravity in their faces, a new consecration in their hearts. They had made a vow, and they would keep it—yes, even though it meant sharing the fate of their heroic German comrades!

—And then in the morning they opened their papers, looking eagerly for more details about the fate of the heroic German comrades, and they found none. Day after day, morning and afternoon, they looked for more details, and found none. On the contrary, to their unutterable bewilderment, they learned that the leaders of the German Social-democracy had voted for the war-budgets, and that the rank and file of the movement were hammering out the goose-step on the roads of Belgium and France! They could not bring themselves to believe it; even yet they have not brought themselves to realise that the story which thrilled them so on that fatal Sunday afternoon was only a cunning lie sent out by the German war-lords, in the hope of causing the Socialists of Belgium and France and England to revolt, and so give the victory to Germany!

CHAPTER III

JIMMIE HIGGINS DEBATES THE ISSUE

I

THE grey flood of frightfulness rolled over Belgium; and every morning, and again in the afternoon, the front page of the Leesville newspaper was like the explosion of a bomb. Twenty-five thousand Germans killed in one assault on Liége; a quarter of a million Russians massacred or drowned in the swamps of the Masurian lakes; so it went, until the minds of men reeled. They saw empires and civilisations crumbling before their eyes, all those certainties upon which their lives had been built vanishing as a mist at sunrise.

Hitherto, Jimmie Higgins had always refused to take a daily paper. No capitalist lies for him; he would save his pennies for the Socialist weeklies! But now he had to have the news, and tired as he was after the day's work, he would sit on his front porch with his ragged feet against a post, spelling out the despatches. Then he would stroll down to the cigar-stand of Comrade Stankewitz, a wizened-up little Roumanian Jew who had lived in Europe and had a map, and would show Jimmie which was Russia, and why Germany marched across Belgium, and why England had to interfere. It was good to have a friend who was a man of travel and a linguist—especially when the fighting became centred about places such as Przemysl and Przasnyaz!

Then every Friday night would be the meeting of the local. Jimmie would be the first to arrive, eager to hear every word the better informed comrades had to say, and thus to complete the education which society had so cruelly neglected.

Before the war was many weeks old, Jimmie's head was in a state of utter bewilderment; never would he have thought it possible for men to hold so many conflicting opinions, and to hold them with such passionate intensity! It seemed as if the world-conflict were being fought out in miniature in Leesville.

At the third meeting after the war began, the prosperous Dr. Service arose, and in his impressive oratorical voice moved that the local should send a telegram to the National Executive Committee of the party, requesting it to protest against the invasion of Belgium; also a telegram to the President of the United States, requesting him to take the same action. And then what pandemonium broke loose! Comrade Schneider, the brewery-worker, demanded to know whether Local Leesville had ever requested the National Executive Committee to protest against the invasion of Ireland. Had the Socialist party ever requested the President of the United States to protect Egypt and India from oppression?

Comrade Dr. Service, who had remained on his feet, began a passionate denunciation of the outrages perpetrated by the German army in Belgium; at which Comrade Schneider's florid face turned purple. He demanded whether all men did not know that France had first invaded Belgium, and that the Belgians had welcomed the French? Weren't all the Belgian forts turned toward Germany? Of course! answered the doctor. But what of that? Was it a crime for a man to know who was going to attack him?

The purple-faced brewer, without heeding this question, demanded: Did not all the world know that the French had begun the war with an aeroplane bombardment of the German cities? The Comrade Doctor, his face also purpling, replied that all the world knew this for a tale sent out by the German propaganda machine. *How* did all the world know it? roared Schneider. By a cable-censorship controlled by British gold?

Jimmie was much excited by this dispute. The only trouble was that he found himself in agreement with both sides, and with an impulse to applaud both sides. And also he applauded the next speaker, young Emil Forster, a pale, slender, and fair-haired youth, a designer in the carpet-factory. Emil was one who seldom raised his voice in the meetings, but when he did, he was heard with attention, for he was a student and a thinker; he played the flute, and his father, also a member of the local, played the clarinet, so the pair were invaluable on "social evenings." In his gentle, dispassionate voice he explained how it was not easy for people in America to understand the dilemma of the German Socialists in the present crisis. We must remember that the Germans were fighting, not merely England and France, but Russia; and Russia was a huge, half-civilised land, under perhaps the most cruel government in the world. How would Americans feel if up in Canada there were three hundred millions of people, ignorant, enslaved, and being drilled in huge armies?

All right, retorted Dr. Service. But then why did not the Germans fight Russia, and let France and Belgium alone?

Because, answered Emil, the French would not permit that. We in America thought of France as a republic, but we must remember that it was a capitalist republic, a nation ruled by bankers; and these bankers had formed an alliance with Russia, the sole possible aim of which was the destruction of Germany. France had loaned something like four billions of dollars to Russia.

And then Schneider leaped up. Yes, and it was that money which had provided the cannon and shells that were now being used in laying waste East Prussia, the land of Schneider's birth!

II

The temper of both sides was rising higher and higher, and the neutrals made efforts to calm the dispute. Comrade Stankewitz, Jimmie's cigar-store friend, cried out in his shrill, eager voice: Vy did ve vant to git mixed up vit them European fights? Didn't ve know vat bankers and capitalists vere? Vat difference did it make to any vorkingman vether he vas robbed from Paris or Berlin? "Sure, I know," said Stankewitz, "I vorked in both them cities, and I vas every bit so hungry under Rothschild as I vas under the Kaiser."

Then Comrade Gerrity, organiser of the local, took his turn. Whatever they did, said Gerrity, they must keep their neutrality in this war; the one hope of the world just now was in the Socialist movement—that it would preserve the international spirit, and point a war-torn world back to peace. Especially just now in Local Leesville they must keep their heads, for they were beginning the most important move in their history, the establishment of a weekly paper. Nothing must get in the way of that!

Yes, said Comrade Service, but they would have to determine

the policy of the paper, would they not? Were they going to protest against injustice at home, and pay no attention to the most flagrant act of international injustice in the history of the world? Was a workingman's paper to say nothing against the enslavement of the workingmen of Europe by the Kaiser and his militarist crew? He, Dr. Service, would wash his hands of such a paper.

And then the members of the local gazed at one another in dismay. Every man and woman of them knew that the prosperous doctor had headed the list of subscribers for the soon-to-be-born Leesville "Worker" with the sum of five hundred dollars. The thought of losing this munificent contribution brought consternation even to the Germans!

But there was one member of the local whom no menace ever daunted. He rose up now—lean, sallow almost to greenness, with black hair falling into his eyes, and a cough that racked him at every other sentence. Bill Murray was his name; "Wild Bill," the papers called him. The red card he carried had been initialled by the secretaries of some thirty locals all over the country. He had lost a couple of toes under a tractor-plough in Kansas, and half a hand in a tin-plate mill in Alleghany County; he had been clubbed insensible in a strike in Chicago, and tarred and feathered in a free speech fight in San Diego. And now he told the members of Local Leesville what he thought of those tea-party revolutionists who pandered to the respectability of a church-ridden community. "Wild Bill" had watched the discussions over "Section Six," the provision in the constitution of the party against sabotage and violence; the very same persons who had been enthusiastic for that bit of middle-class fakery were now trying to line up the local for the defence of the British sea-power! What the hell difference did it make to any workingman whether or not the Kaiser got a railroad to Bagdad? Of course, if a man had been to school in Britain, and had a British wife, and felt himself a British gentleman—you could feel the shudder that went through the gathering, for every one knew that this was Dr. Service—all right, let that man take the first ship across the ocean and enlist; but let him not try to turn an American Socialist local into a recruiting-agency for British landlords and aristocrats.

This brought to his feet Comrade Norwood, the young lawyer who had helped to put through "Section Six" in the National

Convention of the party. If there were people so keen against this Section, why couldn't they get out of the party and form an organisation of their own?

"Because," answered Murray, "we prefer sabotage to striking!"

"In other words," continued Norwood, "you stay in the local, and by a campaign of sneering and personalities you drive your opponents out!"

"This is the first meeting for some months that we have had the pleasure of seeing Comrade Norwood," said "Wild Bill," with venomous placidity. "Perhaps he knew that we were to be asked to raise a regiment for Kitchener!"

And then again Comrade Stankewitz was on his feet, with distress in his thin, eager face. "Comrades, all this vill not get us anyvere! There is but vun question ve have to answer, are ve internationalists, or are ve not?"

"It seems to me," continued Norwood, "the question is, are we anti-nationalists?"

"All right!" shrilled the little Jew. "I vill leave it so—I am an anti-nationalist! Such must all Socialists be!"

"But I don't understand it so," declared the young lawyer. "It is easy for some who belong to a race which has not had a country for two thousand years——"

"And who's dealing in personalities now?" sneered "Wild Bill."

III

So matters went in Local Leesville. The upshot of the debate was that Comrade Dr. Service declared that he washed his hands of the Socialist Party from that time on. And the Comrade Doctor buttoned his handsome black coat over his stately chest and stalked out of the room. The greater part of the remainder of that meeting was devoted to a discussion of him and his personality and his influence in the local. He was no Socialist at all, declared Schneider, he was an English aristocrat, or the next thing to it—his wife had two brothers in the British Expeditionary Force, and a nephew already enlisted in the Territorials, and a visiting cousin on the point of setting out for Canada, as the quickest way of getting into the mix-up. But in spite of all these damaging circumstances, the local was not disposed to give up its most generous supporter, and Comrade Gerrity, the organiser, and Comrade Goldstein of the Ypsels were constituted a committee to go and plead with him and try to bring him back into the fold.

As for Jimmie Higgins, his problem was not so complicated. He had no relatives anywhere that he knew of; and if he had any "country", the country had failed to make him aware of the fact. The first thing the "country" had done for him was to put him into the hands of a negro woman who fed him gruel and water and gave him no blanket in winter. To Jimmie this country was an aggregation of owners and bosses, who made you sweat hard for your wages, and sent the police to club you if you made any kick. A soldier Jimmie thought of as a fellow who came to help the police when they got hard pushed. This soldier walked with his chest out and his nose in the air, and Jimmie referred to him as a "tin willie", and summed him up as a traitor to the working class.

And so it was easy for our little machinist to agree with the Roumanian Jewish cigar-seller in calling himself an "anti-nationalist". It was easy for him to laugh and applaud when "Wild Bill" demanded what the hell difference it made to any workingman whether or not the Kaiser got a railroad to Bagdad. He did not thrill in the least over the story of the British army falling back step by step across France, and holding ten times their number of invaders. The papers called this "heroism"; but to Jimmie it was a lot of poor boobs who had had a flag waved in their eyes, and had sold themselves for a shilling to the landlords of their country. In one of the Socialist papers that Jimmie read, there appeared every week a series of comic pictures in which the workingman was figured as a guileless fool by the name of "Henry Dubb". Poor Henry always believed what he was told, and at the end of each adventure he got a thump on the top of his nut which caused stars to sprout over the page. And of all the many adventures of Henry Dubb, the most absurd were when he got himself into a uniform. Jimmie would cut these pictures out and pass them round in the shop, and among his neighbours in the row of tenement-shacks where he lived.

Nor did it make much difference in Jimmie's feelings when he read of German atrocities. To begin with, he did not believe in them; they were just a part of the poison-gas of war. When men were willing to stab one another with bayonets, and to blow one another to pieces with bombs, they would be willing to lie about one another, you might be sure; the governments would lie deliberately, as one of the ways of making the soldiers fight harder. What? argued Jimmie: tell him that Germans were a lot of savages? When he lived in a city with hundreds of them, and met them all the time at the local?

Here, for instance, was the Forster family; where would you find a kinder lot of people? They were much above Jimmie in social standing—they owned their own home, and had whole shelves full of books, and a pile of music as high as yourself; but recently Jimmie had stopped on a Socialist errand, and they had invited him in to supper, and there was a thin, worn, sweet-faced little woman, and four growing daughters—nice, gentle, quiet girls—and two sons younger than Emil; they had a pot-roast of beef, and a big dish of steaming potatoes, and another of sauer-kraut, and some queer pudding that Jimmie had never heard of; and then they had music—they were fairly dippy on music, that family, they would play all night if you would listen, old Hermann Forster with his stout, black-bearded face turned up as if he were seeing heaven. And you wanted Jimmie to believe that a man like that would carry a baby on a bayonet, or rape a girl and then cut off her hands!

Or there was Comrade Meissner, a neighbour of Jimmie's, a friendly little chatter-box of a man who was foreman in charge of a dozen women from as many different races of the earth, packing bottles in the glass-works. The tears would come into Meissner's pale blue eyes when he told how he was made to drive these women, sick, or in the family way, or whatever it might be. And remember, it was an American superintendent and an American owner who gave Meissner his orders—not a German! The little man could not quit his job, because he had a brood of children and a wife with something the matter with her—nobody could tell what it was, but she took all kinds of patent medicines, which kept the family poor. Sometimes Lizzie Higgins would go over to see her, and the two would sit and exchange ideas about ailments and the prices of food; and meantime Meissner would come over to where Jimmie was minding the Jimmie babies, and the two would puff their cobs and discuss the disputes between the "politicians" and the "direct actionists" in the local. And you wanted Jimmie to believe that men like Meissner were standing old Belgian women against the walls of churches and shooting them full of bullets!

IV

But as the weeks passed, the evidence of atrocities began to pile in, and so Jimmie Higgins was driven to a second line of defence. Well, maybe so, but then all the armies were alike. Somebody told Jimmie the saying of a famous general, that war was hell; and Jimmie took to this—it was exactly what he wanted to believe! War was a return to savagery, and the worse it became, the better Jimmie's argument went. He was not interested in men's efforts to improve war, by agreeing that they would kill in this way but not in that way, they would kill this kind of people but not that kind.

These ideas Jimmie got from his fellow members in the local, and from the Socialist papers which came each week, and from the many speakers he heard. These speakers were men and women of burning sincerity, and with a definite and entirely logical point of view. Whether they talked about war, crime, prostitution, political corruption, or any other social evil, what they wanted was to tear down the old ramshackle structure, and to put in its place something new and intelligent. You might possibly bring them to admit slight differences between capitalist governments; but when it came to a practical issue, to an action, you found that to these people all governments were alike—and never so much alike as in war-time!

Nor was there ever such need for Socialist protest! Very quickly it became apparent that it was not going to be an easy matter for America to keep out of this world-vortex. Because American workingmen did not get a living wage, and could not buy what they produced, there was a surplus product which had to be sold abroad; so the business of American manufacturers depended upon foreign markets—and here suddenly were all the principal trading nations of the world plunging in to buy all the American products they could, and to keep their enemies from buying any at all!

A woman speaker came to Leesville, a shrewd little body with a sharp tongue, who had these disputes figured out, and gave them in a dialogue, as in a play. Kaiser Bill says, "I want cotton." John Bull says, "You shan't have it." Uncle Sam says,

"But he has a right to have it. Get out of the way, John Bull." But John Bull says, "I will hold up your ships and take them into my ports." Uncle Sam says, "No, no! Don't do that!" But John Bull does it. And then the Kaiser says, "What sort of a fellow are you, to let John Bull steal your ships? Are you a coward, or are you secretly a friend of this old villain?" And Uncle Sam says, "John Bull, give me my German mail, and my German newspapers, at least." But John Bull answers, "You've got a lot of German spies in your country—that's why I can't let you have your mail. You can't have German papers because the Kaiser fills them full of lies about me." And the Kaiser says, "If John Bull won't let me have my cotton and my meat and all the rest of it, why don't you stop sending anything to him?" He waits a while, and then he says: "If you won't stop sending things to that old villain, I'll sink the ships, that's all." And Uncle Sam cries, "But that's against the law!" "Whose law?" says the Kaiser. "What sort of a law is it that works only one way?" "But there are Americans on those ships!" cries Uncle Sam. "Well, keep them off the ships!" answers the Kaiser. "Keep them off till John Bull obeys the law."

Put in this way, the situation was easy for any Jimmie Higgins to understand; and month by month, as the debate continued, Jimmie's own point of view became clearer. He was not interested in sending cotton to England, and still less in sending meat. He thought he was lucky if he had a bit of meat twice a week himself, and it was plain enough to him that if the fellows who owned the meat were not allowed to ship it abroad, they might sell it in America at a price that a workingman could pay. Nor was that just greediness on Jimmie's part; he was perfectly willing to go without meat where an ideal was involved —look at the time and money and energy he gave to Socialism! The point was that by sending goods to Europe, you helped to keep up the fighting; whereas, if you quit, the fools must come to their senses. So the Jimmie Higginses worked out their campaign-slogan: "Starve the War and Feed America!"

V

In the third month of the war, disturbing rumours began to run about Leesville. Old Abel Granitch had taken on a contract with the Belgian government, and the Empire Machine Shops were going to make shells. Nothing appeared about this in the local papers, but everybody claimed to have first-hand knowledge, and although no two people told the same story, there must be some basis of truth in them all. And then one day, to Jimmie's consternation, he heard from Lizzie that the agent of the landlord had called and served notice that they had three days to vacate the premises. Old man Granitch had bought the land, and the Shops were to build out that way. Jimmie could hardly credit his ears, for he was six city blocks from the nearest part of the Shops; but it was true, so every one declared; all that land had been bought up, and half a thousand families, children and old people and sick people, men on their death-beds and women in child-birth—all had three days in which to move themselves to new quarters.

Let any one imagine the confusion, the babel of tongues, the women on their porches calling to one another, asking and giving advice! The denunciations and the scoldings and the threats to resort to law! The raids upon landlords, and how the prices went up! Jimmie hurried off to Comrade Meissner, who had bought a home and was paying instalments on it; Meissner, being a Socialist, did not try to gouge him, but was glad to have help in making his payments. There were no partitions in the garret which Jimmie rented, but they would hang curtains and make out somehow, and Lizzie would use Mrs. Meissner's stove until they could get something fixed upstairs. And then to the corner grocery, to borrow a hand-cart and get started at moving the furniture; for to-morrow everybody would be moving, and you would not be able to get anything on wheels for love or money. Until after midnight Jimmie and Meissner worked at transporting babies and bedding and sauce-pans and chairs and chicken-coops piled on the hand-cart.

And next morning at the shop, more excitement! It was four years now that Jimmie had been in the employ of old man Granitch, and in all that time he had done but one thing; standing in a vast room amid a confusion of whirling belts and wheels, a roar and screech and grumble and whir that completely annulled one of the five senses. There came in front of him, mechanically propelled, a tray full of small oblong blocks of steel, which he fed, one with each hand, into two places in a machine; the machine took these blocks, and rounded off one end, and ground the rest a little smaller, and put a thread on it, and it dropped into a tray on the other side, a bolt. Because Jimmie had to watch the machine, and keep the oil-cups full, his was classed as semi-skilled labour, and was paid nineteen and a half cents an hour. Some time ago an expert had studied the process, and figured that with labour at that price it was one-eighth of a cent per hour cheaper to have the work done by hand than to install a machine to do it; and so for four years Jimmie had his job, standing on one spot from seven to twelve, and again from twelve-thirty to six, and carrying home every Saturday night the sum of twelve dollars and twenty-nine cents. You might have thought that the huge machine-works would have made it twelve-thirty for good measure; but if so, you do not understand large scale production.

And now, all of an instant and without warning, Jimmie's precisely ordered and habitual world came to an end. He was at his post when the whistle blew, but the machinery did not move. And presently came the Irish foreman with the curt announcement that the machinery would never move again, at least not on that spot; it was to be cleared out of the way, and new machinery set up, and they were to fall to forthwith with wrenches and hammers and crow-bars to make a new world!

So for a week they did; and meantime, every night as he went home, Jimmie saw people's homes being wrecked—roofs falling in clouds of dust, and gangs of men loading the debris into huge motor-trucks. Before long they had got acetylene torches, and were working all night—gangs of labourers who lived in tents on vacant lots outside the city and kept their canvas cots warm with double shifts of sleepers. Jimmie Higgins realised the dreadful truth, that in spite of all the agitation of Socialists, the war had actually come to Leesville!

CHAPTER IV

JIMMIE HIGGINS STRIKES IT RICH

I

IT was some time before Jimmie understood the nature of the new machinery he was helping to set up. It was nobody's business to explain, for he was only a pair of hands and a strong back; he was not supposed to be a brain—while as for a soul or a conscience, nobody was supposed to be that. Russian agents had come to Leesville with seventeen millions of the money which the Paris bankers had put up; and so over-night whole blocks of homes were swept out of existence, and a huge new steel structure was rising, and on the spot where for four years Jimmie had made certain motions of the hands, they were preparing to manufacture new machinery for the quantity production of shell-casings.

When Jimmie had definitely learned what was in process, he was brought face to face with a grave moral problem. Could he, as an international Socialist, spend his time making shells to kill his German comrades? Could he spend his time making the machinery to make the shells? Would he take the bribe of old man Granitch, a workingman's share of the hideous loot—an increase of four cents an hour, with the prospect of another four when the works got started? Jimmie had to meet this issue, just when it happened that one of his babies was sick, and he was cudgelling his head to think how he could ever squeeze out of his scanty wage the money to pay the doctor!

The answer was easy to Comrade Schneider, the stout and sturdy brewer, who stood up in the local and spoke with bitter scorn of those Socialists who stayed on in the pay of that old hell-devil Granitch. Schneider wanted a strike in the Empire Machine Shops, and he wanted it that very night! But then rose Comrade Mabel Smith, whose brother was a bookkeeper for the concern. It was all very well for Schneider to talk, but suppose some one were to demand that the brewery-workers should strike and refuse to make beer for munition-workers? That was a mere quibble, argued Schneider; but the other denied this, declaring that it was an illustration of what the worker was up against, with no control of his own destiny, no voice as to what use should be made of his product. A man might say that he would have nothing to do with munition-work, and go out into the fields as a farmer—to raise grain to be shipped to the armies! The solidarity of capitalist society was such that nowhere could a man find work that would not in some way be helping to kill his fellow-workers in other lands.

Jimmie Higgins talked solemnly to Lizzie of moving to Hubbardtown—tempted thereto by the signs he saw in an agency which had been set up in a vacant store on Main Street. The Hubbard Engine Company was trying to steal old man Granitch's workers, and was offering thirty-two cents an hour for semi-skilled labour! Jimmie made inquiry and learned that the company was extending its plant for gas-engines; for what purpose was not told, but men suspected that the engines were to go into motor-boats and be used for the sinking of submarines. So Jimmie decided that Comrade Mabel Smith was right; he might as well stay where he was. He would take as much money as he could get and use his new-found prosperity to make trouble for the war-profiteers. It was the first time in his life that Jimmie had ever been free from money-fear. He could now get a job anywhere at good wages, and so he did not care a hang what the boss might say. He would talk to his fellow-workers, and explain the war to them: a war of the capitalists at present, but destined perhaps to turn into another kind of war, which the capitalists would not find to their taste!

II

It was wonderful, incredible, the thing which had befallen Leesville. Full of hatred for the system as Jimmie Higgins was, he could not but be thrilled by what he saw. Thousands of men pouring into the once commonplace little city—men of a score of races and creeds, men old and young, white and black—even a few yellow ones! It was a boom like San Francisco in '49; the money which the Paris bankers had paid to the Russian government, and which the Russian government had paid to old man Granitch, spread out in a golden flood over the city. The speculators raised the price of land, the house-owners raised rents, the hotels doubled their prices, and even so, had to put people to bed on pool tables! Even Tom Callahan of the "Buffeteria" had to hire two assistants, and build an extension, and move his kitchen into the back yard.

At night the hordes of strangers roamed the streets, and Lipsky's "Picture Palace" was packed to the doors, and the "Bon Marché Shoe Store" had a new bankruptcy sale every week, and the swinging doors of the saloons were never still for hours on end. Of course, where so many men were gathered, there came women—swarms of women of as many races as the men. Leesville had some two score churches, and had kept hitherto a careful pretence of decency; but now all barriers went down, the police-force of the city was overwhelmed by the new population—or was it by the golden flood from Paris by way of Russia? Anyway, you saw sights on Main Street which confirmed your distrust of war.

Never had there been such an opportunity for Socialist propaganda! All these hordes of men, collected from the ends of the earth, torn loose from home ties, from religion, from old habits of every sort, thrown together promiscuously, living in any old way, ready for any old thing that might come along! In former days these men had taken what was handed out to them by their newspaper editors and preachers and politicians; they had engaged in commonplace and respectable activities, had lived tame and unadventurous lives. But now they were making munitions; and you might say what you pleased, but there was a certain psychological condition incidental to the making of munitions. An employer could look pious and talk about law and order, so long as he was setting his men to hoeing weeds or shingling roofs or grading track; but what could he say to his men when he was making shells to be used in blowing men to pieces?

So came the Socialist and the Anarchist and the Syndicalist and the Industrial Unionist. Look at these masters, look at this civilisation they have produced! In the world's oldest centres of culture ten or twenty millions of wage-slaves have been hurled together—and then the Socialist or Anarchist or Syndicalist or Industrial Unionist would describe in detail the bloody and bestial operations which these ten or twenty millions of men were performing. And each day's papers would bring fresh details for them to cite—famine and pestilence, fire and slaughter, poison gas, incendiary bombs, torpedoed passenger-ships. Look at these pious hypocrites, the masters, with their refinement, their culture, their religion! These are the people you are asked to follow, it is for such as these that you have been chained to the machines all these weary, toil-crowded years!

III

On every street corner, in every meeting-room, in every spot where the workers gathered at the noon hour, you would hear such arguments; and you would find men listening to them—men who perhaps had never listened to such arguments before. They would nod, and their faces would become grim—yes, the people up on top must be a rotten lot! Here in America, supposed to be a land of liberty and all that—here they were just the same, they were crowding to the trough to drink the blood that was poured out in Europe. Of course, they covered their greed with a camouflage of sympathy for the Allies; but did anybody believe that old man Granitch loved the Russian government? Certainly nobody in Leesville did; they knew that he was "getting his," and their hearts hardened with a grim resolve to "get theirs."

At first they thought they were succeeding. Wages went up, almost for the asking; never did the unskilled man have so much money in his pocket, while the man who could pretend to any skill at all found himself in the plutocratic class. But quickly men discovered the worm in this luscious war-fruit; prices were going up almost as fast as wages—in some places even faster. The sums you had to pay to the landlord surpassed belief; a single workingman would be asked two or three dollars a week for twelve hours' use of a mattress and blanket, which in the old days he might have got for fifty cents. Food was scarce and of poor quality; before long you found yourself being asked to pay six cents for a hunk of pie or a cup of coffee—and then seven cents, and then ten. If you kicked, the proprietor would tell you a long tale about what he had to pay for rent and labour and supplies; and you could not deny that he was probably right. About the only thing that did not go up was a postage-stamp;

and the Socialist would point to this and explain that the Post Office was run by Uncle Sam, instead of by Abel Granitch!

Every rise in price was a fresh stick of fuel for the Socialist machine, and gave new power to their propaganda of "Starve the War and Feed America!" The Socialist saw millions of tons of goods being loaded onto steamships and sent to Europe to be destroyed in war; he saw the workers of Europe becoming enslaved by a bonded debt to a class of parasites in America. he saw America being drawn closer and closer to the abyss of the strife. The Socialist loved no part of this process. He clamoured for an embargo—not merely on munitions, but on food and everything, until the war-lords of Europe came to their senses. He urged the workers to strike, and thus force the politicians to declare the embargo.

Especially, of course, he urged this if he were a German or an Austrian, a Hungarian or a Bohemian. The latter were subject races, but they could not in these early days see beyond the fact that their fathers and brothers and cousins were being killed by the shells that were made in the Empire Machine Shops. With them stood also the Jews, who hated the Russian government so bitterly that nothing else mattered; also the Irish, whose first idea in life was to pay back John Bull for his sins of several centuries, and whose second idea was to take part in any sort of shivaree that was going. It was quite bewildering to Jimmie Higgins; he had wrestled with Catholics of several nations and got nothing but hard words for his pains, but now all of a sudden Tom Callahan of the "Buffeteria" and Pat Grogan of the grocery on the corner made the discovery that maybe he was not such a fool after all!

IV

As a result of this ferment among the workers, the local had doubled its membership, and was holding soap-box meetings on a corner off Main Street on two evenings every week. The plans for the weekly paper, however, still hung fire. Comrade Dr. Service had lost his two brothers-in-law—one in the battle of Mons, and the other in the first frightful gas-attack at Ypres, where whole regiments of men were caught unprepared, and died in awful torments. Also two of his wife's cousins had paid the price—one was blind, and the other a prisoner at Ruhleben, the worst fate of all. So Dr. Service made one last indignant speech in the local, and took his five hundred dollars to start a chapter of the Red Cross!

But now the Germans and the war-haters in the local were asking themselves, was Socialism to languish in the city of the Empire Machine Shops, just because one rich man with an English wife had proved a renegade? Such a question answered itself! The work of collecting subscription lists was taken up more vigorously than ever; and already more than half the lost five hundred had been made up, when one evening John Meissner came home with a most amazing story.

It was his custom to stop at Sandkuhl's for one glass of beer on his way home in the evening; and when anybody in the saloon got to arguing about the war, he would take his chance to put in a little propaganda. This time he had made a regular speech, declaring that the workers would soon put an end to the munition-business; and a fellow had got to talking with him, asking him all sorts of questions about himself, and about the local. How many members did it have? How many of them felt as Meissner did? What were they doing about it? Pretty soon the man had drawn Meissner to a table in the back part of the place, asking about the proposed paper, and what its policy was to be; also about the unions in the city, and their policy, and the personalities of the leaders.

The man had said he was a Socialist, but Meissner did not believe him. Meissner thought he must be some kind of union organiser. There had been talk of various unions making an effort to break into the domain of old man Granitch; and, of course, there was always the I. W. W. trying to break in everywhere with its programme of the "one big union."

Meissner went on to tell how this mysterious stranger had stated to him that it would be possible to get plenty of money to back the proposition of a strike in the Empire Shops. The new plant was just ready to start up, and fresh swarms of men were coming in; what was wanted was some live fellows to get in with them and root for an eight hour day and a minimum wage scale of sixty cents an hour. Men who were willing to do that could get good money, and plenty of it; if the Leesville "Worker" would advocate such a policy, there was no reason why it should not start up the very next week, and publish a big edition and flood the town. The one essential was that arrangements should be made secretly. Meissner must trust no one save dyed-in-the-wool "reds," who would be willing to hustle, and not say where the pay came from. As earnest of his intentions, the stranger pulled out a roll of bills, and casually drew off half a dozen and slipped them into Meissner's hands. They were for ten dollars each—more money than a petty boss at the glass-works had ever got into his hands at one time in all his life!

Meissner exhibited the roll, and Jimmie stared with wide-open eyes. Here indeed was a new development of the war—ten dollar bills for Socialist propaganda to be picked up in the back rooms of saloons! What was this fellow's name? And where did he hang out? Meissner offered to take Jimmie to meet him, and so the two bolted their suppers and set out at top speed.

V

Jerry Coleman had mentioned several saloons where he was known, and in one of these they found him, a smooth-faced, smooth-spoken young fellow whom Jimmie would have taken for a detective or "spotter"—having had dealings with such in his days "on the road." The man wore good clothes, and his finger-nails were cared for, something which, as we know, is seldom permitted to workingmen. But he did not put on airs, and he bade them call him by his first name. He talked to Jimmie a while, enough to make sure of his man, and then he peeled off some more bills, and told Jimmie to find more fellows who could be trusted. It wouldn't do for any one person to have too much money, for that would excite suspicion; but if they would go to work and spend that much for dodgers to be distributed among the munition-workers, and for street-meetings, and for the proposed radical paper—well, there was plenty more money in the place where this had come from.

Where was that place? Jimmie asked; and Jerry Coleman looked wise and winked. Then, after further consideration, he decided it might be well to tell them, provided they would pledge themselves not to mention it to others without his permission. This pledge they gave, and Jerry stated that he was a national organiser for the American Federation of Labour, which had resolved to unionise these munition-plants, and to establish the eight hour day. But it was of the utmost importance that the bosses should not get wind of the matter; it must not be revealed to any one save those whom Coleman saw fit to trust. He was trusting Jimmie and Meissner, and they might know that the great labour organisation was behind them, and would see them through, regardless of expense. Of course, it would be expected that they would use the money honestly.

"Gee!" exclaimed Jimmie. "What do you take us for? A bunch of crooks?"

No, said the other, he was not such a poor judge of character. And Jimmie remarked grimly that anybody who was looking for easy money did not go into the business of Socialist agitation. If there was anything a Socialist could boast of, it was that their workers and elected officials never touched any graft. Mr. Coleman—that is, Jerry—would be handed a receipt for every dollar they spent.

It chanced that that same night there was a meeting of the Propaganda Committee of the local, which consisted of half a dozen of the most active members. Jimmie and Meissner hurried to this place, with their new-found wealth burning a hole in their pockets. They informed the committee that they had been collecting money for the propaganda fund, and produced before the eyes of the astounded comrades the sum of one hundred dollars.

It happened that the chairman of the committee had just received from the National Office of the party in Chicago a sample of a new leaflet entitled "Feed America First"; this leaflet could be had in quantities for a very low price, a dollar or two per thousand; as a result of Jimmie's contribution, a telegram was sent for ten thousand of the leaflets to be shipped by express. And then there was a proposition from the state office, for Comrade Seaman, author of a book against war, to speak every night for two weeks in Leesville. The local had voted to turn down this proposition for lack of funds; but now, with the new contributions, the propaganda committee felt equal to the fifty dollars involved. And then there was the idea of Comrade Gerrity, the organiser, who was conducting street meetings every Wednesday and Saturday nights; if he could have an assistant, at fifteen a week, the soap-boxing could go on every night. John Meissner here put in—he was sure that contributions could be got for that purpose, provided the decision was made without delay. So the decision was made.

VI

The meeting was adjourned, and then Meissner and Jimmie went into conference with Gerrity, the organiser, and Schneider, the brewer, and Comrade Mary Allen, all three of whom happened to be on the committee entrusted with the affairs of the "Worker." Jimmie explained that they had met a union organiser—they could not tell about him, but the committee would have a chance to meet him—who would put up the balance of the money needed, provided that the paper would be willing to call at once for a strike of the Empire employés. Could that promise be made? And Comrade Mary Allen laughed, indicating her scorn for anybody who could cherish a doubt on that question! Comrade Mary was a Quaker; she loved all mankind with religious fervour—and it is astonishing how bitter people can become in the cause of universal love. Her sharp, pale face flushed, and her thin lips set, as she answered that the "Worker" would most surely fight the war-profiteers, so long as she was on the managing committee!

It was finally decided that Comrade Mary should call on Jerry Coleman in the morning, and satisfy herself that he really meant business; if so, she would get the full committee together on the following evening. The committee had authority to go ahead, as soon as the necessary fund was made up, so if Coleman was all right, there was no reason why the first issue of the paper should not appear next week. Comrade Jack Smith, a reporter on the "Herald," the capitalist paper of Leesville, was to resign and become editor of the "Worker," and he already had his editorials written—had been showing them about in the local for the past month!

Jimmie and Meissner set out for home, happy in the feeling that they had accomplished more for Socialism on that one night than in all the rest of their lives. But then, as they walked, there came suddenly a clamour of bells on the night air; a fire! They knew the signals, and counted the strokes, and made the discovery that it was in the neighbourhood of their own home! An engine went by on the gallop, with sparks streaming out behind, and they broke into a run. Before they had gone a couple of blocks, they saw a glare in the sky, and their hearts were in their throats; poor Meissner panted that he had neglected to pay his last month's insurance!

But as they ran, in the ever-growing throng of people, they realised that the fire was too near for their own home; also, it was a bigger blaze than could have been made by any number of shacks. And presently there were shouts in the crowd, "It's the Empire! The Old Shops!" There came a hook and ladder truck, rushing by with shrieking siren, and then the fire-chief in his automobile with a fiercely clanging bell; they turned the corner, and far down the street before them was the building in which for four years Jimmie had tended the bolt-making machine. They saw that one whole end of it was a towering, leaping, sweeping pillar of flames!

CHAPTER IV

JIMMIE HIGGINS HELPS THE KAISER

I

JIMMIE HIGGINS regarded with the utmost resentment the determination of the war to come to Leesville, in spite of all his labours to keep it out. Take the most preposterous thing you could imagine—the most idiotic thing on the face of the earth—take German spies! When Jimmie heard people talking about German spies, he laughed in their faces, he told them they were a bunch of boobs, they belonged in the nursery; for Jimmie classed German spies with goblins, witches and sea-serpents. And here suddenly the bewildered little man found himself in the midst of a German spy mania, the like of which he could never have dreamed!

Everybody seemed to take it for granted that the Empire Machine Shops had been burned by German agents; they just knew it, and by the time the fire was out they had a hundred various stories to support their conviction. The fire had leaped from place to place in a series of explosions; the watchman, who had passed through the building only two minutes before, had rushed back and seen blazing gasoline, and had almost lost his life in the sweep of the flames. And next morning the Leesville "Herald" was out with letters half a foot high, telling these tales and insisting that the plant had been full of German agents, disguised as workingmen.

Before the day was by the police had arrested a dozen perfectly harmless German and Austrian labourers; at least that was the way it seemed to Jimmie, because of the fact that two of the men were members of the Socialist local. Somebody told Mrs. Meissner that all the Germans in Leesville were to be arrested, and the poor woman was trembling with terror. She wanted her husband to run away, but Jimmie persuaded them that this would be the worst possible course; so Meissner stayed in the house, and Jimmie kept his mouth shut for three whole days—an extraordinary feat for him, and a trial more severe than being in jail.

He had lost his job—forever, he thought. But in this again he misjudged the forces which had taken his life in their grip—the power of the gold which had come to Leesville by way of Russia. The day after the fire he received word to report for work again; old man Granitch was so anxious to keep his workers out of the clutches of the Hubbard Engine Company that he put them all, skilled and unskilled, at the job of clearing away the debris of the fire! And five days later came the first carloads of new material, brought on motor-trucks, and the rebuilding of the Empire Shops began. Would you believe it—some of the machinery which had not been damaged too much in the fire was fixed up, and at the end of a couple of weeks was starting up again, covered by a temporary canvas shelter, and with the walls of the new building rising round it.

That was the kind of thing which made America the marvel of the world. It had made old man Granitch young again, people said; he worked twenty hours a day in his shirt-sleeves, and the increase in his profanity was appalling. Even Lacey Granitch, his dashing son, quitted the bright lights of Broadway and came home to help the old man keep his contracts. The enthusiasm for these contracts became as it were the religion of Leesville; it spread even to the ranks of labour, so that Jimmie found himself like a man in a surf, struggling to keep his feet against an undertow.

II

The plans for the "Worker" were delayed, for the reason that when Comrade Mary Allen, the Quaker, went to look for Jerry Coleman the day after the fire, that dispenser of ten dollar bills had mysteriously disappeared. It was a week before he showed up again; and meantime fresh events had taken place, both in the local and cutside. To begin with the latter, as presumably the more important: an English passenger liner, the pride of the Atlantic fleet, loaded to the last cabin with American millionaires, was torpedoed without warning by a German submarine. More than a thousand men, women and children went down, and the deed sent a shudder of horror through the civilised world. At the meeting of Local Leesville, which happened to take place the evening afterward, it proved a difficult matter to get business started.

The members stood about and argued. What could you say about a government that ordered a crime like that? What could you say about a naval officer who would carry out such an order? Thus Comrade Norwood, the young lawyer; and Schneider, the brewer, answered that the German government had done everything that any reasonable man could ask. It had published a notice in the New York papers, to the effect that the vessel was subject to attack, and that any one who travelled on her would do so at his peril. If women and children would ride on munition-ships——

"Munition-ships?" cried Norwood; and then Schneider pointed to a news-despatch, to the effect that the *Lusitania* had had on board a shipment of cartridge-cases.

"A fine lot of munitions!" jeered the lawyer.

Well, was the reply, what were cartridge-cases for, if not to kill Germans? The Germans had been attacked by the whole world, and they had to defend themselves. When you looked at Comrade Schneider, you saw a man who felt himself attacked by the whole world; his face was red up to the roots of his hair, and he was ready to defend himself with any weapon he could get hold of.

Comrade Koeln, a big glass-blower, broke into the discussion. The German government was authority for the statement that the *Lusitania* had been armed with guns. And when Norwood hooted at this, every German in the room was up in arms. What did he have to disprove it? The word of the British government! Was not "perfidious Albion" a bye-word!

"The thing that beats me," declared the young lawyer, "is the way you Germans stand up for the Kaiser now, when before the war you couldn't find enough bad things to say about him."

"What beats me," countered Schneider, "is how you Americans stand up for King George. Every newspaper in Wall Street howling for America to go into the war—yust because some millionaires got killed!"

"You don't seem to realise that the greater number of the men who lost their lives on that ship were workingmen!"

"Ho! Ho!" hooted Comrade Stankewitz. "Vall Street loves so the vorkingmen!"

Comrade Mary Allen, who loved all men, took up the argument. If those workingmen had been killed in a mine disaster, caused by criminal carelessness and greed for profits; if they had died of some industrial disease which might easily have been prevented; if they had been burned in a factory without fire-escapes—nobody in Wall Street would have wanted to go to war. And, of course, every Socialist considered this was true; every Socialist saw quite clearly that the enormity of the *Lusitania* sinking lay in the fact that it had reached and injured the privileged people, the people who counted, who got their names in the papers and were not supposed to be inconvenienced, even by war. So it was possible for Jimmie Higgins, even though shocked by what the Germans had done, to be irritated by the fuss which the Wall Street newspapers made.

Young Emil Forster spoke, and they listened to him, as they always did. It was a quarrel, he said—and as usual in quarrels, both sides had their rights and wrongs. You had to balance a few English and American babies against the millions of German babies which the British government intended to starve. It was British sea-power maintaining itself—and of course controlling most of the channels of publicity. It appealed to what it called "law"—that is to say, the customs it had found convenient in the past. British cruisers were able to visit and search vessels, and to take off their crews; but submarines could not do that, so what the British clamour about "law" amounted to was an attempt to keep Germany from using her only weapon. After all, ask yourself honestly if it was any worse to drown people quickly than to starve them slowly.

And then came "Wild Bill." This wrangling over German and British gave him a pain in the guts. Couldn't they see, the big stiffs, that they were playing the masters' game? Quarrelling among themselves, when they ought to be waking up the workers, getting ready for the real fight. And wizened-up little Stankewitz broke in again—that vas vy he hated var, it divided the vorkers. There vas nothing you could say for var. But "Wild Bill" smiled his crooked smile. There were several things you could say. War gave the workers guns, and taught them to use them; how would it be if some day they turned these guns about and fought their own battles?

III

Comrade Gerrity now took the chair and made an effort to get things started. The minutes of the last meeting were read, new members were voted on, and then Comrade Mary Allen rose to report for the "Worker" committee. The fund had been completed, the first number of the paper was to appear next week, and it was now up to every member of the local to get up on his toes and hustle as never in his life before. Comrade Mary, with her thin, eager face of a religious zealot, made every one share her fervour.

All save Lawyer Norwood. Since the retirement of Dr. Service he was the chief pro-ally trouble-maker, and he now made a little speech. He had been agreeably surprised to learn that the money had been raised so quickly; but then certain uncomfortable doubts having occurred to him, he had made inquiries and found there was some mystery about the matter. It was stated that the new paper was to demand a general strike in the Empire; and of course everybody knew there were powerful and sinister forces now interested in promoting strikes in munition-factories.

"Wild Bill" was on his feet in an instant. Had the comrade any objection to munition-workers demanding the eight hour day?

"No," said Norward, "of course not; but if we are going into a fight with other people, we surely ought to know who they are and what their purpose is. I have been informed—there seems to be a little hesitation in talking about it—that a lot of money has been put up by one man, and nobody knows who that man is."

"He's an organiser for the A. F. of L.!" The voice was Jimmie's. In his excitement the solemn pledge of secrecy was entirely forgotten!

"Indeed!" said Norward. "What is his name?"

Nobody answered.

"Has he shown his credentials?" Again silence.

"Of course I don't need to tell men as familiar with union affairs as the comrades here that every bona-fide organiser for a union carries credentials. If he does not produce them, it is at least occasion for writing to the organisation and finding out about him. Has anybody done that?"

Again there was silence.

"I don't want to make charges," said Norwood——

"Oh, no!" put in "Wild Bill." "You only want to make insinuations!"

"What I want to do is merely to make sure that the local knows what it is doing. It is no secret anywhere in Leesville that money is being spent to cause trouble in the Empire. No doubt this money has passed through a great many hands since it left the Kaiser's, but we may be sure that his hands are guiding it to its final end."

And then what an uproar! "Shame! Shame!" cried some; and others cried, "Bring your proofs!" The "wild" members shouted, "Put him out!" They had long wanted to get rid of Norwood, and this looked to be their chance.

But the young lawyer stood his ground and gave them shot for shot. They wanted proofs, did they? Suppose they had learned of a capitalist conspiracy to wreck the unions in the city; and suppose that the Leesville "Herald" had been clamouring for "proofs"—what would they have thought?

"In other words," shouted Schneider, "you know it's true, yust because it's Yermany!"

"I know it's true," said Norwood, "because it would help Germany to win the war. One doesn't have to have any other evidence—if a certain thing will help Germany to win the war, one knows that thing is being done. All you Germans know that, and what's more, you're proud of it; it's your efficiency, that you boast."

Again there was a cry of "Shame! Shame!" But the cry came from Comrade Mary, the Quaker lady, and it was evident that she had expected a chorus, and was disconcerted at being alone.

Young Norwood, who knew his Germans, laughed scornfully. "Just now your government is selling bonds in America, supposed to be for the benefit of the families of the dead and wounded. Some of those bonds have been taken in this city, as I happen to know. Does anybody really believe the money will reach the families of the dead and wounded?"

This time the Germans answered. "I belief it!" roared Comrade Koeln. "And I! And I!" shouted others.

"That money is staying right here in Leesville!" proclaimed the lawyer. "It is preparing a strike in the Empire!"

A dozen men wanted the floor at once. Schneider, the brewer, got it, for the reason that he could outbellow any one else. "What does the comrade want?" he demanded. "Is he not for the eight hour day?"

"Has he got any of old man Granitch's money?" shrilled "Wild Bill." "Or maybe he doesn't know that Granitch is spending money to get smart young lawyers to help keep his munition-slaves at work?"

IV

Norwood, having thrown the fat into the fire, sat down for a while and let it blaze. When the Germans taunted him with being afraid to say what he really meant—that the local should oppose the demand for the eight hour day—he merely laughed at them. He had wanted to make them show themselves up, and he had done it. Not merely were they willing to do the work of the Kaiser—they were willing to take the Kaiser's pay for doing it!

"Take his pay?" cried "Wild Bill." "I'd take the devil's pay to carry on Socialist propaganda!"

Old Hermann Forster rose and spoke, in his gentle, sentimental voice. If it were true that the Kaiser was paying money for such ends, he would surely find he had bought very little. There were Socialists in Germany, one must remember——

And then came a shrill laugh. Those tame German Socialists! It was Comrade Claudel, a Belgian jeweller, who spoke. Would any rabbit be afraid of such revolutionists as them? Eating out of the Kaiser's hand—having their papers distributed in the trenches for government propaganda! Talk to a Belgian about German Socialists!

So you saw the European national lines splitting Local Leesville in two: on the one side the Germans and the Austrians, the Russian Jews, the Irish and the religious pacifists; on the other side two English glass-blowers, a French waiter, and several Americans who, because of college-education or other snobbish weakness, were suspected of tenderness for John Bull. Between these extreme factions stood the bulk of the membership, listening bewildered, trying to grope their way through the labyrinth.

It was no easy job for these plain fellows, the Jimmie Higgenses. When they tried to think the matter out, they were almost brought to despair. There were so many sides to the question—the last fellow you met always had a better argument than any one you had heard before! You sympathised with Belgium and France, of course; but could you help hating the British ruling classes? They were your hereditary enemies—your school-book enemies, so to speak. And they were the ones you knew most about; since every American jack-ass that got rich quick and wanted to set himself up above his fellows would proceed to get English clothes and English servants and English bad manners. To the average plain American, the word English stood for privilege, for ruling class culture, the things established, the things against which he was in rebellion; Germany was the I. W. W. among the nations—the fellow who had never got a chance and was now hitting out for it. Moreover, the Germans were efficient; they took the trouble to put their case before you, they cared what you thought about them; whereas the Englishman, damn him, turned up his snobbish nose, not caring a whoop what you or anybody might think.

Moreover, in this controversy the force of inertia was on the German side, and inertia is a powerful force in any organisation. What the Germans wanted of American Socialists was simply that they should go on doing what they had been doing all their lives. And the Socialist machine had been set up for the purpose of going on, regardless of all the powers on earth, in the heavens above the earth, or in hell beneath. Ask Jimmie Higgins to stop demanding higher wages and the eight hour day! Wouldn't anybody in his senses know what Jimmie would answer to that proposition? Go chase yourself!

V

But, on the other hand, it must be admitted that Jimmie was staggered by the idea that he might be getting into the pay of the Kaiser. It was true that the traditions of the Socialist movement were German traditions, but they were German anti-Government traditions: Jimmie regarded the Kaiser as the devil incarnate, and the bare idea of doing anything the Kaiser wanted done was enough to make him stop short. He could see also what a bad thing it would be for the movement to have any person believe that it was taking the Kaiser's money.

Suppose, for example, that a report of this evening's discussion should reach the "Herald"! And with the public inflamed to madness over the *Lusitania* affair!

After the discussion had proceeded for an hour or so, Norwood made a motion to the effect that the "Worker" committee should be instructed to investigate thoroughly the sources of all funds contributed, and to reject any that did not come from Socialists, or those in sympathy with Socialism. The common-sense of the meeting asserted itself, and even the Germans voted for this motion. Sure, let them go ahead and investigate! The Socialist movement was clean, it had always been clean, it had nothing to conceal from anyone.

But then came another controversy. Claudel moved that Norwood should be made a member of the committee; and this, of course, was bitterly opposed by the radicals. It was an insult to the integrity of the committee. Then, too, suggested Baggs, an Englishman, perhaps Norwood might really find out something! The Jimmie Higginses voted down the motion—not because they feared any disclosures, but because they felt that a quiet, sensible fellow like Gerrity, their organiser, might be trusted to protect the good faith of the movement, and without antagonising anybody or making a fuss.

The investigation took place, and the result of it was that the money which Jerry Coleman had contributed for the "Worker" was quietly returned to him. But the difference was at once made up by the Germans in the local, who regarded the whole thing as a put-up job, an effort to block the agitation for a strike. These comrades took no stock whatever in the talk about "German gold"; but on the other hand they were keenly on the alert for the influence of Russian gold, which they knew was being openly distributed by old Abel Granitch. And so they put their hands down into their pockets and dug out their scanty wages, so that the demand for social justice might be kept alive in Leesville.

The upshot of the whole episode was that the local rejected the Kaiser's pay, but went on doing what the Kaiser wanted without pay. This could hardly be considered a satisfactory solution, but it was the best that Jimmie Higgins was able to work out at this time.

VI

The first issue of the "Worker" appeared, with Jack Smith's editorial spread over the front page, calling upon the workers of the Empire to take this occasion to organise and demand their rights. "Eight hours for work, eight hours for sleep, eight hours for play!" proclaimed Comrade Jack; and the "Herald" and the "Courier," stung to a frenzy by the appearance of a poacher on their journalistic preserves, answered with broadsides about "German propaganda." The "Herald" got the story of what had happened in the local; also it printed a picture of "Wild Bill," and an interview with that terror of the West, who declared that he was for war on the capitalist class with the aid of any and every ally that came along—even to the extent of emery powder in ball-bearings and copper nails driven into fruit trees.

The "Herald" charged that the attitude of the Socialists toward "tainted wealth" was all a sham. What had happened was simply that the German members of the local were getting German money, and making it "Socialist money" by the simple device of passing it through their consecrated hands. As this had been hinted by Norwood in the local, the German comrades now charged that Norwood had betrayed the movement to the capitalist press. And so came another bitter controversy in the local. The young lawyer laughed at the charge. Did they really believe they could take German money in Leesville, and not have the fact become known?

"Then you think we *are* taking German money?" roared Schneider; and he clamoured furiously for an answer. The other would not answer directly, but he told them a little parable. He saw a tree, sending down its roots into the ground, spreading everywhere, each tiny rootlet constructed for the purpose of absorbing water. And on the top of the ground was a man with a supply of water, which he poured out; he poured and poured without stint, and the water seeped down toward the rootlets, and every rootlet was reaching for water, pushing toward the places where water was likely to be. "And now," said Norwood, "you ask me do I believe that tree has been getting any of that water?"

And here, of course, was the basis of a bitter quarrel. The hot-heads would not listen to subtle distinctions; they declared that Norwood was accusing the movement of corruption, he was making out his anti-war opponents to be villains! He was providing the capitalist press with ammunition. For shame! for shame! "He's a stool-pigeon!" shrieked "Wild Bill." "Put him out, the Judas!"

The average member of the local, the perfectly sincere fellow like Jimmie Higgins, who was wearing himself out, half starving himself, in the effort to bring enlightenment to his class, listened to these controversies with bewildered distress. He saw them as echoes of the terrible national hatreds which were rending Europe, and he resented having these old world disputes thrust into American industrial life. Why could he not go on with his duty of leading the American workers into the co-operative commonwealth?

Because, answered the Germans, old man Granitch wanted to keep the American workers as munition-slaves; and to this idea the overwhelming percentage of the membership agreed. They were not pacifists, non-resistants; they were perfectly willing to fight the battles of the working-class; what they objected to was having to fight the battles of the master-class. They wanted to go on, as they had always gone, opposing the master-class and paying no heed to talk about German agents. Jimmie Higgins believed—and in this belief he was perfectly correct—that even had there been no German agents, the capitalist papers of Leesville would have invented them, as a means of discrediting the agitators in this crisis. Jimmie Higgins had lived all his life in a country in which his masters starved and oppressed him, and when he tried to help himself, met him with every weapon of treachery and slander. So Jimmie had made up his mind that one capitalist country was the same as another capitalist country, and that he would not be frightened into submission by tales about goblins and witches and sea-serpents and German spies.

CHAPTER VI

JIMMIE HIGGINS GOES TO JAIL

EVERY evening now the party held its "soap-box" meetings on a corner just off Main Street. Jimmie, having volunteered as one of the assistants, would bolt his supper in the evening and hurry off to the spot. He was not one of the speakers, of course—he would have been terrified at the idea of making a speech; but he was one of those whose labours made the speaking possible, and who reaped the harvest for the movement.

The apparatus of the meeting was kept in the shop of a friendly carpenter nearby. The carpenter had made a "soap-box" that was a wonder—a platform mounted upon four slender legs, detachable, so that one man could carry the whole business and set it up. Thus the speaker was lifted a couple of feet above the heads of the crowd, and provided with a hand-rail upon which he might lean, and even pound, if he did not pound too hard. A kerosene torch burned some distance from his head, illuminating his features, and it was Jimmie's business to see that this torch was properly cleaned and filled, and to hold it erect on a pole part of the time. The rest of the time he peddled literature among the crowd—copies of the Leesville "Worker," and five and ten cent pamphlets supplied by the National Office.

He would come home at night, worn out from these labours after his daily toil; he would fall asleep at Lizzie's side, and have to be routed out by her when the alarm-clock went off next morning. She would get him a cup of hot coffee, and after he had drunk this, he would be himself again, and would chatter about the adventures of the night before. There was always something happening, a fellow starting a controversy, a drunken man, or perhaps a couple of thugs in the pay of old man Granitch, trying to break up the meeting.

Lizzie would do her best to show that sympathy with her

husband's activities which is expected from a dutiful wife. But all the time there was grief in her soul—the eternal grief of the feminine temperament, which is cautious and conservative, in conflict with the masculine, which is adventurous and destructive. Here was Jimmie, earning twice what he had ever earned before, having a chance to feed his children properly and to put by a little margin for the first time in his harassed life; but instead of making the most of the opportunity, he was going out on the streets every night, doing everything in his power to destroy the golden occasion which fate had brought to him! Like the fellow who climbs a tree to saw off a limb, and sits on the limb and saws between himself and the tree!

In spite of her best efforts, Lizzie's broad, kindly face would sometimes become hard with disappointment, and a big tear would roll down each of her sturdy cheeks. Jimmie would be sorry for her, and would patiently try to explain his actions. Should a man think only of his own wife and children, and forget entirely all the other wives and children of the working-class? That was why the workers had been slaves all through the ages, because each thought of himself, and never of his fellows. No, you must think of your class! You must act as a class—on the alert to seize every advantage, to teach solidarity and stimulate class-consciousness! Jimmie would use these long words, which he had heard at meetings; but then, seeing that Lizzie did not understand them, he would go back and say it over again in words of one syllable. They had old man Granitch in a hole just now, and they must teach him a lesson, and at the same time teach the workers their power. Lizzie would sigh, and shake her head; for to her, old man Granitch was not a human being, but a natural phenomenon, like winter, or hunger. He, or some other like him, had been the master of her fathers for generations untold, and to try to break or even to limit his power was like commanding the tide or the sun.

II

Events moved quickly to their culmination, justifying the worst of Lizzie's fears. The shops were seething with discontent, and agitators seemed fairly to spring out of the ground; some of them paid by Jerry Coleman, no doubt, others taking their pay in the form of gratification of those grudges with which the profit-system had filled their hearts. Noon-meetings would start up, quite spontaneously, without any prearrangement; and presently Jimmie learned that men were going about taking the names of all who would agree to strike.

The matter was brought to a head by the Empire managers, who, of course, were kept informed by their spies. They discharged more than a score of the trouble-makers; and when this news spread at noon-time, the whole place burst into a flame of wrath. "Strike! strike!" was the cry. Jimmie was one of many who started a procession through the yards, shouting, singing, hurling menaces at the bosses, challenging all who proposed to return to work. Less than one-tenth of the working force made any attempt to do so, and for that afternoon the plant of the Empire Machine Shops, which was supposed to be turning out shell-casings for the Russian government, was turning out labour-union, Socialist, and I. W. W. oratory.

Jimmie Higgins was beside himself with excitement. He danced about and waved his cap, he shouted himself hoarse, he almost yielded to the impulse to jump upon a pile of lumber and make a speech himself. Presently came Comrades Gerrity and Mary Allen, who had got wind of the trouble, and had loaded a whole edition of the "Worker" into a Ford; so Jimmie turned newsboy, selling these papers, hundreds of them, until his pockets were bursting with the weight of pennies and nickels. And then he was pressed into service running errands for those who were arranging to organise the workers; he carried bundles of membership-cards and application-blanks, following a man with a bull voice and a megaphone, who shouted in several languages the location of union headquarters, and the halls where various foreign language meetings would be held that evening. Evidently some one had foreseen the breaking of this trouble, and had been at pains to plan ahead.

Late in the afternoon Jimmie was witness of an exciting incident. In one of the shops a number of the men had persisted in returning to work, and an immense throng of strikers had gathered to wait for them. They were afraid to come out, but stayed in the building after the quitting-whistle, while those outside jeered and hooted, and the bosses telephoned frantically for aid. The greater part of the Leesville police-force was on hand, and in addition, the company had its own guards and private detectives. But they were needed all over the place. You saw them at the various entrances, menacing, but not quite so sure of themselves as usual; their hands had a tendency to slip back to the bulge on their right hips.

Jimmie and another fellow had got themselves an empty box and were standing on it, leaning against the wall of the building and shouting "Ya! Ya!" at every "scab" head that showed itself. They saw an automobile come in at the gate, its horn honking savagely, causing the crowd to leap to one side or the other. The automobile was packed with men, sitting on one another's knees, or hanging to the running boards outside. There came a second car, loaded in the same fashion. They were guards, sent all the way from Hubbardtown; for of course the Hubbard Engine Company would help out its rivals in an emergency such as this. That was the solidarity of capitalism, concerning which the Socialists never wearied of preaching.

The men leaped from the cars, and spread themselves fan-wise in front of the door. They had nightsticks in their hands, and grim resolution in their faces; they cried, "Stand back! Stand back!" The crowd hooted, but gave slightly, and a few minutes later the doors of the building opened, and the first of the timid workers emerged. There was a howl, and then from somewhere in the throng a stone was thrown. "Arrest that man!" shouted a voice, and Jimmie's attention was attracted to the owner of this voice—a young man who had arrived in the first automobile, and was now standing up in the seat, from which position he could dominate the throng. "Arrest that man!" he shouted again, pointing his finger; and three of the guards leaped into the crowd at the spot indicated. The man who had thrown the missile started to run, but he could not go fast in the crowd, and in a moment, as it seemed, the guards had him by the collar. He tried to jerk away, and they struck him over the head, and laid about them to keep the rest of the throng at bay. "Take him inside!" the young man in the car kept shouting. And one of the guards twisted his hand in the collar of the wretched stone-thrower, until he grew purple in the face, and so half dragged and half ran him into the building.

III

The young man in the car turned toward the crowd which was blocking the way to the exit. "Get those men out of the way!" he yelled to the guards. "Drive them along—God damn them, they've got no business in here." And so on, with a string of dynamic profanity, which stung both guards and policemen into action, and made them ply their clubs upon the crowd.

"Do you know who that is?" asked Jimmie's companion on the box. "That's Lacey Granitch."

Jimmie started, experiencing a thrill to the soles of his ragged shoes. Lacey Granitch! In the four years that the little machinist had worked for the Empire, he had never caught a glimpse of the young lord of Leesville—something which may easily be believed, for the young lord considered Leesville "a hole of a town," and honoured it with his presence only once or twice a year. But his spirit brooded over it; he was to Leesville a mythological figure, either of wonder and awe, or of horror, according to the temperament of the contemplator. One day "Wild Bill" had arisen in the local, and held aloft a page from the "magazine supplement" of one of the metropolitan "yellows." There was an account of how Lacey Granitch had broken the hearts of seven chorus-girls by running away with an eighth. He fairly "ate 'em alive," according to the account; in order to give an idea of the atmosphere in which the young hero abode, the whirl of delight which was his life, the artist of the Sunday supplement had woven round the border of the page a maze of feminine ankles and calves in a delirium of lingerie; while at the top was a supper-table with champagne-corks popping, and a lady clad in inadequate veils dancing amid the dishes.

This had happened while the local was in the midst of an acrimonious controversy over "Section Six." Should the Socialist party bar from its membership those who advocated sabotage, violence and crime? Young Norwood was pleading for orderly methods of social reconstruction; and here stood "Wild Bill," ripping to shreds the reputation of the young plutocrat of the Empire Shops. "That's what you geezers are sweating for! That's why you've got to be good, and not throw monkey-wrenches in the machinery—so the seven broken-hearted chorus-girls can drown their sorrows in champagne!"

And now here was the hero of all these romantic escapades, forsaking the white lights of Broadway, and coming home to help the old man keep his contracts. He stood in the seat of the automobile, glancing this way and that, swiftly, like a hunter on the alert for dangerous game. His dark eyes roamed here and there, his proud face was pale with anger, his tall, perfectly groomed figure was eloquent of mastership, of command. He was imperious as a young Cæsar, terrible in his vengeance; and poor Jimmie, watching him, was torn between two contradictory emotions. He hated him—hated him with a deadly and abiding hatred. But also he admired him, marvelled at him, cringed before him. Lacey was a wanton, a cursing tyrant, a brutal snob; but also he was the master, the conqueror, the proud, free, rich young aristocrat, for whom all the rest of humanity existed. And Jimmie Higgins was a poor little worm of a proletarian, with nothing but his labour-power to sell, trying by sheer force of his will to lift himself out of his slave-psychology!

There is an old adage that "a cat may look at a king." But this can only have been meant to apply to house-cats, cats of the palace, accustomed to the etiquette of courts; it cannot have been meant for proletarian cats of the gutter, the Jimmie Higgins variety of red revolutionary yowlers. Jimmie and his companion stood on their perch, shouting "Ya! Ya!" and suddenly the crowd melted away in front of them, exposing them to the angry finger of the young master. "Get along now! Beat it! Quick!" And Jimmie, poor little ragged, stunted Jimmie, with bad teeth and toil-deformed hands, wilted before this blast of aristocratic wrath, and made haste to hide himself in the throng. But it was with blazing soul that he went; every instant he imagined himself turning back, defying the angry finger, shouting down the imperious voice, even smashing it back into the throat from which it came!

IV

Jimmie did not even stop for supper. The greater part of the night he worked at helping to organise the strikers, and all next day he spent arranging Socialist meetings. He worked like a man possessed, lifted above the limitations of the flesh. For everywhere that day he carried with him the image of the proud, free, rich young aristocrat, with his dark eyes roaming swiftly, his tall, perfectly groomed figure eloquent of mastership, his voice ringing with challenge. Jimmie was for the time utterly possessed by hatred; and he saw about him thousands of others sharing the mood and shouting it aloud. Every speaker who could be found was turned loose to talk till he was hoarse, and in the evening there were to be half a dozen street meetings. That was always the way when there were strikes; then the working-man had time to listen—and also the desire!

So came the final crisis, when the little machinist had to show the stuff he was made of. He was holding aloft the torch at the regular meeting-place on the corner of Main and Third Streets, and Comrade Gerrity was explaining the strike and the ballot as two edges of the sword of labour, when four policemen came suddenly round the corner and pushed their way through the crowd. "You'll have to stop this!" declared one.

"Stop?" cried Gerrity. "What do you mean?"

"There's to be no more street-speaking during the strike."

"Who says so?"

"Orders from the Chief."

"But we've got a permit."

"All permits revoked. Cut it out."

"But this is an outrage!"

"We don't want any argument, young man——"

"But we're within our rights here."

"Forget it, young feller!"

Gerrity turned swiftly to the throng.

"Fellow-citizens," he cried, "we are here in the exercise of our rights as American citizens! We are conducting a peaceable and orderly political meeting, and we know our rights and propose to maintain them. We——"

"Come down off that box, young feller!" commanded the officer; and the crowd hooted and booed.

"Fellow-citizens!" began Gerrity again; but that was as far as he got, for the policeman seized him by the arm and pulled; and Gerrity knew the ways of American policemen too well to resist. He came down—but still talking. "Fellow-citizens——"

"Are you goin' to shut up?" demanded the other, and as Gerrity still went on orating, he announced: "You are under arrest."

There were half a dozen Socialists with the party, and this was a challenge to the self-respect of every one of them. In an instant Comrade Mabel Smith had leaped onto the stand. "Fellow-workers!" she cried. "Is this America, or is it Russia?"

"That'll do, lady," said the policeman, as considerately as he dared; for Comrade Mabel wore a big picture-hat, and many other signs of youth and beauty.

"I have a right to speak here, and I mean to speak," she declared.

"We don't want to have to arrest you, lady——"

"You either have to arrest me, or else allow me to speak."

"I'm sorry, lady, but it's orders. You are arrested."

Then came the turn of Comrade Stankewitz. "Vorkingmen, it is for the rights of the vorkers ve are here." And so they jerked him off.

And then "Wild Bill." This hundred per cent, middle-of-the-road proletarian had been hanging on the outskirts of the meeting, having been forbidden by the local to take part in the speaking, because of the intemperate nature of his utterances; but now, of course, all rules went down, and Bill leaped onto the shaking platform. "Are we slaves?" he yelled. "Are we dogs?" And it would seem that the police thought so, for they yanked him off the platform, and one of them seized him by the wrist and twisted so that his oration ended in a shriek of pain.

Then came Johnny Edge, a shy youth with an armful of literature, which he hung onto in spite of police violence; and then—then there was one more!

Poor Jimmie! He did not in the least want to get arrested, and he was terrified at the idea of making even so short a speech as was here the order of the night. But of course, his honour was at stake, there was no way out. He handed his torch to a by-stander, and mounted the scaffold. "Is this a free country?" he cried. "Do we have free speech?" And Jimmie's first effort at oratory ended in a jerk at his coat-tail, which all but upset the frail platform upon which he stood.

There were four policemen, with six prisoners, and a throng about them howling with indignation, perhaps ready to become violent—who could say? The guardians of order had been prepared, however. One of them stepped to the corner and blew his whistle, and a minute later came the shriek of a siren, and round the corner came swinging the city's big patrol-wagon, the "Black Maria." The crowd gave way, and one by one the prisoners were thrust in. One of them, "Wild Bill," feeling himself for a moment released from the grip of his captors, raised his voice, shouting through the wire grating of the wagon: "I denounce this outrage! I am a free American——" And suddenly Jimmie, who was next in the wagon, felt himself flung to one side, and a policeman leaped by him, and planted his fist with terrific violence full in the orator's mouth. "Wild Bill" went down like a bullock under the slaughter-man's axe, and the patrol-wagon started up, the cry of its siren drowning the protests of the crowd.

Poor Bill! He lay across the seat, and Jimmie, who had to sit next to him, caught him in his arms and held him. He was quivering, with awful motions like a spasm. He made no sound, and Jimmie was terrified, thinking that he was dying. Before long Jimmie felt a hot wetness stealing over his hands, first slimy, then turning sticky. He had to sit there, almost fainting with horror; he dared not say anything, for maybe the policeman would strike him also. He sat, clutching in his arms the shaking body, and whispering under his breath, "Poor Bill! Poor Bill!"

V

They came to the station-house, and Bill was carried out and laid on a bench, and the others were stood up before the desk and had their pedigrees taken. Gerrity demanded indignantly to be allowed to telephone, and this demand was granted. He routed lawyer Norwood from a party, and set him to finding bail; and meantime the prisoners were led to cells.

They had been there only a couple of minutes when there came floating through the row of steel cages the voice of a woman singing. It was Comrade Mabel Smith, in that clear sweet voice they had so often listened to on "social evenings" in the local. She was singing the Internationale:

> Arise, ye prisoners of starvation,
> Arise, ye wretched of the earth!

The sound thrilled them to the very bones, and they joined in the chorus with a shout. Then, of course, came the jailer: "Shut up!" And then again: "Shut up!" And then a third time: "Will ye shut up?" And then came a bucket of water, hurled through the cell bars. It hit Jimmie squarely in the mouth, and in the words of the poet, "the subsequent proceedings interested him no more!"

About midnight came Lawyer Norwood and Dr. Service. Both of these men had protested against the street-speaking at this time; but of course, when it came to comrades in trouble, they could not resist the appeal to their sympathies. Such is the difficulty of entirely respectable and decorous "parlour" Socialists, in their dealings with the wayward children of the movement, the "impossibilists" and "direct actionists" and other sowers of proletarian wild oats. Dr. Service produced a wad of bills and bailed out all the prisoners, and delivered himself of impressive indignation to the police-sergeant, while waiting for an ambulance to carry "Wild Bill" to the hospital. Jimmie Higgins, who had always hitherto shouted with the "wild" ones, realised suddenly how pleasant it is to have a friend who wears black broadcloth, and carries himself like the drum-major of a band, and is reputed to be worth a couple of hundred thousand dollars.

Jimmie went home; and there was Lizzie, pacing the floor and wringing her hands in anxiety—for there had been no way to get word to her what had happened. She flung herself into his arms, and then recoiled in fright when she discovered that he was wet. He told her the story; and would you believe it—Lizzie, being a woman, and only in the A-B-C stage of revolutionary education, actually did not know that it was a glorious and heroic adventure to be arrested! She thought it a disgrace, and tried to persuade him to keep the dreadful secret from the neighbourhood! And when she found that he was not through yet, but had to go to court in the morning and be tried, she wept copiously, and woke up Jimmie Junior, and started him to bawling. She was only to be pacified when Jimmie Senior agreed to take off his wet clothes at once, and drink a cup or two of boiling hot tea, and let himself be covered up with blankets, so that he might not die of pneumonia before he could get to court.

Next morning there was a crowded court-room and a stern and solemn judge frowning over his spectacles, and Lawyer Norwood making an impassioned defence of the fundamental American right of free speech. It was so very thrilling that Jimmie could hardly be kept from applauding his own lawyer!

And then Comrade Dr. Service arose, and in his most impressive voice gave the professional information that "Wild Bill's" nose had been broken, and three of his front teeth knocked out, and that he was in the hospital and unable to come to court; and all the other prisoners were called upon to testify what "Wild Bill" had done to bring this fate upon him. The policeman who had struck the blow testified that the prisoner had resisted arrest; a second policeman testified, "I seen the prisoner hit him first, your Honour,"—which caused Comrade Mabel Smith to cry out, "Oh, the ungrammatical prevaricator!"

The upshot of the trial was that each of the defendants was fined ten dollars. Comrade Gerrity led off with an indignant refusal to pay the fine; the rest of them followed suit—even Comrade Mabel! This caused evident distress of mind to the judge, for Comrade Mabel with her indignant pink cheeks and her big picture-hat looked more than ever the lady, and it is a fact known even to judges that American jails have not been constructed for ladies. The matter was settled by Lawyer Norwood paying her fine, in spite of her protests, and her demand to be sent to jail.

VI

The five men were led away, over the "Bridge of Sighs," as it was called, to the city jail, where they had their pedigrees taken again, and their pictures and their finger-prints—which for the first time impressed upon their minds the fact that they were dangerous criminals. Their clothes were taken away, and shirts and trousers given them, whose faded blue colour seemed to have been impregnated with the misery of scores of previous wearers. They were led through steel-barred doors, and along dark, steel-barred passages to one of the "tanks." A "tank," you discovered, was one floor of this four-storied packing box; on each side of it were a row of a dozen barred cells, each with four bunks, so that the total maximum population which might be crowded into the central space of the "tank" was ninety-six; however, this only happened on Monday mornings, when the "drunks" had all been brought in, and before the courts had had time to sort them out.

After you had lain down on your bunk for a few minutes, or had leaned against the wall of the "tank," you felt an annoying stinging sensation somewhere on you. You began to rub and scratch; before long you would be rubbing and scratching in a dozen different places, and then you would observe your neighbour watching you with a grin. "Seam-squirrels?" he would say; and he would bid you take off your coat, and engage in the popular hunting game of the institution. Jimmie remembered having heard a speaker refer to the city jail as the "Leesville Louse-ranch"; he had thought that a good joke at the time, but now it seemed otherwise to him.

It was splendid to stand up in court and to take your stand as a martyr; but now Jimmie discovered, as many an unfortunate has discovered before him, that being a martyr is not the sport it is cracked up to be. There were no heroics now, no singing. If you even so much as hummed, they took you out and shut you up in a dark hole called the "cooler"! Nor could you read, for there was no light in your cell, and perpetual twilight in the central gathering place of the "tank." Apparently the only things the authorities of Leesville wished you to do were to hunt "seam-squirrels," to smoke cigarettes, to "shoot craps," and to make the acquaintance of a variety of interesting young criminals, so that when you were ready to resume your outside life you might decide whether you wanted to be a hold-up man, a safe-cracker, a forger, or a second-story operator.

Jimmie Higgins, of course, brought a different psychology from that of the average jail-inmate. Jimmie could do his kind of work just as well in jail as anywhere else; and barring the torment of vermin, the diet of bread and thin coffee and ill-smelling greasy soup, and the worry about his helpless family outside, he really had a happy time—making the acquaintance of hoboes and pickpockets, and explaining to them the revolutionary philosophy. A man who went in to remedy social injustice all by himself could never get very far. It was only when he realised himself as a member of a class, and stood as a class and acted as a class, that he could accomplish a permanent result. Some of the workers had discovered this, and had set out to educate their fellows. They brought the wondrous message, even to those in jail; holding out to them the vision of a world made over in justice and kindness, the co-operative commonwealth of labour, in which every man should get what he produced, and no man could exploit his fellows.

VII

Three days passed, and then one afternoon Jimmie was summoned to see a visitor. He could guess who the visitor was, and he went with his heart in his throat, and looked through the dark mesh of wire, and saw Lizzie standing—stout, motherly Lizzie, now very pale, and breathing hard, and with tears running in little streamlets down her cheeks. Poor Lizzie, with her three babies at home, and her plain, ordinary, non-revolutionary psychology, which made going to jail a humiliation instead of a test of manhood, a badge of distinction! Jimmie felt a clutch in his own throat, and an impulse to tear down the beastly wire mesh and clasp the dear motherly soul in his arms. But all he could do was to screw his face into a dubious smile. Sure, he was having the time of his life in this jail! He wouldn't have missed it for anything! He had made a Socialist out of "Dead-eye Mike," and had got Pete Curley, a fancy "con" man, to promise to read "War, What For?"

There was only one thing which had been troubling him, and that was, how his family was making out. They had had practically nothing in the house, he knew, and poor Meissner could not feed four extra mouths. But Lizzie, also screwing her face into a smile, assured him that everything was all right at home, there was no need to worry. In the first place, Comrade Dr. Service had sent her a piece of paper with his name written on it; it appeared that this was called a check, and the groceryman had exchanged it for a five dollar bill. And in the next place there was a domestic secret which Lizzie had to confide—she had put by some money, without letting Jimmie know it.

"But how?" cried Jimmie, in wonder—for he had thought he knew all about his household and its expenses.

So Lizzie explained the trick she had played. Jimmie had committed an extravagance, treating her to a new dress out of his increased earnings: a gorgeous contrivance of several colours, looking like silk, even if it wasn't. Lizzie had stated that the cost was fifteen dollars, and he, the dub, had believed it! The truth was she had bought the dress in a second-hand shop for three dollars, and had put twelve dollars away for the time of the strike!

And Jimmie went back to his "tank," shaking his head and philosophising: "Gee! Can you beat these women?"

CHAPTER VII

JIMMIE HIGGINS DALLIES WITH CUPID

I

THE strike was over when Jimmie came out of jail; it had been settled by the double-barrelled device of raising the wages of the men and putting their leaders behind bars. Jimmie presented himself at his old place of working, and the boss told him to go to hell; so Jimmie went to Hubbardtown, and stood in the long line of men waiting at the gate of the engine company. Jimmie knew about black-lists, so when his time came to be questioned, he said his name was Joe Aronsky, and he had last worked in a machine-shop in Pittsburg; he had come to Hubbardtown because he had heard of high pay and good treatment. While he was answering these questions, he noticed a man sitting in the corner of the room studying his face, and he saw the boss turn and glance in that direction. The man shook his head, and the boss said: "Nothin' doin'." So Jimmie understood that the Hubbard Engine Company was taking measures to keep its shops clear of the agitators from Leesville.

He spent a couple of days trying other places in his home town, but all in vain—they had him spotted. At the brewery they were slower than elsewhere—they took him on for two hours. Then they found out his record, and "fired" him; and Jimmie "kidded" the boss, saying that they were too late—he had already given a Socialist leaflet to every man in the room!

On Jefferson Street, an out of the way part of the town, was a bicycle-shop kept by an old German named Kumme. One of the comrades told Jimmie that he wanted a helper, and Jimmie went there and got a job at two dollars a day. That was poor pay at present prices, but Jimmie liked the place, because his boss was a near-Socialist, a pacifist—for all countries except Germany. He got round it by saying that every nation had a right to defend itself; and Germany was the nation which had been attacked in this war. A good part of the energies of the old man went into proving this to his customers; if there were any customers who did not like it, they could go elsewhere.

Those who came were largely Germans, and so Jimmie was kept fully supplied with arguments against the munitions-industry, which they called a trade in murder, and in favour of the programme of "Feed America First." Among those who frequented the place was Jerry Coleman, who was still on the job, and as well supplied with ten dollar bills as ever. He had now revealed himself as an organiser for a new propaganda society, called "Labour's National Peace Council." Inasmuch as Labour and Peace were the phrases upon which Jimmie lived, he saw no reason why he should not back this organisation. Coleman assured Jimmie he hated the Kaiser, but that the German "people" must be defended. So Jimmie became, without having the least idea of it, one of the agencies whereby the Kaiser was subsidising social discontent in America.

But Jimmie was more careful now in his agitations. He had brought such distress into his home by his jail sentence, that he had been forced to make promises to Lizzie. Her anxiety for her children could no longer be kept to herself; and this caused a certain amount of friction between them, and sent Jimmie out grumbling at his lot in life. What was the use of trying to educate a woman, who could see no farther than her own kitchen-stove? When you wanted to be a world-saviour, to walk tip-toe on the misty mountain-tops of heroism, she dragged you down and chained you to the commonplace, taking all the zest and fervour out of your soul! The memories of "seam-squirrels" and of thin and ill-smelling and greasy soup had slipped somewhat into the background of Jimmie's mind, and he lived again the sublime hour when he had confronted the court and stood for the fundamental rights of an American citizen. He wanted to have that act of daring appreciated at its true value. Poor, blind, home-keeping Lizzie, who could not fufil these deeper needs of her husband's soul!

Jimmie had been, so far in his married life, as well domesticated as could be expected of a proletarian propagandist. He had yearned to own a home of his own, and meantime had manifested his repressed wish by getting a big packing-box and some broken shingles, and building a model play-house for

Jimmie Junior in the back yard. He had even found time on his tired and crowded Sundays to start a garden in mid-summer, the season when the local was least active. But now, of course, the war had come to obsess his mind, driving him to terror for the future of humanity, tempting him to martyrdoms and domestic irritations.

II

It was at this critical period in Jimmie's life that there appeared in Leesville a vivid young person by the name of Evelyn Baskerville. Evelyn was no tired kitchen slave—with her fluffy brown hair, her pert little dimples, her trim figure, her jaunty hat with a turkey-feather stuck on one side of her head. Evelyn was a stenographer, and proclaimed herself an advanced feminist; at her first visit she set the local upside down. It happened to be "social evening," when all the men smoked, and this "free" young thing took a cigarette from her escort and puffed it all over the place. This, of course, would not have made a stir in great centres of culture such as London and Greenwich Village; but in Leesville it was the first time that the equality of women had been interpreted to mean that the women should adopt the vices of the men.

Then Evelyn had produced from her handbag some leaflets on Birth Control, and proposed that the local should undertake their distribution. This was a new subject in Leesville, and while the members supposed it was all right, they found it embarrassing to have the matter explained too fully in open meeting. Evelyn wanted a "birth strike," as the surest means of ending the war; she wanted the "Worker" to take up this programme, and did not conceal her contempt for reactionaries in the movement who still wanted to pretend that babies were brought by storks. The delicate subject was finally "tabled," and when the meeting adjourned and the members walked home, every one was talking about Miss Baskerville—the men mostly talking with the men, and the women with the women.

Pretty soon it became evident that the vivid and dashing young person was setting her cap for Comrade Gerrity, the organiser. As Gerrity was an eligible young bachelor, that was all right. But then, a little later, it began to be suspected that she had designs upon Comrade Claudel, the Belgian jeweller.

Doubtless she had a right to make her choice between them; but some of the women were of the opinion that she took too long to choose; and finally one or two malicious ones began to say that she had no intention of choosing—she wanted both.

And then fell a thunderbolt into Jimmie's life. It was just after his arrest, when fame still clung to him; and after the meeting Comrade Baskerville came up and engaged him in conversation. How did it feel to be a jailbird? When he told her that it felt fine, she bade him not be too proud—she had served thirty days for picketing in a shirt-waist strike! As she looked at him, her pretty brown eyes sparkled with mischief, and her wicked little dimples lost no curtain-calls. Poor, humble Jimmie was stirred to his shoe-tips, for he had never before received the attentions of such a fascinating creature—unless perchance it had been to sell her a newspaper, or to beg the price of a sandwich in his hobo days. Here was one of the wonderful things about the Socialist movement, that it broke down the barriers of class, and gave you exciting glimpses of higher worlds of culture and charm!

Comrade Baskerville continued to flash her dimples and her wit at Jimmie, despite the fact that Comrade Gerrity and Comrade Claudel and several other moths were hovering about the candle-flame, and all the women in the local watching out of the corners of their eyes. Finally, to Jimmie's unutterable consternation, the vivid young goddess of Liberty inquired, "Wouldn't you like to walk home with me, Comrade Higgins?" He stammered, "Yes"; and they went out, the young goddess plying him with questions about conditions in the jail, and displaying most convincing erudition on the subject of the economic aspects of criminology—at the same time seeming entirely oblivious to the hoverings of the other moths, and the disgust of the unemancipated ladies of Local Leesville.

III

They walked down the street together, and first Comrade Baskerville shivered with horror at the "seam-squirrels," and then exclaimed with delight over the conversion of "Dead-eye Mike" to Socialism, and then made merry over the singing of the Internationale in the police-station. Had she discovered a "character" in this seemingly insignificant little machinist? At any rate, she plied him with questions about his past life and his ideas. When he told her of his starved and neglected childhood, she murmured sympathetically, and it seemed to the fascinated Jimmie that here was a woman who understood instinctively all the cravings of his soul. She laid her hand on his arm, and it was as if an angel were touching him—strange little thrills ran like currents of electricity all over him.

Yes, Comrade Baskerville could appreciate his sufferings, because she had suffered too. She had had a step-mother, and had run away from home at an early age, and fought her own way. That was why she stood so firmly for woman's emancipation—she knew the slavery of her sex through bitter experience. There were many men who believed in sex-equality as a matter of words, but had no real conception of it in action; as for the women—well, you might see right here in the local the most narrow, bourgeois ideas dominating their minds. Jimmie did not know what ideas Comrade Baskerville meant, but he knew that her voice was musical and full of quick changes that made him shiver.

He was supposed to be taking her home; but he had no idea where she lived, and apparently she had no idea either, for they just wandered on and on, talking about all the wonderful new ideas that were stirring the minds of men and women. Did Comrade Higgins believe in trial marriages? Comrade Higgins had never heard of this wild idea before, but he listened, and bravely concealed his dismay. What about the children? The eager feminist answered there need not be any children. Unwanted children were a crime! She proposed to get the working-class women together and instruct them in the technique of these delicate matters; and meantime, lacking the women, she was willing to explain it to any inwardly embarrassed and quaking man who would lend his ear.

Suddenly she stopped and cried, "Where are we?" And there came a peal of merry laughter, as she discovered they had gone far astray. They turned and set off in the right direction, and meantime the lecture on advance feminism continued. Poor Jimmie was in a panic—tumbled this way and that. He had considered himself a radical, because he believed in expropriating the expropriators; but these plans for overthrowing the conventions and disbanding the home—these left him aghast. And trilled into his ear by a vivid and amazing young thing with a soft hand upon his arm and a faint intoxicating perfume all about her! Why was she telling these things to him? What did she mean? What? *What?*

IV

They came to the house where she lived. It was late at night, and the street was deserted. It was up to Jimmie to say good night, but somehow he did not know how to say it. Comrade Evelyn gave him her hand, and for some reason did not take it away again. Of course it would not have been polite for Jimmie to have pushed it away. So he held it, and looked at the shadowy form before him, and felt his knees shaking. "Comrade Higgins," said the brave, girlish voice, "we shall be friends, shall we not?" And of course, Jimmie answered that they would—always! And the girlish voice replied, "I am *glad!*" And then suddenly it whispered, "Good night!" and the shadowy form turned and flitted into the house.

Jimmie walked away with the strangest tumult in his soul. It was something which the poets had been occupied for centuries in trying to portray, but Jimmie Higgins had no acquaintance with the poets, and so it was a brand new thing to him, he was left to experience the shock of it and to resolve the problems of it all alone. To be rolled and tossed about like a man in a blanket at a college hazing! To be a prey to bewilderment and fear, hope and longing, despair and rebellion, delicious excitement, angry self-contempt and tormenting doubt! Truly did that poet divine who first conceived the symbol of the mischievous little god, who steals upon an unsuspecting man and shoots him through the heart with a sharp and tormenting arrow!

The worst of it was, Jimmie couldn't tell Lizzie about it. The first time in four years that he had had a trouble he could not tell Lizzie! He even felt ashamed, as he came home and crawled into bed—as if he had done some dreadful wrong to Lizzie; and yet, he would have been puzzled to tell just what the wrong was, or how he could have avoided it. It was not he who had made the young feminist so delicious and sweet and frank and amazing. It was not he who had made the little god, and brewed the poison for the arrow's tip. No, it was some power greater than himself that had prepared this situation, some power cruel and implacable, which plots against domestic tranquillity; perhaps it was some hireling of capitalism, which will not permit a propagandist of social justice to do his work in peace of soul!

Jimmie tried to hide what was going on; and of course—poor, naïve soul—he had never learned to hide anything in his life, and now was too late to begin. The next time the local met, the women were saying that they were disappointed in Comrade Higgins; they had thought he was really devoted to the cause, but they saw now he was like all the rest of the men—his head had been turned by one smile on a pretty face. Instead of attending to his work, he was following that Baskerville creature about, gazing at her yearningly, like a moon-calf, making a ninny of himself before the whole room. And he with a wife and three babies at home, waiting for him and thinking he was hustling for the cause. When the meeting adjourned, and the Baskerville creature accepted the invitation of Comrade Gerrity to escort her home, the dismay of Comrade Higgins was so evident as to be ludicrous to the whole room.

V

In the interest of common decency it was necessary for the women of the local to take action on this matter. At least, a couple of them thought so, and quite independently and without prearrangement they called on Lizzie next day and told her that she should come more frequently to meetings, and keep herself acquainted with the new ideas of advanced feminism. And so when Jimmie came home that night, he found his wife dissolved in tears, and there was a most harrowing scene.

For poor Elizabeth Huszar, pronounced Eleeza Betooser, had had no chance whatever to familiarise herself with the new ideas of advanced feminism. Her notions of "free unions" had been derived from a quite different world, whose ideas were not new, but on the contrary very, very old, and were "advanced" only on the road to perdition. She judged Jimmie's behaviour according to thoroughly old standards, and she was broken-hearted, overwhelmed with grief and shame. He was like all the rest of men—and when she had fondly thought he was different! He despised her and spit upon her—a woman he had picked up in a brothel.

Poor Jimmie was stunned. He was conscious of no disrespect for Lizzie, it had not occurred to him to think that she might take the matter that way. But so she had taken it, beyond doubt, and with intensity that frightened him. He would not have believed that so many tears could stream from one woman's eyes—nor that his good, broad-faced, honest wife could be so abject in her misery. "Oh, I knowed it, I knowed it all along—it would be that way! I hadn't never ought to married you—you know I told you so!"

"But, Lizzie!" pleaded the husband. "You're mistaken. That hadn't nothin' to do with it."

She turned upon him wildly, her fingers stuck out as if she would claw him. "You mean to tell me if you hadn't 'a married a woman off the street, you'd 'a gone chasin' a fluffy-haired girl? If you'd 'a had a decent wife, that you knowed had some rights——"

"Lizzie!" he protested, in consternation. "Listen here——"

But she was not to be stopped. "Everybody said I was a fool; but I went an' done it, 'cause you swore you'd never hold it up to me! An' I went an' had them children"—Lizzie swept her arm at the children, as if to wipe them off the earth, to which they had come by a cruel mistake. Jimmie Junior, who was old enough to know that something serious was happening, and whose instinct was all against being wiped off the earth, began to howl wildly; and that set off the little ones—soon they were all three of them going at the top of their lungs. "Boo-hoo-hoo!"

It was truly a terrible climax to a romance. Jimmie, almost distracted, seized the hand of his injured spouse. "It's all nonsense!" he cried. "What they been tellin' you? I ain't done a thing, Lizzie! I only walked home with her one night."

But Lizzie answered that one night was plenty enough—she knew that from intimate and hateful experience. "And I know them fluffy-headed kind that frizzes their hair. What does she want to walk home at night with married men fer? And talkin' about the things she does——"

"She don't mean no harm, Lizzie—she's tryin' to help workin' women. It's what's called birth control—she wants to teach women——"

"If she wants to *teach* women, why don't she *talk* to the women? What's she all the time talkin' to *men* fer? You think you can tell me tales like that—me, that's been what I have?" And Lizzie went off into another fit, worse than ever.

VI

Jimmie found that it was with romance as with martyrdom —there was a lot of trouble about it which the romancers did not mention. He really felt quite dreadful, for he had a deep regard for this mother of his little ones, and he would not have made her suffer for anything. And she was right, too, he had to admit—her shots went deep home. "How'd you feel, if you was to find out I'd been walkin' home with some man?" When it was put to him that way, he realised that he would have felt very badly indeed.

A flood of old emotions came back to him. He went in memory with his group of roystering friends to the house of evil where he had first met Elizabeth Huszar, pronounced Eleeza Betooser. She had taken him to her room, and instead of making herself agreeable in the usual way, had burst into tears. She had been ill-treated, and was wretchedly lonely and unhappy. Jimmie asked why she did not quit the life, and she answered that she had tried more than once, but she could not earn a living wage; and anyhow, because she was big and handsome, the bosses would never let her alone, and what was the difference, if you couldn't keep away from the men?

They sat on the bed and talked, and Jimmie told her a little about his life, and she told about hers—a pitiful and moving story. She had been brought to America as an infant; her father had been killed in an accident, and her mother had supported several children by scrub-work. Lizzie had grown up in a slum of the far east side of New York, and she could not remember a time when she had not been sexually preyed upon; lewd little boys had taught her tricks, and men would buy her with candy or food. And yet there had been something in her struggling for decency; of her own volition she had tried to go to school, in spite of her rags; and then, when she was thirteen, she had answered an advertisement for work as a nurse-maid. That story had made an especial impression upon Jimmie—it was truly a most pitiful episode.

Her place of employment had been a "swell" apartment,

with a hall-boy and an elevator—the most wonderful place that Lizzie had ever beheld; it was like living in heaven, and she had tried so hard to do what she was told, and be worthy of her beautiful mistress and the lovely baby. But she had been there only two days when the mistress had discovered vermin on the baby, and had come to Lizzie and insisted on examining her head. And of course she had found something. "Them's only nits!" Lizzie had said; she had never heard of anybody who did not have "nits" in their hair. But the beautiful lady had called her a vile creature, and ordered her to pack up her things and get out of the house at once. And so Lizzie had had to wait until she became an inmate of a brothel before anybody took the trouble to teach her how to get the "nits" out of her hair, and how to bathe, and to clean her finger-nails and otherwise be physically decent.

Jimmie recalled all that, and he fell on his knees before his wife, and caught her two hands by main force, and swore to her that he had not done any wrong; he went on to tell her exactly what wrong he had done, which was the best way to convince her that he had not done any worse. He vowed again and again that he would never, never dally with Cupid again—he would see Comrade Baskerville at once and tell her it was "all off."

And so Lizzie looked up through her tears. "No," she said, "you don't need to see her at all!"

"What shall I do, then?"

"Just let her alone—don't tell her nothin'. She'll know it's off all right."

VII

But when you have a dead romance, you cannot leave it to rot on the highway; you are driven irresistibly to bury it decently. In spite of his solemn promises, Jimmie found himself thinking all the time about Comrade Baskerville, and how he would act when he met her next time—all the noble and dignified speeches he would make to her. He must manage to be alone with her; for of course he could not say such things with the jealous old hags of the local staring at him. The best thing, he decided, would be to tell her the frank and honest truth; to tell her about Lizzie, and how good and worthy she had been, and how deeply he realised his duty to her. And then tears would come into Comrade Baskerville's lovely eyes, and she would tell him that she honoured his high sense of marital responsibility. They must renounce; but of course they would be dear and true friends—always, always. Jimmie was holding her hands, in his fancy, as he said these affecting words: Always! Always! He knew that he would have to let go of the hands, but he was reluctant to do so, and he had not quite got to the point of doing it when, walking down Jefferson Street on his way home from work—behold, in front of him a trim, eager little figure, tripping gaily, with a jaunty hat with a turkey-feather stuck on one side! Jimmie knew the figure a block away, and as he saw it coming nearer, his heart leaped up and hit him in the bottom part of his neck, and all his beautiful speeches flew helter-skelter out of his head.

She saw him, and the vivid, welcoming smile came upon her face. She came up to him, and their hands clasped. "Why!" she cried. "What a pleasant meeting!"

Jimmie gulped twice, and then began, "Comrade Baskerville——" And then he gulped again, and began, "Comrade Baskerville——"

She stopped him. "I'm not Comrade Baskerville," she declared.

He could not get the meaning of these unexpected words. "What?" he asked.

"Haven't you heard the news?" she said, and beamed on him. "I'm Comrade Mrs. Gerrity."

He stared at her, utterly bewildered. "I've been that for twenty-four whole hours! Congratulate me!"

Little by little the meaning of the words began to dawn in Jimmie's stupid head. "Comrade Mrs. Gerrity!" he echoed. "But—but—I thought you didn't believe in marriage."

There came the most bewitching smile, a smile decorated with two rows of pearly white teeth. "Don't you understand, Comrade Higgins? No woman believes in marriage—until she meets the right man."

This was much too subtle. Jimmie was still gaping openmouthed. "But then, I thought—I thought——" he stopped again; for in truth, he had not known quite what he thought, and anyway, it seemed futile to try to formulate it now.

But of course, she knew, without his telling her; she knew

the meaning of his look of dismay, and of his stammering words. Being a kind little creature, she laid her hand on his arm. "Comrade Higgins," she said, "don't think I'm too mean!"

"Mean?" he cried. "Why, no! What? How——"

"Try to imagine you were a girl, Comrade Higgins. You can't propose to a man, can you?"

"Why, no—that is——"

"That is, not if you want him to accept! You have to make him do it. And maybe he's shy, and don't do it, and you have to put the idea in his head for him. Or maybe he's not sure he wants you, and you have to make him realise how very desirable you are! Maybe you have to scare him, making him think you're going to run off with somebody else! Don't you see how it is with a girl?"

Jimmie was still badly dazed, but he saw enough to enable him to stammer, "Yes." And Comrade Baskerville—that is, Comrade Mrs. Gerrity—gave him her hand again. "Comrade Higgins," she said, "you're a dear, sweet fellow, and you won't be too angry with me, will you? We'll be friends, won't we, Comrade Higgins?"

And Jimmie clasped the soft, warm hand, and gazed into the shining brown eyes, and he made a part of the wonderful speech which he had been planning as he walked. He said: "Always! Always!"

CHAPTER VIII

JIMMIE HIGGINS PUTS HIS FOOT IN IT

I

THE world struggle continued with constantly increasing ferocity. All summer long the Germans hammered at the French and British lines; while the British hammered at the gates of Constantinople, and the Italians at the gates of Trieste. The Germans sent their giant airships to drop loads of bombs on London, and their submarines to sink passenger-steamers and hospital-ships. Each fresh outrage against international law became the occasion of more letters of protest from the United States, and of more controversies in the newspapers, and in Congress, and in Kummé's bicycle-shop on Jefferson Street, Leesville.

In this last place, to be sure, the discussions were rather one-sided. Practically all who came there regarded the munitions industry as an accursed thing, and made no secret of their glee at the misfortunes which befell it; at shipyards which caught fire and burned up, at railroad-bridges and ships at sea destroyed by mysterious explosions. Kumme, a wizened-up, grizzle-haired old fellow with a stubby nose and a bullet-head, would fall to cursing in a mingling of English and German when any one so much as mentioned the fleets of ships that went across the water, loaded with shells to kill German soldiers; he would point a skinny finger at whoever would listen to him, declaring that the Germans in this country were not slaves, and would protect their Fatherland from the perfidious British and their Wall Street hirelings. Kumme took a newspaper printed in German, and a couple of weeklies published in English for the promotion of the German cause; he would mark passages in these papers and read them aloud—everything that the mind of man could recall or invent that was discreditable to Britain, to France and Italy, to Wall street, and to the nation which allowed Wall Street to bamboozle and exploit it. There were many Americans who had "muck-raked" their own country in the interests of social reform, and had praised the social system of Germany. These arguments the German propagandists now found useful, and Jimmie would take them to the Socialist local and pass them about. From the meeting of the local he and Meissner would go to the saloon where they had rendezvous with Jerry Coleman, who would distribute more ten dollar bills to be used in the printing of anti-war literature.

Old Kumme had a nephew by the name of Heinrich, who paid him a visit now and then. He was a tall, fine-looking fellow, who spoke much better English than his uncle, and wore better clothes. Finally he came to stay, and Kumme announced that he was to help in the shop. They didn't need any help that Jimmie could see, and certainly not from a fellow like Heinrich, who couldn't tell a spoke from a handle-bar; but it was none of Jimmie's business, so Heinrich put on working clothes, and spent a couple of weeks sitting behind the counter conversing in low tones with men who came to see him. After a while he took to going out again, and finally announced that he had secured a job in the Empire.

II

And then to the hangers-on in the shop there was another addition—an Irish workingman named Reilly. The Irishman was a peculiar problem in the war—the thorn in the Allied conscience, the weak spot in their armour, the broken link in their chain of arguments; and so every German was happy when an Irishman entered the room. This fellow Reilly came to have a punctured tire mended, and stopped to tell what he thought about the world-situation. Old man Kumme slapped him over the back, and shook him by the hand, and told him he was the right sort, and to come again. So Reilly took to hanging about; he would pull from his pocket a paper called "Hibernia," and Kumme would produce from under the counter a paper called "Germania," and the two would denounce "perfidious Albion" by the hour. Jimmie, bending over the straightening of a sprocket, would look up and grin, and exclaim, "You bet!"

It was winter-time, and darkness came early, and Jimmie was doing his work by electric light in the back of the shop, when Reilly came and mysteriously drew him into a corner. Did he really mean what he said about hatred of war, and willingness to fight against it? The Empire Shops were now turning out thousands of shell-casings every day, to be used in the murder of men. It was useless to try to start a strike, there were so many spies at work, and they fired every man who opened his mouth; if an outsider tried it they would send him to jail—for of course old Granitch had the city government in his vest-pocket.

All this was an old story to Jimmie; but now the Irishman went on to a new proposition. There was a way to stop the work of the Empire, a way that had been tried in other places, and had worked. Reilly knew where to get some T.N.T.—an explosive many times more powerful than dynamite. They could make bombs out of the steel tubing of bicycles, and Jimmie, knowing the Empire Shops as he did, could find a way to get in and arrange matters. There was big money in it—the fellows who did that job might live on Easy Street the rest of their lives.

Jimmie was stunned. He had been perfectly sincere in classifying German spies with sea-serpents; and here was a sea-serpent right before his eyes, raising his head through the floor of Kumme's bicycle-shop!

Jimmie answered that he had never had anything to do with that sort of thing. That wasn't the way to stop war; that was only making more war. The other began to argue with him, showing that it wouldn't hurt anybody; the explosion would take place at night, and all that would be damaged would be Abel Granitch's purse. But Jimmie was obdurate; fortunately one thing that had been incessantly pounded into his head at the local was that the movement could not use conspiracy, it must work by open propaganda, winning the minds and consciences of men.

First the Irishman became angry, and called him a coward and a molly-coddle. Then he became suspicious, and wanted to know if Jimmie would sell him out to the Empire. Jimmie laughed at this; he had no love for Abel Granitch—the damned old skunk might do his own spying. Jimmie would simply have nothing to do with the matter, one way or the other.

And so the project was dropped; but the little machinist was moved to keep his eyes open after that, and he made note of how many Germans, all strangers, were making the shop a meeting place; also the quick intimacy which had developed between the Irishman and Heinrich, Kumme's nephew who held himself so straight and had no back to his head.

Matters came to a climax with startling suddenness—the explosion of a bomb, though not the kind which Jimmie was expecting. It was an evening in February, just as he was about to close up, when he saw the door of the shop open, and four men walk in. They came with a peculiar, business-like air, two of them to the puzzled Jimmie, and the other two to Kumme. One turned back the lapel of his coat, showing a large gold star, and announcing, "I am an agent of the government, and you are under arrest." And at the same time the other seized Jimmie's arms and slipped a pair of handcuffs over his wrists. He passed his hands over his prisoner, a ceremony known as "frisking"; and at the same time the other men had seized Kumme. Jimmie saw two more men enter at the rear door of the shop, but they had nothing to do, for both Jimmie and Kumme had been too much startled to make any move to escape.

They were led out to an automobile, shoved in and whirled away. No questions were answered, so after a bit they stopped asking questions and sat still, reflecting upon all the sins they had ever committed in their lives, and upon the chances of these sins being known to the police.

III

Jimmie thought he was going to jail, of course; but instead they took him to the Post Office building, to an upstairs room. Kumme was taken to another room, and Jimmie did not see him again; all that Jimmie had time to know or to think about was a stern-faced young man who sat at a desk and put him on a griddle. "It is my duty to inform you that everything you state may be used against you," said this young man; and then, without giving Jimmie a chance to grasp the meaning of these words, he began firing questions at him. All through the ordeal the two detectives stood by his side, and in a corner of the room, at another desk, a stenographer was busily recording what he said. Jimmie knew there were such things as stenographers—for had he not come near falling in love with one only a short time before?

"Your name?" said the stern-faced young man; and then, "Where do you live?" And then, "Tell me all you know about this bomb-conspiracy."

"But I don't know nothin'!" cried Jimmie.

"You are in the hands of the Federal government," replied the young man, "and your only chance will be to make a clean breast. If you will help us, you may get off."

"But I don't know nothin'!" cried Jimmie, again.

"You have heard talk about dynamiting the Empire Shops?"

"Y-yes, sir."

"Who?"

"A man——" Jimmie got that far, and then he recollected the promise he had given. "I—I can't tell!" he said.

"Why not?"

"It wouldn't be right."

"Do you believe in dynamiting buildings?"

"No, sir!" Jimmie put into this reply a note of tense sincerity; and so the other began to argue with him. Atrocious crimes had been committed all over the country, and the government wished to put a stop to them; surely it was the duty of a decent citizen to give what help he could. Jimmie listened until a sweat of anxiety stood out on his forehead; but he could not bring himself to "peach" on a fellow-workingman. No, not if he were sent to jail for ten or twenty years, as the stern-faced young man told him might happen.

"You told Reilly you wouldn't have anything to do with bombs?" asked the young man; and Jimmie answered, "Sure, I did!" And his poor head was so addled that he didn't even realise that in his reply he had told what he had been vowing he would never tell!

The questioner seemed to know all about everything, so it was easy for him to lead Jimmie to tell how he had heard Kumme cursing the Empire Shops, and the country, and the President; how he had seen Kumme whispering to Reilly, and to Germans whose names he had not learned, and how he had seen Heinrich, Kumme's nephew, cutting up lengths of steel tubing. Then the questioner asked about Jerry Coleman. How much money had Jimmie got, and just what had he done with it? Jimmie refused to name other people; but when the young man made the insinuation that Jimmie might have kept some of the money for himself, the little machinist exclaimed with passionate intensity—not one dollar had he kept, nor his friend Meissner either; they had given statements to Jerry Coleman, and this though many a time they had been hard up for their rent. The police could ask Comrade Gerrity and Comrade Mary Allen, and the other members of the local.

So the questioner led Jimmie on to talk about the Germans in the movement. Schneider, the brewer, for example—he was one of those who cursed the Allies most vehemently, and he had been in this bomb-conspiracy. Jimmie was indignant; Comrade Schneider was as good a Socialist as you could find, and Socialists had nothing to do with bombs! But young Emil Forster—he had been making explosives in his spare hours, had he not? At which Jimmie became still more outraged. He knew young Emil well; the boy was a carpet-designer and musician, and if anybody had told such tales about him, they were lying, that was all. The questioner went on for an hour or so, tormenting poor Jimmie with such doubts and fears; until finally he dropped a little of his sternness of manner, and told Jimmie that he had merely been trying him out, to see what he knew about various men whose pro-German feelings had brought them under suspicion. No, the government had no evidence of crime against Schneider or Forster, or any of the bona-fide Socialists. They were just plain fools, letting themselves be used as tools of German plotters, who were spending money like water to make trouble in munitions factories all over the country.

IV

The questioner, who explained himself as a "special agent" of the Department of Justice, went on to read Jimmie a lecture. A sincere man like himself ought to be ashamed to let himself be taken in by German conspirators, who were trying to break up American industry, to lead American labour by the nose.

"But they want to stop the making of munitions!" cried Jimmie.

"But that's only so that Germany can make more munitions!"

"But I'm opposed to their being made in Germany, too!"

"What can you do to stop it in Germany?"

"I'm an international Socialist. When I oppose war in my own country, I help the Socialists to oppose it in other countries. I ain't a-going to stop—not so long as I've got any breath left in me!" And here was Comrade Jimmie, delivering a sermon on pacifism to the "special agent" of the government, who held his fate in his hands! But no one was going to defend war to Jimmie Higgins and not be answered—even though Jimmie might go to jail for the rest of his life!

The young man laughed—more genially than Jimmie would have thought possible at the start of this grilling. "Higgins," he said, "you're a good-natured idiot. You can thank your lucky stars that one of the men you trusted happened to be a government detective. If we didn't know the truth about you, you might have had a hard time clearing yourself."

Jimmie's jaw had fallen. "A government detective! Who is the government detective?"

"Reilly," said the young man.

"Reilly? But it was him that tempted me!"

"Well, congratulate yourself that you resisted temptation!"

"But maybe he tempted Heinrich too!"

"No—Heinrich didn't have to be tempted. It was on account of Heinrich that we began the investigation. He has been making explosives and planting them all over the country. His name isn't Heinrich, and he isn't a nephew of Kumme; his name is von Holtz, and he's a Prussian officer, a personal friend of the Kaiser."

Jimmie was speechless. For the love of Mike! He had been sitting in the back part of old Kumme's bicycle-shop, filling his pipe from the tobacco-pouch of a personal friend of the Kaiser! He had called this personal friend of the Kaiser a dub and a jack-ass, informing him that a real mechanic could put a ball-bearing together while he, the personal friend of the Kaiser, was spitting on his hands. Could you beat it?

Mr. Harrod, the "special agent," informed Jimmie that he would have to testify as to what he knew; and Jimmie was so indignant at the way he had been taken in that he was willing to do so. He would have to give bond to appear, added the other; did he know any one who would vouch for him? Jimmie racked his harassed brain. Comrade Dr. Service might consent, if he were quite sure that Jimmie had not really meant to help the Germans. Mr. Harrod kindly consented to give this assurance, and called up Dr. Service, whom he seemed to know, and told him the circumstances: Dr. Service finally said that he would put up a couple of thousand dollars to guarantee Jimmie's appearance before the grand jury and at the trial. Mr. Harrod added that if Dr. Service would promise to come in the morning and attend to the matter, the government would take his word and let the witness go for the night. The doctor promised, and Jimmie was told that he was free till ten o'clock next morning. He went out, like a sky-lark escaping from a cage!

V

He had been warned not to talk to any one, so he told Lizzie that he had been kept late to make repairs on a motorcycle. And next morning he got up at the usual hour, to avoid exciting suspicion, and went and stared at the shop, which was locked up, with a policeman on guard. He bought a copy of the Leesville "Herald," and read the thrilling story of the German plot which had been unearthed in Leesville. There were half a dozen conspirators under arrest, and more than a dozen bombs had been found, all destined to be set off in the Empire Shops. Franz Heinrich von Holtz, who had blown up a bridge in Canada and put an infernal machine on board a big Atlantic liner, had been nailed at last!

Half an hour before time, Jimmie was waiting at the Post Office building, and when Comrade Dr. Service arrived, they went in and signed the bond. Coming out again, the grim and forbidding doctor ordered Jimmie into his car, and oh, what a dressing-down he did give him! He had Jimmie where he wanted him—right over his knees—and before he let him up he surely did make him burn! The little machinist had been so cock-sure of himself; going ahead to end the war, by stopping the shipping of munitions, and paying no heed to warnings from men older and wiser than himself! And now see what he had got himself in for—arrested with a gang of fire-bugs and desperadoes, under the control and in the pay of a personal friend of the Kaiser!

Poor Jimmie couldn't put up much of a defence: he was

cowed, for once. He could only say that he had had no evil intention—he had merely been agitating against the trade in munitions—a wicked thing——

"Wicked?" broke in the Comrade Doctor. "The thing upon which the freedom of mankind depends!"

"W-what?" exclaimed Jimmie; for these words sounded to him like sheer lunacy.

The other explained. "A nation that means to destroy its neighbours sets to work and puts all its energies into making guns and shells. The free peoples of the world won't follow suit—you can't persuade them to do it, because they don't believe in war, they can't realise that their neighbours intend to make war. So, when they are attacked, their only chance for life is to go out into the open market and buy the means of defence. And you propose to deprive them of that right—to betray them, to throw them under the hoofs of the war-monster! You, who call yourself a believer in justice, make yourself a tool of such a conspiracy! You take German money——"

"I never took no German money!" cried Jimmie, wildly.

"Didn't Kumme pay you money?"

"But I worked in his shop—I done my ten hours a day right straight!"

"And this fellow Jerry Coleman? Hasn't he given you money?"

"But that was for propaganda—he was agent for Labour's National Peace Council——"

And the Comrade Doctor fairly snorted. "How could you be such an ass? Don't you read the news? But no—of course you don't—you only read German dope!" And the Comrade Doctor drew out his pocket-book, which was bursting with clippings, and selected one from a New York paper, telling how the government was proceeding against the officials of an organisation called "Labour's National Peace Council" for conspiring to cause strikes and violence. The founder of the organisation was a person known as "the Wolf of Wall Street"; the funds had been furnished by a Prussian army officer, an attaché of the German legation, who had used his official immunity to incite conspiracy and wholesale destruction of property in a friendly country. What had Jimmie to say to that?

And poor Jimmie for once had nothing to say. He sat,

completely crushed. Not merely the money which he had got from Kumme on Saturday night, but also the ten dollar bills which Jerry Coleman had been slipping into his hand—they too had come from the Kaiser! Was the whole radical movement to be taken over by the Kaiser, and Jimmie Higgins put out of his job?

CHAPTER IX

JIMMIE HIGGINS RETURNS TO NATURE

I

KUMME'S bicycle-shop went out of business, and its contents were sold at auction. Jimmie Higgins watched the process wistfully, reflecting how, if he had not wasted his substance on Socialist tracts, if he had saved a bit of his wages like any normal human being, he might have bought this little business and got a start in life. But alas, such hopes were not for Jimmie! He must remain in the condition which the President of his country described as "industrial serfdom"; he must continue to work for some other man's profit, to be at the mercy of some other man's whim.

He found himself a job in the railroad-shops; but in a couple of weeks came an organiser, trying to start a union in the place. Jimmie, of course, joined; how could he refuse? And so the next time he went to get his pay he found a green slip in his envelope, informing him that the Atlantic Western Railroad Company would no longer require his services. No explanation was given, and none sought—for Jimmie was old in the ways of American wage-slavery, euphemistically referred to as "industrial serfdom."

He got another start as helper to a truckman. It was the hardest work he had yet done—all the harder because the boss was a dull fellow who would not talk about politics or the war. So Jimmie was discontented; perhaps the spring-time was getting into his blood; at any rate, he hunted through his Sunday paper, and came on an advertisement of a farmer who wanted a "hand." It was six miles out in the country, and Jimmie, remembering his walk with the Candidate, treated himself to a Sunday afternoon excursion. He knew nothing about farm-work, and said so; but the munition-factories had drained so much labour from the land that the farmer was glad to get anybody. He had a "tenant-house" on his place, and on Monday morning Jimmie hired his former boss—the truckman—to move his few sticks of furniture; he bade farewell to his little friend Meissner, and next day was learning to milk cows and steer a plough.

So Jimmie came back to the bosom of his ancient Mother. But alas, he came, not to find joy and health, not as a free man, to win his own way and make a new life for himself; he came as a soil-slave, to drudge from dawn to dark for a hire that barely kept him going. The farmer was the owner of Jimmie's time, and Jimmie disliked him heartily, because he was surly-tempered and stingy, abusing his horses and nagging at his hired man. Jimmie's education in farm-economics was not thorough enough to enable him to realise that John Cutter was as much of a slave as himself—bound by a mortgage to Ashton Chalmers, President of the First National Bank of Leesville. John drudged from dawn to dark, just as Jimmie did, and in addition had all the worry and fear; his wife was a sallow and hollow-chested drudge, who took as many bottles of patent-medicine as poor Mrs. Meissner.

But Jimmie kept fairly cheerful because he was learning new things, and because he saw how good it was for the babies, who were getting fresh air and better food than they had ever had in their little lives before. All summer long he ploughed and harrowed and hoed, he tended horses and cows and pigs and chickens, and drove to town with farm-truck to be sold. He would be too tired at night even to read his Socialist papers; for six months he let the world go its way unhindered—its way of desperate strife and colossal anguish. It was the time when the German hordes hurled themselves against the fortifications of Verdun. For five horrible months they came on, wave upon endless wave; the people of France set their teeth and swore, "They shall not pass!" and the rest of civilisation waited, holding its breath.

II

The only chance Jimmie had to talk about these matters was of a Saturday night when he strolled up to the store at a near-by cross-roads. The men he met here were of a new type to him—as different from factory people as if they came from another planet. Jimmie had been taught to laugh at them as "hayseeds"; intellectually he regarded them as relics of a vanished age, so of course he could not listen to their talk very long without "butting in." He began with the declaration that the Allies were as bad as the Germans. He got away with that, because they had all been taught to hate the "Britishers" in their schoolbooks, and they didn't know very much about Frenchmen and "Eye-talians." But when Jimmie went on to say that the American government was as bad as the German government—that all governments were run by capitalists, and all went to war for foreign markets and such plunder—then what a hornets' nest he brought about his ears! "You mean to say American armies would do what them Proosians done in Belgium?" And when Jimmie answered Yes, an indignant citizen rose from his seat on a cracker-box, and tapped him on the shoulder and said: "Look here, young feller, you better run along home. You'll git yerself a coat of tar and feathers if you talk too much round these parts."

So Jimmie shut up for a while; and when he went out with his armful of purchases, an aged, white-whiskered patriarch who had been listening got up and followed him out. "I'm goin' your way," he said. "Git in with me." Jimmie climbed into the buggy; and while the bony old mare ambled along through the summer-night the driver asked questions about Jimmie's life. Where had he been brought up? How had it been possible for a man to live all his life in America, and know so little about his native land?

Peter Drew was this old farmer's name, and he had been in the first battle of Bull Run, and had fought with the Army of Northern Virginia all the way to Richmond. So he knew how American armies behave; he could tell Jimmie about a million free men who had rushed to arms to save their nation's integrity, and had made a clean job of it, and then gone quietly back to their work at farm and forge. Jimmie had heard Comrade Mary Allen, the Quaker, make the statement that "Force never settled anything." He repeated this now, and the other replied that an American ought to be the last person in the world to make such a statement, for his country had provided the best illustration in history of the importance of a good job of spanking. It was force that had settled the slavery question—and settled it so that now you might travel in the

South and have a hard time to find a man that would want to unsettle it.

But Jimmie knew nothing about all that; he knew nothing about anything in America. The old man said it frightened him to realise that the country had let a man grow up in it with so little understanding of its soul. All that precious tradition, utterly dead so far as Jimmie was concerned! All those heroes who had died to make free the land in which he lived, and to keep it free—and he did not know their names, he did not even know the names of the great battles they had fought! The old man's voice trembled and he laid his hand on Jimmie's knee.

The little Socialist tried to explain that he had dreams of his own. He was fighting for international freedom—his patriotism was higher and wider than any one country. And that was all right, said the other, but why kick down the ladder by which you had climbed—and especially when you had perhaps not entirely finished climbing? Why not know the better side of your own country, and appeal to it? Peter Drew went on to tell of a speech he had heard Abraham Lincoln make, and to quote things Lincoln had said; could Jimmie doubt that Lincoln would have opposed the rule of the country by Wall Street? And when a country had been shaped and guided by such men as Lincoln, why trample its face and besmirch its good name—just because there were in it some evil men contending against its ideals of freedom and democracy?

This old soldier lived about a mile from Jimmie, and asked his new friend to come and see him. So the next afternoon, which was Sunday, Lizzie put on a newly starched dress, and Jimmie packed the two littlest infants in the double perambulator, and took Jimmie Junior's chubby hand, and they trudged down the road to the farm-house which the old man's father had built. Mrs. Drew was a sweet-faced, rather tired looking old lady, but her pale eyes seemed to smile with hospitality, and she brought out a basket of ripe peaches, and sat and chatted sympathetically with Lizzie about the care of babies, while Jimmie and the old man sat under the shade of an elm tree by the kitchen-door and discussed American history. Jimmie listened to stories of battle and imprisonment, of monster heroisms and self-immolations. Up to this time he had been looking at war from the outside, as it were; but now he got a glimpse of the soul of it, he began to understand how a man might be willing to leave his home and his loved ones, and march out to fight and suffer and die to save his country in which he believed.

And here was another new idea: this old fellow had been a soldier, had fought through four years of incessant battles, and yet he had not lost his goodness. He was kind, gentle, generous; he gave dignity to the phrases at which Jimmie had been taught to mock. It was impossible not to respect such a man; and so little by little Jimmie was made to reflect that there might be such a thing as the soul of America, about which Peter Drew was all the time talking. Perhaps there was really more to the country than Wall Street speculators and grafting politicians, policemen with clubs and militiamen with bayonets to stick into the bodies of workingmen who tried to improve their lot in life!

III

In the course of the summer Jimmie had to take several days off and go into Leesville to attend the trial of the German plotters. He had to take the witness-stand and tell all he know about Kumme and Heinrich and the other men who had frequented the bicycle-shop. It was a very serious experience, and before it was over Jimmie was heartily glad that he had rejected the invitation to help blow up the Empire Machine Shops. The trial ended with a sentence of six months for Jimmie's old employer, and of two years each for Heinrich and his pals. The law allowed no more—to the intense disgust of the Leesville "Herald." The "Herald" was in favour of a life-sentence for any one who interfered with the industry upon which the prosperity of the city depended.

Among those who came to the trial was Comrade Smith, editor of the "Worker," and Jimmie sat with him in Tom's "Buffeteria," and heard an account of the latest developments in the Empire Shops. The movement of discontent had been entirely crushed; the great establishment was going at full blast, both day and night. They were taking on hundreds of new hands, mostly women and girls, speeding them faster and faster, turning out tens of thousands of shell-casings every day. And still they were not satisfied; new buildings were going up, the concern was spreading like a huge blot over the landscape. There was talk of an explosives factory nearby, so that shells might be filled as fast as they were made.

The "boom" conditions continued in Leesville; speculators were reaping harvests, it seemed as if the masters of the city were all on a spree. Comrade Smith advised Jimmie to stay where he was, for it was getting to be harder and harder for the workers in Leesville to get anything to eat. But out on the heights along the river front, the part of the city called "Nob Hill," new palaces were rising. And it was that way all over the Eastern part of the country, said the young editor; the rich no longer knew what to do with their millions.

On the day the trial ended, Jimmie stayed in town to attend a meeting of the local and pay his back dues. So he met all his old friends, and heard "Wild Bill" get up and deliver one of his tirades. Bill had in his hand a newspaper clipping telling of the amazing madness that had struck Wall Street. Munition-stocks were soaring to prices beyond belief; "war-babies," men called them, with unthinkably cynical wit. On the "Great White Way," to which they rushed to celebrate these new Arabian Nights, there was such an orgy of dissipation as the world had never seen. "And this is what we have to slave for!" yelled "Wild Bill"—looking wilder than ever since the police had broken his nose and knocked out his three front teeth. "This is why we are chained to our jobs—shut up in jail if we so much as open our mouths! Piling up millions for old man Granitch, so that young Lacey can marry chorus-girls and divorce them—or steal away another man's wife, as they say he's doing just now!"

Then young Emil Forster spoke, explaining to Jimmie the inner significance of terrific world-events. Russia was in the midst of a gigantic offensive, which was meant to overwhelm Austria; England at the same time was hurling in her new armies on the Somme; for these two giant movements they wanted shells—millions and millions of shells from America, which alone could make enough of them. The railroads were clogged with them, they were piled mountain-high at the terminals and ports; whole fleets of steamers were loading up with them, and proceeding to England and France, and to Russia by way of Archangel. And of course the German submarines were out to stop them; the whole world was like a powder-magazine over the issue. The President, by his series of notes, had forced Germany to agree not to sink passenger-vessels; but this promise was not easy to keep—accidents kept happening, and the temper of the peoples was rising, America was being drawn nearer every hour to the vortex of this dreadful strife.—Such was the picture which Jimmie carried back to the farm; you could hardly wonder if he missed that peace and joy which men are supposed to imbibe at the bosom of their Mother Nature!

CHAPTER X

JIMMIE HIGGINS MEETS THE OWNER

I

IT was late at night when Jimmie left the Socialist local, and took the trolley out into the country. He had to walk nearly two miles from where he got off, and a thunder-storm had come up; he got out and started to trudge through the darkness and the floods of rain. Several times he slipped off the road into the ditch, and once he fell prone, and got up and washed the mud from his eyes and nose with the stream of fresh water pouring about his head. While he was thus occupied he heard the sound of a horn, and saw a glare of light rushing up. He jumped into the ditch again, and a big automobile went by at a fast pace, spattering showers of mud all over him. He plodded on, swearing to himself. Some of them munition-millionaires, no doubt—tearing over the country at night, honking their horns like they owned the roads, and covering poor walking people with their splashings!

And so on, until Jimmie came round a turn of the road, and saw the white glare of light again, this time standing still. It seemed to be pointing up into the trees; and when he got nearer he made out the reason—it had run off the road into the ditch, and then up the other slope, and there rolled over onto its side.

"Hello!" said a voice, as Jimmie came slopping up.

"Hello!" he answered.

"How far is it to the nearest house?"

"Maybe half a mile."

"Who lives there?"

"I do."

"Have you got a horse and buggy?"

"There's one at the big house, just a piece beyond."

"Do you suppose we could get enough men to turn this car over?"

"I dunno; there ain't many about here."

"Damn!" muttered the man to himself. Then, after a moment, "Well, there's no use staying here." This to his companion, whom Jimmie made out to be a woman. She was standing still, with the cold rain pouring over her. The man put his arm about her, and said to Jimmie, "Lead the way, please." So Jimmie set out, slopping through the mud as before.

Nothing more was said until they reached the "tenant-house" where the Jimmies lived. But meantime the little Socialist's mind was busy; it seemed to him that the man's voice was familiar, and he was trying to recall where and how he had heard it before. They came to the house, which was dark, and the couple stood on the porch while Jimmie went in and groped for a match and lighted the single smoky oil-lamp on which the household depended. Carrying it in his hand, he went to the door and invited the couple in. They came; and so Jimmie got a glimpse of the face of the man, and almost dropped the lamp right there where he stood. It was Lacey Granitch!

II

The young lord of Leesville was too much occupied with his own affairs to notice the look on the face of the yokel before him; or perhaps he was so used to being recognised, and to being stared at by yokels. He looked about the room and saw a stove. "Can you get us a fire, so this lady can get dry?"

"Y-yes," said Jimmie. "I-I suppose so." But he made no move; he stood rooted to the spot.

"Lacey," put in the woman, "don't stop for that. Get the car started, or get another." And Jimmie looked at her; she was rather small, and very beautiful—quite the most beautiful human creature that Jimmie had ever looked at. One could see that she was expensively dressed, even though everything she had on was soaked with rain.

"Nonsense!" exclaimed Lacey. "You can't travel till you get dry—you'd be ill." And he turned upon Jimmie. "Get a fire, won't you?" he exclaimed. "A big fire. I'll make it worth while to you for whatever you do. Only don't stand there gaping all night," he added impatiently.

Jimmie leaped to obey; partly because he had been in the habit of leaping to obey all his life—but also partly because he was sorry for the beautiful wet lady, and because, if he stood and stared any longer, Lacey Granitch might recognise him. The moment when Jimmie had been singled out in the herd of strikers and cursed by the young master of the Empire Machine Shops was one of the most vivid memories of Jimmie's rebellious life, and it did not occur to him that the incident might not have equally impressed the other participant.

In a few minutes the stove was hot; and urged by her escort, the lady took off her driving-coat and hat, and hung them over a chair. Everything underneath was wet, and the man urged her to take off her skirt and waist. "What does he matter?" he argued, referring to Jimmie; but the lady would not do it. She stood by the stove, shivering slightly, and pleading with her escort to make haste, to find some way to get the car running again. They might be followed——

"Oh, nonsense, Helen!" cried Lacey. "You are tormenting yourself with nightmares. Be sensible, and get dry." He piled the wood into the stove, and ordered Jimmie to get another armful; and Jimmie obeyed with his hands and feet—but meantime his rebellious little brain was taking in every detail of the situation, putting this and that together.

The talking had waked up Lizzie, so Jimmie rushed into the next room and whispered, "Lacey Granitch is here!" If he had told her that the Angel Gabriel was there, or Jehovah with all his thunders and his retinue of seraphim, poor Lizzie could not have been more stunned. Jimmie ordered her to get up, and get on her dress and shoes, and get a cup of coffee for the lady; the dazed woman obeyed—though she would rather have crawled under the bed than face the celestial personages who had taken possession of her home.

III

Lacey ordered Jimmie to accompany him, to find some help to get the car into travelling condition. They went out together, and on the porch, before they braved the rain again, young Granitch stopped and spoke: "See here, my man; I want you to help me get a gang together, and I want you to keep quiet, please—say nothing about who was in the car. If any other people come along and ask questions, keep your mouth shut, and I'll make it worth while to you—well worth while. Do you understand?"

Every instinct in Jimmie Higgins was ready to answer, "Yes, sir." That was what he had always answered to such commands—he, and his father, and his father's fathers before him. But something else within him resisted this instinct—the new revolutionary psychology which he had so painfully acquired, and which made continual war upon his old-time docilities. It seemed that this was the moment, if ever in his life, to show the stuff he was made of. He clenched his hands, and everything in him turned to iron. *"Who is that lady?"* he demanded.

Lacey Granitch was so taken aback that he started visibly. "What do you mean?"

"I mean—is she your wife? Or is she some other man's wife?"

"Why you damned——" And the young lord of Leesville stopped, speechless. Jimmie fell back a couple of steps, as a matter of precaution, but he did not weaken in his rigid resolve.

"I know you, Mr. Granitch," he said; "and I know what you're doing. You might as well know you ain't foolin' nobody."

"What the hell is it to you?" cried the other; but then he stopped again, and Jimmie heard him breathing hard. Evidently he made an effort to keep his self-control; when he spoke again, his voice was quieter. "Listen, my good fellow," he said. "You have a chance to make a good deal of money to-night——"

"I don't want your money!" broke in Jimmie. "I wouldn't touch your filthy money, that you get by murdering men!"

"My God!" said Lacey Granitch; and then, weakly: "What have you got against me?"

"What have I got? I was workin' in the Empire, an' I went on strike for my rights, an' you cursed me like I was a dog, an' you sent the police an' had me arrested, an' they smashed Wild Bill's nose, an' sent me up for ten days when I hadn't done nothin'——"

"Oh! So that's it, is it?"

"Yes, that's it; but I wouldn't mind that so much—if it

wasn't for them shells you're makin' to kill men over in Europe. And you spendin' the money drinkin' champagne with chorus-girls, an' running off with other men's wives!"

"You——" and Lacey uttered a foul oath, and leaped at Jimmie; but Jimmie had expected that, he was looking out for himself. There was no railing to the little porch on which he stood, and he leaped off to the ground and away. Because he knew the lay of the land, he could run faster in the darkness than his pursuer.

He sped down the path and out into the road—and there was the headlight of an automobile, almost upon him. The vehicle came to an instant stop, and a startled voice cried, "Hey, there!"

"Hey, there!" answered Jimmie, and stopped in the light; for he did not believe that his enemy would dare pursue him there.

The voice from the car spoke again. "There's an automobile off the road a ways back here. Do you know anything about who the people are that were driving it?"

"Sure I do!" answered Jimmie promptly.

"Where are they?"

"They're up in that house—Lacey Granitch an' a lady named Helen——"

And instantly the door of the car was flung open. A man leaped out, and another man, and another; they kept coming—Jimmie would not have believed that an automobile could have held so many people. Not one of them said a word, but all started on the run for Jimmie's house as if they were charging in a battle.

IV

Jimmie followed behind. He heard sounds of a scuffle on the lawn, and screams from inside. At first the little farm-hand could not make up his mind what to do, but finally he ran to the house; and there in the front room he saw the beautiful lady, with her wet hair streaming down her back, and the tears streaming down her face, sunk on her knees before the man who had hailed Jimmie from the automobile. She had caught his coat with her two hands, and clung to it with such desperation that when he tried to draw away he dragged her along the floor. "Paul!" she was screaming. "What are you going to do?"

"Be quiet! Be quiet!" commanded the man. He was young, tall and superhumanly handsome; his face had the white light of a passionate resolve, his lips were set like those of a man who is marching to his death in battle. "Answer me!" cried the woman again and again; until finally he said: "I shan't kill him; but I mean to teach him his lesson."

"Paul, Paul, have mercy!" sobbed the woman; she went on pleading hysterically, in the most dreadful distress that Jimmie had ever seen or heard. "It wasn't his fault, Paul, it was mine! I did it all! Oh, for Christ's sake! You are driving me mad!" She moaned, she implored, she sobbed till she choked herself; and when the man tried to tear her hands loose she fought with him, he could not get free of her.

"You're not going to move me, Helen," he declared. "You might as well get that clear."

"But I tell you it was my fault, Paul! I ran away with him!"

"All right," answered the man, grimly. "I'll fix him so no other man's wife will ever run away with him."

Her clamour continued more wildly than ever, until two other men came into the room. "Joe," said Paul, to one of them, "take her down to the car and keep her there. Don't let her call for help—if anybody comes along, keep her quiet, keep your hand tight over her mouth."

"Paul, you're a fiend!" shrieked the woman. "I'll kill you for this!"

"You're welcome to," answered the man. "I shouldn't care—but I'm going to do this job before I die." And he tore the woman's hands away from him, and by his stern anger he gave the other two men the necessary resolution. They carried her, half fainting, out of the room.

All this time Jimmie Higgins had been standing like one turned to stone; and Lizzie had shrunk into a far corner of the room, all but paralysed with terror. Now the man turned to them. "My good people," he said, "we want to borrow your room for a half hour or so. We'll pay you well for it—enough to buy the whole house if you want to."

"W-w-what are you goin' to do?" stammered Jimmie.

"We're going to teach a little fundamental morality to a

young man whose education has been neglected," replied the other. That somehow did not tell Jimmie very much, but he forbore to speak again, for never in all his life had he seen a man who conveyed to him the impression of such resistless force as this man. He was truly a superhuman creature, terrifying, panoplied in lightnings of wrath.

The door of the house opened again, and Lacey Granitch came in, with a man on each side holding him by the arms, and a pair of handcuffs on his wrist. Of all the dreadful spectacles that Jimmie had seen that dreadful night, the worst was the face of the young master of the Empire Machine Shops. It was green—absolutely and literally green. His knees trembled so that he seemed about to sink to the floor, and his dark eyes were those of an animal in a trap.

There came another man behind him carrying two black cases in his hands. He opened one, and took out some instrument with wires attached, and hung part of it to a hook on the wall; he pressed a switch, and a soft white radiance flooded the room. The man who was in command, the one whom the lady had called "Paul," now turned to Jimmie and his wife. "You may take your lamp," he said. "Go into the other room and stay there till we call you, please."

"W-w-what are you goin' to do?" Jimmie found courage to stammer again. But the other merely bade him to go into the other room and stay, and it would be all right, and he would be well paid for his time and trouble. There was no use trying to interfere; no use trying to get away, for the house would be watched.

V

Jimmie Junior had been wakened by the uproar, and was whimpering; so Lizzie hurried to quiet him, and Jimmie set the little smoky lamp on the dresser, and went and sat on the bed beside her, holding her hand in his. Both their hands were shaking in a way that was amazing.

Every sound from the other room was plainly audible. Lacey was pleading, and "Paul" commanded him to hold his tongue. There was a scuffle, and then terrified moans, which died away. There began to steal into the Higgins bed-room a most ghastly odour; they could not imagine what it was.

And then they began to hear wild clamour from Lacey Granitch, as if he were suffering in hell. It was awful beyond words; the perspiration came out in beads on the faces of the listeners, and Jimmie was just about making up his mind that it was his duty to rush in and protest, or perhaps to climb out of the window and make an effort to steal away and summon help, when the door opened and the man called "Paul" came in, closing the door behind him.

"It's all right," said he. "People always make a fuss when they're given an anaesthetic, so don't let it frighten you." And he stood here waiting, rigid, grim, while the sounds went on. Finally they died away and silence fell—a long, long silence. He opened the door and went back into the other room, and the two Jimmies were left holding each other's shaking hands.

Now and then they heard a man speak in a low voice, or some one move across the room; and always that ghastly, overpowering odour kept creeping in, making them think they would die of suffocation, and their three babies also. The suspense and horror had become almost unbearable—when finally they began to hear Lacey Granitch again, moaning, sobbing—most harrowing sounds. "My God! My God!" whispered Lizzie. "What are they doing?" And when Jimmie did not answer, she whispered again. "We ought to stop them! We ought to get help!"

But then once more the door opened, and "Paul" came in. "It's all right now," he said. "He's coming out." Neither of the Jimmies had the least idea what "coming out" meant, but they were reassured to know that the masterful person at least was satisfied. They waited; they heard Lacey vomiting, as it seemed—and then they heard him cursing, in between his feeble gasps. He called the men the same foul name that he had called Jimmie; and that somehow made the whole affair seem better—it brought one down to earth again!

"Paul" went out and stayed for a while, and when he came back, he said, "We're going now; and understand, there's nothing for you to worry about. We shall leave the patient here, and as soon as we get to a telephone, we'll notify the hospital to send an ambulance. So all you have to do is to wait, and keep quiet and don't worry. And here's something for the use of your house——" The man put out his hand with a roll of bills, which Jimmie mechanically took—"and if anybody asks you about what happened to-night, just say you didn't see anything and don't know anything whatever about it. I'm sorry to have troubled you, but it couldn't be helped. And now, good night."

And so the masterful young man went out, and they heard him and his companions tramping down the porch-steps. They listened, until they heard the automobile start up and disappear in the darkness. Then from the next room they heard a moan.

Trembling with terror, Jimmie got up and stole to the door, and opened it a tiny crack. The room was in utter darkness. "Get me some water!" the voice of Lacey groaned; and Jimmie tiptoed back, and got the little smoky lamp, and came to the door again. He peered in, and saw that Lacey was lying on the floor with a sheet over him—everything but his head, which was resting on a pillow. His face was yellow and twisted with pain. "Water! Water!" he sobbed; and Jimmie rushed to get a glass and fill it from the pail. When he brought it, Lacey first tried to drink, and then began to vomit; then he lay, sobbing softly to himself. He saw Jimmie staring at him, and his eyes filled with sudden hate and he whispered, "This is what you got me in for, you damned little skunk!"

CHAPTER XI

JIMMIE HIGGINS FACES THE WAR

I

THE ambulance arrived, and the two attendants who came with it brought in a stretcher and carried young Granitch away. Jimmie opened the windows to get rid of the odour of ether, and meantime he and Lizzie sat for hours, discussing every aspect of the dreadful scene they had witnessed, and speculating as to its meaning. When Jimmie investigated the roll of bills which had been slipped into his hand, he found that there were ten of them, new, crisp, and bright yellow, each having the figure twenty printed upon it. It was more money than these two humble little people had ever had or expected to have in all their lives. It was literally blood-money, they felt, but it would be hard to see who would be benefited if they rejected it. Certainly the deed which had been done that night could not be undone—not for all the money that old Granitch had heaped up in his vaults.

Jimmie kept quiet, as he had been bidden, and apparently no one told about his part in the affair—no reporters came out to his country home to ask for interviews. But when he went to the cross-roads store a couple of nights later he found that the story was all over—nobody was talking or thinking about anything else. The news, in fact, had gone by telegraph all over the world, and wherever people read it they shuddered with horror, and the Socialists had a choice illustration of the effect of excessive wealth upon morals.

There were half a dozen versions of the story, Jimmie found; some declared that the outraged husband had caught young Granitch in his home and had fetched a surgeon there; others that he had taken him to a hospital; others that the operation had been performed in a road-house nearby. But none mentioned the tenant-house on the farm of John Cutter, and Jimmie wrapped himself in his pride of superior knowledge, and let the loungers in the country store chatter on. He would go back each night for new gossip; and first he heard that old man Granitch was meaning to have all the conspirators arrested and sent to jail; but then it was said that young Lacey had left the hospital and vanished, no one knew where. And they never knew; never again did he appear to curse the strikers at the Empire, nor to break the hearts of chorus-girls on the Great White Way! His grim old father's hair turned grey in a few weeks; and while he went on to fill his contracts with the Russian government, all men knew that his heart was eaten out with grief and rage and shame.

Jimmie and his wife held numerous confabulations over those twenty dollar bills. What should they do with their fortune? The "Worker," always in need of funds, was just now issuing bonds in small denominations, and Jimmie could not imagine any better financial investment than a working-class paper; but Lizzie, alas, could not be made to see it. And then his eye was caught by an advertisement of an oil-company, published in a Socialist paper, which lifted it above suspicion. But again Lizzie blocked the way. She begged her visionary husband to turn the money over to her; she argued that half of it belonged to her anyhow—had she not done her part to earn it? "What part?" Jimmie asked; and she answered that she had kept quiet—and what more had he done?

Eleeza Betooser wanted that treasure to insure safety for the children through whatever troubles might come to their propagandist father. And finally the propagandist father gave way, and the woman proceeded to secure the money in the ancient way of her sex. She took the ten crisp bills and sewed them in a layer of cloth, and wound the cloth about the ankle of her right leg, and sewed it there, and put a stocking over it to hide it. And that apparatus would stay there—day or night, winter or summer, it would never part from its owner. She would be a walking bank, a bank that she knew was safe from panic or crisis; the feeling of the two hundred dollars about her ankle would be communicated to every part of Lizzie—warming her heart, delighting her brain, and stimulating her liver and digestion.

II

And soon the chances of life caused Jimmie to be glad of the innate conservatism of the feminine nature. The giant British offensive was drowned in mud and blood on the Somme, and the Russian offensive went to pieces before Lemberg; and meantime John Cutter stowed his barrels of apples in the cellar, and got the last of his corn-crop husked, and drove his load of pumpkins to market; and then one Saturday night, after the cows had come in, wet and steaming with November rain, he informed his hired man that he would not need his services after that month, he would no longer be able to afford "help." Jimmie stared at him in consternation—for he had thought that he had a permanent job, having learned the work, and having heard no serious complaints.

"But," explained Cutter, "the work's all done. Do you expect me to pay you to sit round? I'll be glad to take you on next spring, of course."

"And what'll I do in the meantime?" Jimmie glared, and all his hatred of the villainous profit-system welled up in his heart. So much food he had helped to raise and store away—and not a pound of it his! "Say," he remarked, "I know what you want! Some kind of a trained bear, that'll work all summer, and go to sleep in winter an' not eat nothin'!"

The little Socialist was all the crosser, because he knew that his boss had just made a lucky stroke—they were running a spur of the railroad out to the vast explosives plant they were constructing in the country, and Cutter had got the price of his mortgage for a narrow strip of land that was nothing but wood-lot. Jimmie had seen the trade made, and had put in a useful word as to the value of that "timber," but now he had no share in the deal. He must be content with an offer of the tenant-house for five dollars a month through the winter, and a job with the railroad-company, grading track.

There came rain and snow and blizzards, but the railroad construction stopped for nothing. It went on in three shifts, day and night; for half the world was clamouring for the means to blow itself up, and the other half must work like the devil to furnish the means. At least that was the way the matter presented itself to Jimmie Higgins, who took it as a personal affront the way this diabolical war kept pursuing him.

He had fled into the country from it, bringing his little family to a tenant-house on an obscure, worn-out farm, several miles from the nearest town; but here all of a sudden came a gang of Dagoes with picks and shovels. They lifted up and set to one side the chicken-house where Lizzie kept her eleven hens and one rooster, and the pig-sty where one little shoat gobbled up their table-scraps; and two days later came a huge machine, driven by steam, creeping on a track, picking up rails and ties from a car behind it, swinging them round and laying them in front of it, and then rolling ahead over the bed it had made. So the railroad just literally walked out into the country, and before long whole train-loads of cement and sand and corrugated iron walls and roofing came rattling and banging past the Higgins back-door. Day and night this continued; and a little ways beyond they knew that a two mile square of scrubby waste was being laid out with roads and tracks and little squat buildings, set far apart from each other. In a few months the frightened family would lie awake at night and listen to trains rattling past, coming out from the explosives plant, piled to the tops with loads of trinitrotoluol, and such unpronounceable instruments of murder and destruction. And this was the fate which capitalism had handed out to an ardent anti-militarist, a propagandist of international fraternity!

III

Jimmie Higgins went into the Socialist local now and then, to pay his dues and to refresh his soul on pacifist speeches. Just before Christmas the President of the United States wrote a letter to all the warring nations, pleading with them to end the strife; intimating that all the belligerents were on a par as to badness, and stating explicitly that America had nothing to do with their struggle. This, of course, brought intense satisfaction to the members of Local Leesville of the Socialist party; it was what they had been proclaiming for two years and four months! They had never expected to have a capitalist president in agreement with them, but when the opportunity came, they made the most of it; clamouring that the capitalist president should go farther—should back up his words by actions. If the warring nations would not make peace, let America at least clear her skirts by declaring an embargo, refusing to furnish them with the means of self-destruction!

But for some reason incomprehensible to Jimmie Higgins, the capitalist president would not take this further step; and time moved on, and at the end of January fell a thunder-bolt, in the shape of a declaration from the German government that beginning next day it rescinded its agreement to visit and search steamers, and declared war to the death against all vessels sailing in barred zones. Jimmie went to a meeting of the local a few days after that, and found the gathering seething with excitement. The President had appeared before Congress that day and made a speech calling for war; and the Germans and Austrians in the local were wild with indignation, shaking their fists and clamouring against the unthinkable outrage of an attack upon the Fatherland. There was a new edition of the "Worker" just out, filled with bitter protests, and the Germans and the pacifists wanted to pledge the local to a movement for a general strike of labour throughout the country. Street-meetings had been resumed—for of course, since the strike in the Empire had been settled, the police had had no pretext to prevent them. The extremists now wanted anti-war speakers on every corner, and anti-war leaflets shoved under every door-step; they were willing to put up the money and to pledge their time for these activities.

Lawyer Norwood rose and revealed the split that was now full-grown in the party. For the United States to lie down before that insolent declaration of the German government would be to imperil everything which a lover of liberty held dear. It would mean that Britain would be starved out of the war, and British sea-power shattered—that British sea-power upon which free government had based itself throughout the world. Norwood was unable to get any further, for the tempest of jeering and ridicule that overwhelmed him. "Freedom in Ireland!" shrieked Comrade Mary Allen. "And in India! And in Egypt!" bellowed Comrade Koeln, the glass-blower, whose mighty lungs had been twenty years preparing for this emergency.

It was hard to stop the laughter—it seemed so funny that a man who called himself a Socialist should be defending British battleships! But Comrade Gerrity, the chairman, pounded with his gavel, and insisted that the meeting should give fair play, that every speaker should be heard in his turn. So Norwood went on. He understood that no government in this world was perfect, but some were better than others, and it was a fact of history, whether or not they chose to admit it, that such freedom as had already been secured in the world —in Britain and Canada and Australia and New Zealand and the United States—had rested under the protection of British battle-ships. If those battle-ships went down, it would mean that every one of those free communities would begin building up a military force many times as strong as they had now. If the United States did not maintain the established customs of sea-commerce in the present crisis, it would mean one thing and one only—that America would spend the next thirty years devoting her energies to preparing for a life-and-death struggle with German Imperialism. If we were not to fight later, we must fight now——

"All right, you fight!" shouted Comrade Schneider, the brewer, his purple face more purple than ever before in the history of Local Leesville.

"I'm going to fight all right," answered the young lawyer. "This is my last speech here or anywhere else—I'm leaving for an officers' training-camp to-morrow. I have come here to do my duty, to warn you comrades—even though I know it will be in vain. The time for debate has passed—the country is going into war——"

"*I'm* not going into war!" roared Schneider.

"Be careful," answered the other. "You may find yourself in before you know it."

And the big brewer laughed to shake the plaster off the walls. "I'd like to see them send me! To fight for the British sea-power! Ho! Ho! Ho!"

IV

It was a stormy speech young Norwood made, but he persisted to the end, so that, as he said, his conscience might be clear, he might know that he had done what he could to protect the movement from its greatest blunder. He warned them that the temper of the country was rising; you could see it rising hour by hour, and things which had been tolerated in the past would be tolerated no longer. Democracy would protect its life —it would show that in a crisis it was as strong as militarism—

"Yes, and turn itself into militarism to do it!" cried Comrade

Mary Allen. The Quaker lady was almost beside herself; she, more even than the Germans, saw in what was transpiring the violation of her most sacred convictions. America, her own country, was giving itself to war, making ready to turn its resources to the wholesale mutilation of men! Comrade Mary's thin face was white; her lips were tight with resolve, but her feelings betrayed themselves by the quivering of her nostrils. And oh, what a speech she made! Such torrents of furious hatred in the cause of universal love! Comrade Mary quoted a Socialist writer who had said that just as gladiatorial combats had continued until Christian monks were willing to throw themselves into the arena, so war would continue until Socialists were willing to throw themselves beneath the hoofs of the cavalry. And in this Quaker spinster you saw one Socialist who was ready to go out that very night and throw herself beneath the hoofs of cavalry, infantry, or artillery, or even of a police-automobile.

And that was the sentiment of the meeting as a whole. If America entered the European strife, it would be because the Socialist organisation had exhausted its means of protest in vain. They would call meetings, they would distribute literature, they would voice their convictions on the streets and in the shops and wherever the people might be reached. They would have no part in this wicked strife, either now or later; they would continue in the future, as in the past, to denounce and to expose the capitalist politicians and the capitalist newspapers who caused war and thrived upon war. And in proportion to the intensity of their feelings would be their bitterness and contempt for the few renegades who in this hour of crisis, this test of manhood and integrity, were deserting the movement and going to enrol themselves in officers' training-camps!

And so when Jimmie went home that night he carried with him an armful of revolutionary literature, which during the noon-hour he proceeded to distribute among the workers on the construction-job, which was now inside the preserves of the explosives company. So naturally in the course of the afternoon he was summoned before the boss and fired; they escorted him to the limits of the property, and told him that if he ever returned he would be shot on sight. And then at night he went up to the cross-roads store and tried to give out his literature there, and got into a controversy with some of the cracker-box loungers, one of whom jumped up and shook his fist in Jimmie's face, shouting, "Get out of here, you dirty little louse! If you don't stop talking your treason round here, we'll come down some night and ride you out of the country on a rail!"

CHAPTER XII

JIMMIE HIGGINS MEETS A PATRIOT

I

THE country, it seemed, was hell-bent for war; and Jimmie Higgins was hell-bent for martyrdom. If the great madness were to take possession of America, it would not be without his having done what he could to prevent. He would stand in the path of the war-chariot; he would throw himself beneath the hoofs of the cavalry, and block the road with his dead body. To which vivid programme there was only one obstacle—or, to be precise, four obstacles, one large and three small, the large one being Eleeza Betooser.

Poor Lizzie of course had no real comprehension of the world-forces against which her husband was contending; to Lizzie, life consisted of three babies, whom it was her duty to feed and protect, and a husband, who was her instrument for carrying out this duty. The world outside of these was to her a vague and shadowy place, full of vague and shadowy terrors. Somewhere up in the sky was a holy virgin who would help when properly appealed to, but Lizzie was handicapped in appealing to this virgin by the fact that her husband despised the holy one, and would cast insulting doubts upon her virtue.

Now the shadowy terrors of this vast outside world were moving to ends of their own, and her poor, puny husband persisted in putting himself in their way. He had got turned out of his job, for the fourth or fifth time since Lizzie had known him, and he was in imminent danger of getting into jail, or into a coat of tar and feathers. As the controversy grew hotter and the peril greater, Lizzie came to a condition which might have been diagnosed as chronic impending hysteria. Her eyes were red from secret weeping, and at the slightest provocation she would burst into floods of tears and throw herself into her husband's arms. This would start off Jimmie Junior, and the little ones, who always took their cue from him.

And Jimmie Senior would stand perplexed and helpless. Here was a new aspect of the heroic life, not dealt with in the books. He wondered—had there ever in history been such a thing as a married martyr? If so, what had this martyr done with his family?

Jimmie would try to explain to his distressed spouse. It was a question of saving a hundred million people from the horrors of war; what did one man matter, in comparison with that? But alas, the argument did not carry at all, the simple truth being that the one man mattered more to Lizzie than all the other ninety-nine million, nine hundred and ninety-nine thousand, nine hundred and ninety-nine. And besides, what could the one man do? One poor, obscure, helpless workingman out of a job——

"But it's the organisation!" he cried. "It's all of us together—it's the party! We promised to stand together, so we got to do it! If I drop out, I'm a coward, a traitor! We must make the workers understand——"

"But you can't!" cried Lizzie.

"But we're doin' it! Come see!"

"And what can they do?"

Which of course started Jimmie off on a propaganda speech. What could the workers do? Say rather, what could they not do! How could any war be fought without the workers? If only they would stand together, if they would rise against their capitalist oppressors——

"But they won't!" sobbed the woman. "They got no use for you at all! You go an' get fired—or you get your face beat in, like poor Bill Murray——"

"But is that any worse than goin' to war?"

"You ain't got to go to war!"

"Who says I ain't? I got to go, if the country goes. They'll drag me off an' make me! If I refuse they'll shoot me! Ain't they doin' that in England an' France an' Roosia an' all them countries?"

"But will they do it here?" cried Lizzie, aghast.

"Sure they will! That's exactly what they're gettin' ready for—what we're fightin' to stop them from! You don't know what's goin' on in this country—listen here!"

And Jimmie hauled out the last issue of the "Worker," which quoted speeches made in Congress, calling for conscription, declaring that such a measure was an essential war-step. "Don't you see what they're up to? An' if we're goin' to stop them, we gotta act now, before it's too late. Hadn't I just as good go to jail here in Leesville as be shipped over to Europe to be shot—or maybe drowned by a submarine on the way?"

And thus a new terror was introduced into Lizzie's life—robbing her of sleep for many a night thereafter, planting in her mother-heart for the first time the idea that she might be concerned in the world-war. "What'd become of the babies?" she wailed; and Jimmie answered: Whose business was it to bother about working-class babies, under the hellish capitalist system?

II

So Jimmie had his way for a bit—he went into Leesville and helped distribute literature, and held the torch at street-meetings, where some people hooted at them and others defended them, and the police had to interfere to prevent a riot. It was at this time that a militant majority was trying to drive through the Senate a declaration of war against Germany, and a handful of pacifists blocked the way in the closing hours of the session, thus causing a delay of several weeks. How you regarded this action depended upon your point of view. The President denounced them as "wilful men," and the Wall Street newspapers apparently wanted them lynched; whereas Jimmie and his fellows in the local hailed them as heroes and friends of mankind. The Socialists argued that the President had been re-elected, only four months before, by pacifist votes, and upon a pacifist platform; and now he was sweeping the country into war, and denouncing those who stood upon his former convictions!

On top of this came another event which set Jimmie almost beside himself with excitement. For three days all news from Petrograd was cut off; and then came a report, electrifying the world—the Tsar had been overthrown, the Russian people were free! Jimmie could hardly believe his eyes; he went in to the meeting of the local three nights later, to find the comrades celebrating as if the world were theirs. Here was the thing they had been preaching, day in and day out, all these weary years, amid ridicule, hatred and persecution; here was the Social Revolution, knocking at the gates of the world! It would spread to Austria and Germany, to Italy, France, England—and so to Leesville! Everywhere the people would come into their own, and war and tyranny would vanish like a hateful nightmare!

Speaker after speaker got up to proclaim this glorious future; they sang the Marseillaise and the Internationale, and the Russians who were present clasped one another in their arms, with tears running down their cheeks. It was voted that they must hold a mass-meeting immediately, to explain this epoch-making event to the people of the city; also they must stand more firmly than ever by their programme of opposition to war. Now, with Social Revolution knocking at the gates of the world, what was the use of America's going in for militarism?

So Jimmie set to work with redoubled fervour, giving all his time to agitation. He had apparently no chance of getting a job, and for the moment he gave up trying. The keeper of the cross-roads store, being down on him because of his ideas, refused him any more credit; and so poor Lizzie was driven to do what she had vowed never to do—take off the stocking from her right leg, and unsew the bandage from her ankle, and extract one of the ten precious twenty dollar bills. Their bright yellow was considerably faded now, their beautiful crispness gone entirely; but the store-keeper made no kick on that account—he returned the change, and incidentally took occasion to give her a friendly warning concerning her husband's reckless talk. There was trouble coming to him, and his wife had better shut him up before it was too late. So poor Lizzie ceased being a pacifist, and went home to have more hysterics on her husband's bosom.

III

Being unable to hold him back, she sent word by the mail-carrier to old Peter Drew to come up and help; the old farmer hitched up his bony mare and drove to see them, and for a couple of hours talked America while Jimmie talked Russia. Was America to lie down before the Kaiser? Jimmie would answer that they were going to bring down the Kaiser in the same way they had brought down the Tsar. The workers of Russia having shown the way, nevermore would the workers of any nation bow to the yoke of slavery. Yes, even in the so-called republics, such as France, which was ruled by bankers, and America, which was ruled by Wall Street—even here, the workers would read the lesson of revolt!

"But in America the people can get anything they want!" cried the bewildered old man. "They only have to vote——"

"Vote?" snarled Jimmie. "An' have their votes thrown out by some rotten political gang, like they got here in Leesville? Don't talk to me about votin'—they told me I'd moved into a new district an' lost my vote—lost it because I lost my job! So it's old man Granitch has the say whether I can vote or not! You'll find the same thing true of two-thirds of the men in the Empire Shops—half the unskilled men in the country got no votes, because they got no home, no nothin'."

"But," argued the old soldier, "how will you run your new working-class government, if not by votes?"

"Sure, we'll run it by votes," Jimmie answered—"but first we'll turn out the capitalists; they won't have the money to buy political machines; they won't own the newspapers an' print lies about us. Look at this Leesville 'Herald' right now—just plain downright lies they print—we can't get any truth at all to the people."

And so it went. It was of no use for the old man to plead for the "country"; to Jimmie the "country" had let itself be lost, suppressed, taken over by the capitalists, the "plutes." Jimmie's sense of loyalty was not to his country, but to his class, which had been exploited, hounded, driven from pillar to post. In past times the government had allowed itself to be used by corporations; so now it was in vain that the President made appeals for justice and democracy, using the beautiful language of idealism. Jimmie did not believe that he meant it; or anyhow, Wall Street would see that nothing came of his promises. The "plutes" would take his words and twist them into whatever sense they wished; and meantime they went on pouring out abuse on Jimmie Higgins—throwing the same old mud into his eyes, blinding him with the same old hatred. So there was no way for an old soldier and patriot to break through the armour of Jimmie's prejudice.

IV

Next day was to be the great mass-meeting in celebration of the Russian revolution; and would you believe it, Lizzie was hoping to persuade Jimmie to stay away; she had brought Mr. Drew to help persuade him! Poor Lizzie had visions of everybody in the hall being carted off to jail, of Jimmie getting up and shouting something, causing the police to fall on him and beat in his skull with their clubs. It was in vain he declared that he was going to do nothing more romantic than sell literature and act as usher. She clasped him in her arms, weeping copiously, and when he was still obdurate, she declared that she would go with him. She would try to persuade Mrs. Drew to take care of the babies for one night.

Old Peter Drew answered that he would be interested to attend the meeting himself. How would it do for him to come for Lizzie and the little ones, and leave the latter at his home, and then drive with Lizzie to the meeting? They could meet Jimmie at the Opera-house, where he would be spending the day decorating. Then after the meeting they could all drive back together. Fine! said Jimmie, who had visions of the old soldier becoming infected with revolutionary fever.

But alas, it did not work out that way. To Jimmie's consternation the old man turned up at the Opera-house in a faded blue uniform with brass buttons all over it! Everybody stared, of course; and they stared all the harder because they saw this military personage in company with Comrade Higgins. The old boy gazed about at the swarms of people, many of them with red buttons, the women with red ribbons or sashes; he gazed at the decorations—the huge flag and the long red streamers, the banner of the Karl Marx Verein, and the banner of the Ypsels, or Young Peoples' Socialist League of Leesville, and the banner of the Machinists' Union, Local 4717, and of the Carpenters' Union, District 529, and of the Workers' Co-operative Society. He turned to Jimmie and said, "Where's the American flag?"

The Liederkranz sang the Marseillaise, and after the audience had cheered and waved red handkerchiefs and shouted itself hoarse, Comrade Gerrity, the chairman, made a little speech. For many years all Socialists had been accustomed to employ a metaphor by which to describe conditions in their country, and now they would no longer be able to use it, for Russia was free, and America would follow her example when she had the sense. He introduced Comrade Pavel Michaelovitch, who had come all the way from New York to tell them the meaning of the greatest event of history. Comrade Pavel, a slender, frail, scholarly-looking man with a black beard and black-rimmed spectacles, said a few words in Russian, and then he talked for an hour in broken English, explaining how the Russians had won their way to freedom, and now would use it to set free the rest of the proletariat. And then came Comrade Schultze, of the Carpet Weavers' Union, assuring them that there was no need to go to war with Germany, because the German workers had been shown the way to freedom, and would follow very soon; Schultze knew, because his brother was editor of a Socialist paper in Leipzig, and he had inside information as to what was going on in the Fatherland.

Then Comrade Smith, the editor of the "Worker," was introduced, and the trouble began. The young editor wasted no time in preliminaries; he was an international revolutionist, and no capitalist government was going to draft him for its bloody knaveries. Never would he be led out to murder his fellow-workers, whether in Germany, Austria, Bulgaria or Turkey; the masters of Wall Street would find that when they set out to drive American freemen to the slaughter-pen, they had made the mistake of their greedy lives. "Understand me," declared Comrade Smith—though there seemed so far to have been nothing in which any one could possibly have misunderstood him—"understand me, I am no pacifist, I am not opposed to war—it is merely that I purpose to choose the war in which I fight. If they try to put a gun into my hands, I shall not refuse to take it—not much, for I and my fellow wage-slaves have long wished for guns! But I shall use my own judgment as to where I aim that gun—whether at enemies in front of me, or at enemies behind me—whether at my brothers, the working-men of Germany, or at my oppressors, the exploiters of Wall Street, their newspaper lackeys and military martinets!"

The sentences of this speech came like the blows of a hammer, and they struck forth a clamour of applause from the audience. But suddenly the cheering crowd became aware that something out of the ordinary was happening. An aged, white-whiskered man clad in a faded blue uniform had risen from his seat in the middle of the hall and was shouting and waving his arms. People near him were trying to pull him down into his seat, but he would not be squelched, he went on shouting; and the audience in part fell silent out of curiosity. "Shame!

Shame!" they heard him cry. "Shame upon you!" And he pointed a trembling finger at the orator, declaring, "You are talking treason, young man!"

"Sit down!" shrieked the crowd. "Shut up!"

But the old man turned upon them. "Are there no Americans at all in this audience? Will you listen to this shameless traitor without one word?"

People caught him by the coat-tails, men shook their fists at him; at the other side of the hall "Wild Bill" leaped up on a chair, shrieking: "Cut his throat, the old geezer!"

Two policemen came running down the aisle, and the "old geezer" appealed to them: "What are you here for, if not to protect the flag and the honour of America?" But the policemen insisted that he stop interrupting the meeting, and so the old man turned and stalked out from the hall. But he did not go until he had turned once more and shaken his fist at the crowd, yelling in his cracked voice, "Traitors! Traitors!"

V

Poor Jimmie remained in his seat, overwhelmed. That he, the most devoted of workers for Socialism, should have been the cause of such a disgraceful scene—bringing to this revolutionary meeting a man in the uniform of a killer of the working-class! He could not stay and face the comrades; before the speaking had finished he gave Lizzie a nudge, and the two got up and stole out, dodging every one they knew.

Outside they stood in perplexity. They thought, of course, that the old man would have driven away without them; they pictured the long walk from the trolley-line in the darkness and mud—and with Lizzie dressed in her only Sunday-go-to-meeting! But when they went to the place where Mr. Drew had left his buggy, to their surprise they found him patiently waiting for them. Seeing them hesitate, he said, "Come! Get in!" They were much embarrassed, but obeyed, and the old mare started her amble towards home.

They rode for a long time in silence. Finally Jimmie could not stand it, and began, "I'm so sorry, Mr. Drew. You don't understand——" But the old man cut him off: "There's no use you and me tryin' to talk, young man." So they rode the rest of the way without a sound—except that once Jimmie imagined he heard Lizzie sobbing to herself.

Jimmie really felt terribly about it, for he had for this old soldier a deep respect, even an affection. Mr. Drew had made his impression not so much by his arguments, which Jimmie considered sixty years out of date, as by his personality. Here was one patriot who was straight! What a pity that he could not understand the revolutionary point of view! What a pity that he had to be made angry! It was one more of the horrors of war, which tore friends apart, and set them to disputing and hating one another.

At least, that was the way it seemed to Jimmie that night, while he was still full of the speeches he had heard. But at other times doubts assailed him—for of course a man cannot defy and combat a whole community without sometimes being led to wonder whether the community may not have some right on its side. Jimmie would hear of things the Germans had done in the war; they were such dirty fighters, they went out of their way to do such utterly revolting and useless, almost insane things! They made it so needlessly hard for any one who tried to defend them to think of them even as human beings. Jimmie would argue that he did not mean to help the Germans; he would resent bitterly the charges of the Leesville newspapers that he was a German agent and a traitor; but he could not get away from the uncomfortable fact that the things he was doing *did* have a tendency to further German interests, at least for a time.

When that was pointed out to him by some patriot in a controversy, his answer would be that he was appealing to the German Socialists to revolt against their military leaders; but then the patriot would begin to find fault with the German Socialists, declaring that they were much better Germans than Socialists, and citing utterances and actions to prove it. One German Socialist had stood up in the Reichstag and declared that the Germans had two ways of fighting—their armies overcame their enemies in the field, while their Socialists undermined the morale of the workers in enemy countries. When that passage was read to Jimmie, he answered that it was a lie; no such speech had ever been made by a Socialist. He had no way of proving it was a lie, of course; he just knew it! But then, when he went away and thought it over, he began to wonder; suppose it were true! Suppose the German workers had been so drilled and schooled in childhood that even those who called themselves revolutionists were patriots at heart! Jimmie would begin to piece this and that together—things he had heard or read. Certainly these German Socialists were not displaying any great boldness in fighting their government!

The answer was that they could not oppose their government, because they would be put in jail. But that was a pretty poor answer; it was their business to go to jail—if not, what right had they to expect Jimmie Higgins to go here in America? Jimmie presented this problem to Comrade Meissner, who answered that if Jimmie would go first, then doubtless the German comrades would follow. But Jimmie could not see why he should be first; and when they tried to clear up the reason, it developed that down in his heart Jimmie had begun to believe that Germany was more to blame for the war than America. And not merely would Comrade Meissner not admit that, but he became excited and vehement, trying to convince Jimmie that the other capitalist governments of the world were the cause of the war—Germany was only defending herself against them! So there they were, involved in a controversy, just like any two non-revolutionary people! Repeating over the same arguments which had gone on in the local between Norwood, the lawyer, and Schneider, the brewer; only this time Jimmie was taking the side of Norwood! Jimmie found himself face to face with the disconcerting fact that his devoted friend Meissner was a German—and therefore in some subtle way different from him, unable to see things as he did!

CHAPTER XIII

JIMMIE HIGGINS DODGES TROUBLE

I

WAR or no war, the soil had to be ploughed and seed sown; so John Cutter came to his tenant and proposed that he should resume his job as farm-hand. Only he must agree to shut up about the war, for while Cutter himself was not a rabid patriot, he would take no chances of having his tenant-house burned down some night. So there was another discussion in the Higgins family. Lizzie remembered how during the previous summer Jimmie had worked from dawn till dark, and been too tired even to read Socialist papers, to say nothing of carrying on propaganda: which seemed to the distracted wife of a propagandist the most desirable condition possible! Poor Eleeza Betooser—twice again she had been compelled to take down the stocking from her right leg, and unsew the bandage round her ankle, and extract another of those precious yellow twenty dollar bills; there were only seven of them left now, and each of them was more valuable to Lizzie than her eye-teeth.

Jimmie finally agreed that he would gag himself, so far as concerned this country-side. What was the use of trying to teach anything to these barnyard boobs? They wanted war—let them go to war, and be blown to bits or poisoned in the trenches! If Jimmie had propaganding to do, he would do it in the city, where the workingmen had brains, and knew who their enemies were. So once more Jimmie harnessed up John Cutter's horses to the plough, and went out into John Cutter's field to raise another crop of corn for a man whom he hated. All day he guided the plough or the harrow, and at night he fed and cared for the horses and the cows, and then he came home and ate his supper, listening to the rattling of the long freight-train that went through his back yard, carrying materials for the making of TNT.

For the great explosives plant was now working day and night, keeping the war in Jimmie's thoughts all the time, whether he would or not. In the midnight hours the trains of finished materials went out, making Jimmie's windows rattle with their rumble and clatter, and bearing his fancies away to the battle-line across the seas, where men were soon to be blown to pieces with the contents of these cars. One night something went wrong on the track, and the train stopped in his back yard, and in the morning he saw the cars, painted black, with the word "Danger" in flaming red letters. On top of the cars walked a man with a club in his hand and a bulge on his hip, keeping guard.

It appeared that some one had torn up a rail in the night, evidently for the purpose of wrecking the train; so there came a detective to Jimmie, while he was working in the field, to cross-question him. They had Jimmie's record, and suspected him of knowing more than he would tell. "Aw, go to hell!" exclaimed the irate Socialist. "D'you suppose, if I'd wanted to smash anything, I'd 'a done it on the place where I work?" And then, when he went home to dinner, he found that they had been after Lizzie, and had frightened her out of her wits. They had threatened to turn them out of their home; Jimmie saw himself hounded here and there by this accursed war—until it finished by seizing him and dragging him to the trenches!

II

The new Congress had met, and declared a state of war with Germany, and the whole country was rushing into arms. Men were enlisting by hundreds of thousands; but that was not enough for the militarists—they wanted a conscription-law, so that every man might be compelled to go. If they were so sure of themselves and their wonderful war, why weren't they satisfied to let those fight it who wanted to? —So argued the rebellious Jimmie and his anti-militarist associates. But no! the militarists knew perfectly well that the bulk of the people did not want to fight, so they proposed to make them fight. Every energy of the Socialist movement was now concentrated on the blocking of this conscription scheme.

Local Leesville hired the Opera-house again, organising a mass-meeting of protest, and the capitalist papers of the city began clamouring against this meeting. Was the patriotism and loyalty of Leesville to be affronted by another gathering of sedition and treason? The "Herald" told all over again the story of the gallant old civil war veteran who had risen in his seat and shouted his protest against the incitements of "Jack" Smith, the notorious "red" editor. The "Herald" printed a second time the picture of the gallant old veteran in his faded blue uniform, and the list of battles in which he had fought, from the first Bull Run to the last siege of Richmond. Some farmer passing by handed a copy of this paper to Lizzie, adding that if there was any more treason-talk in this locality there was going to be a lynching-bee. So Jimmie found his wife in tears again. She was absolutely determined that he should not go to that meeting. For three days she wept and argued with him, and for a part of three nights.

It would have been comical if it had not been so tragic. Jimmie would use the old argument, that if he did not succeed in stopping the war, he would be dragged into the trenches and killed. So, of course, Lizzie would become a pacifist at once. What right had the war to take Jimmie from her? The little Jimmies had a right to their father! All children had a right to their fathers! But then, after Lizzie had expressed these tearful convictions, Jimmie would say, All right, then he must go to that meeting, he must do what he could to prevent the war. And poor Lizzie would find herself suddenly confronting the terrors of the police with their clubs and the patriots with their buckets of tar and bags of feathers! No, Jimmie must not carry on any propaganda, Jimmie must not go to the meeting! Poor Jimmie would try to pin her down: which way did she want him killed, by the Germans, or by the police and the mobs? But Lizzie did not want him killed either way! She wanted him to go on living!

Jimmie would try to arrange a compromise for the present. He would go to the meeting, but he would promise not to say a word. But that did not console Lizzie—she knew that if anything happened, her man would get into it. No, if he were determined to go, she would go too—even if they had to load the three babies into the perambulator, and push them two or three miles to the trolley! If Jimmie tried to make a speech, she would hang onto his coat-tails, she would clasp her hands over his mouth, she would throw herself between him and the clubs of the policemen!

So matters stood, when on the afternoon before the meeting there came a heavy rain, and the road to the trolley was rendered impossible for a triple-loaded baby-carriage. So there were more hysterics in the family; Jimmie took his wife's hand in his and solemnly swore to her that she might trust him to go to this meeting, he would not do anything that could by any possibility get him into trouble. He would not try to make a speech, he would not get up and shout—no matter what happened, he would not say a word! He would merely sell pamphlets, and show people to their seats, as he had done at a hundred meetings before. To make sure of his immunity, he would even leave off the red badge which he was accustomed to display on Socialist occasions! By these pledges repeated over and over, he finally succeeded in pacifying his weeping spouse, and gently removed her clutch on his coat-tails, and departed, waving his hand to her and the kids.

The last thing he saw through the rain was Jimmie Junior, flourishing a red handkerchief which Lizzie at the last moment had extracted from her husband's pocket. The last sound he heard was Jimmie Junior's voice, shouting: "You be good now! You shut up!" Jimmie went off, thinking about this little tike; he was five years old, and growing so that you could notice the difference over night. He had big black eyes like his mother, and a grin full of all the mischief in the world. The things he knew and the questions he asked! Jimmie and Lizzie never got tired of talking about them; Jimmie recalled them one by one, as he trudged through the mud—and, as always, he set his lips and clenched his hands, and took up anew the task of making the world a fit place for a workingman's child to grow up in!

III

The principal orator of the evening was a young college professor who had been turned out of his job for taking the side of the working-class in his public utterances, and who was therefore a hero to Jimmie Higgins. This young man had the facts of the war at his finger tips; he made you see it as a gigantic conspiracy of capitalists the world over to complete their grip on the raw materials of wealth, and on the bodies and souls of the workers. He bitterly denounced those who had forced the country into the war; he denounced the Wall Street speculators and financiers who had made their billions already, and would be making their tens of billions. He denounced the plan to force men to fight who did not wish to fight, and his every sentence was followed by a burst of applause from the throng which packed the Opera-house. If you judged by this meeting, you would conclude that America was on the verge of a revolution against the war.

The young professor sat down, wiping the perspiration from his pale forehead; and then the Liederkranz sang again—only it was not called the Liederkranz now, it had become known as the "Workers' Singing Society," out of deference to local prejudice. Then arose Comrade Smith, editor of the "Worker," and announced that after the collection the orator would answer questions; then Comrade Smith launched into a speech of his own, to the effect that something definite ought to be done by the workers of Leesville to make clear their opposition to being dragged into war. For his part he wished to say that he would not yield one inch to the war-clamour—he was on record as refusing to be drafted in any capitalist war, and he was ready to join with others to agree that they would not be drafted. The time was short—if anything were to be done, they must act at once—

And then suddenly came an interruption—this time not from an old soldier, but from a sergeant of police who had been standing at one side of the stage, and who now stepped forward, announcing, "This meeting is closed."

"What?" shouted the orator.

"This meeting is closed," repeated the other. "And you, young man, are under arrest."

There was a howl from the audience, and suddenly from the pit in front of the stage, whence ordinarily the orchestra dispensed sweet music, there leaped a line of blue-uniformed men, distributing themselves between the public and the speaker. At the same time down the centre aisle came a dozen soldiers marching, with guns in their hands and bayonets fixed.

"This is an outrage!" shouted Comrade Smith.

"Not another word!" commanded the police official; and

two policemen who had followed him grabbed the orator by each arm and started to lead him off the stage.

Comrade Gerrity leaped to the front of the platform. "I denounce this proceeding!" he shouted. "We are holding an orderly meeting here——"

A policeman laid hold of him. "You are under arrest."

Then came Comrade Mabel Smith, sister of the editor of the "Worker." "For shame! For shame!" she cried. And then, to a policeman, "No, I will not be silent! I protest in the name of free speech! I declare——" And when the policeman seized her by the arm, she continued to shout at the top of her lungs, driving the crowd to frenzy.

There were disturbances all over the audience. Mrs. Gerrity, wife of the organiser, sprang up in her seat and began to protest. It happened that Jimmie Higgins was in the aisle not far from her, and his heart leaped with strange, half-forgotten emotions as he saw this trim little figure, with the jaunty hat and the turkey-feather stuck on one side. Comrade Evelyn Baskerville, of Greenwich Village, she of the fluffy brown hair and the pert little dimples and the bold and terrifying ideas, she who had so ploughed up the soul of Jimmie Higgins and almost broken up the Higgins home—here she was, employing a new variety of coquetry, by which she compelled three soldiers with rifles and bayonets to devote their exclusive attention to her!

And then Comrade Mary Allen, the Quaker lady, who believed in moral force applied through the ear-drums. She stood in the aisle with her armful of pamphlets and her red sash over her shoulder, proclaiming, "In the name of liberty and fair play I protest against this outrage! I will not see my country dragged into war without asserting my right of protest! I stand here, in what is supposed to be a Christian city; I speak in the name of the Prince of Peace——" and so on, quite a little speech, while several embarrassed young men in khaki were trying to find out how to hold their rifles and a shouting Quakeress at the same time.

And then Comrade Schneider, the brewer. He had been up on the stage with the singers, and now got somehow to the front. "Haf we got no rights in America left?" he shouted. "Do we in this audience——"

"Shut up, you Hun!" roared some one in the front of the

crowd, and three policemen at once leaped for Comrade Schneider, and grabbed him by the collar, twisting so hard that the German's face, always purple when he was excited, took on a dark and deadly hue.

Poor Jimmie Higgins! He stood there with his armful of "War, What For?"—trembling with excitement, itching in every nerve and sinew to leap into this conflict, to make his voice heard above the uproar, to play his part as a man—or even as a Comrade Mabel Smith, or a Comrade Mary Allen, or a Comrade Mrs. Gerrity, née Baskerville. But he was helpless, speechless—bound hand and foot by those solemn pledges he had given to Eleeza Betooser, the mother of babies.

He looked about, and near him in the aisle he saw another man, also bound hand and foot—bound by the memory of the smash in the face which had broken his nose and knocked out three of his front teeth! "Wild Bill" saw a policeman watching him now, eager for another pretext to leap on him and pound him; so he was silent, like Jimmie. The two of them had to stand there and see the fundamental constitutional rights of American citizens set at naught, to see liberty trampled in the dust beneath the boots of a brutal soldiery, to see justice strangled and raped in the innermost shrine of her temple.—At least, that was what you had seen if you read the Leesville "Worker"; if on the other hand you read the "Herald"—which nine out of ten people did—then you learned that the forces of decency and order had at last prevailed in Leesville, the propaganda of the Hun was stifled forever, the mouthers of sedition had felt the heavy hand of public indignation.

IV

Outside, a crowd gathered to jeer while the prisoners were loaded into the patrol-wagon; but the police drove them away, keeping everybody moving, and breaking up several attempts at street-oratory. Jimmie found himself with half a dozen other comrades, wandering aimlessly down Main Street, talking over and over what had happened, each explaining why and how he had not shared the crown of martyrdom. Some had shouted as loud as the rest, but had been missed by the police; some had thought it wiser to run away and live to shout another day; some wanted to start that very night to print a leaflet and call another mass-meeting. They adjourned to Tom's "Buffeteria" to talk things over; they took possession of a couple of tables, and got their due quotas of coffee and sandwiches, or pie and milk, and had just got fairly started on the question of raising bail without the help of Comrade Dr. Service—when suddenly something happened which drove all thoughts of the meeting out of their minds.

It was like a gigantic blow, striking the whole world at once; a cosmic convulsion, quite indescribable. The air became suddenly a living thing, which leaped against your face; the windows of the little eating-place flew inward in a shower of glass, and the walls and tables shook as if with palsy. The sound of it all was a vast, all-pervasive sound, at once far off and near, tailing away in the clatter and crash of innumerable panes of glass falling from innumerable windows. Then came silence, a sinister, frightful silence, it seemed; men stared at one another, crying, "My God! What's that?" The answer seemed to dawn upon every one at once: "The powder-plant!"

Yes, that must be it, beyond doubt. For months they had been talking about it and thinking about it, speculating as to the probabilities and the consequences. And now it had happened. Suddenly one of the company gave a cry, and they turned and stared at his white face, and realised the terror that clutched his heart. Comrade Higgins, whose home was so near the place of peril!

"Gee, fellers, I gotta go!" he gasped; and several of the comrades jumped up and ran with him into the street. If there was a single pane of glass left intact in Leesville, you would not have thought it as you trod those side-walks.

If Jimmie had been trained in efficiency, and accustomed to spending money more freely, he might perhaps have found out something by the telephone or by inquiry at the newspaper-offices; but the one thing he thought of was to take the trolley and get to his home. The comrades ran with him, speculating with eager excitement, trying to reassure him—it could be nothing worse than some glass and some dishes smashed. Some had thought of going all the way with him, but they remembered they would be too late for the last trolley back, and they had their jobs in the morning. So they put him on the car and bade him good-bye.

V

The trolley was packed with people going out to see what had happened, so Jimmie had plenty of company and conversation on the way. But when he came to his stop, he got off and walked alone, for the others were going to the explosives plant, and they rode a mile or so farther on the car.

Never would Jimmie forget that journey—that walk of nightmares. The road was pitch-dark, and before he had gone more than half the distance, he stumbled over something, and fell head-foremost. He got up, and groped, and discovered that it was a tree, lying prone across the road. He searched his mind, and remembered a great dead tree that stood at that spot. Could the explosion have knocked it down?

He went on, feeling his way more cautiously, yet goaded to greater speed by his fears. A little way farther was a farm-house, and he went into the yard and shouted, but got no reply. The yard was covered with shingles, apparently blown from the roof. He went on, more frightened than ever.

He came to a turn in the road which he knew was less than half a mile from his home; and here there were several horses and wagons tied, but no one to answer his calls. The road passed through a wood; but apparently there was no road any more—the trees had been picked up bodily and thrown across it. Jimmie had to grope this way and that, and he ran a piece of broken branch into his cheek, and by that time was almost ready to cry with fright. He knew that his home was two miles from the explosives plant, and he could not conceive how an explosion could have done such damage at such a distance.

He saw a lantern ahead, bobbing this way and that, and he shouted louder than ever, and finally succeeded in persuading the bearer of the lantern to wait for him. It proved to be a farmer who lived some ways back; he knew no more than Jimmie did, and they made their way together. Beyond the woods, the road was littered with loose dirt, bushes, bits of fence and rubbish, burned black. "It must have been near here," declared the man, and added words which caused Jimmie's heart almost to stand still, "It must have been on the railroad-track!"

They came to a little rise, from which in day-time the line of the railroad was visible. They saw lanterns, many of them, moving here and there like a swarm of fire-flies. "Come this way," Jimmie begged of the farmer, and ran toward his home. The road was buried under masses of earth, as if thousands of steam-shovels had emptied their contents on it. When they came to where the fence of Jimmie's house ought to have been, they found no fence, but a slide of loose earth that had never been there before. Where the apple-tree had been there was nothing; where the lawn had been there was a pitch down a hill, and where the house had been was a huge valley, seeming in the darkness a bottomless abyss!

VI

Jimmie was distracted. He grabbed the lantern from the other man, and ran this way and that, looking for some of the familiar land-marks of his home—the chicken-house, the pig-sty, the back fence with the broken elm tree in the corner, the railroad beyond. He could not believe that he had come to the place at all—he could not credit the reality of such night-mare sights as his eyes reported to him. He rushed about, stumbling over mountains of upheaved brown dirt, sliding down into craters that were filled with a strange penetrating odour which caused his eyes to smart; and then clambering out again and running after men with lanterns, shouting questions at them and not waiting for an answer. It seemed to him that if he ran just a little farther he must surely find the house and the other things he was looking for; but he found nothing but more craters and more mountains of dirt; and little by little the horrible truth became clear to him, that all the way down the railroad-track, as far as he could see or run, this gigantic trough extended, a valley of raw dirt with mountains on each side, crowned here and there with wheels and axles and iron trucks of blown-up freight-cars, and filled in the bottom with the deadly fumes of trinitrotoluol!

Jimmie cried out to the men and women with lanterns, asking had they seen his wife and babies. But no one had seen them—no one had notified them of the impending explosion! Jimmie was sobbing, calling out distractedly; he ran out to the road, and after much searching found a charred tree-stump which gave him his precise bearings, so that he knew where the house should have been, and could assure himself that it was precisely where that frightful slope started down into the abyss. He slid around on this slope, calling aloud, as if he expected the spirits of his loved ones might have remained there, defying all the power of suddenly expanding gases. He ran back across the road and called, as if they might have fled that way.

At last he ran into Mr. Drew; old Mr. Drew, who a couple of weeks before had taken Eleeza Betooser and her three little ones driving in his buggy! That memory was the nearest Jimmie could get to them, and so he clutched the old soldier's arm, and held on to it, weeping like a little child.

The old man tried to draw him away, to get him to his home. But Jimmie must stay on the spot, he was held by a spell of horror. He wandered about, dragging Mr. Drew with him, pleading with people to no purpose; now and then he would break out with curses against war-makers, and especially those who made explosives and transported them in freight-trains through other men's back yards. For once people heard him without threats of lynching.

So on through this night of anguish. Jimmie lost old man Drew in the darkness, and was all alone when the dawn came, and he could see the sweep of desolation about him, and the awe-stricken faces of the spectators. Soon afterwards came the climax. He saw a crowd gathered, and as he came up, this crowd parted for him. Nobody seemed to want to speak, but they all watched, as if curious to see what he would do. One of the men bore a burden, wrapped in a horse-blanket; Jimmie gazed, and after a moment's hesitation the man threw back part of the blanket, and there before Jimmie's eyes was a most horrible sight—a human leg, a large white leg, the lower half covered with a black stocking tied at the top with a bit of tape. It was such a leg as you see in the windows of stores where they sell pretty things for ladies; only this leg was soft, mangled at the top, smeared with blood, and partly charred black. One glance was enough for Jimmie, and he put his hands over his eyes and turned and ran—out to the road and away, away—anywhere from this place of nightmares!

VII

Jimmie's whole world was wiped out, ended. He had no place to go, no care what became of him. He stumbled on till he came to the trolley-track, and got on the first car which came along. It was pure chance that it happened to be going back to Leesville, for Jimmie had no longer any interest in that city. When the car came to the barn, he got out and wandered aimlessly, until he happened to pass a saloon where he had been accustomed to meet Jerry Coleman, distributor of ten dollar bills. Jimmie went in and ordered a drink of whiskey; he did not tell the saloon-keeper what had happened, but took the drink to a table and sat down by himself. When he had finished, he ordered another, because it helped him not to think; he sat there at the table, drinking steadily for an hour or more. And so upon his confused mind there dawned a strange, a ghastly idea, climax of all that night of horror. Which leg of Lizzie was it the man had been carrying wrapped in a horse-blanket? The right leg or the left? If it was the left leg, why, nothing; but if it was the right, why then, under the stocking was sewed a bandage, and in that bandage was wrapped a package containing seven faded yellow twenty dollar bills!

And what would they do about it? Would they bury the leg without investigation? Or would the man who had found it happen to undress it? And what was Jimmie to do? A hundred and forty dollars was not to be sneezed at by a working-man—it was more money than he had ever had in his life before, or might ever have again. But could he go to the man and say, "Did you find any money on my wife's leg?" Could he say, "Please give me my wife's leg, so that I can undress it and unsew the bandage, and get the money that I was paid for keeping quiet about the surgical operation on Lacey Granitch, that was done in my house before it was blown to pieces by the explosion."

Jimmie thought it all over while he took a couple more drinks, and finally settled it to himself: "Aw hell! What do I want with money? I ain't a-goin' to live no more!"

CHAPTER XIV

JIMMIE HIGGINS TAKES THE ROAD

I

JIMMIE HIGGINS was wandering down the street, when he ran into "Wild Bill," who was, of course, greatly surprised to see his friend in a drunken condition. When he heard the reason, he revealed an unexpected side of his nature. If you judged "Wild Bill" by his oratory, you thought him a creature poisoned through and through, a soul turned rancid with envy, hatred and malice and all uncharitableness. But now the tears came into his eyes, and he put his arm over Jimmie's shoulder. "Say, old pal, that's bum luck! By God, I'm sorry!" And Jimmie, who wanted nothing so much as somebody to be sorry with, clasped Bill in his arms, and burst into tears, and told over and over again how he had gone to what had been his home, and found only a huge crater blown out by the explosion, and how he had gone about calling his wife and babies, until at last they had brought him one leg of his wife.

"Wild Bill" listened, until he knew the story through, and then he said, "See here, old pal, let's you and me quit this town."

"Quit?" said Jimmie, stupidly.

"Every time I open the front of my face now, the police jump in it. Leesville's a hell of a town, I say. Let's get out."

"Where'll we go?"

"Anywhere—what's the diff? It's coming summer. Let's slam the gates."

Jimmie was willing—why not? They went back to the lodging-house where Bill lived, and he tied up his worldly goods in a gunny-sack—the greater part of the load consisting of a diary in which he had recorded his adventures as leader of an unemployed army which had started to march from California to Washington, D. C., some four years previously. They took the trolley, and getting off in the country, walked along the banks of the river, Jimmie still sobbing, and Bill in the grip of one of his fearful coughing spells. They sat down beside the stream, not so far from where Jimmie had gone in swimming with the Candidate; he gave a touching account of this adventure, but fell asleep in the middle of it, and Bill wandered off and begged some food at a farm-house, using his cough as a convenient lever for moving the heart of the house-wife. When night came, they sought the railroad and got on board a southward-moving freight; so Jimmie Higgins went back to the hobo life, at which he had spent a considerable part of his youth.

But there was a difference now; he was no longer a blind and helpless victim of a false economic system, but a revolutionist, fully class-conscious, trained in a grim school. The country was going to war, and Jimmie was going to war on the country. The two agitators got off the train at a mining-village, and got a job as "surface-men," and proceeded to preach their gospel of revolt to the workers in a lousy company boarding-house. When they were found out, they "jumped" another freight, and repeated the performance in another part of the district.

The companies were too vigilant for there to be any chance of a strike; but "Wild Bill" whispered to the young workers that he knew a trick worth two of that—he would teach them the art of "striking on the job"! This idea of course had great charm for embittered men; enabling them to pay back the boss, while at the same time continuing on his pay-roll. Bill had read whole books in which the theory and practice of "sabotage" were worked out, and he could tell any sort of workman tricks to make his employer sweat under the collar. If you worked in a machine-shop, you dropped emery-powder into the bearings; if you worked on a farm, you drove copper nails into the fruit-trees, which caused them to die; if you packed apples, you stuck your thumb-nail into one, which made sure that the whole box would be rotten when it arrived; if you worked in a saw-mill, you drove a spike into a log; if you worked in a restaurant, you served double portions to ruin the boss, and spit in each portion, to make sure the customer did not derive any benefit. All these things you did in a fervour of exaltation, a mood of frenzied martyrdom, because of the blaze of hate which had been fanned in your soul by a social system based upon oppression and knavery.

II

To Jimmie, living the obscure and comparatively peaceful life of a Socialist propagandist, the question of "sabotage, violence and crime" had been a more or less academic one, about which the comrades debated acrimoniously, and against which they voted by a large majority. But now Jimmie was out among the "wobblies," the "blanket-stiffs"—the unskilled workers who had literally nothing but their muscle-power to sell; here he was in the front-line trenches of the class war. These men wandered about from one job to another, at the mercy of the seasons and the fluctuations of industry. They were deprived of votes, and therefore of their status as citizens; they were deprived of a chance to organise, and therefore of their status as human beings. They were lodged in filthy bunk-houses, fed upon rotten food, and beaten or jailed at the least word of revolt. So they fought their oppressors with any and every weapon they could lay hands on.

In the turpentine-country, in a forest, Jimmie and his pal came to a "jungle," a place where the "wobblies" congregated, living off the country. Here around the camp-fires Jimmie met the guerrillas of the class-struggle, and learned the songs of revolt which they sang—some of them parodies on Christian hymns which would have caused the orthodox and respectable to faint with horror. Here they rested up, and exchanged data on the progress of their fight, and argued over tactics, and cussed the Socialists and the other "politicians" and "labour-fakirs," and sang the praises of the "one big union," and the "mass strike," and "direct action" against the masters of industry. They told stories of their sufferings and their exploits, and Jimmie sat and listened. Sometimes his eyes were wide with consternation, for he had never met men so desperate as these.

For example, "Strawberry" Curran—named for his red hair and innumerable freckles—an Irish boy with the face of a choir-singer, and eyes that must have been taken straight out of the blue vault of heaven. This lad told about a "free speech fight" in a far Western city, and how the chief of police had led the clubbing, and how they had got back at him. "We bumped him off all right," said "Strawberry"; it was a favourite phrase of his—whenever anybody got in his way, he "bumped him off." And then "Flathead Joe," who came from the Indian country, was moved to emulation, and told how he had put dynamite under the supports of a mine-breaker, and the whole works had slid down a slope into a canyon a mile below. And then a lame fellow, "Chuck" Peterson, told about the imprisonment of two strike-leaders in the hop-country of California, and of the epidemic of fires and destructions that had plagued that region for several years since.

All such things these men talked about quite casually, as soldiers would talk about the events of the last campaign. This class-war had been going on for ages, and had its own ethics and its own traditions; those who took part in it had their heroisms and sublimities, precisely like any other soldiers. They would have been glad to come into the open and fight, but the other side had all the guns. Every time the "wobblies" succeeded in organising the workers and calling a big strike, all the agencies of capitalist repression were called in—they were beaten by capitalist policemen, shot by capitalist sheriffs, starved and frozen in capitalist jails, and so their strike was crushed and their forces scattered. After many such experiences, it was inevitable that the hot-headed ones should take to secret vengeance, should become conspirators against capitalist society. And society, forgetting all the provocations it had given, called the "wobblies" criminals, and let it go at that. But they were a strange kind of criminal, serving a far-off dream. They had their humours and their humanities, their literature and music and art. Among them were men of education, graduates of universities both in America and abroad; you might hear one of the group about these camp-fires telling about slave-revolts in ancient Egypt and Greece; or quoting Strindberg and Stirner, or reciting a scene from Synge, or narrating how he had astounded the family of some lonely farmhouse by playing Rachmaninoff's "Prelude" on a badly out-of-tune piano.

Also you met among them men who had kept their gentleness, their sweetness of soul; men of marvellous patience, whose dream of human brotherhood no persecution, no outrage had been able to turn sour. They clung to their vision of a world redeemed, made over by the outcast and lowly; a vision that was brought to the world by a certain Jewish carpenter, and has haunted mankind for nineteen hundred years. The difference was that these men knew precisely how they meant to do it; they had a definite philosophy, a definite programme, which they carried as a gospel to the wage-slaves of the world. And they knew that this glad message would never die—not all the jails and clubs and machine-guns in the country could kill it, not obloquy and ridicule, not hunger and cold and disease. No! for the workers were hearing and understanding, they were learning the all-precious lesson of Solidarity. They were forming the "one big union," preparing the time when they would take over industry and administer it through their own workers' councils, instead of through the medium of parliaments and legislatures. That was the great idea upon which the Industrial Workers of the World was based; it was this they meant by "direct action," not the sinister thing which the capitalist newspapers made out of the phrase.

III

The country was going into its own war, which it considered of importance, and it called upon Jimmie Higgins and the rest of his associates to register for military service. In the month of June ten million men came forward in obedience to this call—but Jimmie, needless to say, was not among them. Jimmie and his crowd thought it was the greatest joke of the age. If the country wanted them, let it come and get them! And sure enough, the country came—a sheriff and some thirty farmers and turpentine-workers sworn in as deputies and armed with shot-guns and rifles. Should their sons go over seas to be killed in battle, while these desperadoes continued to camp out on the country, living on hogs and chickens which honest men had worked to raise? They had wanted to break up this "jungle" for some time; now they could do it in the name of patriotism! They surrounded the camp, and shot one man who tried to slip out in the darkness, and searched the rest for weapons, and then loaded them into half a dozen automobiles and took them to the nearest lockup.

So here was Jimmie, confronting a village draft-board. How old was he? The truth was that Jimmie did not know definitely, but his guess was about twenty-six. The draft-limit being thirty, he swore that he was thirty-two. And what were they going to do about it? They didn't know where he had been born, and they couldn't make him tell—because he didn't know it himself! His face was lined with many cares, and he had a few grey hairs from that night of horror when his loved ones had been wiped out of existence. These farmers knew how to tell the age of a horse, but not how to tell the age of a man!

"We'll draft ye anyhow!" vowed the chairman of the board, who was the local justice of the peace, an old fellow with a beard like a billy-goat.

"All right," said Jimmie, "but you'll get nothin' out o' me."

"What d' ye mean?"

"I mean I wouldn't fight; I'm a conscientious objector to war."

"They'll shoot ye!"

"Shoot away!"

"They'll send you to jail for life."

"What the hell do I care?"

It was difficult to know what to do with a person like that. If they did put him in jail, they would only be feeding him at the expense of the community, and that would not help to beat the Germans. They could see from the flash in his eyes that he would not be an easy man to break. Local interest asserted itself, and the old fellow with the wagging beard demanded: "If we let ye go, will ye get out o' this county?"

"What the hell do I care about your old county?" replied Jimmie.

So they turned him loose, and "Wild Bill" also, because it was evident at a glance that he was not long for this world and its wars. The two of them broke into an empty freight-car, and went thundering over the rails all night; and lying in the darkness, Jimmie was awakened by a terrified cry from his companion, and put out his hand and laid it in a mess that was hot and wet.

"Oh, my God!" gasped Bill. "I'm done for!"

"What is it?"

"Hemorrhage."

The terrified Jimmie did not even know what that was. There was nothing he could do but sit there, holding his friend's trembling hand and listening to his moans. When the train stopped, Jimmie sprang out and rushed to one of the brakemen, who came with his lantern, and saw "Wild Bill" lying in a pool of blood, already so far gone that he could not lift his head. "Jesus!" exclaimed the brakeman. "He's a goner, all right."

The "goner" was trying to say something, and Jimmie leaned

his ear down to him. "Good-bye, old pal," whispered Bill. That was all, but it caused Jimmie to burst out sobbing.

The engine whistled. "What the hell you stiffs doin' on this train?" demanded the brakeman—but not so harshly as the words would indicate. He lifted the dying man—no very serious burden—and laid him on the platform of the station. "Sorry," he said, "but we're behind schedule." He waved his lantern, and the creaking cars began to move, and the train drew away, leaving Jimmie sitting by the corpse of his pal. The world seemed a lonely place that long night.

In the morning the station-agent came, and notified the nearest authorities, and in the course of the day came a wagon to fetch the body. What was the use of Jimmie's waiting? One "Potter's field" was the same as another, and there would be nothing inspiring about the funeral. The man who drove the wagon looked at Jimmie suspiciously and asked his age; they were scarce of labour in that country, he said—the rule was "Work or fight." Jimmie foresaw another session with a draft-board, so he leaped onto another freight train, taking with him as a legacy "Wild Bill's" diary of the unemployed army.

IV

It was harvest-time, and Jimmie went West to the wheat country. It was hard work, but the pay made your eyes bulge. Jimmie realised that war was not such a bad thing—for the ones that stayed at home! If you didn't like one farmer's way of speaking to you, or the kind of biscuits his wife offered you, you could move on to the next, and he would take you in at four bits more per day. It was the nearest approach to a workingman's paradise that Jimmie had ever encountered. There was really only one drawback—the pestiferous draft-boards that never stopped snooping round. They were forever hauling you up and threatening and questioning you—putting you through the same scene over and over. Why couldn't the boobs give you a card, showing that you had been through the mill, and let that settle it? But no, they wouldn't give you a card—they preferred to go on jacking you up because you had no card! It was all a trick, thought Jimmie, to wear him out and force him into their army by hook or by crook. But here was one time when they would not get away with it!

However, Jimmie Higgins was not nearly so dangerous a character, now that "Wild Bill" was gone out of his life. It was really not his nature to cherish hate, or to set out deliberately to revenge himself. Jimmie was a Socialist in the true sense of the word—he felt himself a part of society, and that peace and plenty and kindness which he desired for himself he desired for all mankind. He was not dreaming of a time when he could turn the capitalists out of power and treat them as they were now treating him; he meant the world to be just as good a place for the capitalists as for the workers—all would share alike, and Jimmie was ready to wipe out the old scores and start fair any day. His propaganda regained its former idealistic hue, and it was only when somebody tried to drag him into the slaughter-pen that he developed teeth and claws.

So he became fairly happy again—happier than he had thought he could ever be. It was in vain he told himself that he had nothing to live for; he had the greatest thing in the world to live for, the vision of a just and sane and happy world. So long as anybody could be found to listen while he talked about it and explained how it might be achieved, life was worth while, life was real. It was only now and then that his bitter heart-ache returned to plague him—when he wakened in the night with his arms clasped about the memory of the soft, warm, kindly body of Eleesa Betooser; or when he came to a farm-house where there were children, whose prattle reminded him of the little fellow who had been his prime reason for wanting a just and sane and happy world. Jimmie found that he could not bear to work in one farm-house where there were children; and when he told the farmer's wife the reason, he and the woman declared a temporary truce to the class-war, and celebrated it with half a large apple-pie.

V

The Socialists held a National convention at St. Louis, and drew up their declaration concerning the war. They called it the most unjustifiable war in history, "a crime against the people of the United States"; they called on the workers of the country to oppose it, and pledged themselves "to the support of all mass movements in opposition to conscription." This was, of course, a serious step to take at such a time; the comrades realised it, and there were solemn gatherings to discuss the referendum, and not a little disagreement as to the wisdom of the declaration. In the town of Hopeland, near which Jimmie was working, there was a local, and he had got himself transferred from Leesville, and paid up his back dues, and had his precious red card stamped up to date. And now he would go in and listen to debates, just as exciting and just as bewildering as those he had heard at the outbreak of the war.

There were some who pointed out the precise meaning of those words, "all mass movements in opposition to conscription." The leading dry-goods merchant of the town, who was a Socialist, declared that the words meant insurrection and mob violence, and the resolution would be adjudged a call to treason. At which there leaped to his feet a Russian Jewish tailor, Rabin by name; his first name was Scholem, which means Peace, and he cried in great excitement: "Vot business have ve Socialists vit such vords? Ve might leaf dem to de enemy, vot?"—You might have thought you were in Leesville, listening to Comrade Stankewitz. The only difference was that there were not many Germans in this town, and those few confined their discussions to Ireland and India.

Jimmie would hear the arguments, back and forth and back again, and his mind would be in greater confusion than ever. He hated war, as much as ever; but on the other hand, he was learning to hate the Germans too. The American government, going into war, had been forced to assert itself, and the stores and billboards were covered with proclamations and picture-posters, and the newspapers were full of recitals of the crimes which Germany had committed against humanity. Jimmie might refuse to read this "Wall Street dope," as he called it, but the workingmen with whom he was associating read it, and would fire it at him whenever they got into a controversy. Also the daily events in the news despatches—the sinking of hospital-ships filled with wounded, the shelling of life-boats, the dragging away into slavery in coal-mines of Belgian children thirteen and fourteen years old! How could any man fail to hate and to fear a government which committed such atrocities? How could he remain untroubled at the thought that he might be assisting such a government to victory?

Jimmie was honest, he was trying to face the facts as he saw them; and when he stopped to think, when he remembered the things he had done in company with "Wild Bill" and "Strawberry" Curran and "Flathead Joe" and "Chuck" Peterson, he could not deny that he had been, however unintentionally, helping the Kaiser to win the war. In his arguments with others, Jimmie dared not tell all he knew about such matters; so, when he argued with himself, his conscience was troubled, and doubt gnawed at his soul. Suppose it were true, as Comrade Dr. Service had tried to prove to him, that a victory for the Kaiser would mean that America would have to spend the next twenty or thirty years getting ready for the next war? Might it not then be better to forego revolutionary agitation for a while, until the Kaiser had been put out of business?

There were not a few Socialists who argued this way—men who had been active in the movement and had possessed Jimmie's regard before the war. Now they denounced the St. Louis resolution—the "majority report" as it was called. When this report was carried in referendum by a vote of something like eight to one, these comrades withdrew from the party, and some of them bitterly attacked their former friends. Such utterances were taken up by the capitalist press; and this made Jimmie Higgins indignant. A fine lot of Socialists, to quit the ship in the hour of peril! Renegades, Jimmie called them, and compared them with Judas Iscariot and Benedict Arnold and such like celebrities of past ages. They, being exactly the same sort of folks as Jimmie, answered by calling Jimmie a pro-German and a traitor; which did not make it easier to persuade Jimmie to listen to their arguments. So both sides became blinded with anger, forgetting about the facts in the case, and thinking only of punishing a hated antagonist.

VI

All over the country now men were sending their sons to the training-camps, and putting their money into "liberty-bonds." So they were in no mood to listen to argument—they would fly into a rage at the least hint that the cause in which they were making sacrifices was not a perfectly just and righteous cause. There was an organisation called the "People's Council for Peace and Democracy," which attempted to hold a national convention; the gathering was broken up by mobs, and the delegates went wandering over the country, trying in vain to get together. The mayor of Chicago gave them permission to meet in that city, but the governor of the state sent troops to prevent! You see, the people of the country had learned all about the organization for which Jerry Coleman had been working—"Labour's National Peace Council"; and here was another organization, bearing practically the same name, and carrying on an agitation which seemed the same to the average man. The distinction between hired treason and super-idealism was far too subtle for the people to draw in a time of such peril.

It was becoming more and more the fashion to arrest Socialists and to suppress their papers; the government authorities in many places declared the "majority report" unmailable, and indicted state and national secretaries for having sent it out in the ordinary routine of their business. Jimmie received a letter from Comrade Meissner in Leesville, telling him that Comrade "Jack" Smith had been given two years in the penitentiary for his speech in the Opera-house, and the other would-be speakers had been fined five hundred dollars each. Several issues of the "Worker" had been barred from the mails, and now the police had raided the offices and forced the suspension of the publication. All over the country that sort of thing was happening, so now if you argued with Jimmie in favour of the war, his answer was that America was more Prussian than Prussia, and what was the use of fighting for Democracy abroad, if you had to sacrifice every particle of Democracy at home in order to win the fight?

Jimmie really believed this—he believed it with most desperate and passionate intensity. He looked forward to a war won for the benefit of oppression at home; he foresaw the system of militarism and suppression riveted forever on the people of America. Jimmie would admit that the President himself might be sincere in the fine words he used about democracy; but the great Wall Street interests which had run the country for so many decades—they had their secret purposes, for which the war-frenzy served as a convenient cloak. They were going to make universal military service the rule in America; they were going to see to it that every school-child learned the military lessons of obedience and subordination. Also they were going to put the radical papers out of business and put a stop to all radical propaganda. Those Socialists who had been trapped into supporting the President's war-programme would wake up some morning with a fearful dark-brown taste in their mouths!

No, said Jimmie Higgins, the way to fight war was to resist the subterfuges, however cunning and plausible, by which men sought to persuade you to support war. The way to fight war was the way of the Russians. The propaganda of proletarian revolt, the glorious example which the Russian workers had set, would do more to break down the power of the Kaiser than all the guns and shells in the world. But the militarists did not want it broken that way—Jimmie suspected that many of them would rather have the war won by the Kaiser than have it won by the Socialists. The governments refused to give passports to Socialists who wanted to meet in some neutral country and work out the basis of a settlement upon which all the peoples of the world might get together; and Jimmie took the banning of this Socialist conference as the supreme crime of world-capitalism, it was evidence that world-capitalism knew its true enemy, and meant to use the war as an excuse to hold that enemy down.

VII

Day by day Jimmie was coming to place more of his hopes in Russia. His little friend Rabin, the tailor, took a Russian paper published in New York, the "Novy Mir," and would translate its news and editorials. Local Hopeland, thus inspired, voted a message of fraternal sympathy to the Russian workers. In Petrograd and Moscow there was going on, it appeared, a struggle between the pro-ally Socialists and the Internationalists, the true, out-and-out, middle-of-the-road, thick-and-thin proletarians. The former were called Mensheviki, the latter were called Bolsheviki, and of course Jimmie was all for the latter. Did he not know the "stool-pigeon Socialists" at home, who were letting themselves be used by capitalism?

The big issues were two—first, the land, which the peasants wanted to take from the landlords; and second, the foreign debt. The Russian Tsar had borrowed four billion dollars from

France and a billion or two from England, to be used in enslaving the Russian workers and driving several millions of them to death on the battle-field. Now should the Russian workers consider themselves bound by this debt? When anybody asked Jimmie Higgins that question, he responded with a thunderous No, and he regarded as hirelings or dupes of Wall Street all those Socialists who supported Kerensky in Russia.

When the American government, wishing to appeal to the Russian people for loyalty in the war, sent over a commission to them, and placed at its head one of the most notorious corporation lawyers in America, a man whose life, the Jimmies said, had been sold to service in the anti-liberal cause, Jimmie Higgins' shrill voice became a yell of ridicule and rage. Of course Jimmie's organisation saw to it that the Bolsheviki were informed in advance as to the character of this commission—something which was unnecessary, as it happened, because immediately after the overthrow of the Tsar there had begun a pilgrimage of Russian Socialists from New York and San Francisco, men who had seen the seamy side of American capitalism in the slums of our great cities, and who lost no time in providing the Russian radicals with full information concerning Wall Street!

It chanced that in San Francisco a well-known labour leader had been charged with planting a bomb to break up a "preparedness" parade. He had been convicted upon what was proven to be perjured testimony, and the labour unions of the country had been conducting a campaign to save his life—which campaign the capitalist newspapers had been carefully overlooking, according to their invariable custom. But now the returned exiles in Petrograd took up the matter, and organised a parade to the American embassy, with a demand for the freeing of this "Muni." The report, of course, came back to America—to the immense bewilderment of the American people, who had never heard of this "Muni" before. To Jimmie Higgins it seemed just the funniest joke on earth that a big labour-struggle should be on in San Francisco, and Americans should get their first news about it from Petrograd! Look! he would cry—how much real democracy there is in America, how much care for the working-classes!

So all that summer and fall, while Jimmie Higgins slaved

in the fields, getting in his country's wheat-crop, and then his country's corn crop, there was a song of joy and awakening excitement in his soul. Far over the seas men of his own kind were getting the reins of power into their hands, for the first time in the history of the world. It could not be long before here in America the workers would learn this wonderful lesson, would thrill to the idea that freedom and plenty might really be their portion!

CHAPTER XV

JIMMIE HIGGINS TURNS BOLSHEVIK

I

WINTER was coming, and the farm-workers moved to the cities; but this year they did not go as bums and out-o'-works—they went, each man a little king. Jimmie wandered into the city of Ironton, and got himself a job in a big automobile shop at eight dollars a day, and set to work agitating for ten dollars. It was not that he had any need of the extra two dollars, of course, but merely because his first principle in life was to make trouble for the profit-system. The capitalist papers of this middle-Western metropolis were furiously denouncing workingmen who struck "against their country" in war-time; Jimmie, on the other hand, denounced those who used "country" as camouflage for "boss," and made the war a pretext to deprive labour of its most precious right.

There was a Socialist local in Ironton, still active and determined, in spite of the fact that its office had been raided by the police, and most of the party's papers and magazines barred from the mails. You could always get leaflets printed, however; and if you could no longer denounce the war directly, you could jeer at England's exhibition of "democracy" in Ireland, you could point to the profits of the profiteers, and demand conscription of wealth along with conscription of manhood. Some American Socialists became almost as subtle as that German rebel of pre-war days, who, desiring to lampoon the Kaiser, wrote an account of the life of the Roman emperor Agricola, reciting his vanities and insane extravagances.

Late in the fall came an event which should have troubled Jimmie Higgins more deeply than it did. Along the Izonzo river the Italian armies were facing the Austrians, their hereditary enemies; they were at the end of a long, exhaustive, and for the most part unsuccessful campaign, and the Italian Socialists at home were carrying on precisely such a warfare against their own government as Jimmie Higgins was carrying on in America. They were helped by the Catholic intriguers, who hated the Italian government because it had destroyed the temporal power of the Pope; they were helped by the subtle and persistent efforts of Austrian agents in their country, who spread rumours among Italian troops of the friendly intentions of the Austrians, and of the imminence of a truce. These agents went so far as to fake copies of the leading Italian newspapers, with accounts of starvation and riots in the home-cities, and the shooting down of women and children. These papers were given out in the Italian trenches, before a certain mountain-sector where the Austrian troops had been fraternising with the Italians; and then, during the night, the Austrian troops were withdrawn, and picked German "shock-troops" substituted, which attacked at dawn and drove through the Italian lines, sweeping back the army along a hundred mile front, capturing some quarter of a million prisoners and a couple of thousand cannon—practically all the Italians had.

That Jimmie Higgins did not pay more attention to this terrifying incident was in part because he read it in the capitalist papers and did not believe it; but mainly because his whole attention just now was centred on Russia, where the proletariat was about to make its bid for power. Now you would see how wars were to be ended and peace restored to a distracted world!

The moderate Socialist government of Kerensky was pleading with the capitalist masters of the Allied nations for a statement of their peace terms, so that the workers of Russia might know what they were fighting for. The Russian workers wanted a declaration in favour of no annexations, no indemnities, and disarmament; on such terms they would help fight the war, in spite of all the starvation and suffering in distracted Russia. But the Allied statesmen would not make any such declaration, and the Russian workers, backed by all the Socialists of the world, declared that the reason was that these Allied statesmen were waging an imperialist war—they did not intend to stop fighting until they had taken vast territories from the German powers, and exacted a ransom that would cripple Germany for a generation. The Russian workers refused point-blank to fight for such aims, and so in November came the second revolution, the uprising of the Bolsheviki.

Almost their first action when they took possession of the palaces and government archives was to publish to the world the secret treaties which the rulers of England, France and Italy had made with Russia. These treaties formed a complete justification for the attitude of the Russian revolutionists—they showed that the Allied imperialists had planned most shameless plundering; England was to have the German colonies and Mesopotamia, France was to have German territory to the Rhine, Italy was to have the Adriatic coast, and to divide Palestine and Syria with England and France.

And here was the most significant fact to Jimmie Higgins—these enormously important revelations, the most important since the beginning of the war, were practically suppressed by the capitalist newspapers of America! First these papers printed a brief item—the Bolsheviki had given out what they claimed were secret treaties, but the genuineness of these documents was gravely doubted. Then they published evasive and lying denials from the British, French and Italian diplomats; and then they shut up! Not another word did you read about those secret treaties; except for one or two American newspapers with traditions of honour, the full text of those treaties was given in the Socialist press alone! And now, cried Jimmie Higgins, to the workingmen in his shop, what do you think of those wonderful Allies of ours? What do you think of those Wall Street newspapers of ours? Could any workingman who had such facts put before him fail to realise that Jimmie Higgins had a case, and a most important work in the world to do, in spite of all his unreason and his narrowness?

II

Jimmie was now in the seventh heaven, walking as if on air. A proletarian government at last, the first in history! A government of workingmen like himself, running their own affairs, without the help of politicians or bankers! Coming out before the world and telling the truth about matters of state, in language that common men could understand! Disbanding the armies, and sending the workers home! Turning the masters out of the factories, and putting shop-committees in control! Taking away the advertising from the crooked capitalist papers, and so putting them out of business! Our little friend would rush to the corner every morning to get the paper and see what had happened next; he would go down the street, so excited that he forgot his breakfast.

Jimmie had made a new acquaintance in Ironton; the little tailor, Rabin, whose name was Scholem, which means Peace, had given him a letter to his brother, whose name was Deror, which means Freedom. Each afternoon when the automobile factory let out, Jimmie would get an evening paper and take it to Deror's tailor-shop, and the two would spell out the news. By God, look at this! Did you ever hear the like? The man in charge of the Bolshevik foreign office was a Marxian Jew who had helped edit the "Novy Mir," the revolutionary paper which Scholem had read to Jimmie! He had been a waiter in the Waldorf-Astoria hotel, and now he was giving out the secret treaties, and issuing propaganda manifestos to the international proletariat!

The American capitalist press was full of lies about the new revolution, of course; but Jimmie could read pretty well between the lines of the capitalist press, and the few Socialist papers that were still in business, and which he read at the headquarters of the local, gave him the rest of what he wanted. To Jimmie, of course, everything the Bolsheviki did was right; if it wasn't right, it was a lie. The little machinist knew that the Bolsheviki had repudiated the four billion dollar debt which the government of the Tsar had contracted with the bankers of France; and Jimmie knew perfectly well what was the lying power of four billion dollars!

The American papers were shocked because the Russian Socialists were deserting the cause of democracy, and giving Germany a chance to win the war. The American papers called them German agents, but Jimmie did not take any stock in such talk as this. Jimmie was familiar with the "frame up," as it is operated against the workers in America. He saw that the first thing the Bolshevik leaders did was to make an appeal to the revolutionary workers of Germany. The Russian proletariat had shown the way—now let the German proletariat follow! Literature was printed and shipped wholesale into Germany, leaflets were dropped by aviators among the German troops; and when Jimmie and Deror read that the German generals had protested to the Russians against such practices, they laughed aloud with delight. Well might the war-lords squeal; they knew what was coming to them! And when in January Jimmie and Deror read of the revolting of a brigade of German troops, and a strike of several hundred thousand workingmen throughout Germany, they thought the end was at hand. The little tailor got up in Local Ironton and made a motion that it take to itself the name "Bolshevik"—which motion was carried with a whoop. And these American Bolsheviki went on to consult with the labour-unions, suggesting that they should form "shop-committees," and prepare for the taking over of industry à la Russe!

III

But something went suddenly wrong with the newly built revolutionary steam-roller. The German military chiefs seized their strike-leaders at home and threw them into jail, or shipped them off to the front trenches to be slaughtered. By terrorism, shrewdly mixed with cajolery, they broke the strike, and sent the grumbling slaves back to their treadmill. And then the German armies began to march into Russia!

It was the crisis to which Jimmie Higgins had been looking forward ever since the war began. Tolstoi had taught that if one nation refused to fight, it would be impossible for another nation to invade it; and while Jimmie Higgins was no mystic or religious non-resistant, he agreed in this with the great Russian. No workers in an enemy army could possibly be brought to fire upon their peace-proclaiming brothers!

And here at last was the test of the theory; here were German Socialists ordered to march against Russian Socialists—ordered to fire upon the red flag! Would they do what their masters, the war-lords, commanded? Or would they listen to the clamorous appeals of the international proletariat, and turn their guns against their own officers?

All the world saw what happened; it saw the glorious revolutionary machine, in which Jimmie Higgins had put all his trust, run into a ditch and land its passengers in the mud. The German armies marched, and the Socialists in the German armies did exactly what the non-Socialists did—they fired upon the red flag, as they would have fired upon the flag of the Tsar. They obeyed the orders of their officers, like true and loyal Germans; they drove back the Bolsheviki in confusion, taking their guns and supplies, and destroying their cities; they led off the Russian women and children into slavery, precisely as if they were Belgian or French women and children, destined by the German Gott as the legitimate prey of Kultur. They sacked Riga and Reval, they overran all the Eastern portions of Russia—Courland, Livonia, Esthonia; they moved into the rich grain country of Southern Russia, the Ukraine; they landed from their ships and took Finland, wiping out the liberties of that splendid people. They were at the gates of Petrograd, and the Bolshevik government was forced to flee to Moscow. Of all which military feats the German Socialist papers spoke with stern pride!

IV

Poor Jimmie Higgins! It was like the blow of a mighty fist in his face; he was literally stunned—it was weeks before he could grasp the full meaning of what was happening, the debacle of all his hopes. And it was the same with Ironton's Bolshevik local; all the "pep" was gone out of its proceedings. To be sure, some noisy ones went on shouting for revolution the very next day—men who had been talking formulas for twenty or thirty years, and had no more notion of a fact than they had of a pseudopodium. But the sensible men of the group knew that their "St. Louis resolution" was being shot to death over there in the trenches before Petrograd.

It was interesting especially to see Rabin. The common belief of Americans was that a Jew could not be induced to fight; they told a story about one who cried out to his son, asking why he was letting another boy pummel him, and the son whispered in reply, "Keep still, I got a nickel under my foot!" All through the war the Jewish Socialists in America had been, next to the Germans, the most ardent pacifists; but now here was a social revolution managed by Jews, here was a Russian government which gave the Jews their rights for the first time in history! So the little Jewish tailor stood up before these American Bolsheviki, and with tears running down his cheeks declared: "Comrades, I am already tru vit speeches; I am going into dis var! I vill put myself vit de Polish Socialists, vit de Bohemian Socialists—I fight de Kaiser to de death! So vill fight every Jewish Socialist in de vorld!" And this was no mere braggadocio—Comrade Rabin actually proceeded to shut up his tailor-shop, and went away to join the "red brigade" which was being organised by the Jewish revolutionists of New York!

If the German war-lords had set out deliberately to hamstring the American Socialists, to make it impossible for them to go on demanding peace, they could not have acted differently. They dragged the helpless Bolsheviki into a peace-conference at Brest-Litovsk, and forced them to cede away all the territories that Germany had taken, and on top of that to pay an enormous indemnity. They planned to compel the new Russian government to become a vassal to the Central powers, working to help them enslave the rest of the world. The German armies went through the conquered territories, stripping them bare, robbing the peasants of every particle of food, beating them, shooting them, burning their homes if they resisted. They gave to the world such a demonstration of what a German peace would mean, that everywhere free men set their teeth and gripped their hands, and swore to root this infamous thing from out civilisation. Even Jimmie Higgins!

V

Yes, even Jimmie! He made up his mind that he would work as hard as ever he could, and produce as many automobile-trucks as he could. But alas, a man cannot be hounded and oppressed all his life, cannot have hatred and rebellion ground into the deeps of his soul, and then forget it over-night because of certain intellectual ideas, certain new items that he reads in his paper. What happened to Jimmie was that his mind was literally torn in half; he found himself, every twenty-four hours of his life, of two absolutely contradictory and diametrically opposite points of view. He would vow destruction to the hated German armies; and then he would turn about and vow destruction to the men at home who were managing the job of destroying the German armies!

For these men were Jimmie's life long enemies, and were no more able to forget their prejudices over-night than was Jimmie. For example, the lying capitalist paper which Jimmie had to read every morning! When Jimmie had read a patriotic editorial in the "Ironton Daily Sun," it had become utterly impossible for him to help win the war that day! Or the politicians, seeking to use the war-cry of democracy abroad to crush all traces of democracy at home; to "get" the radicals whom they hated and feared, and by means of taxes on necessities and a bonded debt to put the costs of the war onto the poor! Or the capitalists, making fervid speeches about patriotism, but refusing to give up the whip-hand over their wage-slaves!

Jimmie Higgins was working in a factory, making automobile-trucks for the armies in France; and the owners of the factory would not let the men have a union, and so there was a strike. The bosses made an agreement to take everybody back and permit a union, and then proceeded treacherously to violate the agreement, getting rid of the most active organisers on this or that transparent pretext. Jimmie Higgins, trying to help with the skill of his hands to make the world safe for democracy, was turned out of his job and left to wander in the streets, because a big profit-seeking corporation did not believe in democracy, and refused to permit its workers any voice in determining the conditions of their labour! The Government was trying to deal with emergencies such as this, to put an end to the epidemic of strikes which was hindering the war-work everywhere; but the government had not yet got its machinery going, and meantime Jimmie's little feeble sprout of patriotism got a severe chill.

Jimmie got drunk, and wasted a part of his money on a woman of the street. Then, being ashamed of himself, and still plagued by the memory of his dead wife and babies, he straightened up and resolved to start life anew. He found himself thinking about Leesville; it was the only place in the world where he had ever been really happy, and now since Deror Rabin had gone East, it was the only place where he had friends. How were the Meissners making out? How was Comrade Mrs. Gerrity, née Baskerville? What was Local Leesville thinking about Russia and about the war? Jimmie took a sudden resolve to go and find out. He priced a ticket, and found that he had enough money and to spare. He would take the journey—and take it in state, as a citizen and a war-worker, not as a hobo in a box-car!

CHAPTER XVI

JIMMIE HIGGINS MEETS THE TEMPTER

I

WHEN Jimmie Higgins stepped off the train at Leesville, it was a blustery morning in early March, with snow still on the ground and flurries of it in the air. In front of the station was a public square, with a number of people gathered, and Jimmie strolled over to see what was going on. What he saw was a score of young men, some in khaki uniforms, some in ordinary trousers and sweaters, being drilled. Jimmie, being in the mood of a gentleman of leisure, stopped to watch the show.

It was the thing he had been talking and thinking about for nearly three years: this monstrous perversion of the human soul called Militarism, this force which seized hold of men and made them into automatons, moving machines which obeyed orders in a mass, and went out and did deeds of which none of them taken separately would have been capable, even in their dreams. Here was a bunch of average nice Leesville boys, employés of the shops nearby, "soda-jerkers" and "counter-jumpers," clerks who had deftly fitted shoes onto the feet of pretty ladies. Now they were submitting themselves to this deforming discipline, undergoing this devilish transmogrification!

Jimmie's eye ran down the line: there was a street-car conductor he knew, there was a machinist from the Empire, also there was a son of Ashton Chalmers, president of the First National Bank of Leesville. And suddenly Jimmie gave a start. Impossible! It could not be! But—it was! Young Emil Forster! Emil a Socialist, Emil a German, Emil a student and thinker, who had penetrated the hypocritical disguises of this capitalist war, and had fearlessly proclaimed the truth every Friday night at the local—here he was with a suit of khaki on his rather frail figure, a rifle in his hand and a look of grim resolve on his face, going through the evolutions of squad-drill: left, right, left, right, left, right—column left, march—one, two, three, four—left, right, left, right,—squad right about, march—left, right, left, right—squad left oblique, march—and so on. If you are to form any picture of the scene you must imagine the swift tramp of many feet in unison —thump, thump, thump, thump, thump, thump; you must imagine the marchers, with their solemnly set faces, and the orders thundered out by a red-faced young man of desperate aspect, the word *march* coming each time with a punch that hit you over the heart. This red-faced young man was the very incarnation of the military despot as Jimmie had pictured him; watching with hawk-like eye, scolding, pounding, driving, with no slightest regard for the feelings of the slaves he commanded, or for any of the decencies of civilised intercourse.

"Hold those half steps, Casey! Keep your eye on the end man—you'll have him splitting his legs if you don't wait for him. Column left, march—one, two, three, four—now you're all right—off with you—that's better! Put a little pep into your feet, Chalmers, for God's sake—if you go marching into Berlin like that they'll think it's the hospital squad! By the right flank, column fours, march—watch your distance there, end man! How many times do you want me to tell you that?" —And so on and on—tramp, tramp, tramp, tramp—while a small boy standing beside Jimmie, evidently a truant from school, chanted over and over: "Left—left—the soldier got drunk and he packed up his trunk and he left—left! And do you not think he was right—right?"

II

Now if you have ever stood about and watched outdoor exercise or games, on a day in March with snow on the ground and a keen wind blowing, you know how it is—you have to stamp your feet to keep warm; and if in your neighbourhood there are twenty left feet smiting the ground in unison, and then twenty right feet smiting the ground in unison, it is absolutely inevitable that your stamping should keep time to the smiting; also the rhythm of your stamping will be communicated upwards into your body—your thoughts will keep time with the marching squad—tramp, tramp, tramp, tramp—left, right, left, right! The psychologists tell us that one who goes through the actions appropriate to an emotion will begin to feel that emotion; and so it was with Jimmie Higgins. By a process so subtle that he never suspected it Jimmie was being made into a militarist! Jimmie's hands were clenched, Jimmie's jaw was set, Jimmie's feet were tramping, tramping on the road to Berlin, to teach the Prussian war-lords what it meant to defy the free men of a great republic!

But then something would happen to blast these budding excitements in Jimmie's soul. The red-faced fellow would break into the rhythm of the march. "For the love of Mike, Pete Casey, can't you remember those half-steps? Squad, halt! Now look here, what's the matter with you? Step out and let me show you once more." And poor Casey, a meek-faced little man with sloping shoulders, who had been running the elevator in the Chalmers Building up to a week ago, would patiently practise marching without moving, so that the rest of the line could wheel round him as a pivot. The petty tyrant who scolded at him was determined to have his own way; and Jimmie, who had had to do with many such tyrants in his long years of industrial servitude, was glad when this particular one got mixed up in his orders, and ran his squad into the fountain in the middle of the drill-ground, and some of them marched over the parapet, sliding down into the ice-covered basin below. The spectators roared, and so did the marchers, and the red-faced young man had to join in, and to come down off his high horse.

The conflict of impulses went on in Jimmie's soul. These marching men were the "boobs" at whom he had been mocking for something over two years. They did not look like "boobs," he had to admit; on the contrary, they looked quite capable of deciding what they wanted to do. And they had decided; they had quit their jobs several weeks in advance of the time when they would be called for the draft, and had set to work to learn the rudiments of the military art, in the hope of thus getting more quickly to France. Among them were bankers and merchants and real estate dealers, side by side with soda-jerkers and counter-jumpers and elevator-men—and all taking their orders from an ex-blacksmith's helper, who had run away to fight in the Philippines.

Jimmie got this last bit of information from a fellow who stood watching; so he realised that here was the thing he had been reading about in the papers—the new army of the people, that was going forth to make the world safe for democracy! Jimmie had read such words, and thought them just camouflage, a trap for the "boobs." But here, a sight of wonder before his eyes, a son of Ashton Chalmers, president of the First National Bank of Leesville, being ordered about and hauled over the coals by an ex-blacksmith's helper, who happened to know how to shout with the accents of a pile-driver: "Shoulder *humps!* Order *humps!* Present *humps!*"

The squad spread itself out for exercise—grasping their heavy rifles and swinging them this way and that with desperate violence. "Swing over head and return, ready, exercise—one, two, three, four, five, six, seven, eight—eight, seven, six, five, four, three, two, one." It was no joke making those swings in such quick time; the poor little elevator-man Casey was left hopelessly behind, he could only make half the swing, and then couldn't get back to place on the count; he would look about, grinning sheepishly, and then fall into time and try again. Everybody's face was set, everybody's breath was coming harder and harder, everybody's complexion was becoming apoplectic.

"Swing to the right!" shouted the blacksmith-tyrant. "Ready, exercise—one, two"—and so on. And then he would yell: "No, Chalmers, don't punch out with your arms—swing up your gun! Swing it up from the bottom! That's the way! Poke 'em! Poke 'em! Put the punch into 'em!" And over Jimmie stole a cold horror. There was nothing on the end of those guns but a little black hole, but Jimmie knew what was supposed to be there—what would some day be there; the exercise meant that these affable young Leesville store-clerks were getting ready to drive a sharp, gleaming blade into the bowels of human beings! "Poke 'em! Poke 'em!" shouted the ex-blacksmith, and with desperate force they swung the heavy rifles, throwing their bodies to one side and leaping out with one foot. Horrible! Horrible!

III

Man is a gregarious animal, and it is a fundamental law of his being that when a group of his fellows are doing a certain thing, and doing it with energy and fervor, any one who does not do it, who does not share the mood of energy and fervour, shall be the object of ridicule and anger, shall feel within his own heart confusion and distress. This is true, even if the group is doing nothing more worth-while than making itself drunk. How much more shall it be when it is engaged in making the world safe for democracy!

The only way the man can save himself is by holding before his mind the belief that he is right, and that some day this will be recognised; in other words, by appealing to some other group of men, who in some future time will applaud him. If he is sure of this future applause, he can manage to stand the jeers for the moment. But how when he begins to doubt—when his mind is haunted by the possibility that the men of the future may agree with those of the present, who are learning to march in unison, and to poke bayonets into the bodies of Huns?

One of the things which brought this destructive doubt to Jimmie's soul was the sight of Emil Forster, learning to march and to poke. Emil had been one of his heroes, Emil knew a hundred times as much as he—and Emil was going to the war! The squad marched away to the city hall across the square, and deposited its rifles in a room in the basement, and then Emil came out, and Jimmie went up to him. The young carpet-designer of course was delighted to meet his old friend, and asked him to go to lunch. As they walked along the street together Jimmie asked what it meant, and Emil answered: "It means that I have made up my mind."

"You're going to fight the German people?"

"Strange as you'll think it, I'm going to fight them for their own good. Bebel wrote in his memoirs that the way to get democratic progress in autocratic countries is through military defeat; and it seems up to America to provide this defeat for Germany."

"But—you were preaching just the opposite!"

"I know; it makes me feel foolish sometimes. But things have changed, and there's no sense shutting your eyes to facts."

Jimmie waited.

"Russia, more especially," continued Emil, answering the unspoken question. "What's the use of getting Socialism, if you're just throwing yourself down for a military machine to run over you? You're playing the fool, that's all—and you have to see it. What hope is there for Russia now?"

"There's the German Socialists."

"Well, they just didn't have the power, that's all. What's more, we have to face the fact that a lot of them aren't really revolutionists—they're politicians, and haven't dared to stand out against the crowd. Anyhow, whatever the reason is, they didn't save their own country, and they didn't save Russia. They certainly can't expect us to give them a third chance—it costs too much."

"But then," argued Jimmie, "ain't we doin' just what we blame them for doin'—turnin' patriots, supportin' a capitalist government?"

"When you're supporting a government," replied Emil, "it makes a lot of difference what use it's making of your support. We all know the faults of our government, but we know too that the people can change it when enough of them get ready, and that makes a real difference. I've come to realise that if we give the Kaiser a beating, the German people will kick him out, and then we can talk sense to them."

IV

They walked along for a bit in silence, Jimmie trying to assimilate these ideas. They were new—not in the sense that he had not heard them before, but in the sense that he had not heard them from a German. "How does your father feel?" he asked, at last.

"He hasn't changed," replied the other. "And that makes it pretty hard—it's all we can do to keep from quarrelling. He's old, and new ideas don't come to him easily. Yet you'd think he'd be the first to see it—his father was one of the old revolutionists, he was put in jail in Dresden. I don't suppose you know much about the history of Germany."

"No," said Jimmie.

"Well, in those days the German people tried to get free, and they were put down by the troops, and the real revolutionists were driven into exile. Some of them came over here—like my grandfather. But you see, their children have forgotten about their wrongs—they look back on Germany now, and think of it sentimentally, as it's pictured in the stories and songs—a sort of Christmas-tree Germany. They don't know about the Germany that's grown up—the Germany of iron and coal kings, that combines all the cruelty of feudalism with modern efficiency and science—the Beast with the Brains of an Engineer!"

They walked on, Emil lost in thought. "You know," he broke out, suddenly, "this war has been a revelation to me—the most horrible you could imagine. It's as if you loved a woman, and saw her go insane before your eyes, or turn into some sort of degenerate. For I believed in the Christmas-tree Germany; I loved it, and I argued for it, I just couldn't bring myself to believe what I read in the papers. Now I look back, and it seems like a trap that the German war-lords had set for my mind—reaching way over here into America, and making me think what they wanted me to! Perhaps I've gone to the other extreme—I find I distrust everything that's German. Father accused me of it last night; he was singing an old German song that says that when you hear men singing you may lie down in peace, for bad men have no songs. And I reminded him that the nation which taught that idea had marched into Belgium singing!"

"Gee!" exclaimed Jimmie. He could imagine how old Hermann Forster had taken that remark!

The young carpet-designer smiled, rather sadly. "He says it's because I've put on khaki. But the truth is, I'd been full of these thoughts, and all at once they came to a head. I was drafted, and I had to make up my mind one way or the other. I decided I'd fight—and then, when I'd decided, I wanted to get into it right away." Emil paused, and looked at his friend and asked, "What about you?"

Jimmie, of course, was a draft-evader, one of the hated "slackers." Ordinarily, he would have told Emil, and the two of them would have grinned. But now Emil was in khaki, Emil was a patriot; perhaps it would not be wise to trust him entirely! "They haven't got me yet," said Jimmie; and then, "I ain't so sure as I used to be, but I ain't ready to be a soldier—I dunno's I could stand bein' bossed like that fellow does it."

Emil laughed. "Don't you suppose I want to learn?"

"But does he need to call you names?"

"That's part of the game—nobody minds that. He's putting the pep into us—and we want it in."

Jimmie found that such a new point of view that he didn't know what to reply.

"You see," the other went on, "if you really want to fight, you go in for it; it's quite remarkable how your feelings change. You imagine yourself in the presence of the enemy, and you know your success depends on discipline; if there's a leader, and especially if you feel that he knows his business, you're glad to have him to teach you, to make the whole machine do what you want it to. I know it sounds funny from me, but I've learned to love discipline." And Emil laughed, a nervous laugh. "This army means business, let me tell you; and it's got right down to it. They've been fighting three years and a half over in Europe, and they send their best men over to show us, and we dig in and learn—I tell you, we work as if the devil was after us!"

V

It sounded so strange to hear things like this from the lips of Emil Forster! Jimmie could hardly make them real to himself—the world was slipping from under his feet. The Socialist movement was being seduced—won over by the militarists! He didn't quite dare to say this; but he hinted, cautiously, "Ain't you afraid maybe we'll get used to fightin'—to discipline and all that? May be they'll trick us—the plutes."

"I know," said the other. "I've thought of that, and I've no doubt they'll try it—they want universal training for that very purpose. We have to fight them, that's all; we have to fight right now—to make clear why we're going into this war. We have to hold it before the people—that this is a war to bring democracy to the whole world. If we can fix that in people's minds, the imperialists won't have a look in."

"If you could do it, of course——" began Jimmie, hesitatingly.

"But we *are* doing it!" cried Emil. "We're doing it day by day. Look at this strike here in Leesville."

"What strike?"

"Didn't you know there'd been another walk-out in the Empire Shops?"

"No, I didn't."

"The men went out, and the government sent an arbitration

commission, and forced both sides to accept an award. They broke old Granitch down—made him recognise the union and grant the basic eight hour day."

"My God!" exclaimed Jimmie. It was the thing for which he had stood up in the Empire yards and been cursed by young Lacey Granitch; it was the thing for which he had been sent to jail and devoured by lice! And now the government had helped the men to win their demand! It was the first time—literally the first in Jimmie's whole life—that he had been led to think of the government as something else than an enemy and a slave-driver.

"How did Granitch take it?" he asked.

"Oh, awful! He threatened to quit, and let the government run his plant; but when he found the government was perfectly willing, he dropped his bluff. And look here—here's something else." Emil reached into an inside pocket of his overcoat and pulled out a newspaper clipping. "Ashton Chalmers went to a banquet at some bankers' convention the other day and made a speech to them. Read this."

Jimmie, walking along, read some words that Emil had underscored in pencil: "Whether we will or no, we have to recognise that the old order is dead. We face a new era, when labour is coming into its own. If we do not want to be left behind as derelicts, we shall have to get busy and do our part to bring in this new era, which otherwise will come with bloodshed and destruction."

"For the love of Mike!" said Jimmie.

"It just about knocked Leesville out," said Emil. "You ought to have seen the papers that reported the speech! It was as if God in his heaven had gone crazy, and the clergymen in the churches had to tell the news!"

To the little machinist there flashed a sudden idea. He caught his friend by the arm. "Emil!" he exclaimed. "Do you remember that time when Ashton Chalmers and old Granitch came to our meeting at the Opera-House?"

"Sure thing!" said Emil.

"Maybe that done it!"

"Nothing more likely."

"And it was me that sold him the tickets!"

Jimmie was thrilled to the bottoms of his shoes. Such is the reward that comes now and then to the soul of a propagandist; he struggles on amid ridicule and despair—and then suddenly, like a gleam of light, comes evidence that somewhere, somehow, he has reached another mind, he has made a real impression. Ashton Chalmers had listened to the Socialist orator, and he had gone away and read and investigated; he had realised the force of this great world movement for economic justice, he had broken the bonds and barriers of his class, and told the truth about what he saw coming. When Jimmie read the wonderful words which the bank president had spoken, he was nearer to an impulse to fight Germany than at any previous moment of his life!

CHAPTER XVII

JIMMIE HIGGINS WRESTLES WITH THE TEMPTER

I

OF course, not all the Socialists of Leesville had got the "military bug" like Emil Forster. Late in the afternoon, Jimmie ran into Comrade Schneider, on his way home from work at the brewery, and he was the same old Schneider—the same florid Teuton countenance, the same solid Teuton voice, the same indignant Teuton point of view. All Jimmie had to do was to mention the name of Emil, and Schneider was off. A hell of a Socialist he was! Couldn't even wait for the drill-sergeant to come after him, but had to run and hunt for him, had to go and put himself out in the public square, where the town-loafers could watch him playing the monkey!

No, said Schneider, with abundant profanity, he had not moved one inch from his position; they could send him to jail any time they got ready, they could stand him up before a firing-squad, but they'd never get any militarism into him. Pressed for an answer, the big brewer admitted that he had registered; but he wasn't going to be drafted, not on his life! Jimmie suggested that this might be because he had a wife and six children; but the other was too much absorbed in his tirade to notice Jimmie's grin. He blustered on, in a tone so loud that several times people on the street overheard, and gave him a black look. Jimmie, being less in the mood of martyrdom, parted from him and went to see the Meissners.

The little bottle-packer was living in the same place, having rented the upper part of his house to a Polish family to help meet his constantly rising expenses. He welcomed Jimmie with open arms—patted him on the back with delight, and opened a bottle of beer to treat him. He asked a hundred questions about Jimmie's adventures, and told in turn about events in Leesville. The local as a whole had stood firm against the war, and was still carrying on propaganda, in the face of ferocious opposition. The working classes were pumped so full of "patriotic dope," you could hardly get them to listen; as for the radicals, they were marked men—their mail was intercepted, their meetings attended by almost as many detectives as spectators. A number had been drafted—which Meissner considered deliberate conspiracy on the part of the draft-boards.

Who had been taken? Jimmie asked. The other answered: Comrade Claudel, the jeweller—he wanted to go, of course; and Comrade Koeln, the glass-blower—he was a German, but had been naturalised, so they had taken him, in spite of his protests; and Comrade Stankewitz——

"Stankewitz!" cried Jimmie, in dismay.

"Sure, he's gone."

"Was he willing?"

"They didn't ask if he was willing. They just told him to report."

Somehow that seemed to bring the war nearer to Jimmie's consciousness than anything that had happened so far. The little Roumanian Jew had given him the greater part of his education on this world-conflict; it was over the counter of the cigar-store that Jimmie had got the first geography lessons of his life. He had learned that Russia was the yellow country, and Germany the green, and Belgium the pale blue, and France the light pink; he had seen how the railroads from the green to the pink ran through the pale blue, and how the big fortresses in the pale blue all faced towards the green—something which Meissner and Schneider and the rest of the green people considered a mortal affront, a confession of guilt on the part of the pale blue people. Comrade Stakewitz's wizened up, eager little face rose before Jimmie; he heard the shrill voice, trying to compose the disputes in the local. "Comrades, all this vill not get us anyvere! There is but vun question ve have to answer, are ve internationalists, or are ve not!"

"My God!" cried Jimmie. "Ain't that awful?"

He had got to the point where he was willing to admit that perhaps the Kaiser had got to be licked, and maybe it was all right for a fellow that felt like Emil Forster to go and lick him. But to lay hold of a man who hated war with all his heart and soul, to drag him away from the little business he had painfully built up, and compel him to put on a uniform and obey other men's orders—well, when you saw a thing like that, you knew about the atrocities of war!

II

Comrade Meissner went on. Worse than that—they had taken Comrade Gerrity. And Jimmie stared. "But he's married!"

"I know," explained Meissner, "but that ain't what counts. What you got to have is a dependent wife. An' the Gerritys didn't know that—Comrade Evelyn held on to her job as stenographer, and somebody must have told on them, for the board jacked him up, and cancelled his exemption. Of course, it was only because he was organiser of the local; they want to put us out of business any way they can."

"What did Gerrity do?"

"He refused to serve, and they sent a squad of men after him and dragged him away. They took him to Camp Sheridan, and tried to put him in uniform, and he refused—he wouldn't work, he wouldn't have anything to do with war. So they tried him and sentenced him to twenty-five years in jail; they put him in solitary confinement, and he gets nothin' but bread and water—they keep him chained up by his wrists a part of the time——"

"Oh! *Oh!*" cried Jimmie.

"Comrade Evelyn's most crazy about it. She broke down and cried in the local, and she went around to the churches—they have women's sewing-circles, you know, and things for the Red Cross, and her and Comrade Mary Allen gets up and makes speeches an' drives the women crazy. They arrested 'em once, but they turned 'em loose—they didn't want it to get in the papers."

Comrade Meissner could not have foreseen how this particular news would affect Jimmie; Meissner knew nothing about the strange adventure which had befallen his friend, the amatory convulsion which had shaken his soul. Before Jimmie's mind now rose the lovely face with the pert little dimples and the halo of fluffy brown hair; the thought of Comrade Evelyn Baskerville in distress was simply not to be endured. "Where is she?" he cried. He had a vision of himself rushing forthwith to take up the agitation; to raid the church sewing-circles and brave the wrath of the she-patriots; to go to jail with Comrade Evelyn; or perhaps—who could say?—to put about her, gently and reverently, a pair of fraternal and comforting arms.

Jimmie had the temperament of the dreamer, the idealist, to whom it is enough to want a thing to see that thing forthwith coming into being. His imagination, stimulated by the image of the charming stenographer, rushed forth on the wildest of flights. He realised for the first time that he was a free man; while, as for Comrade Evelyn, suppose the worst were to happen, suppose Comrade Gerrity were to perish of the diet of bread and water, or to be dragged into the trenches and killed—then the sorrowing widow would be in need of some one to uphold her, to put fraternal and comforting arms about her——

"Where is she?" Jimmie asked again; and Comrade Meissner dissipated his dream by replying that she had gone off to work for an organisation in New York which was agitating for humane treatment for "conscientious objectors." Meissner hunted up the pamphlet published by this organisation, telling most hideous stories of the abusing of such victims of the military frenzy; they had been beaten, tortured and starved, subjected to ridicule and humiliation, in many cases dragged before courts-martial and sentenced to imprisonment for twenty or thirty years. Jimmie sat up a part of the night reading these stories—with the result that once more the feeble sprout of patriotism was squashed flat in his soul!

III

Jimmie went to the next meeting of the local. It was a slender affair now, for some of the members were in jail, and some in the training-camps, and some afraid to come for fear of their jobs, and some discouraged by incessant persecution. But the old war-horses were there—Comrade Schneider, and gentle old Hermann Forster, and Comrade Mabel Smith, with an account of her brother's mistreatment in the county jail, and Comrade Mary Allen, the Quaker lady. This last was still taking it as a personal affront that America should be going into the bloody mess, in spite of all her denunciations and protests; she was even paler and thinner than when Jimmie had seen her last—her hands trembled and her thin lips quivered as she spoke, you could see that she was burning up with excitement over the monstrous wickedness of the world's events. She read to the local a harrowing story of a boy who had registered as a conscientous objector in New York, and had been taken out to a training-camp and subjected to such indignities that he had shot himself. Comrade Mary had no children of her own, so she had adopted these conscientious objectors, and as she read of their experiences, her soul was convulsed with a mingling of grief and rage.

Jimmie went back to the Empire Shops and applied for a job. They needed thousands of men, so the "Herald" declared —but they did not need a single one like Jimmie! The man to whom he applied recognised him at once, and said, "Nothin' doin'." For the sake of being nasty, Jimmie went to the headquarters of the newly formed union, and asked them to force old Abel Granitch to give him work, according to the terms of the agreement with the government. But the union secretary, after thinking the matter over, decided that the provision against blacklisting applied only to men who had been out on the last strike, not to the strikers of a couple of years before. There was no use going out of one's way to look for trouble, said this secretary. Jimmie went away jeering at the union, and damning the war as heartily as ever.

He was in no hurry to get work, having still some money in his pocket, and being able to live cheaply with the Meissners. He went again to watch young Forster drilling, and went home with him and heard an argument with old Hermann. You could see how this family had been split wide open; the old man had ordered his traitorous son out several times, but the mother had flung herself into the breach, pleading that the boy was going away in a few days, and perhaps would never return. The evening that Jimmie was there, the paper printed a speech of the President, outlining his purposes in the war, the terms of justice for all peoples, a league of nations and universal disarmament. Emil read this triumphantly, finding in it a justification of his support of the war. Wasn't it a great part of what the Socialists wanted?

Hermann answered grudgingly that the words were all right, but how about the deeds? Also, how about the other Allies—did the President imagine he could boss them? No—to the imperialists of England and France and Italy those fine words were just bait for gudgeons; they would serve to keep the workers quiet till the war was won, and then the militarists would kick out the American President and pick the bones of the carcass of Germany. If they really meant to abide by the President's terms, why didn't they come out squarely and say so? Why didn't they repudiate the verdammte secret treaties? Why didn't England begin her career in democracy by setting free Ireland and India?

So it went; and Jimmie listened to both speakers, and agreed with both alternately, experiencing more and more that distressing condition of mental chaos, in which he found himself of two absolutely contradictory and diametrically opposite points of view!

IV

All winter long the papers had been full of talk about a mighty German offensive that was coming in the spring. The German people were being told all about it, and how it was to end the war with a glorious triumph. In America nobody was sure about the matter; the fact that the attack was boldly announced seemed good reason for looking elsewhere. Perhaps the enemy was preparing to overwhelm Italy, and wished to keep France and England from sending troops to the weakened Italian line!

But now suddenly, in the third week of March, the Germans made a mighty rush at the British line in front of Cambrai; army upon army they came, and overwhelmed the defenders, and poured through the breach. The British forces fell back—every hour it seemed that their retreat must be turned into a rout. Day by day, as the despatches came in, Jimmie watched the map in front of the "Herald" office, and saw a huge gap opening in the British line, a spear-head pointing straight into the heart of France. Three days, four days, five days, this ghastly splitting apart went on, and the whole world held its breath. Even Jimmie Higgins was shaken by the news—he had got enough into the war by this time to realise what a German triumph would mean. It took a strong pacifist stomach indeed to contemplate such an issue of events without flinching.

Comrade Mary Allen had such a stomach; to her religious

fervour it made no difference whatever which set of robbers ruled the world. Comrade Schneider had it also; he knew that Germany was the birth-place and cradle of Socialism, and believed that the best fate that could befall the world was for the Germans to conquer it, and let the German Socialists make it into a co-operative commonwealth bye and bye. Comrade Schneider was now openly gloating over this new proof of German supermanity, the invincibility of German discipline. But most of the other members of the local were awed—realising in spite of themselves the seriousness of the plight which confronted civilisation.

Jimmie would inspect the bulletin-board, and go over to watch the drilling, and then to Tom's "Buffeteria" with Emil Forster. He had always had an intense admiration for Emil, and now the young designer, distressed by the strife at home, was glad of some one to pour out his soul to. He would help Jimmie to realise the meaning of the British defeat, the enormous losses of guns and supplies, the burden it would put upon America. For America would have to make up these losses, America would have to drive the Germans out of every foot of this newly conquered territory.

Jimmie would listen, and study the matter out on the map; and so gradually he learned to be interested in a new science, that of military strategy. When once you have fallen under the spell of that game, your soul is lost. You think of men, no longer as human creatures, suffering, starving, bleeding, dying in agony; you think of them as chess-pawns; you dispose of them as a gambler of his chips, a merchant of his wares; you classify them into brigades and divisions and corps, moving them here and there, counting off your losses against the losses of the enemy, putting in your reserves at critical moments, paying this price for that objective, wiping out thousands and tens of thousands of men with a sweep of your hand, a mark of your pencil, a pressure on an electric button! Once you have learned to take that view of life, you are no longer a human heart, to be appealed to by pacifists and humanitarians; you are a machine, grinding out destruction, you are a ripe apple, ready to fall into the lap of the god of war, you are an autumn leaf, ready to be seized by the gales of patriotism, and blown to destruction and death.

CHAPTER XVIII

JIMMIE HIGGINS TAKES THE PLUNGE

I

JIMMIE went home one evening to the Meissners, and there got a piece of news that delighted him. Comrade Stankewitz had come back from Camp Sheridan! The man to whom he had sold his tobacco-store having failed to pay up, Stankewitz had got a three days' furlough to settle his business affairs. "Say, he looks fine!" exclaimed Meissner; and so after supper Jimmie hurried off to the little store on the corner.

Never had Jimmie been so startled by the change in a man; he would literally not have known his Roumanian Jewish friend. The wrinkles which had made him look old had filled out; his shoulders were straight—he seemed to have been lifted a couple of inches; he was brown, his cheeks full of colour—he was just a new man! Jimmie and he had been wont to skylark a bit in the old days, as young male creatures do, putting up their fists, giving one another a punch or two, making as if they were going to batter in one another's noses. They would grip hands and squeeze, to see which could hold out longest. But now, when they tried it, there was "nothing to it"—Jimmie got one squeeze, and hollered quits.

"Vat you tink?" cried Stankewitz. "I veigh tventy pounds more already—tventy pounds! They vork you like hell in that army, but they treat you good. You don't never have such good grub before, not anyvere you vork."

"You like it?" demanded Jimmie, in amazement.

"Sure I like it, you bet your money! I learn lots of things vat I didn't know before. I get myself straight on this var, don't you ferget it."

"You believe in the war?"

"Sure I believe in it, you bet your money!" Comrade Stankewitz, as he spoke, pounded with an excited fist on the counter.

"Ve got to vin this var, see? Ve got to beat them Yunkers! I vould have make up my mind to that, even if I don't go in the army—I vould have make it up ven I see vat they do vit Russia."

"But the revolution——"

"The revolution kin vait—maybe vun year, maybe two years already. It don't do us no good to have a revolution if the Yunkers walk over it! No, sir—I vant them Germans put out of Roumania und out of Russia und out of Poland—und I tell you, in this American army you got plenty Roumanian Socialists, plenty Polish Socialists, und the Kaiser vill be sorry ven he meets them in France, you bet your money!"

So Jimmie got another dose of patriotism, a heavy dose this time; for Stankewitz was all on fire with his new conviction, as full of the propaganda impulse as he had been when he called himself an "anti-nationalist." He could not permit you to differ with him—became irritated at the bare mention of those formula-ridden members of the local who were still against the war. They were fools—or else they were Germans; and Comrade Stankewitz was as ready to fight the Germans in Leesville as in France. He got so excited arguing that he almost forgot the cigars and the show-cases which he had to get rid of in two days. To Jimmie it was an amazing thing to see this transformation—not merely the new uniform and the new muscles of his Roumanian Jewish friend, but his sense of certainty about the war, his loyalty to the President for the bold deed he had done in pledging the good faith of America to securing the freedom and the peaceful future of the harassed and tormented subject-races of Eastern Europe.

II

Jimmie got a sheet of letter paper, and borrowed a scratchy pen and a little bottle of ink from Mrs. Meissner, and wrote a painfully misspelled letter to Comrade Evelyn Gerrity, née Baskerville, to assure her of his sympathy and undying friendship. He did not tell her that he was beginning to wabble on the war; in fact, when he thought of Jack Gerrity, chained up to the bars of a cell-window, he un-wabbled—he wanted the social revolution right away. But then as he went to drop the letter into the post-office, so that it might go more quickly, he bought a paper and read the story of what was happening in France. And again the war-fervour tempted him.

By desperate, frenzied fighting the British had succeeded in holding up for a few days the colossal German drive. But help was needed—instant help, if civilisation was to be saved. The cry came across the seas—America must send assistance—guns, shells, food, and above all else men. Jimmie's blood was stirred; he had an impulse to answer the call, to rush to the rescue of those desperate men, crouching in shell-holes and fighting day and night for a week without rest. If only Jimmie could have gone right to them! If only it had not been necessary for him to go to a training-camp and submit himself to a military martinet! If only it had not been for war-profiteers, and crooked politicians, and lying, predatory newspapers, and all the other enemies of democracy at home!

Jimmie dropped his letter in the slot, and turned to leave the post-office, when his eye was caught by a sign on the wall—a large sign, in bold, black letters: "YOUR COUNTRY NEEDS YOU!" Jimmie thought it was more "Liberty Bond" business; they had been after him several times, trying to separate him from his earnings, but needless to say they hadn't succeeded. However, he stopped out of curiosity, and read that men were needed to go to France—skilled men of all sorts. There was a long list of the trades, everything you could think of—carpenters, plumbers, electricians, lumbermen, stevedores, railwaymen, laundrymen, cooks, warehousemen—so on for several columns. Jimmie came to "machinists," and gave a guilty start; then he came to "motor-cycle drivers" and "motor-cycle repairers" —and suddenly he clenched his hands. A wild idea flashed over him, causing such excitement that he could hardly read on. Why should he not go to France—he, Jimmie Higgins! He was a man without a tie in the world—as free as the winds that blew across the ocean! And he was looking for a job—why not take one of these?

It was a way he might share all the adventures, see the marvellous sights of which he had been reading and hearing, and without the long delay in a training-camp, without waiting to be bossed about by a military martinet! Jimmie looked to see what pay was offered; fifty-one dollars a month and an "allowance" for board and expenses. At the bottom of the sign he read the words: "Why not work for your Uncle Sam?" Jimmie as it happened was in a fairly friendly mood towards his Uncle Sam at that moment; so he thought, why not give him a chance as a boss? After all, wasn't that what every Socialist was aiming at—to be an employé of the community, a servant of the public, rather than of some private profiteer?

III

Jimmie went to the window to inquire, and the clerk told him that the "war-labour recruiting office" was at the corner of Main and Jefferson. He came to the corner designated, and there in a vacant store was a big recruiting sign, "War Labour Wanted," and a soldier in khaki walking up and down. A week ago Jimmie could not have been bribed to enter a place presided over by a soldier; but he had learned from Emil and Stankewitz that a soldier might be a human being, so he went up and said, "Hello."

"Hello, yourself," said the soldier, looking him over with an appraising eye.

"If I was to hire here, when would I start for France?"

"To-night," said the soldier.

"You kiddin' me?"

"They ain't payin' me to kid people," said the other; and then, "What's your hurry?"

"Well, I don't want to be stalled in a trainin' camp."

"You won't be stalled if you know your business. What are you?"

"I'm a machinist; I've repaired bicycles, an' I know a bit about motor-cycles."

"Walk in," said the soldier, and led the way, and presented Jimmie to a sergeant at the desk. "Here's a machinist," he said, "and he's in a hurry to get to work. Runnin' away from his wife, may be."

"There's a bunch of men starting for the training-camp to-night," said the sergeant.

"Trainin'-camp?" echoed Jimmie. "I want to go to France."

The other smiled. "You wouldn't expect us to send you till we'd tried you out, would you?"

"No, I suppose not," replied Jimmie, dubiously. He was on his guard against tricks. Suppose they were to enlist him as a worker, and then make him fight!

The other went on. "If you're competent, you'll get to France all right. We need men over there in a hurry, and we won't waste your time."

"Well now," said Jimmie, "I dunno's you'll want me at all when you hear about me. I'm a Socialist."

"Thought you was a machinist," countered the sergeant.

"I'm a Socialist, too. I was in the strike at the Empire a coupla years ago, and they blacklisted me. I can't get no work in the big places here."

"Well," said the sergeant, "it's a good town for you to quit, I should say."

"You want a man like that?" persisted Jimmie.

"What we want is men that know machinery, and'll dig in and work like hell to beat the Kaiser. If you're that sort, we don't ask your religion. We've got a bunch that start to-night."

"Holy smoke!" said Jimmie. He had thought he would have time to ask questions and to think matters over, time to see his friends and say good-bye. But the sergeant was so efficient and business-like; he took it so completely for granted that any man who was worth his salt must be anxious to help wallop the Hun! Jimmie, who had come in full of hurry, was now ashamed to back water, to hem and haw, to say, "I dunno; I ain't so sure." And so the trap snapped on him—the monster of Militarism grabbed him!

IV

"Sit down," said the sergeant, and the anxious little Socialist took the chair beside the desk.

"What's your name?"

"James Higgins."

"Your address?"

"I'm just stayin' with a friend."

"The friend's address?" and so on: where had Jimmie worked last, what work had he done, what references had he to offer. Jimmie could not help grinning as he realised how his record must sound to a military martinet. He had been fired and blacklisted at the motor-truck factory in Ironton, his last job; he had been fired and blacklisted at the Empire Shops; he had been arrested and sent to jail for soap-boxing on the streets of Leesville; he had been arrested in the bomb-conspiracy of Kumme and Heinrich von Holst. The sergeant entered each of these items without comment, but when he came to the last, he stared up at the applicant.

"I didn't have nothin' to do with it," declared Jimmie.

"You got to prove that to me," said the sergeant.

"I proved it once," replied Jimmie.

"Who to?"

"Mr. Harrod, the agent of the Department of Justice here."

The other took up the telephone and called the post office building. Jimmie listened to one half of the conversation—would Mr. Harrod look up the record of James Higgins, who was applying for enlistment in the Mechanical Department of the Motor Corps? There was some delay—Mr. Harrod was talking—while Jimmie sat, decidedly nervous; but it was all right apparently—the sergeant hung up the receiver, and remarked reassuringly, "He says you're just a dub. He told me to congratulate you on having got some sense."

Jimmie made the most of this more than dubious statement, and proceeded to answer questions as to his competence. Was there anybody at the Empire who could certify as to this? The sergeant was about to call up the Empire Shops, but reconsidered; if Jimmie had actually worked in a machine-shop and in a bicycle-shop, they would surely be able to find something for him in the army. In an hour of such desperate need they took most every one. "How tall are you?" demanded the sergeant, and added, "Weight don't matter so much, because we'll feed you."

The office of the medical examiner was upstairs in the same building, and Jimmie was escorted upstairs, and invited to remove his coat and shirt, and have his chest measured, and his heart and lungs listened to, and his teeth counted, and his nose peered into, and a score of such like stunts. He had things wrong with him, of course, but not too many for army purposes, it appeared. The doctor jotted down the figures on a sheet and signed it, after which Jimmie and the soldier went back to the recruiting-office.

And now suddenly the little Socialist found himself with an enlistment-paper before him, and a wet pen in his hand. He had never once been asked: "Is your mind made up? Do you really mean to take this irrevocable step?" No, the sergeant had taken it for granted that Jimmie meant business. He had done all this inquiring and writing down of information, this weighing and measuring and what not, and now he sat with a stern, compelling eye fixed on his victim, as much as to say: "Do you mean to tell me that I've done all that for nothing?" If Jimmie had actually refused to sign his name, what a blast of scorn would have withered him!

So Jimmie did not even stop to read all the paper; he signed. "And now," said the sergeant, "the train leaves at nine-seventeen this evening. I'll be there to give you your ticket. Don't fail to be on hand. You understand you're under military discipline now." There was a new tone in these last words, and Jimmie quaked inwardly, and went out with a sort of hollow feeling in the pit of his stomach.

V

He rushed away to tell Comrade Stankewitz, who hugged him with delight, and shouted that they would meet in France! Then he went to tell Emil Forster, who was equally glad. He found himself with an impulse to hunt up Comrade Schneider and tell him. Jimmie discovered in himself a sudden and curious antagonism to Schneider; he wanted to have matters out with him, to say to him: "Wake up, you mutt—forget that fool dream of yours that the Kaiser's goin' to win the war!"

There were others Jimmie thought of, upon whom he would not call. Comrade Mary Allen, for example—he would let her get the news after he was out of the reach of her sharp tongue! Also he thought of Comrade Evelyn; he might never see her again; if he did see her, she might refuse to speak to him! But Jimmie repressed the pang of dismay which this realisation brought him. He was going to war, and the longings and delights of love must be put to one side!

He went to the Meissners for supper, and broke the news to them. He had expected protests and arguments, and was surprised by the lack of them. Had the little bottler-packer been impressed by the experiences of Comrade Stankewitz? Or could it be that he was afraid to voice his full mind to Jimmie—just as Jimmie had been afraid in the case of Emil Forster?

Jimmie had some commissions to entrust to the Meissners;

he would leave with them the diary of "Wild Bill," which he had hung on to, but which seemed hardly the sort of literature to take on a transport.

"Sure," assented Meissner. "Besides, the subs might get it."

And Jimmie gave a sudden start. By heck! It was the first time the idea had occurred to him. He would have to pass through the barred zone! He might be in some fighting after all! He might never get to France! "Say!" he exclaimed. "That ocean must be cold this time of year!"

For a moment he wavered. Surely it would have been more sensible to wait till later in the season, when the consequences of a plunge overboard would be less distressing! But Jimmie remembered the armies, locked in their grip of death; never would despatch-riders need their motor-cycles more urgently than now! Also Jimmie remembered the sergeant at the recruiting-office. "You understand, you're under military discipline now!" He set his jaw in a grim resolve. The "subs" be damned, he would go and do his part! Already he felt the thrill of his responsibility in this mighty hour of history; he was a military man, with a stern duty to do, with the destinies of nations depending upon his behaviour!

CHAPTER XIX

JIMMIE HIGGINS PUTS ON KHAKI

I

THERE were seven fellows who boarded the train that evening, under the temporary charge of a blacksmith from the nearby country. At seven o'clock next morning they presented their papers at the entrance-gate of the training-camp, and under the escort of a soldier were marched down the main street, hanging on to their bundles and suit-cases, and staring about them at the sights.

It was a city, inhabited by some forty thousand men, on a site which a year ago had been waste scrub-land. Long rows of wooden buildings stretched in every direction—barracks, dining-rooms, study-rooms, offices, store-houses—with great stretches of exercise and training grounds between. Just to see this city, with its swarming population of young men, all in uniform, erect, eager, well set-up and vivid with health, every man of them busy, and every man seemingly absorbed in his job—that alone was a worth-while experience. It was a new kind of city—a city without a loafer, without a drunkard, without a parasite. The seven workingmen from Leesville felt suddenly slouchy and disgraced, with their ill-fitting civilian clothes and their miscellaneous bundles and suit-cases.

The first thing they did with the new arrivals was to make them clean, to fumigate and vaccinate them. In a Socialist local one meets all sorts of eccentrics, the lunatic-fringe of the movement, and so it happened that Jimmie had listened to a tirade against the diabolical practice of inoculation, which caused more deadly diseases than it was supposed to prevent. But the medical officers of this camp did not stop to ask Jimmie's conclusions on that vital subject; they just told him to roll up the sleeve of his left arm, and proceeded to wipe his skin clean and scratch it with a needle.

And then came the tailor, to do him up in khaki. This also was something the little machinist had not bargained for; he had taken it as a matter of course that he would be allowed to work for Uncle Sam in any old clothes, just as he had done for Abel Granitch. But no—he must have an outfit, complete even to a tooth-brush, which they would show him how to use. Having been done up neat and tight in khaki, with a motor-wheel on his sleeve to show his branch of the service, he stood and looked at himself in the glass, experiencing a demoralising and unworthy excitement. He was every bit as handsome as Comrade Stankewitz! When he walked down the street, would the girls giggle, and turn to look at him, as they did at the sedate and proper Comrade Emil? So the meshes of Militarism were being woven about the soul of Jimmie Higgins.

II

Jimmie was in quarantine, not allowed to go out of camp on account of his typhoid and other vaccinations. There was enough about the place to have interested him; but, alas, he became suddenly very sick, and was terrified to realise that the opponent of inoculation must have been right. His health had been undermined forever, he would suffer from a dozen obscure diseases! He went to the hospital, miserable in body and still more miserable in mind; but in a couple of days he began to feel better, and listened to the nurses, who told him cheerfully that everybody felt that way for a bit. Then he got up, and had several free days in which to complete his recovery—days which he spent wandering about the camp, watching the fascinating sights.

It was like a circus with hundreds of rings. The drilling and marching he had seen in the Leesville square were here going on wholesale. Hundreds of groups were being put through squad-drill and the manual, while other groups were having special kinds of exercises—climbing up walls, digging trenches, making roads, shooting at targets. It rained every other day, and the ground was a morass, but no one paid the least attention to that; the men came in plastered with mud, and steaming like lard-vats. They seemed to enjoy it; nothing ever interfered with their bantering and jokes.

Jimmie watched them with alternating moods of curiosity

and horror; for the things that were done here brought the war, with its infinite and multiform wickedness, before his very eyes. Here was a group of men being taught to advance under fire; crawling on their bellies on the ground, jumping from one hummock to another, flinging themselves down and pretending to fire. A man in front, supposed to have a machine-gun, was shouting when he had "got" them. Now they unslung their little trenching-tools, and began to burrow themselves like woodchucks into the ground. "Dig, you sons o' guns, dig!" the officer would shout. "Keep your head down, Smith! Make the dirt fly! Put the jazz into it! That's the stuff!"

Jimmie had never watched football practice, so he had no conception of the efforts to which men could be goaded by "coaching." It was abhorrent—yet also it was fascinating, the spell of it got hold of him. He saw what these men were doing; they were learning to act in masses, to act with paralysing and terrific force. Whatever it was they did, they did with the smash of a battering-ram. You saw the fire in their eyes, the grim, set look on their faces; you knew that they were not going to war with any hesitations or divided minds.

You would move over a rise in the ground, and come upon a bunch of them at bayonet-practice. You didn't require imagination to get the hang of this; they had dummies made of leather, and they rushed at these figures, hacking, stabbing—and here was the most amazing part of it, shouting with rage. Actually, the officers taught them to yell, to snarl, to work up their feelings to a fury! It was blood-curdling—Jimmie turned away from it sick. It was just what he had been arguing for three years and a half—you had to make yourself into a wild beast in order to go to war!

Also Jimmie watched the target-ranges, from which came all day a rattle of shots, like the whir of many typewriters. Companies of men came marching, and spread themselves out along the firing-steps, and under the direction of instructors proceeded to contribute their quota to the noise. Over by the targets were others who kept score and telephoned the results; so all day long, winter or summer, rain or shine, men were learning to kill their fellows, mechanically, as if it were a matter of factory routine. At other ranges were moving targets, where sharp-shooters were acquiring skill; you noticed that their targets were never birds and deer, as at the shooting-galleries which Jimmie had seen at the beaches and at Socialist picnics. No, they were the heads or bodies of men, and each body painted a greenish grey, matching the uniforms of the enemy.

III

So day by day Jimmie lived with the idea of killing, confronting the grim and ferocious face of war. He had thought that repairing motor-cycles would be pretty much the same anywhere you did it; but he found that it was one thing to repair motor-cycles to be ridden by errand-boys and workingmen out for a holiday with their sweethearts, and another and entirely different thing to repair them for fighting-men and despatch-couriers. Jimmie was driven more insistently than ever to make up his mind about this war. It was every day less easy for him to hold two contradictory sets of opinions.

All the men he now met were of one opinion, and by no possibility to be persuaded to consider any other. Jimmie found that he could get them to agree that after this war for democracy there would be vast changes in this world, the people would nevermore let themselves be hoodwinked and exploited as they had; he found that he could interest them in the idea of having the government run the great industries, producing food and clothing for the people as it was now producing them for the troops. But when he tried to give this programme the name of Socialism, then the trouble began. Weren't Socialists the loons who wanted to have America "lay down" like Russia? The premise from which all discussion started with these men was that America was going to win the war; if you tried to hint that this matter could so much as be hesitated over, you met, first sharp mockery, and then angry looks, and advice to go and take a pill and get the Hun poison out of your system.

Nor was there any use trying to talk about the dangers of militarism. These men knew all about the dangers of militarism—for the Kaiser. The man who is at the butt-end of a gun, and knows how to aim it so as to pick off a cat at six hundred yards—that man will let the cat do the worrying. So, at any rate, the matter seemed to these husky young recruits, who were learning to march in the mud and sleep in the rain and chew up carpet-tacks and grind Huns into leber-wurst. They were putting through the job with a fierce and terrifying gaiety;

they exulted in their toughness, they called themselves "grizzlies" and "mountain cats" and what not; they sang wild songs about their irritability, their motto was "Treat 'em rough!" It was a scary atmosphere for a dreamer and utopian; Jimmie Higgins shrank into himself, afraid even to reach about for some fellow-Socialist with whom he might exchange opinions about the events of the outside world.

IV

In the evening there were picture-shows, concerts, lectures—nearly all dealing with the war, of course. They were held in big halls built by the Y. M. C. A., an organisation for which Jimmie had a hearty contempt. He regarded it as a device of the exploiting classes to teach submission to their white-collar slaves. But nobody could live in a training-camp without being aware of the "Y." Jimmie was invited to a lecture, and out of boredom he went.

It was Sergeant Ebenezer Collins, imported from Flanders to tell the "doughboys" about the wiles of the Hun. Sergeant Collins spoke a weird language which Jimmie had never heard before, and not all of which he could understand; it served, however, to convince him that the sergeant was genuine—for nobody could possibly have faked such a form of utterance! "When yer gow inter Wipers naow," said the orator, "yer see owld, grye-headed lydies an' bybies like little wite gowsts, an' yer sye ter them, 'Gow a-wye, the 'Un may be 'ere ter-dye,' but they wown't gow, they got now 'omes ter gow ter!"

But in spite of the difficulties of a foreign language, you realised that this cockney sergeant was a man. For one thing he had a sense of humour; he had kept it in the midst of terror and death—kept it standing all night in trenches full of icy cold water, with icy cold water pouring down his collar. Also the sergeant had a sense of honour—there were things he could not do to a 'Un, even though the 'Un might do them to him. Jimmie had listened to excited debates in Local Leesville, as to whether the Allies were really any better than the Germans; whether, for example, the Allies would have sunk passenger-liners with women and babies on board, if it had been necessary in order to win the war. Sergeant Collins did not debate this question, he just revealed himself as a fighting man. "It's because we plye gymes, an' they down't," he remarked. "If yer plye gymes, yer now 'ow to plye fair."

For three years and eight months Jimmie had been hearing stories about atrocities, and for three years and eight months he had been refusing to believe them. But now the cockney sergeant told about a pal who had been wounded in a night attack by the 'Uns, and the sergeant had tried to carry him back and had had to leave him; towards dawn they made a counter-attack, and retook the village, and there they found the sergeant's pal, still alive, in spite of the fact that he was spiked to a barn-door with bayonets through his hands and feet. When that story was told, you heard a low murmur run through the room, and saw a couple of thousand young men clenching their hands and setting their jaws, getting ready for their big job in France.

Just now, said the sergeant, the Germans were making the most desperate attack of the war. The British were at bay, with their backs against the wall. It was upon the men in the training-camps of America that the decision rested; there was no one but them to save the day, to save the rest of the world from falling under the hoofs of the Hun monster. Would they do their part? Jimmie Higgins heard the answer from those two thousand young throats, and the pacifist in him shrunk deeper out of sight.

But the pacifist was never entirely silent. War was wrong! War was wrong! It was a wicked and brutal way for human beings to settle their disagreements. If human beings were not yet intelligent enough to listen to reason—well, even so, that didn't make war right! A man had to have principles, and to stand by them—how else could he make the world come his way? Yes, war was wrong! But, meantime, war was here; and calling it wrong did not put a stop to it! What the devil was a fellow to do?

V

As soon as Jimmie was able to work, they took him to the part of the camp where a motor-cycle division was training. Here was a big repair shop, with plenty of damaged machines upon which he might display his skill. He did not know the particular engine they used here, but he soon learned the secrets of it, and satisfied the officers in charge that he knew how to take one apart and put it together again, to replace and mend tires, to clean ball-bearings and true crooked rims. "You're all right," they said. "And you're needed like the devil over there. You won't have to wait long."

There was a platform where the trains came into the camp, and every few hours now there came a long train to be loaded with men. Jimmie got his notice, and packed his kit and answered roll-call and took his place; at sun-down of the next day he was detrained at a "mobilisation-camp"—another huge city, described in the cautious military fashion as "Somewhere in New Jersey," though everybody within a hundred miles knew its exact location. Here was a port, created for the purposes of war, with docks and wharves where the fleets of transports were loaded with supplies and troops. The vessels sailed in fleets, carrying thirty or forty thousand men at once. From the port of New York alone there was going out a fleet like this every week—the answer of America to the new drive of the Hun.

One met here, not merely the fighting-men, but the forces of all the complicated service behind the lines: gangs of lumbermen from the far Northwest, who were to fell the forests of France and make them into railroad-ties and timbers for trenches; railway-men, miners, and construction-gangs, engineers and signalmen, bridge-builders and road-makers, telephone-linemen and operators, the drivers of forty thousand motor-cars and of five thousand locomotives; bakers and cooks, menders of shoes and of clothing, farmers to till the soil of France, and doctors and nurses to tend its sick and wounded. There was nothing which the skill and knowledge of a nation of a hundred million people had to offer that was not gathered into this vast encampment. All the youngest and keenest were here, eager to do their part, laughing at danger, tingling with excitement, on tiptoe with curiosity and delight. Jimmie Higgins, watching them, found his doubts melting like an April snow-storm. How could any man see this activity and not be caught up in it? How could he be with these laughing boys and not share their mood?

Jimmie himself had not had a merry childhood, he did not know the youth of his own country—the breezy, slangy, rather shocking, utterly irrepressible youth of this democratic world. If there was anything they did not know—well, they did not know it; if there was anything they could not do—their motto was: "Show me!" Jimmie, not having been to school, found himself having a hard time with their weird slang. When one of these fellows hailed you, "Hey, pimp!" it did not necessarily mean that he did not like you; when he greeted you, "Hey, sweetness!" it did not mean that he felt for you any overpowering affection. If he referred to his officer as "hard-boiled," he did not have in mind that this officer had been exposed to the action of water at 212 degrees Fahrenheit; he merely meant that the officer was a snob. When he remarked, "Good-night!" in broad daylight, he meant you to understand that he disagreed with you.

He disagreed frequently and explosively with Jimmie Higgins, trying to point out a difference between the German rulers and the German people! Such subtleties had no interest for these all-knowing boys. When Jimmie persisted, they called him a "nut," a "poor cheese"; they told him that he was "cuckoo," that his "trolley was twisted"; they made whirling motions with their hands to indicate that he had "wheels in his head," they made flapping motions over him to signify that there were "bats in his belfry." So Jimmie subsided, and let them talk their own talk—imploring one another to "have a heart," or to "get wise," or to "make it snappy," or to "cut out the rough stuff." And he would sit and listen while they sang with zest a song telling about what they were going to do when they got to France:

Bring the good old bugle, boys, we'll sing another song,
Sing it with a spirit that will move the world along,
Sing it as we love to sing it, just two million strong—
While we are canning the Kaiser.

CHORUS:

Oh, Bill! Oh, Bill! We're on the job to-day!
Oh, Bill! Oh, Bill! We'll seal you so you'll stay!
We'll put you up in ginger in the good old Yankee way—
While we are canning the Kaiser.

Hear the song we're singing on the shining roads of France;
Hear the Tommies cheering, and see the Poilus prance;
Africanders and Kanucks and Scots without their pants—
While we are canning the Kaiser. (Chorus)

Bring the guns from Bethlehem, by way of old New York;
Bring the beans from Boston, and don't leave out the pork;
Bring a load of soda-pop, and pull the grape-juice cork—
While we are canning the Kaiser. (Chorus)

Come you men from Dixieland, you lumberjacks of Maine;
Come you Texas cowboys, and you farmers of the plain;
Florida to Oregon, we boast the Yankee strain—
While we are canning the Kaiser. (Chorus)

Now we've started on the job, we mean to put it through;
Ship the kings and kaisers all, and make the world anew;
Clear the way for common folk, for men like me and you—
While we are canning the kaiser.

CHORUS:

Oh, Bill! Oh, Bill! We're on the job to-day!
Oh, Bill! Oh, Bill! We'll seal you so you'll stay!
We'll put you up in ginger in the good old Yankee way—
While we are canning the Kaiser.

CHAPTER XX

JIMMIE HIGGINS TAKES A SWIM

I

YOU did not stop very long in the mobilisation-camp, for the arrival of your train was timed with the arrival of the ship on which you were to sail. You had a meal, sometimes you slept a night, then you marched to the docks. Nor was there much of the traditional "sweet sorrow" about the departure of these great fleets; the weeping mothers and sisters had not been notified to be present, and the ladies of the canteen-service had given coffee and sandwiches, cigarettes and chocolate, to so many tens of thousands that they had forgotten about tears. It was like the emigration of a nation; the part of America that was now on the other side was so large that nobody would need to feel homesick.

Jimmie's embarking was done at night; on the long, covered piers lighted by arc-lights, the soldiers set down their kits and stood about, munching food, singing songs, and keeping one another's wits sharpened for battle. They filtered on board, and then without a light or a sound the vessel stole down the long stretches of the harbour, and out to sea. One never knew at what hour the enemy submarines might attempt a raid on the American side, so the entrance to the harbour was mined and blockaded, a narrow passage being opened when the ships passed through.

When morning came the convoy was out at sea, amid glorious green rollers, and Jimmie Higgins was lying in his narrow berth, cursing the fates that had lured him, the monster of Militarism into whose clutches he had been snared. The army medical service had a serum to prevent small-pox and another to prevent typhoid, but they had nothing for sea-sickness as yet; so for the first four days of the trip Jimmie wished that a submarine would come and end his misery once for all.

At last, however, he came on deck, an utterly humbled Socialist agitator, asking only a corner to lie in the sunshine—preferably where he could not see the Atlantic surges, the very thought of which turned him inside out. But gradually he found his feet again, and ate with permanence, and looked out over the water and saw the other vessels of the convoy, weirdly painted with many-coloured splotches, steaming in the shape of a gigantic V, with two cruisers in front, and another on each side, and another bringing up the rear. Day and night the look-outs kept watch, and the wig-wag men and the heliograph men were busy, and the wireless buzzed its warnings of the movements of the underwater foe. The U-boats had not yet got a transport, but they had made several tries, and every one knew that they would continue trying. Twice a day the clanging of bells sounded from one end of the vessel to the other, and the crews rushed to the boat-drill; each passenger had his number, and unless he was ill in his berth he had to take his specified place, with his life-preserver strapped about his waist.

The passengers played cards, and read and sang and skylarked about the decks. Up on the top deck, to which Jimmie was not invited, were officers, also a number of women and girls belonging to the hospital and ambulance units. "Janes" was the term by which the soldier-boys described these latter; you could see they were a good sort of "Janes," serious and keen for their job, looking businesslike and impressive in their uniforms with many pockets. Among them were suffragists, answering the taunt of the other sex, showing that in war as well as in peace the world needed them; it had to find a place for them on board the most badly crowded transport.

Never having been on an ocean-liner before, Jimmie did not know that it was crowded; it did not trouble him that there was hardly room for a walk on the decks. He watched the sea and the great white gulls and the piebald ships; he watched the crew at work, and got acquainted with his fellow-passengers. Before long he found a driver of an ambulance who was a Socialist; also an I. W. W. from the Oregon lumber-camps. Even the "wobblies," it appeared, had come to hate the Kaiser; a bunch of them were in France, and more would have come, if the government had not kept them cross by putting their leaders into jail. An army-officer with some sense had gone into the spruce-country of the far North-west, and had appealed to the patriotism of the men, giving them decent hours and wages, and recognizing their unions; as a result, even the dreaded I. W. W. organization had turned tame, and all the lumber-jacks had pitched in to help in "canning the Kaiser"!

II

The fleet was nearing the submarine-zone and it was time for the convoying destroyers to arrive. Everybody was peering out ahead, and at last a cry ran along the decks: "There they are!" Jimmie made out a speck of smoke upon the horizon, and saw it turn into a group of swiftly flying vessels. He marvelled at the skill whereby they had been able to find the transports on this vast and trackless sea; he marvelled at the slender vessels with their four low, rakish stacks. These sea-terriers were thin skins of steel, covering engines of enormous power; they tore through the water, literally with the speed of an express-train, leaving a boiling white wake behind. Seeing them rock and swing from side to side in the waves, hurled this way and that, you marvelled that human beings could live in them and not be jerked to pieces. Jimmie never tired of observing them, nor did they tire of racing in and out between the vessels of the convoy, weaving patterns of foam, the men on their decks watching, watching for the secret foe.

Every one on board the transports of course was on the alert. Jimmie in his secret heart was scared stiff, but he did not reveal it to these mocking soldier-boys, who made merry over German U-boats as they did over sauerkraut and pretzels and limburger and "wienies," otherwise known as "hot dogs." Actually, Jimmie found, they were hoping to encounter a submarine; not to be hit, of course, but to have the torpedo pass within a foot or two, so that they might have something thrilling to write to the folks at home!

There came storms, and blinding sheets of rain across the water, and mists that hid everything from view; but still the little sea-terriers dashed here and there, winding their foam wakes about the fleet, by night as well as by day. How they managed to avoid collisions in the dark was a mystery beyond imagining; Jimmie lay awake, picturing one of them plunging like a sharp spear into the rows of bunks in the steerage where he had been stowed. But when morning dawned, his berth was unspeared, and the watch-dogs of the sea were still weaving their patterns.

It was a day of high wind, with clouds and fitful bursts of sunshine in which the waves shone white and sparkling. Jimmie was standing by the rail with his "wobbly" friend, watching the white-caps, when his companion called his attention to a sparkle that seemed to persist, hitting one in the eye. They pointed it out to others, and as the orders were strict to report anything out of the way, some one shouted to the nearest look-out. A cry went over the ship, and there was hasty wigwagging of the signalmen, and three of the destroyers leaped away like hounds on the chase.

There were some on board who had glasses, and they cried out that it was a black object, and finally reported it a raft with people on it. Later, when Jimmie reached port, he heard an explanation of the sparkle which had caught his eye—a woman on the raft had a little pocket-mirror, and had used this to flash the sun's rays upon the vessel, until at last she had attracted attention.

Those who had glasses were mostly on the upper deck, so Jimmie did not see anything of the rescue; the transports of course did not swerve or delay, for their orders forbade all altruisms. Even the little destroyers would not approach the raft until they had scoured the sea for miles about, and then they did not stop entirely, but slid by and tossed ropes to the people on the raft, dragging them aboard one by one. A seaman standing near Jimmie explained this procedure; it appeared that the submarines were accustomed to lurk near rafts and life-boats, preying upon those vessels which came to their rescue. Distressed castaways were bait—"live bait," explained the seaman; the U-boats would lurk about for days, sometimes for a week, watching the people in the life-boats struggle against the waves, watching them die of exposure and starvation and thirst, watching them signal frantically, waving rags tied onto oars, shouting and praying for help. One by one the castaways would perish, and when the last of them was gone, the U-boat would steal away. "Dead bait's no good," explained the seaman.

III

This mariner, Toms by name, came from Cornwall; for the transport was British, and so also the convoying war-ships—Jimmie's fate had been entrusted to "perfidious Albion"! Seven times this Toms had been torpedoed and seven times rescued, and he had most amazing tales to tell to landlubbers, and a new light to throw on a subject which our Socialist landlubber had been debating for several years—the torpedoing of passenger-vessels with women and children on board. Somehow Jimmie found it a different proposition when he heard of particular women and children, how they looked and what they said, and what happened when they took to open boats in midwinter, and the boats filled up with water, and the children turned blue and then white, and were rescued with noses and ears and hands and feet frozen off.

Jimmie was a workingman, and understood the language of workingmen, their standards and ways of looking at life. And here was a workingman; not a conscious Socialist, to be sure, but a union man, sharing the Socialist distrust of capitalists and rulers. What this weather-bitten toiler of the sea told to Jimmie, Jimmie was prepared to understand and believe; so he learned, what he had refused to learn from prostitute newspapers, that there was a code of sea-manners and sea-morals, a law of marine decency, which for centuries had been unbroken save by pirates and savages. The men who went down to the sea in ships were a class of their own, with instincts born of the peculiar cruelties of the element they defied—instincts which broke across all barriers of nations and races, and even across the hatreds of war.

But now these sea-laws had been defied, and the Hun who had defied them had placed himself outside the pale of the human race. In the souls of seamen there had been generated against him a hatred of peculiar and unique ferocity; they hunted him as men hunt vipers and rattle-snakes. The union to which this Toms belonged had pledged itself, not merely for the war, but for years afterwards, that its members would not sail in German ships, nor in any ship in which a German sailed, nor in any ship which sailed to a German port, nor which carried German goods. It had refused to carry Socialist delegates desiring to attend international conferences with German Socialists; it had refused to carry for any purpose labour leaders whom it considered too mercifully disposed towards Germany.

When Jimmie learned this, you can imagine the arguments, continuing far into the night! Quite a crowd gathered about, and they gave it to the little Socialist hot and heavy. The upshot of it was that somebody reported him, and the officer in command of his "motor-unit" read him a stern lecture. He was not here to settle peace-terms, but to do his work and hold his tongue. Jimmie, awed by the fangs and claws of the monster of Militarism, answered, "Yes, sir," and went away and sulked by himself the whole day, wishing that the submarines might get this transport, with everybody on board except two Socialists and one "wobbly."

IV

It was the morning of the day they were due in port. Everybody wore life-preservers, and stood at his station; when suddenly came a yell, and a chorus of shouts from the side of the ship, and Jimmie rushed to the rail, and saw a white wake coming like a swift fish directly at the vessel. "Torpedo!" was the cry, and men stood rooted to the spot. Far back, where the white streak started, you could see a periscope, moving slowly; there was a volley of cracking sounds, and the water all about it leaped high, and the little sea-terriers rushed towards it, firing, and getting ready their deadly depth-bombs. But of all that Jimmie got only a glimpse; there came a roar like the opening of hell in front of him; he was thrown to the deck, half-stunned, and a huge fragment of the rail of the vessel whirled past his head, smashing into a stateroom behind him.

The ship was in an uproar; people rushing here and there, the members of the crew leaping to get away the boats. Jimmie sat up and stared about him, and the first thing he saw was his friend the "wobbly," lying in a pool of blood, with a great gash in his head.

Suddenly somebody began to sing: "Oh, say, can you see by the dawn's early light——" Jimmie had always hated that song, because jingoes and patrioteers used it as an excuse to bully and humiliate radicals who did not jump to their feet with sufficient alacrity. But now it was wonderful to see the effect of the song; everybody joined, and the soldier-boys and workingmen and nurses and lady ambulance-drivers, no matter how badly scared, recalled that they were part of an army on the way to war. Some helped the crews to get the boats into the water; others bound up the wounds of the injured, and carried them across the rapidly slanting decks.

The great ship was going down. It was horrible to realise—this mighty structure, this home for two weeks of several thousand people, this moving hotel with its sleeping-berths, its dining-saloons, its kitchens with lunch ready to be eaten, its mighty engines and its cargo of every kind of necessity and comfort for an army—all was about to plunge to the bottom of the sea! Jimmie Higgins had read about the torpedoing of scores of ocean-liners, but in all that reading he had learned less about the matter than he learned in a few minutes while he clung half-dazed to a stay-rope, and watched the life-boats swing out over the sides and disappear.

V

"Women first!" was the cry; but the women would not go until the wounded had been taken, and this occasioned delay. Jimmie helped to get his friend the "wobbly," and passed him on to be lowered with a rope. By that time the deck had got such a slant that it was hard to walk on it; the bow was settling, and the stern rearing up in the air. Never could you have realised the size of an ocean-liner, until you saw it rear itself up like a monstrous mountain, preparatory to plunging beneath the waves! "Jump for it!" shouted voices. "They'll pick you up from the other vessels. Jump and swim."

So Jimmie rushed to the rail. He saw a life-boat below, trying to push away, and being beaten against the vessel by the heavy waves. He heard a horrible scream, and saw a man slip between the boat and the side of the liner. People on every side of him were jumping—so many that he could not find a clear spot in the water. But at last he saw one, and climbed upon the rail and took the plunge.

He struck the icy water and sank, and a wave rolled over him. He came up quickly, owing to his life-preserver, and gasped for breath, and was choked by another rushing wave and then pounded on the head by an oar in the hands of a struggling sailor. He managed to get out of the way, and struck out to get clear of the vessel. He knew how to do this, thanks to many "swimmin'-holes"—including the one he had visited with the Candidate. But he had never before swam in such deadly cold as this; it was colder than he had dreamed when he had talked about it with Comrade Meissner! Its icy hand seemed to smite him, to smite the life out of him; he struggled desperately, as one struggles against suffocation.

The waves beat him here and there; and then suddenly he was seized as if by the falls of Niagara, drawn along and drawn under—down, down. He thought it was the end, and when again he bobbed up to the surface, his breath was all but gone. The great bulk of the vessel was no longer in sight, and Jimmie was struggling in a whirlpool, along with upset boats and oars and deck-chairs and miscellaneous wreckage, and scores of people clinging to such objects, or swimming frantically to reach them.

Jimmie was just about ready to roll over and let his face go under, when suddenly there loomed above him on the top of a wave a boat rowed swiftly by sailors. One in the boat flung a rope to him, and he tried to catch it, but missed; the boat plunged towards him, and an arm reached out, and caught him by the collar. It was a strong and comforting arm, and Jimmie abandoned himself to it, and remembered nothing more for a long time.

VI

When Jimmie opened his eyes again he was in a most extraordinary position. At first he could not make it out, he was only aware of endless bruises and blows, as if some one were shaking him about in a gigantic pepper-cruet. As nature protested desperately against such treatment, Jimmie fought his way back to consciousness, and caught hold of something, in his neighbourhood, which presently turned out to be a brass railing; he struggled to ward off the blows of his tormentors, which turned out to be the aforesaid railing, plus a wall, plus two other men, one on each side of him, the three of them being lashed to the brass railing with ropes. The wall and railing and Jimmie and the other men were behaving in an incredible fashion—swinging down, as if they were plunging into a bottomless abyss, then swinging up, as if they were going to part altogether from this mundane sphere; the total enormous swing, from bottom to top, being mathematically calculated to occupy a period of five and one half seconds of time.

Jimmie discovered before long that there were a whole row of men, lashed fast and subjected to this perplexing form of torture. They made you think of a row of carcasses in a butcher-shop—only, who could picture a butcher-shop whose floor careened to an angle of forty-five degrees in one direction, and then, in a space of precisely five and a half seconds, careened to an angle of forty-five degrees in the opposite direction?

And they kept bringing more carcasses and hanging them in this insane butcher-shop! Two sailors in uniforms would come staggering, carrying a man between them, clinging to the railing, to Jimmie, to the other men, to anything else they could grab. They would make a desperate rush while the swing was right, and get to a new place on the railing, where they would tie the new man with a bit of rope about his waist, and leave him there to be mauled and pounded. One side of the room was lined solid with carcasses, and then the other side, and still they came. This was apparently a dining-saloon, there being a table down the middle, and two rows of chairs; they lashed people into these chairs, they brought others and lashed them to the bottom of the chairs—any old place at all! There were some who thought they could hold on for themselves; but after the sailors were gone they discovered that it took more skill to hold on than they realised, and they would come hurtling across the floor, winding up with a crash on top of some one else.

It was not the first time in Jimmie's life that he had had to scramble for himself in some uncomfortable situation; he got his wits together quickly. He was shivering as if with ague, and he managed to get out of his wet coat. There being a couple of ladies strapped into chairs in front of him, he did not like to go further; but presently came sailors with armfuls of blankets, and made him perform the complicated feat of getting out of his dripping icy uniform and getting the blanket wrapped around his middle, so that the rope would not saw him into halves. Then came a steward with a pot of hot coffee; being marvellously expert at holding this at all angles of the ship, he poured it into cups with little funnels for drinking, and thus got some down Jimmie's throat.

The little machinist felt better after that, and was able to devote attention to the man on his right, who had hit his nose so many times that it was bleeding in a stream, and had been tilted at so many angles that the blood had run into his eyes and made him blind. The man on the other side of him apparently could make no effort at all to keep his face from being pounded, or his feet from being thrown into the pit of Jimmie's stomach; after Jimmie made a number of protests, an officer came along, and put his ear to the man's chest and pronounced him dead. They brought another rope, and lashed him tighter, so that he would behave himself.

For several hours Jimmie clung to that railing. The destroyer would soon be in port, they kept telling him; meantime they brought him hot soup to keep up his strength. Some people fainted, but there was nothing that could be done for them. The first boat-loads of the rescued had filled up the berths of both officers and crew; the rest must hang on to the railings as best they could. They should be thankful it was decent weather, said one of the sailors; the vessel didn't roll any faster in bad weather, but it rolled much farther in the same time—a distinction which struck Jimmie as over-subtle.

The poor fellow's arms were numb with exhaustion, he had lost hope that anything in the world ever could be still, when the announcement was made that the harbour was in sight, and everybody's troubles would soon be over. And sure enough, the rolling gradually became less. The little vessel still quivered from stem to stern with the movement of her enormous engines, but Jimmie didn't mind that—he was used to machinery; he got himself untied from the railing, and lay down on the floor, right there where he was, and fell asleep. Nor did he open his eyes when they came with a stretcher, and carried him onto a pier and slid him into a motor-truck and whisked him off to a hospital.

CHAPTER XXI

JIMMIE HIGGINS ENTERS SOCIETY

I

WHEN Jimmie took an interest in life again he was lying in a bed: a bed that actually was still, that did not rise with a leaping motion to the ceiling, and then sink like a swift elevator into the basement. Better yet was the fact that this bed had clean sheets, and a lovely angel in spotless white hovering about it. You who read of Jimmie Higgins' adventures have perhaps been blessed with some of the good things of life, and may need to have it explained to you that never before had Jimmie known what it was to sleep between sheets—to say nothing of clean sheets; never had he known what it was to sleep in a night-gown; never had he had hot broth fetched to him by a snow-white angel with a bright smile and an aureole of golden-brown hair! This marvellous creature waited on his slightest nod, and when she was not busy running errands for him, she sat by his bedside and chatted, asking him all sorts of questions about himself and his life. She thought he was a soldier, and he, shameless wretch, discovered what she thought, and delayed to tell her that he was a common repairer of motor-cycles!

This was a war-hospital, and there were terrible sights to be seen here, terrible sounds to be heard; but Jimmie for a long time missed them almost entirely—he was so comfortable! He lay like a nice dozy cat; he ate good things and drank good things, and then he fell asleep, and then he opened his eyes in the sunshine of a golden brown aureole. It was only gradually that he realised that somewhere in the ward a man was choking and gasping all night, because the inside of his lungs had been partly eaten out with poisonous acids.

Jimmie inquired and was told that more than a hundred people on the transport had lost their lives, including several women; the nurse brought a paper with a list of the casualties, among which he read the name of Mike Angoni—his friend the "wobbly" from the far West! Also the name of Peter Toms—the seaman from Cornwall, caught at the eighth attempt! Jimmie read that the submarine which had sunk the transport had been shattered by a depth-charge, and the sea all strewn with the wreckage of it; and strange and terrible as it might seem, Jimmie, the pacifist, the Socialist, experienced a thrill of satisfaction! Not once did he stop to reflect that on board this underwater craft might have been some German comrade, some poor, enslaved, unhappy internationalist like himself! Jimmie wanted the sneaking, treacherous terrors of the sea exterminated, regardless of everything!

The nurse with the halo of golden-brown hair got interested in her American patient, and would sit and talk with him every chance she got. She learned about Eleeza Betooser and the babies who had been blown to pieces in the explosion. Also she learned about Jimmie's being a Socialist, and asked him questions about it. Wasn't he just a little hard on the leisure classes? Might it not be that some of the capitalists would be as glad as he to know about a better social system? The young lady pronounced the word "capitalists" with the accent on the "it," which puzzled Jimmie for a time; also she assured him that "wage shedules" would never go back to what they were before the war, and Jimmie had to ask what a "shedule" might be. He did not have to ask what she meant by a "tart," because there it was on his tray—a delicious little strawberry pie.

II

This meant that the destroyer had come to an English port; the nurse was a Britisher. If Jimmie had had tact, he would have remembered that Britishers have an outfit of earls and dukes and lords and things, to which they are sentimentally attached. But tact is not the leading virtue of Socialists; in fact Jimmie made a boast of scorning it—if people asked his opinion, he "gave it to 'em straight." So now he caused this white angel to understand that he regarded the effete aristocracies of the old world with abysmal contempt; he meant to put them out of business right off the bat. In vain the white angel pleaded that some of them might be useful people, or at any rate well-meaning; Jimmie pronounced them a bunch of parasites and grafters; the thing to do was to make a clean sweep of them.

"You won't cut off their heads?" pleaded the nurse. "Surely they ought to have a chance to reform!"

"Oh, sure!" answered Jimmie. "All I mean is, everybody's got to go to work—the dooks an' aristercrats like the rest."

The nurse went off, carrying Jimmie's chamber to be emptied; and while she was gone, the man in the next bed, a gun-pointer from an American destroyer with his head bandaged up so that he looked like a Hindoo swami, turned his tired eyes upon Jimmie and drawled: "Say, you guy, you better can that line o' talk!"

"Whaddyer mean?" demanded Jimmie, scenting controversy with some militarist.

"I mean that there young lady belongs to the nobility herself."

"Go on!" said Jimmie.

"Straight!" said the other. "Her father's the earl of Skyeterrier, or some such damn place."

"Aw, cut it out!" growled the little machinist—for you never knew in dealing with these soldier boys whether you were being "kidded" or not.

"Did you ask her name?"

"She told me it was Miss Clendenning."

"Well, you ask her if she ain't the Honourable Beatrice Clendenning, and see what she says."

But Jimmie could not get up the nerve to ask. When the young lady came back, carrying his chamber washed clean, her pet patient was lying still, but so red in the face that she suspected that he had been trying to get out of bed without permission.

III

Nor was that the end of wonders. Next day there ran a murmur of excitement through the ward, and everything was cleaned up fresh, though there was really nothing that needed cleaning. Flowers were brought in, and each nurse had a flower pinned on her waist. When Jimmie asked what was "up," the

Honourable Beatrice looked at him with a quizzical smile. "We're going to have some distinguished visitors," she said. "But you won't be interested—a class-conscious proletarian like you."

And she would not tell him; but when she went out, the fellow in the next bed told. "It's the king and queen that's comin'," said the gun-pointer.

"Aw, ferget it!" said Jimmie—quite sure he was being "kidded" this time.

"Comin' to see the submarine victims," said the gun-pointer. "You cut out your Socialist rough stuff for to-day."

Jimmie asked the nurse when she came back; and sure enough, it was true—the king and queen were to visit the hospital, and pay their respects to the victims of the U-boat. But that wouldn't interest Jimmie Higgins. Would he not rather be carried away and put in a private room somewhere, so that his revolutionary eyes would not be offended? Or would he stay, and make a soap-boxer of His Majesty?

"Sure, he won't have no time to talk to a feller like me!" said Jimmie.

"Don't you be too sure," replied the other. "He's got nothing to do but talk, you know!"

Jimmie didn't venture any farther, because he knew that the Honourable Beatrice was laughing at him, and he had never been laughed at by a woman before, and didn't know quite how to take it. He could not have been expected to understand that the Honourable Beatrice was a suffragette, and laughed at all men on general principles. Jimmie lay quietly in his bed and concealed the unworthy excitement in his soul. Wasn't that the devil now? Him, a little runt of a workingman from nowhere in particular, that had been brought up on a charity-farm, and spent a good part of his life on the bum—him to be meeting the king of England! Jimmie had a way of disposing of kings that was complete and final; he called them "kinks," and when he had called them that he had settled them, wiped them clean out. "None o' them kinks fer me!" he had said to the Honourable Beatrice.

But now a "kink" was coming to the hospital! And what was Jimmie going to do? How the devil did you talk to 'em? Did you have to say, "Your Majesty"? Jimmie gripped his hands under the bed-covers, "I'll be damned if I do!" He summoned his revolutionary fervour, he called up the spirits of his "wobbly" friends, "Wild Bill" and "Strawberry" Curran and "Flathead Joe" and "Chuck" Peterson. What would they do under these circumstances? What would the Candidate do? Somehow, Jimmie's revolutionary education had been neglected—nothing had ever been said in any Socialist local as to how a comrade should behave when a "kink" came to visit him!

Jimmy was naturally a kindly human being; he was ready to respond to the kindness of other human beings. But was it in accord with revolutionary ethics to be polite to a "kink"? Was it not his duty to do something to show his contempt for "kinks"? Maybe his Royal Nibs never had anybody to "stand up to him" in all his life before. Well, let him have it to-day!

IV

A nurse rushed into the ward in great excitement, and whispered, "They're coming!" And after that the nurses all stood round, twisting their hands together nervously, and the patients lay with their eyes glued on the door where the apparition was to appear.

At last there came in sight a man dressed in uniform, who Jimmie would never have dreamed could be a king—except that he had seen his picture in the illustrated papers. He was a medium-sized, rather stoop-shouldered little gentleman, decidedly commonplace-looking, with a closely trimmed brown beard turning grey, and rosy cheeks such as all Englishmen have. He was escorted by the head of the hospital-staff; and behind him came a lady, a severe-looking lady dressed in black, with a couple more doctors escorting her, and behind them several officers in uniform.

The king and queen stopped at the head of the room, and looked down the rows of beds. Each of them wore a friendly smile, and nodded, and said, "How do you do?" And of course everybody smiled back, and the nurses curtsied and said, "How do you do, Your Majesties?" And then His Majesty said, "I hope everybody is doing well?" And the doctor called the head nurse in charge of the ward, who came up smiling and bowing, and answered that everybody was doing beautifully, thank you; at which both His Majesty and Her Majesty declared that they were *so* pleased. The queen looked about, and seeing a man with many bandages, went to him and sat by his bedside and began to ask him questions; the king moved down the centre of the room, until suddenly his eye happened on the Honourable Beatrice.

She had not moved; she stood at her place like the other nurses. But Jimmie, watching, saw a smile come upon the king's face, and he moved towards her, saying, "Oh! How do you do?" The young lady went to meet him, quite as if she were used to meeting kings every day.

"How are your patients doing?" inquired His Majesty.

"Beautifully," said she; and His Majesty said that he was pleased—just as if he had not said the same words only a minute before. He looked at the patients with benevolent but tired-looking eyes; and the Honourable Beatrice, by those subtle methods known to women, brought it about that he looked especially at her favourite. She knew that he would wish to talk to some of the patients, and by ever so slight a movement she brought it about that it was towards Jimmie Higgins he advanced.

"What is your name?" he asked, and then, "Well, Higgins, how are you feeling?"

"Sure, I'm all right," said Jimmie sturdily; "I wanner get up, only she won't let me."

"Well," said His Majesty, "the time was when the king was the tyrant, but now it's the nurse." He smiled at the Honourable lady. "Are you an American soldier?"

"Naw," replied Jimmie, "I'm only a machinist."

"This is a war of machines," replied His Majesty, graciously.

"I'm a Socialist!" exclaimed Jimmie, right off the bat.

"Indeed!" said His Majesty.

"You bet!" was the reply.

"But you're not one of those Socialists who oppose their country, I see."

"I done it for a long time," said Jimmie. "I didn't see we had no business in this here war. But I been changin'—a bit."

"I'm glad to hear that," remarked His Majesty. "Doubtless your recent experience has helped you to change."

"Sure," replied Jimmie. "But I'm still a Socialist, don't you make no mistake about that, Mr. King."

"I won't," said His Majesty; and he looked at the Honourable Beatrice, and between them there flashed one of those subtle messages which highly sophisticated people know how to give and to catch—entirely over the heads of Socialist machinists from Leesville, U. S. A. To the Honourable Beatrice the message conveyed, "How perfectly delicious!" To His Majesty it conveyed, "I knew you'd enjoy it!"

Jimmie's mind was of course occupied entirely with the idea of propaganda. He must make the most of this strange opportunity! "Things is goin' to be changed after this here war!" said he. "Fer the workin' people, I mean."

"They'll be changed for all of us," said His Majesty. "The dullest of us know that."

"The workin' people got to get what they earn!" persisted Jimmie. "Why, Mr. King—back home where I come from a feller could work twelve hours a day all his life, an' not have enough saved up to bury himself with. An' they say it was worse here in England."

"We have had terrible poverty," admitted His Majesty. "We shall have to find some way of getting rid of it."

"There ain't no way but Socialism!" cried Jimmie. "Look into it, an' you'll see! We gotter get rid o' the profit-system. The feller that does the work has gotter get what he produces."

"Well," said His Majesty, "you'll agree with me this far at least—we must beat the Germans first." And then he turned to the Honourable Beatrice. "We shall learn much from our American visitors," he said, and flashed her another of those subtle messages, which indicated that perhaps it was not a good thing for patients in hospitals to become excited over Socialist propaganda! So the Honourable Beatrice turned to the man in the other bed, and His Majesty turned also; he ascertained that the man's name was Deakin, and that he came from Cape Cod. His Majesty remarked how badly England needed good Yankee gun-pointers, and how grateful he was to those who came to help the British navy. Jimmie listened, just a tiny bit jealous —not for himself, of course, but because he knew that Socialism was so much more important than gun-pointing!

V

At the foot of the bed there stood a military officer. He had been there for some time, but Jimmie did not notice him till the king arose and moved away. The officer was just the sort of hand-made aristocrat that Jimmie imagined all officers to be; smooth-shaven, except for a little toy moustache, with serene, impassive features, a dapper and immaculate uniform, and a queer little fancy stick in his hand, to show that he never did anything resembling work. He was eyeing the machinist, with what the machinist suspected to be a superior air. "Well, my good man," said he, "you had a talk with the king!"

That seemed obvious enough. "Sure!" said Jimmie.

"Generally," continued the officer, "when one talks with the king, one addresses him as 'Your Majesty'—not as 'Mr. King'."

Jimmie was tired now, and not looking for controversy; so he did not bridle as he might otherwise have done. "Nobody told me," said he.

"Also," continued the other, "one is not supposed to volunteer opinions. One waits for the king to ask a question, and then one answers."

Jimmie's eyes were closed, and he only half opened them as he answered. "They been tellin' me this here is a war for Democracy!" said he.

CHAPTER XXII

JIMMIE HIGGINS WORKS FOR HIS UNCLE

I

THEY gave Jimmie Higgins a couple of days to lie about on the grounds of the hospital, and make the acquaintance and hear the experiences of men who had lost arms and legs in battle, or had been burned by flame-throwers, or ruined for life by poison-gases. Strange as it might seem, Jimmie found among these men not a few with whom he could talk, whose point of view was close to his own. These Britishers had been through the mill; they knew. None of the glory stuff for them! Leave that for the newspaper scribblers, the bloody rascals who stayed at home and beat on tomtoms, driving other men to march in and die. You went and got yourself battered up, ruined for life—and then what would they do for you? It was a hard world to a man who was crippled and helpless. Yes, said Jimmie; the same hard world that it was to a Socialist, a dreamer of justice.

But there was the old dilemma, from which he had never been able to find escape, whether in Leesville, U. S. A., or on the high seas, or here in old England. What were you going to do about the Huns? To hold out your hand to them was like putting it into a tiger's cage. No, by God, you had to fight them, you had to lick them, cost what it might! And the speaker would go on and tell of things he had seen: a Prussian officer who had shot a British surgeon in the back, after this surgeon had bound up his wounds; a commandant of a prison-camp who had withdrawn all medical aid in a typhus-epidemic, and allowed his charges to perish like rats.

So, hell though it was, you had to go through with it; if you were a man, you had to set your teeth and grip your hands and take your share of the horror, whatever it might be. And Jimmie, being something of a little man in his way, would set his teeth and grip his hands and take, in imagination, the share of the particular human wreck who happened to be talking to him. So Jimmie Higgins was battered back and forth, like a tennis-ball between the two forces of Militarism and Revolution.

Just now was another crisis—the Huns had begun a furious drive in Flanders, the third battle of Ypres, and the British were falling back, not in rout, but in retreat which might become rout at any hour. The bulletins came in several times a day, and people on the streets would stop and read them, their faces full of fear. When the wind was right you could hear the guns across the channel; Jimmie would lie at night and listen to the dull, incessant thunder—a terrific, man-made storm, in which showers of steel were raining down upon the heads of soldiers hiding in shell-holes and hastily dug trenches. The war seemed very near indeed when the wind was right!

II

Still, a fellow has to live. Jimmie was in a foreign land for the first time in his life, and when they turned him loose, he and a couple of other American chaps went wandering about the streets, staring at the sights of this town, which had been a small harbour before the war, but now was a vast centre of the world's commerce, one of the routes by which large sections of Britain were moved across the channel every day.

You saw on the streets no men out of uniform, except a few old ones; you saw nobody at all idle, except the young children. The women were driving the trucks, and operating the street-cars, which were called "trams," and the elevators, which were called "lifts." Everybody's face was sober and drawn, but they lightened up when they saw the Americans, who had come so far to help them in their trouble. In the cake-shops, and the queer little "pubs" where rosy-cheeked girls sold very thin beer, they could not be polite enough to the visitors from over-seas; even the haughtiest-looking "bobby" would stop to tell you the way about the streets. "First to the roight, third to the left," he would say, very fast; and when you looked bewildered, he would say it again, as fast as ever.

But they needed motor-cycles so badly in the new American armies that they didn't give Jimmie much time to be a hero; he got his orders, and a new outfit, and bade farewell to the

Honourable Beatrice, promising to write to her now and then, and not to be too hard on the aristocracy. He crossed the channel, alive with boats like the Hudson River with its ferries, and came to another and still bigger port, which the Americans had taken and made over new for the war. Long vistas of docks had been built since the fighting began; Jimmie saw huge cranes that dipped down into the hold of a ship, and pulled out whole locomotives, or maybe half a dozen automobile trucks in one swoop. Behind these docks was a tangle of railroad-yards and tracks, and miles upon miles of sheds, piled to the top with stores of every sort you could imagine. A whole encampment-city covered the surrounding hills, crowned by an old, creaking, moss-grown windmill—the Middle Ages looking in dismay upon these modern times.

Nobody took the trouble to invite Jimmie to inspect these marvels, but he got glimpses here and there, and men with whom he chatted told him more. One man had been directing the unloading of canned tomatoes; for six months he had seen nothing but crates upon crates and car-loads upon car-loads of canned tomatoes, coming into one end of a shed and going out at the other. Somewhere in the higher regions dwelt a marvellous tomato-brain, which knew exactly how many cans a division of dough-boys in a training-camp would consume each day, how many would be needed by patients in hospitals, by lumbermen in French forests, by revellers in Y. M. C. A. huts. Every now and then a ship brought another supply, and the man who told Jimmie about it bossed a gang of negroes who piled the crates on trucks.

And then Jimmie met a Frenchman, who had been a waiter in a Chicago hotel, and now was bossing a gang of wire-haired Korean labourers. Jimmie had thought he knew all the races of the earth in the shops and mills and mines of America; but here he heard of new kinds of men—Annamese and Siamese, Paythans and Sikhs, Madagascans and Abyssinians and Algerians. All the British empire was here, and all the French colonies. There were Portuguese and Brazilians and West Indians, bushmen from Australia and Zulus from South Africa; and these not having proven enough, America was now pouring out the partly melted contents of her pot—Hawaiians and Porto Ricans, Filipinos and "spiggoties," Esquimaux from Alaska, Chinamen from San Francisco, Sioux from Dakota, and plain black plantation niggers from Louisiana and Alabama! Jimmie saw a gang of these latter mending a track which had been blown out of place by a bomb from an aeroplane; their black skins shining with sweat, their white teeth shining with good-nature as they swung their heavy crow-bars, a long row of them moving like a machine, chanting to keep in unison. "Altogether—heave!" the officer would call, and the line would swing into motion——

"Get a *mule*
An' a *jack!*
No *slow,*
No *slack!*
Put the *hump*
In yo' *back*——"

III

For nearly four years Jimmie had been reading about France, and now he was here, and could see the sights with his own eyes. People with wooden shoes, for example! It was worth coming across the seas to see women and kids going clatter, clatter along the cobbled streets. And the funny little railroad-coaches, with rows of doors like rabbit-pens. It was a satisfaction to notice that the train had a real man-sized engine, with U. S. A. painted thereon. Jimmie owned a share in that engine, and experienced socialistic thrills as he rode behind it.

He had got separated from his "unit," thanks to the submarine and the sojourn in the hospital. They had given him a pass, with orders to proceed to a certain town, travelling on a certain train. Now Jimmie sat looking out of the window, as happy as a boy out of school. A beautiful country, the fresh green glory of spring everywhere upon it; broad, straight military highways lined with poplars, and stone houses with queer steep roofs, and old men and women and children toiling in the fields.

Jimmie chattered with the men in the compartment, soldiers and workers, each a cog in the big machine, each bound upon some important errand. Each had news to tell—tales of the fighting, or of the progress of preparation. For more than a year now America had been getting ready, and here, in the most desperate crisis of the war, what was she going to do? Everybody was on tip-toe with excitement, with impatience to get into the scrap, to make good in the work upon which his soul was set. Every man knew that the "dough-boys" would show themselves the masters of "Fritz"; they knew it as religious people know there is a God in Heaven—only, unlike most religious people, they were anxious to get to this heaven and meet this God at the earliest possible moment. Next to Jimmie sat a Wisconsin farmer-boy, German in features, in name, even in accent; yet he was ready to fight the soldiers of the Kaiser—and quite sure he could lick them! Had he not lived since childhood in a free country, and been to an American public-school?

Everybody had funny stories to tell about the adventures of soldiers in a foreign land. The French were all right, of course, especially the girls; but the shop-keepers were frugal, and you had better count your change, and bite the coins they offered you. As for their language—holy smoke! Why did a civilised people want to talk a lingo that made you grunt like a pig—or like a penful of pigs of all sizes? Across the way sat a Chicago street-car conductor with a little lesson-book, and now and then he would read something out loud. *An, in, on, un,* that many different sizes of pigs! When you wanted bread, you asked for a pain, and when you wanted a dish of eggs, you asked for a cat-roof omelette. How was this for a tongue-twister—say five hundred and fifty-five francs in French!

Fortunately, you didn't have to say that many—not on the pay of a dough-boy, put in a plumber from up-state in New York. For his part, he did not bother to grunt—he would make drinking motions or eating motions, and they would bring him things till they found what he wanted. One time he had met a girl that he thought was all right, and he wanted to blow her to a feed, so he drew a picture of a chicken, thinking he would get it roasted. She had chattered away to the waiter, and he had come back with two soft-boiled eggs. That was the French notion of taking a girl out to dinner!

IV

They loaded Jimmie into a motor-lorry and whirled him away. You knew you were going to war then, by heck; there were two almost solid processions of wagons and trucks, loaded with French soldiers and materials going, and damaged French soldiers returning. It was like Broadway at the most crowded hour; only here everything went by in a whirl of dust—you got quick glimpses of drivers with tense faces and blood-shot eyes. Now and then there would be a blockade, and men would swear and fume in mixed languages; staff-cars in an extra hurry would go off the road and bump along across country, while gangs of negro labourers, French colonials, seized the opportunity to fill up the ruts worn in the highway.

They put Jimmie off at a village where his motor-unit was located, in a long shed made of corrugated iron, the sort of shed which the army threw up over night. Here were a score of men working at repairs, and Jimmie stopped for no formalities, but took off his coat and pitched in. There was plenty of work, he could see; the machines came, sometimes whole truck-loads of them, damaged in every way he had ever seen before, and in new ways not dreamed of in Kumme's bicycle-shop—tires torn to shreds by fragments of shrapnel, frames twisted out of shape by explosions, and nasty splotches of blood completing the story.

It was one of the many places where American units had been taken to plug the damaged French lines. There was a reserve battalion nearby, and outside this village a group of men at work, putting up tents for a hospital. Some thirty miles ahead was the front, and you heard the guns off and on, a low sullen roar, punctuated with hammer-strokes of big fellows. Millions of dollars every hour were being blown to nothingness in that fearful inferno; a gigantic meat-mill that was grinding up the bodies of men, and had never ceased day or night for nearly four years. You could be a violent pacifist in sound of those guns, or you could be a violent militarist, but you could not be indifferent to the war, you could not be of two minds about it.

And yet—Jimmie Higgins was of two minds! He wanted to beat back the Huns, who had made all this fearful mess; but also he wanted to beat the profiteers who were making messes at home. It happened that Jimmie had reached the army at a trying moment, when there were no American big guns, and when promises of machine-guns and aeroplanes had failed. There was wild excitement in the home papers, and not a little grumbling in the army. It was graft and politics, men said; and Jimmie caught eagerly at this idea. He pointed out how the profiteers at home were intrenching themselves, making ready to exploit the soldiers returning without jobs. That was a line of talk the men were ready for, and the little machinist rejoiced to see the grim look that come upon their faces. They would attend to it, never fear; and Jimmie would go on to tell them exactly how to attend to it!

V

But that was only now and then, when the wind was the other way, and you did not hear the guns. For the most part Jimmie's thoughts were drawn irresistibly to the front; about him were thousands of other men, all their thoughts at the front, their hands clenched, their teeth set, their beings centred upon the job of holding the Beast at bay. Jimmie saw the grey ambulances come in, and the wounded lifted out on stretchers, their heads bandaged, their bodies covered with sheets, their faces a ghastly waxen colour. He saw the poilus, fresh from the trenches, after God alone knew what siege of terror. They came staggering, bent double under a burden of equipment. The first time Jimmie saw them was a day of ceaseless rain, when the dust ground up by the big lorries was turned into ankle-deep mud; the Frenchmen were plastered with it from head to foot; you saw under their steel helmets only a mud-spattered beard, and the end of a nose, and a pair of deep-sunken eyes. They stopped to rest not far from the place where Jimmie worked; they sank down in the wet, they fell asleep in pools of water, where not even beasts could have slept. You did not have to know any French to understand what these men had been through. Good God! Was that what was going on up there?

Jimmie thanked his stars he was no nearer. But that coward's comfort did not last him long, for Jimmie was not a coward, he was not used to letting other men struggle and suffer for him. His conscience began to gnaw at him. If that was what it cost to beat down the Beast, to make the world safe for democracy, why should he be escaping? Why should he be warm and dry and well fed, while workingmen of France lay out in the trenches in the rain?

Jimmie went back and worked overtime without extra pay—something that old man Granitch had never got out of him, you bet, nor old man Kumme either. For three whole days he stayed a militarist, forgetting his life-long training in rebellion. But then he got into an argument with a red-headed Orangeman in his unit, who expressed the opinion that every Socialist was a traitor at heart, and that after the war the army should be used to make an end of them all. Jimmie in his rage went farther than he really meant, and again got a "calling down" from his superior officer; so for several days his proletarian feelings blazed, he wanted the revolution right away, Huns or no Huns.

VI

But most of the time now the spirit of the herd mastered Jimmie; he wanted what all the men about him wanted—to hold back the Beast from these fair French fields and quaint old villages, and these American hospitals and rest-camps and Y. M. C. A. huts—to say nothing of motor-cycle repair-sheds with Jimmie Higgins in them! And the trouble was that the Beast was not being held back; he was coming nearer and nearer—one bull rush after another! Jimmie's village was near the valley of the Marne, and that was the road to Paris; the Beast wanted to get to Paris, he really expected to get to Paris!

The sound of guns grew louder and louder, and rumour flew wild-eyed and wild-tongued about the country. The traffic in the roads grew denser, but moving more slowly now, for the Germans were shelling the road ahead, and blockades were frequent; one huge missile had fallen into a French artillery-train only a couple of miles away. "They'll be moving us back, if this keeps up," said Jimmie's sergeant; and Jimmie wondered: suppose they didn't move them! Suppose they forgot all about it! Was there any person whose particular duty it was to remember to see that motor-cycle units got moved in the precise nick of time? And what if the Germans were to break through and sweep over all calculations? This was a little more than Jimmie Higgins had bargained for when he entered the recruiting-office in Leesville, U. S. A.!

They gave out gas-masks to every one in Jimmie's unit, and put an alarm-bell in the shed, and made everybody practise putting on the masks in a hurry. Jimmie was so scared that he thought seriously of running away; but—such is the perversity of human nature—what he did was to run in the opposite direction! His officer in command came into the shed and demanded, "Can any of you men ride?" And imagine any fellow who worked at repairing motor-cycles admitting that he couldn't ride! "I can!" said Jimmie. "I can!" said every other workman in the place.

"What is it?" asked Jimmie—always of the forward and pushing sort.

"The French ask for half a dozen men in a rush. They've had several motor-cycle units wiped out or captured."

"Gee!" said Jimmie. "I'll go!"

"And me!" said another. "And me!" "And me!"

"All right," said the officer, and told them off: "You and you and you. And you, Cullen, take command. Report to French headquarters at Chatty Terry. You know where it is!"

"Sure Mike!" said Cullen. "I been there." Jimmie hadn't been to "Chatty Terry," but he knew it was somewheres across the Marne. The officer gave him a map, showing the villages through which he would go. Jimmie and his companions named these villages, using sensible language, without concession to the fool notions of the natives. Wipers, Reems, Verdoon, Devil Wood, Arm-in-tears, Saint Meal—all these Jimmie had heard about; also a place where the Americans had won their first glorious victory a week ago, and which they called, sometimes Cantinny, sometimes Tincanny. And now Jimmie was going to "Chatty Terry," in charge of a red-headed Orangeman who a few days ago had expressed the opinion that all Socialists were traitors and should be shot!

The officer gave them passes, one for each man, in case they got separated, and they started towards the place where the new machines were lined up. On the way Jimmie had a moment of utter panic. What was this he was getting himself in for, idiot that he was? Going up there where the shells were falling, wiping out motor-cycle units! And shells that were full of poison gases, most of them! Of all the fool things he had done in his life, this was the crown and climax! His knees began to shake, he turned sick inside. But then he glanced about, and caught Pat Cullen's menacing blue eye; Jimmie returned the glare, and the spirit of battle flamed up in him, he laid hold of the handles of a motor-cycle and strode towards the door. Was any Irish mick going to catch him in a funk, and "bawl him out" before this crowd, and put the Socialist movement to shame? Not much!

CHAPTER XXIII

JIMMIE HIGGINS MEETS THE HUN

I

THE six motor-cyclists leaped onto their machines and went chugging down the road. Of course they raced one another; all motor-cyclists always race—and here was the best of all possible excuses, the French army in dire need of them, several of its precious cycle-units wiped out or captured! They tore along, dodging in and out between trucks and automobiles, ambulances and artillery caissons, horse-wagons and mule-wagons, achieving again and again those hair's-breadth escapes which are the joy in life of every normal motor-cyclist. Now and then, when things were too slow, they would try a crawl in the ditches, or push their machines over the ploughed fields. So it happened that Jimmie found himself competing with his red-headed Irish enemy; there was a narrow opening between two stalled vehicles, and Jimmie made it by the width of his hand, and vaulted onto his machine and darted away, free and exulting—his own boss! He shoved in the juice and made time, you bet; no "mick" was going to catch up and shout orders at him!

There were long trains of refugees streaming back from the battle-fields; pitiful peasant-people with horse-carts and dog-carts and even wheel-barrows, toothless old men and women trudging alongside, children and babies stuck in amidst bedding and furniture and sauce-pans and bird-cages. This was war, as the common people saw it; but Jimmie could not stop now to think about it—Jimmie was on his way to the front. There were big observation balloons up over his head, looking like huge grey elephants with broad ears; there were aeroplanes whirring about, performing incredible acrobatic feats, and spraying each other with showers of steel; but Jimmie had no time for a single glance at these marvels—Jimmie was on his way to the front!

He swept around a curve, and there directly in front of him was a hole in the middle of the road, as big as if a steam-shovel had been working for a week. Jimmie clapped on the brakes, and swerved side-ways, missing a tree and plunging into a cabbage-patch. He got off and said, Gee! once or twice; and suddenly it was as if he were whacked on the side of the ear with a twelve-inch board—the whole world about him turned into a vast roar of sound, and a mountain of grey smoke leaped into being in front of him. Jimmie stared, and saw out of a little clump of bushes a long black object thrust itself out, like the snout of a gigantic tapir from some prehistoric age. It was a ten-inch gun, coming back from its recoil; and Jimmie, smelling its fumes, struggled back to the road with his machine, before the monster should speak again and stifle him entirely.

There was a frame house in the distance, and in front of it a barnyard, and sheds with thatched roofs. There came a scream, exactly like the siren of Hook and Ladder Company Number One that used to go tearing about the streets in Leesville, U. S. A.; a light flashed in one of the sheds, and everything disappeared in a burst of smoke, which spread itself in the air like a huge duster made from turkey-feathers. There came another shriek, a little nearer, and the ground rose in a huge black mushroom, which boiled and writhed like the clouds of an advancing thunderstorm. Boom! Boom! Two vast, all-pervading roars came to Jimmie's ears; and his knees began to quake. By heck! He was under fire! He looked ahead; there must be Germans just up there! Was a fellow supposed to ride on without knowing?

There was a big battle on, that much was certain; but the uproar was so distributed that one could hardly tell whether it was in front or behind. However, the transport was steadily advancing—horse-wagons, mule-wagons, motor-wagons, all plodding patiently, paying no heed to the shellbursts. And then Jimmie took a look behind, and saw that infernal red-headed Orangeman! He imagined a raucous voice, shouting: "C'mon here! Whatcher waiten' fer?" Jimmie bounced onto his machine and turned her loose!

He came to a place where something had hit a load of ammunition, and there were pieces of a wagon and a driver scattered about; it was a horrible mess, but Jimmie passed it without much emotion—his whole soul was centred on beating

Pat Cullen into "Chatty Terry"! He came to the outskirts of a village, and there was a peasant's cottage with the roof blown off, and a smell fresh out of the infernal regions, and a terrified old woman standing by the road-side with two terrified children clinging to her skirts. Jimmie stopped his machine and shouted: "Chatty Terry?" When the old woman did not answer quickly, he shouted again: "Chatty Terry? Chatty Terry? Don't you understand French? Chatty Terry?" The old woman apparently did not understand French.

He rode up the street of the village, and came to a military policeman directing traffic at a crossing. This fellow understood English, and said: "Chatty Terry? Eet ees taken!" And when Jimmie stood dismayed, wondering what he was to do now, the policeman told him that headquarters had been shifted to this village—it was in the château; he did not say "chatty," so Jimmie did not understand his kind of English. But Jimmie rode as directed, and came to a place with iron gates in front, and a big garden, and a sentry in front, and a bustle of coming and going, so he knew that he had reached his destination, and had beaten his Irish enemy!

II

Jimmie's pass was in duplicate French and English, so the sentry could read it, and signed him to pass in. At the door of the château he showed the paper again, and a French officer in the hall-way espied him, and exclaimed, "A cyclist? Mon dieu!" He half ran Jimmie into another room, where another officer sat at a big table with a chart spread out on it, and innumerable filing cabinets on the walls. "Un courier Americain!" he exclaimed.

"Only one?" asked the officer, in English.

"Five more's comin'," said Jimmie quickly. He hated Pat Cullen like the devil, but he wouldn't have any French officer think that Pat would lie down on his job. "The road's cut up, an' there's lots o' traffic. I come as fast——"

"See!" interrupted the officer—not quite as polite as Frenchmen are supposed to be. "This packet contains maps, which we make from aeroplane-photographs—you comprehend? It is for the artillerist——"

The officer paused for a moment; there came a deafening

crash outside, and the window of the room collapsed, and something grazed Jimmie's face.

"Violà!" remarked the officer. "The enemy draws nearer. Our wires are cut; we send couriers, but they perhaps do not arrive; it needs that we send many—what you say?—duplicates. You comprehend?"

"Sure!" said Jimmie.

"It is most urgent; the battle depends upon it—the war, it may be. You comprehend?"

"Sure!" said Jimmie again.

"You are brave, mon garçon?"

Jimmie did not reply so promptly to that; but the officer was too tactful to wait. Instead he asked, "You know French?" And when Jimmie shook his head: "It needs that you learn. Say this: Botteree Normb Cott. Try it, if it pleases you: Botteree Normb Cott."

Jimmie, stammering like a schoolboy, tried: the officer made him repeat the sounds, assuring him gravely that he need have no doubts whatever; if he would make those precise sounds, any Frenchmen would know what he was looking for. He was to take the main road east from the village and ride till he came to a fork; then he was to bear to the right, and when he came to the edge of a dense wood, he was to take the path to the left, and then say to everybody he met: "Botteree Normb Cott!"

"Is it that you have a weapon?" inquired the officer; and when Jimmie answered no, he pressed a button, and spoke quick words to an orderly, who came running with an automatic revolver and a belt, which Jimmie proceeded to strap upon him, with thrills, half of delighted pride and half of anguished terror. "You will say to the men of the botteree that the Americans come soon to the rescue. You will find them, my brave American?" The officer spoke as if to a son whom he dearly loved; and Jimmie, who had never received an order in that tone of voice, reciprocated the affection, and clenched his hands suddenly and answered, "I'll do my best, sir." He turned to leave the room, when whom should he see coming in—Mike Cullen! Jimmie gave him a wink and a grin, and hustled outside and leaped upon his machine.

III

And now here was the little machinist from Leesville, U. S. A., flying down the battered street of this French village with something like a mid-western cyclone going on in his head. They say that a drowning man remembers everything that ever happened in his life; perhaps that was not true of Jimmie, but certainly he remembered every pacifist argument he had ever heard in his life. For the love of Mike, what was this he had let himself in for? Bound for the spot where the whole German army was trying to break through—upon an errand the most dangerous of any in the war! How in the name of Karl Marx and the whole revolutionary hierarchy had he managed to get himself into such a pickle? He, Jimmie Higgins, Bolshevik and wobbly!

And he was going through with it! He was going to throw his life away—just because he had started—because he had pledged himself—because he was carrying maps which might enable a "botteree" to win the war! Did he really care that much about this infernal capitalist war? So cried out the proletarian demons in the soul of Jimmie Higgins; and meantime the engine hammered and chugged, and a miraculous power in the depths of his subconsciousness moved the handle-bars so that he dodged shell-holes and grazed automobiles.

The air was full of the scream of shells and the clatter of their bursting, an infernal din out of which he could hardly pick individual sounds. The road ahead was less crowded; the vehicles had left it, spreading out to one side or the other. How much farther ahead was that fork? And suppose the Germans had got there, and had captured "Botteree Normb Cott"—was he going to present them with a brand new motor-cycle in addition? There were other "botterees" which he passed; why couldn't he give them the maps? Jimmie rode on, raging inwardly. If he had been a despatch-rider he would have known all about this, but he was only a repair-man, and they had had no business to put such a job off on him!

There were woods about him now, the trees smashed up by shells, and Jimmie considered it the part of prudence to get off his machine and steal forward and peer out to see if there were Germans in the opening beyond. And suddenly his knees gave way, because of the fright he was in, with all this deadly racket.

He became violently sick at his stomach, and began to act as he had acted on the first three days of his ocean passage from New York. At the same time all the other functions of his body began to operate. A group of Frenchmen passing by burst into hilarious laughter; it was ridiculous and humiliating, but Jimmie was powerless to help it—he wasn't cut out for a soldier, he hadn't agreed to be a soldier, they had had no business sending him up here where vast craters of shell-holes were opening in the ground, and whole trees were being lifted out of the earth, and the air was full of a stink which might require a gas-mask or might not—how was poor Jimmie to tell?

IV

He mastered the awful trembling of his knees and the grotesque efforts of his body to get rid of everything inside him, and got on his machine again and stole ahead. He could only go a few rods at a time, because the road was so cut up. Should he leave the machine and run for it? Or should he go back and tell them their infernal maps were all wrong, there was no fork in the road? No—for there at last was the fork, and after Jimmie had ridden and run a hundred yards farther, there was a wheat-field, and a line of woods, and at the edge of it four guns belching flame and smoke and racket. Jimmie stood his machine in a ditch and went tearing across the fields, wild with relief, because he had found his "Botteree Normb Cott," and could hand over his precious packet and get out of this mess as fast as two wheels would take him.

But to his dismay he found that it wasn't the French battery, it was an American battery; the French battery was farther ahead, and a little to the right; the officer gave directions, taking it entirely for granted that Jimmie would go on to his goal.

But then came another officer. "What have you got there?" And when Jimmie answered maps, he demanded them; he seemed as greedy for maps as a child for his gifts on Christmas morning. He ripped open the packet—what is called "cutting red tape" in the army—and spread out the papers and began to call out figures to another officer who sat on a camp-stool at a little folding table, with many sheets of figures in front of him. This officer went on noting down the information—and the men at the guns went on shoving in shells and stepping back while the screaming messengers were hurled upon their way. In the rear were other men, wheeling up ammunition, unloading one of the big camions which Jimmie had been dodging on the roads. It was a regular factory, set up there in the middle of the fields, despatching destruction to the unseen foe.

"We're having the hell of a time," remarked the officer, as he folded up the maps again and handed them to Jimmie. "Our wires have been cut three times in the last half hour, and we have to shoot blind."

"Where are the Germans?" asked Jimmie.

"Somewhere up ahead there."

"Have you seen them?"

"Good Lord, no! We hope to move before they're that near!"

Jimmie felt a bit reassured by the quiet, business-like demeanour of all the men in this death-factory. If they could stand the racket, no doubt he could; only, they were all together, while he had to go off by himself. Jimmie wished he had enlisted in the artillery!

He shoved the maps into the inside pocket of his jacket, and chased back to his machine and set out. He took a side-path as directed, and then a wood-road—and then he got lost. That was all there was to it—he was hopelessly lost! The path didn't behave at all as the one he was looking for. It went through a long stretch of woods with shattered trees lying this way and that; then it crossed a field of grain, and then it plunged down into a ravine, and climbed to the other side, and up a ridge and down again. "Hell!" said Jimmie to himself. And if you could imagine all the noises in all the boiler-factories in America, you would have something less than the racket in that woods through which Jimmie was wandering, saying "Hell!" to himself.

V

He got to the top of the ridge, puffing and panting and dripping perspiration; and there suddenly he jumped from his machine and ran with it behind a tree-trunk and stood anxiously peering out. There were men ahead; and what sort of men? Jimmie tried to remember the pictures of Germans he had seen, and did they look like this? The air was full of smoke, which made it hard to decide; but gradually Jimmie made out one group, dragging a machine-gun on wheels; they placed it behind a ridge of ground, and began to shoot in the direction of Germany. So Jimmie advanced, but with hesitation, not wanting to interfere with the aiming of the gun, which was making a noise like a rivetting machine, only faster and louder. It had a big round cylinder for a barrel, and the men were feeding it long strips of cartridges out of a box, and were so intent on the process that they paid no attention whatever to Jimmie. He stood and stared, spell-bound. For these creatures seemed not men, but hairy monsters out of caves—ragged, plastered with mud, grimed and smoke-blackened, with their faces drawn, their teeth shining like the teeth of angry dogs. Jimmie forgot all about the enemy, he saw only this roaring, flame-vomiting machine, and the men who were a part of it.

Suddenly one of the men leaped up, a little hairier and a little blacker than the rest, and shouted, "Ah derry-air! Ah derry-air!" And the gun stopped roaring and vomiting flame, and the men laid hold and began to tug and strain to draw it back. The leader continued exhorting them; until suddenly an amazing thing happened—right in the midst of his shouting, the whole of his mouth and lower jaw disappeared. You did not see what became of it—it just vanished into nothingness, and there in the place of it was a red cavern, running blood. The man stood with his startled eyes shining white in his black and hairy face, and gurgling noises coming out—as if he thought he was still shouting, or could if he tried harder.

The others paid not the least attention to this episode; they continued tugging at the gun. And would you believe it, the man with no mouth and jaw fell to helping again! The wheels struck a rise in the ground, and he waved his hands in impotent excitement, and then rushed at Jimmie, exposing to the horrified little machinist the full ghastliness of that red cavern running blood.

Jimmie tried his magic formula: "Botteree Normb Cott." But the man waved his hands frantically and grabbed Jimmie by the arm—the very incarnation of that Monster of Militarism which the little machinist had been dodging for four years! He pushed Jimmie towards the gun, and the other men shouted: "Asseestay!" So of course there was nothing for Jimmie to do but lay hold and tug with the rest.

Presently they got the wheels to moving, and rolled the thing up the ridge. A wagon came bumping through the woods, and the men at the gun gave a gasp which was meant to be a cheer, and one of them laid hold of Jimmie again, crying: "Portay! Portay!" He dragged out a heavy box and loaded it into Jimmie's arms, and carried another himself, and so in a few moments the machine-gun was drumming, and Jimmie went on carrying boxes. The men who were driving the wagon leaped upon the horses and drove away; and still Jimmie carried boxes, blindly, desperately. Was it because he was afraid of the little French demon who was shouting at him? No, not exactly, because when he went back with a box he saw the little demon suddenly double up like a jack-knife and fall forward. He did not make a sound, he did not even kick; he lay with his face in the dirt and leaves—and Jimmie ran back for another box.

VI

He did it because he understood that the Germans were coming. He had not seen them; but when the gun fell silent he heard whining sounds in the air, as if from a litter of elephantine puppies. Sometimes the twigs of trees fell on him, the dirt in front of him flew up into his face; and always, of course, everywhere about him was that roar of bursting shells which he had come to accept as a natural part of life. And suddenly another man went down, and another—there were only two left, and one of them signalled to Jimmie what to do, and Jimmie did not say a word, he just went to work and learned to run a machine-gun by the method favoured by modern educators—by doing.

Presently the man who was aiming the gun clapped his hand to his forehead and fell backwards. Jimmie was at his side, and the gun was shooting—so what more natural than for Jimmie to move into position and look along the sights? It was a fact that he had never aimed any sort of gun in his life before; but he was apt with machinery—and disposed to meddle into things, as we know.

Jimmie looked along the sights; and suddenly it seemed as if the line of distant woods leaped into life, the bushes vomiting grey figures which ran forward, and fell down, and then leaped up and ran and fell down again. "Eel vienn!" hissed the man at Jimmie's side. So Jimmie moved the gun here and there, pointing it wherever he saw the grey figures.

Did he kill any Germans? He was never entirely sure in his own mind; always the idea pursued him that maybe he had been making a fool of himself, shooting bullets into the ground or up into the air—and the poilus at his side thinking he must know all about it, because he was one of those wonderful Americans who had come across the seas to save la belle France! The Germans kept falling, but that proved nothing, for that was the method of their advance anyway, and Jimmie had no time to count and see how many fell and how many got up again. All he knew was that they kept coming—more and more of them, and nearer and nearer, and the Frenchmen muttered curses, and the gun hammered and roared, until the barrel grew so hot that it burned. And then suddenly it stopped dead!

"Sockray!" cried the two Frenchmen, and began frantically working to take the gun to pieces; but before they had worked a minute one of them clapped his hand to his side and fell back with a cry, and a second later Jimmie felt a frightful blow on his left arm, and when he tried to lift it and see what was wrong, half of it hung loose, and blood ran out of his sleeve!

VII

That was too much for the remaining Frenchman. He caught Jimmie by the other arm, exclaiming, "Vennay! Vennay!" Apparently that meant to run away; Jimmie didn't want to run away, but the Frenchman chattered so fast, and tugged so hard, and Jimmie was half dazed anyhow with pain, so he let himself be dragged back. And presently they came to a dead soldier lying with a gun by his side, and the Frenchman grabbed the gun and unstrapped the cartridge-belt, and then threw himself down behind a big rock. Jimmie remembered the automatic which he had strapped at his waist; he held it out to the Frenchman, shaking his head and saying, "No savvy! No work!"—as if he thought the Frenchman would understand bad English better than good English! But the Frenchman understood the head-shaking, and showed Jimmie how to move the little catch which released the trigger for firing. With hasty fingers he tore off the sleeve of Jimmie's shirt, and bound up his arm tightly with a bandage from his kit; then he raised up over the rock, and cursed the sockray Bosh and began to fire.

Jimmie got up the nerve to peer out, and there were the grey figures, much nearer now, and he knew they were Germans because they were like the pictures he had seen. They were running at him, firing as they came, and Jimmie fired his revolver, shutting his eyes because he was scared of it. But then, finding that it behaved all right, he fired again, and this time he did not close his eyes, because he saw a big German running straight towards him, the fury of battle in his face. It was plain what this German meant to do—to leap on Jimmie with his sharp bayonet; and somehow Jimmie never once thought of his pacifist arguments—he fired, and saw the German fall, and was murderously glad at the sight.

There were shots from behind him; apparently there had been a lot of Frenchmen hidden in these woods, and the enemy was not finding it easy to advance. Jimmie's companion jumped up and ran again, and Jimmie followed, and a hundred yards or so back they came to a shell-hole with half a dozen poilus in it. Jimmie tumbled in, and the men chattered at him, and gave him more cartridges, so that when the Germans appeared again he did his part. A bullet took a lump of hair off his temple, and shrapnel exploding nearby almost split his ear-drums; but still he went on shooting. His heart was really in the job now, he was going to stop these Bosh or bust. With five Frenchmen, two of them wounded, he held the shell-hole for an hour; one of them ran back and staggered up with a supply of ammunition, and loaded up a rifle for Jimmie, and laid it so that he could manage it with one hand. So Jimmie went on shooting, half-dead, half-blind, half-choked with powder smoke.

The sockray Bosh made another charge, and this was the end, every man in the shell-hole knew. There were literally swarms of the grey figures, their bullets came like a shower of hail. Jimmie decided to wait till the enemy was near enough for him to aim the revolver with effect. He crouched, watching a Frenchman with the life-blood oozing out of a hole in his chest; then he raised up and emptied his automatic, and still there were Germans rushing on.

Jimmie was so very tired now, he really did not care very much what happened; he knelt in the hole, looking up, and suddenly he saw the huge figure of a German looming above him, his rifle poised. Jimmie closed his eyes and waited for the blow, and suddenly the German came down with a crash on top of him.

Jimmie thought for sure he must be dead; he lay wondering, was this immortality? But it did not seem like either heaven or hell as he had imagined them, and gradually he realised that the German was writhing and moaning. Jimmie wriggled from under, and looked up, just in time to see another German loom over the shell-hole, and pitch forward and hit on his face.

It was evident that somebody farther back was attending to these Germans; so Jimmie lay still, with a feeble flicker of hope in his heart. The rattle of shots went on, a battle that lasted ten or fifteen minutes, but Jimmie was too tired to peer out and see how matters were going. Presently he heard some one running up behind him, and he looked around and up, and saw two men jump into the shell-hole. He took one glance, and his heart leaped. The doughboys!

VIII

Yes, sir, there were two doughboys in the shell-hole! Jimmie had seen so many tens of thousands of them that he had no doubt. Compared with the war-battered poilus, they were like soldiers out of a fashion-plate: smooth-shaven, with long chins and thin hips, and a thousand other details which made you realise that home was home, and better than any other place in the world! And oh, the beautiful business-like precision of these fashion-plate soldiers! They never said a word, they never even glanced about; they just threw themselves down at the edge of the shell-hole, and leaned their rifles over and set to work. You didn't need to see—you could tell from the look on these men's faces that they were hitting something!

Presently came two more, leaping in. Without so much as a nod of greeting, they settled down and went to shooting; and when they had used up most of their cartridges, one of them got up and shouted to the rear, and there came a man running with a fresh supply in a big pouch.

Later on came three more with rifles. Apparently there were not so many Germans now, for these newcomers found time for words. "They told us to hold a line back there," said one. "But hell!"

"There's more Huns up ahead," said another. "Let's get 'em."

"Just as well now as later," said a third.

"You stay behind and get that finger tied up," said the first speaker; but the other told him to go and get his own fingers tied up.

Then one of them looked about and spied Jimmie. "Why, here's a Yank!" he cried. "What you doin' here?"

Jimmie answered: "I'm a motor-cycle man, and they sent me with maps for a battery, but I think it's been captured long ago."

"You're wounded," said the other.

"It ain't much," said Jimmie, apologetically. "It was a long time ago anyhow."

"Well, you go back," said the doughboy. "We're here now—it'll be all right." He said it, not boastingly, but as a simple matter of fact. He was a mere boy, a rosy-cheeked kid with a little ugly pug-nose covered with freckles, and a wide, grinning mouth. But to Jimmie he seemed just the loveliest boy that had ever come out of the U. S. A. "Can you walk?" he asked.

"Sure!" said Jimmie.

"And these Frenchies?" The doughboy looked at the others. "You savvy their lingo?" When Jimmie shook his head, he turned to the battle-worn hairy ones. "You fellows go back," he said. "We don't need you now." When they stared uncomprehending, he asked: "Polly voo Francy?"

"We, we!" cried they, in one voice.

"Well then," said the doughboy, "go back! Go home! Toot sweet! Have sleep! Rest! We lick 'em Heinies!" As the poilus did not show much grasp of this kind of "Francy," the doughboy boosted them to their feet, pointed to the rear, patted them on the back, and grinned with his wide mouth. "Good boy! Go home! American! American!"—as if that was enough to make clear that the work of France in this war was done! The poilus looked over the top of the shell-hole, and saw a swarm of those new fashion-plate soldiers, darting forward through the woods, throwing themselves down and shooting at the sockray Bosh. They looked at the rosy-cheeked boy with the grateful faces of dogs, and shouldered their packs and rifles and set out for the rear, helping Jimmie, who suddenly found himself very weak, and with a splitting headache.

IX

These doughboys had a song that Jimmie had heard all the time: "The Yanks are coming!" And now the song needed to be rewritten: "The Yanks are here!" All these woods through which Jimmie had blundered with his motor-cycle were now swarming with nice, new, clean-shaven, freshly-tailored soldier-boys, turned loose to get their first chance at the Hun. Four years they had been reading about him and hating him, a year and a half they had been getting ready to hit him—and now at last they were turned loose and told to go to it! Back on the roads was an endless procession of motor-trucks, with doughboys, and also marines, or "leather-necks," as they were called. They had started at four o'clock that morning, and ridden all day packed in like sardines; and here, a mile or two back in the woods, the trucks had come to a halt, and the sardines had jumped out and gone into this war!

Jimmie did not realise till long afterwards what a world-drama he had been witnessing. For four months the Beast had been driving at Paris; irresistibly, incessantly, eating his way like a forest fire, spreading ever wider and more fearful desolation—this Beast with the Brains of an Engineer! The world had shuddered and held its breath, knowing that if he got to Paris it would mean the end of the war, and of all things that free men value. And now here he made his last supreme rush, and the French lines wavered and cracked and gave way; and so in this desperate crisis they had brought up the truck-loads of doughboys for their first real test against the Beast.

The orders had been to hold at all hazards; but that had not been enough for the doughboys, they and the leather-necks had seized the offensive and sent the Germans reeling back. The very pride of the Prussian army had been worsted by these new troops from overseas, at whom they had mocked, whose very existence they had scouted.

It was a blow from which "Fritz" never recovered; he never gained another foot, and it was the beginning of a retreat that did not stop until it reached the Rhine. And the Yanks had done it—the Yanks, with the help of Jimmie Higgins! For Jimmie had got there first; Jimmie had held the fort while the Yanks were coming! Yes, truly; if he had n't stuck by that machine-gun and helped to work it, if he hadn't hid in that shell-hole, emptying the contents of a rifle and an automatic pistol into the charging Huns, if he hadn't held them up that precious hour—why, they might have swept over this position, and the Yanks might not have had a chance to deploy, and the victory of "Chatty Terry" might not have gone resounding down the ages! The whole course of the world's history might have been different, if one little Socialist machinist from Leesville, U. S. A., had not chanced to be wandering through "Bellow Wood" in search of a fabulous and never-discovered "Botteree Normb Cott!"

CHAPTER XXIV

JIMMIE HIGGINS SEES THE OTHER SIDE

I

BUT these exultations and glory-thoughts were reserved for a later stage of Jimmie Higgins's life. At present he was weak, and his head was splitting, and his left arm burning like fire. And on top of this came a happening so strange that it drove the whole battle from his thoughts. He was walking on a path with his French companions, when one of them noticed a man in a French uniform lying on the ground a little way to one side. He was not a soldier, but a hospital-orderly or stretcher-bearer, as you could tell by the white bandage with a red cross on his arm. He had been shot through the shoulder, and some one had plugged up the wound and left him; so now the French soldiers helped him to his feet and started to lead him back. Jimmie watched them, and when he saw the man's face, the conviction stole over him that he had seen the face before. He had seen it, or one incredibly like it—and under circumstances of intense emotion. The old emotion stirred in the deeps of his subconsciousness, and suddenly it burst to the surface, an explosion of excitement. It could not be! The idea was absurd! But—it must be! It was! The wounded French stretcher-bearer was Lacey Granitch!

The young heir of the Empire Machine Shops might never have known the little Socialist machinist; but recognition was so evident on Jimmie's face, that Lacey was set groping in his own mind. Now and then as the party walked along he stole an uneasy glance at his fellow-countryman; and presently when they struck a road, and sat down to rest and wait for a vehicle of some sort, Lacey put himself beside Jimmie and began: "You're the fellow that was in the house that night, aren't you?"

Jimmie nodded; and the young lord of Leesville looked at him uneasily, looked away, and then looked back. "I've got something I want to ask you," he said.

"What's that?"

"Don't give me away."

"How do you mean?"

"Don't tell who I am. There's no reason why anybody should know. I'm trying to get away from it."

"I see," said Jimmie. "I won't tell."

"You promise?"

"Sure."

Then was a silence. Then suddenly, with no reason that Jimmie could see, the other exclaimed: "You'll tell!"

"But I won't!" protested Jimmie. "What makes you say so?"

"You hate me!"

Jimmie hesitated, as if investigating his own mind. "No," he said, "I don't hate you—not any more."

"God!" exclaimed the other. "You don't need to—I've paid all I owe!"

Jimmie studied his face. Yes, you could see that was true. Not merely was Lacey haggard, his features drawn with the pain he was enduring; there were lines in his face that had not been put there by a few days of battle, nor even by a couple of years of war. He looked twenty years older than the insolent young aristocrat whom Jimmie had seen hurling defiance at the Empire strikers.

His eyes were searching Jimmie's anxiously, pleadingly. "I had to get away," he said. "I couldn't face it—everybody staring at me, grinning at me behind my back! I tried to enlist in the American army, but they wouldn't have me—not to do any sort of work. So I came to France, where they need men badly—they let me carry a stretcher. I've been through it all now—more than a year. I've been wounded twice before, but I can't seem to get killed, no matter where I go. It's the fellows that want to live that get killed—damn it!"

The speaker paused, as if seeing visions of the men whom he had seen die when they wanted to live. When he went on, it was in a voice of humble entreaty. "I've tried to pay for my blunders. All I ask now is to be let alone, and not have everybody gossiping about me. That's fair, isn't it?"

Jimmie answered: "I give you my word—I won't tell a soul about it."

"Thank you," said Lacey; and then, after a moment's pause, "My name is Peterson. Herbert Peterson."

II

A truck came along and gave them a lift to the nearest dressing-station: a couple of tents with big red crosses on them, and a couple more being put up, and motor-cars bringing nurses and supplies, and others with loads of wounded, French and American. Jimmie was so weak now that he hardly cared about anything; he took his place in a row of wounded men, waiting patiently, trying not to make a fuss, because this was war, and the Hun had to be licked, and everybody was doing his best. He lay down on the ground, and shut his eyes; and gradually there came to him a familiar odour. At first he thought it was the product of his imagination—because he had just met Lacey Granitch, and been reminded of the night when he and Lizzie had crouched in the room of the lonely farm-house, and listened to the sounds and smelled the odour through the door. And presently Jimmie heard the very same sounds from the tent—moans and shrieks, babbling as of insane men. How strange that both times when he smelt this odour and heard these cries he should be with the young master of the Empire Shops!

Jimmie's turn came, and they led him into the tent, making short work with him—merely ascertaining that no artery was cut and that he would not bleed to death, and then tagging him for the brigade hospital. They loaded him into a truck with a score of other "sitting cases," including Lacey Granitch, and treated him to a long ride which he did not at all enjoy. At the hospital, which was a big group of tents, now swarming with activity, Jimmie waited his turn again—so many wounds all at once, and so few to tend them!

At last he was led into the operating-place; the first sight that greeted his eyes being a couple of orderlies carrying out a tub filled with sawed off arms and legs and miscellaneous fragments of men. There was a surgeon with a white costume smeared with blood, and a white mask over his face, and several nurses with white masks also. Nobody greeted him, or stopped for preliminaries—they laid him on the operating-table, and covered all but his shattered arm with a rubber sheet, and slit off his bandages, and then a nurse put something over his face and said, "Breathe deeply, please."

It was that ghastly odour again, but overpowering now. Jimmie breathed, and everything began to rock and swim, his head began to roar, worse than when he had fought the machine-gun. He could not stand any more of it; he cried and struggled to get loose, but they had strapped his feet, and some one held his other arm, so his frantic efforts were of no avail.

He began to fall; head over heels he went tumbling, into vast bottomless abysses—down, down, down. He heard a strange voice saying: "Their collars are too tight." The words rang in his ears, they assumed monstrous and overwhelming significance, they became a whole universe by themselves—"Their collars are too tight!" All the rest of creation ceased, the lamp of being went out; there remained only a voice, pronouncing amid whirling infinitics: "Their collars are too tight!"

III

Somewhere in the vast spaces of chaos was a snore. Then, ages afterwards, out of the void there arose a mysterious forgotten effort to get something out of a choking throat. After several such unaccountable manifestations, the feeble flame of consciousness that called itself Jimmie Higgins flickered up, and he realised that it was he who was trying desperately not to be choked. Also he realised that he was become one horrible pain; somebody had driven a nail through his arm, and fastened him tight to the ground by it; also they had blown up his stomach, so that it was threatening to burst, and when he choked, it was an agony. He gasped for help, but no one paid any attention to him; he was all alone in the dungeon-house of pain, buried and forgotten forever.

Gradually he emerged from the misty regions of anæsthesia, and realised that he was on a stretcher, and being carried. He moaned for water, but no one would give it to him. He pleaded that there was something dreadful wrong with him, he was going to burst inside; but they told him that was only ether gas, and not to worry he would soon be all right. They laid him on a cot in a room, one of a long row, and left him to wrestle with the demons all alone. This was war, and a man who had only a shattered arm might count himself among the lucky.

So through a night and a day Jimmie lay and made the best of a bad situation. There were two nurses in this tent, and Jimmie, having nothing to do but watch them, conceived a bitter rage at them both. One was lean and angular and sallow; she went about her duties grimly, with no nonsense, and Jimmie did not realise that she was ready to drop with exhaustion. The other was pretty, with fluffy yellow hair, and was flirting shamelessly with a young doctor. Perhaps Jimmie should have reflected that men were being killed rapidly these days, and it was necessary that some should concern themselves with supplying the future generations; but Jimmie was in no mood to probe the philosophy of flirtation—he remembered the Honourable Beatrice Clendenning, and wished he was back in Merrie England. Also he remembered his pacifist principles, and wished he had kept out of this hellish war!

But his pain became somewhat less, and they loaded him into an ambulance and took him farther back, to a big base hospital. Here, before long, he was able to sit up, and to be wheeled out into the sunshine, and to discover the unguessed raptures of convalescence—the amazing continuous appetite, the amazing continuous supply of good things to eat and drink; the bliss of looking at trees and flowers, and listening to the singing of birds, and telling other people how you rode out on a motor-cycle to look for "Botteree Normb Cott"—what the hell was that, anyhow?—and ran into the whole Hun army, and held it up for a couple of hours, and won the battle of Chatty Terry all alone!

IV

One of the first persons Jimmie saw was Lacey Granitch, and Lacey took him off to a corner of the park and said: "You haven't told any one?"

"No, Mr. Granitch," said Jimmie.

"My name is Peterson," said Lacey.

"Yes, Mr. Peterson," said Jimmie.

It was a strange acquaintance between these two, chosen from the opposite poles of social life, and brought together in the democracy of pain. Jimmie had the young lord of Leesville down, and might have walked on his face; but strange as it might seem, Jimmie took towards him an attitude of timid humility. Jimmie felt that he had betrayed him to a cruel and hideous vengeance; moreover, in spite of all his revolutionary fervours, Jimmie could not forget that he was talking to one of the masters of the world. You might hate with all your soul the prestige and power that went with the Granitch millions, but you couldn't be indifferent to it, you could never feel natural in the presence of it.

As for Lacey, he was no longer the proud, free, rich young aristocrat; he had suffered, and learned respect for his fellowmen, regardless of money. He heard how this little Socialist machinist, whom once he had cursed in a herd of strikers, had ridden into the jaws of death and helped to nail the Beast through the snout! So he wanted to know about him, and these two sat conversing for hours, each of them discovering a new world.

Just now all Europe and America were engaged in furious argument on the subject of the Bolsheviki. Had they betrayed democracy to the Hun, or were they, as they claimed, leading the way for mankind to a newer and broader kind of democracy? Lacey, of course, believed the former—everybody in the American army believed it, and in fact everybody in France, except a few dyed-in-the-wool reds. When Lacey found that Jimmie was one of these reds, he questioned him, and they had it hot and heavy for days. How could men have done what Lenine and Trotzky had done, unless they were paid German agents? So Jimmie had to set forth the theory of internationalism; the Bolsheviki were making propaganda in Germany, they were doing more to break the power of the Kaiser than even the Allied armies. How did Jimmie know that? He didn't know the details, of course, but he knew the soul of internationalism; he could tell what Lenine and Trotzky were doing, because he knew what he would be doing, were he in their place!

They talked on and on, and the young lord of Leesville, who would some day fall heir to an enormous fortune, and had been trained to think of it as his by every right, human and divine, heard a little runt of a machinist from the shops explain how he was going to seize that mass of property—he and the rest of his fellows combined into one big union—and how they were going to run it, not for Lacey's benefit, but for the benefit of all society. Jimmie forgot all respect for persons when he got on this theme; this was his dream, this was the proletariat expropriating the expropriators, and he told about it with shining eyes. In times past the young lord of Leesville would have answered him with insolent serenity, perhaps with a threat of machine-guns; but now he said hesitatingly that it was a large programme, and he feared it couldn't be made to work.

V

He was moved to question Jimmie about his past life, so as to understand how such fanaticism had come to be. So Jimmie told about starvation and neglect, about overwork and unemployment, about strikes and jails and manifold oppressions. The other listened, nodding his head. Yes, of course, that was enough to drive any man to extremes. And then, thinking further, "I wonder," said he, "which of us two got the worse deal from life."

Jimmie was without means of understanding that remark. Lacey had had everything, hadn't he? To which Lacey answered, "I had too much, and you had too little; and which is worse for a man?"

By way of making clear what was in his mind, he told Jimmie a little about his own life. He pictured a big household, with a father beset by business cares, and turning over the managing of his home to employés. "My mother was a fool," said Lacey. "I suppose it sounds bad for a man to say that, but I've known it all my life. Maybe the old man was too busy to look up a woman with sense—or maybe he didn't believe there were any. Anyhow, my mother's idea was to be seen spending more money than any other woman in town; that was her 'position,' and her children were part of the show—we must wear more clothes and bully more servants than anybody else's children. I've thought it all out—I've had lots of opportunity for thinking of late. I can't remember when I didn't hit my nurse in the face if she tried to take away a toy from me. I never had to ask for anything twice—if I did, I went into a tantrum and got it. I learned to smoke and to drink wine, and then came the women—the women finished me, as you know."

He paused; and Jimmie nodded sympathetically, remembering the story of the eight chorus-girls about whom "Wild Bill" had read out in the local.

"It's hell for a boy to have a lot of money," said Lacey, "and to be preyed on by women. You have your human emotions, of course—you're absolutely compelled to believe in some woman; and they're all perfectly cold-blooded—at least the kinds that a rich boy meets. I don't mean only adventuresses—I mean the society-girls, the ones you're supposed to marry. Their damned old harpies of mothers are pushing behind them, of course—laying out everything they own for clothes, and not knowing how they can pay the bills for last season. They set out to catch you, they're mad with the determination, they don't care about reputation, they'll do any damned thing. You take them out in your car, and then they want to get out and pick flowers, and they draw you into the woods, and presently you've got hold of their hands, and then you're hugging and kissing them, and then you go the limit. But then you've got to marry them; and when they find you won't, they have hysterics, and say they're going to shoot their heads off; only they don't shoot their heads off, they kiss you some more, and borrow your diamond scarf-pin and forget to return it."

The young lord of Leesville fell silent. Sombre memories possessed him, and Jimmie, darting a swift glance at him, saw the look of weary age on his face. "I've never talked with anybody about what happened at the end," said he, "and I never mean to; but I'll say this much—the time I loved a married woman was the only honest love I ever had, because she was the only woman who wasn't looking to marry me!"

That was of course too subtle for a man like Jimmie Higgins. But this much the little Socialist got—that the heir of the Granitch fortune had been in truth a miserably unhappy mortal. And this was an extraordinary revelation to Jimmie, who had taken it for granted that the rich were the lucky ones of earth. He had hated them on the supposition that they were without care; they were the Lotus-eaters, of whom the poet wrote that they

"live and lie reclined
On the hills like Gods together, careless of mankind,
For they lie beside their nectar, and the bolts are hurl'd
Far below them in the valleys, and the clouds are lightly curl'd
Round their golden houses, girdled with the gleaming world:

Where they smile in secret, looking over wasted lands,
Blight of famine, plague and earthquake, roaring deeps and fiery sands,
Clanging fights and flaming towns, and sinking ships and praying hands.
But they smile, they find a music centred in a doleful song
Steaming up, a lamentation and an ancient tale of wrong,
Like a tale of little meaning tho' the words are strong;
Chanted from an ill-used race of men that cleave the soil,
Sow the seed, and reap the harvest with enduring toil,
Storing yearly little dues of wheat, and wine and oil.

But now Jimmie had crossed the social chasm, he had seen the other side of the problem of riches and poverty. After that revelation, he would be more merciful in his judgments of his fellow-mortals; he would understand that the system in which we are trapped makes true happiness impossible—for those who have too much as well as for those who have too little.

CHAPTER XXV

JIMMIE HIGGINS ENTERS INTO DANGER

I

WHILE Jimmie wandered through the streets of this French town, letting his broken arm get strong again, the death-grapple of the war continued. In mid-July the Germans made a last desperate lunge at the Marne; they were stopped dead in a couple of days by the French and Americans combined; and then the Allied commander-in-chief struck back, smashing in the side of the German salient, and driving the enemy, still fighting furiously, but moving back from the soil of France. All France caught its breath with excitement, with relief mingled with dread. So many times they had hoped, through these four weary, hideous years, and so many times their hopes had been dashed! But this time there was no mistake—it was really the turning of the tide. The enemy resisted at every step, but he went on moving out of the salient, and the Allies went on lunging—now here, now there, see-sawing back and forth, and keeping their opponents bewildered.

Jimmie read about it in the army paper, the "Stars and Stripes"; and now, for the first time in four years, Jimmie's mind was one mind on the war. Jimmie was on the field of every battle, his teeth set, his hands clenched, his whole soul helping at the job. He had got over the disorders of anæsthesia, and was forgetting the shock of his wound; he had realised that wounds, and even death, were something a man could bear—not cheerfully, of course, not lightly, but you could bear them, if only you knew that the Beast was being put out of business.

In the old days the word German had meant to Jimmie fellows like Meissner and Forster and Schneider; but now it meant a huge grey form looming over the edge of a shell-hole, its face distorted with hate, its bayonet poised to plunge. Perhaps the most vivid impression of Jimmie's whole life was the relief he had felt when he realised that some doughboy had shot a bullet into that looming figure. Let there be more doughboys, more and more, until the last figure had been shot! Jimmie knew, of course, that the policy he had been advocating in America had not tended to that end; if Jimmie in Leesville had had his way, there would have been no doughboys to rescue Jimmie at Chatty Terry! Jimmie was quite clear on that point now, and for the time being the pacifist was dead in him.

He listened to the talk of the men in this hospital. They had all been through the mill, they had got their wounds, light or severe, but it had not broken their spirit—not a bit of it; there was hardly one among them who was not hoping to get cured and to get back into the game before it was over. That was how they took it—a game, the most sensational, the most thrilling that a man would ever play. These boys had been brought up on foot-ball, the principal training and only real interest in life of some hundreds of thousands of young Americans every year. They had brought the spirit and the method of foot-ball with them into the army, and communicated it to those less fortunate millions who had been neither to college nor to high school: the team-work, the speed, the incessant, gruelling drill, the utter, unquestioning loyalty, the persistent searching of eager young minds for new combinations, new tricks; and above all the complete indifference to the possibility of a broken collar-bone or a damaged heart-valve, provided only that the game should be won!

This army was attacking a foe who relied on machine-guns to break formations and give time to withdraw stores and big guns to safety; so the life of young America for the moment had become a study of the arts of rushing machine-guns. Jimmie listened to the conversation of the new men, and saw the technique being worked out before his eyes. Tanks were all right, aeroplanes were all right, when you had them; but mostly you did not have them in time, so the doughboy was learning to take machine-guns with the bayonet. You had a little squad, trained like a foot-ball team, with its own system of signals, its formations worked out by young heads put together at night. It was a costly game—you would be lucky if a third of the players came out alive; but if you could get one man to the machine-gun with a bayonet, you had won the game—because he would take the gun and turn it about on the retreating Germans, and could kill enough of them in a minute to make up for the losses of his squad.

II

Lacey Granitch's shoulder healed, and he went back to his job. He told Jimmie what it had meant to him to meet a Socialist; if he could believe what Jimmie believed, he wouldn't mind living, even with his shame. Jimmie gave him the names of books to read, and Lacey promised to read them; of course Jimmie was proud and happy—seeing a vision of the Empire Machine Shops turned over to the control of the workers, the capitalist system committing hari-kari in one American industry!

Jimmie got a letter from one of the workingmen in the repair station where he had last worked, telling him that the Americans had taken over this sector, and now there was a big shop established, and when was he coming back? But Jimmie was not so eager to come back; working on motorcycles did not seem a thrilling prospect to one who had held up the whole Hun army and won the battle of Chatty Terry. Having proven his mettle as a fighting man, Jimmie wondered if there mightn't be some way for him to get into the real army, and do a real man's work?

He wrote a letter to the officer in command of his motor-unit, telling what had happened to him, and couldn't it be arranged? In reply the officer said that he would have an investigation made, and if Jimmie's story could be verified, he would have honourable mention, and promotion of some sort. And sure enough, a month later, when Jimmie was ready to leave the hospital, came official notice that he was promoted to be a sergeant of motor-transport, and ordered to report to headquarters in a certain harbour on the English channel for assignment. Sergeant Jimmie Higgins!

Jimmie reported, of course, and was put in charge of a dozen cyclists and repair-men, newly arrived on a transport. These men looked up to Jimmie as a veteran and hero, and Jimmie, who had never enjoyed authority in his life before—

except you count Jimmie Junior and the two kids—may have had his head turned just a little bit. But there was real work to be done, and no time for strutting. There was excitement in the air, wild rumour and speculation; this little unit of Jimmie's, composed of specially fit men, was going somewhere on a special errand—an expedition, evidently by sea. Nobody was told where—that wasn't the way in the army; but presently there were issued sheepskin-lined coats and heavy wool-lined boots—in the middle of August! So they knew that they were bound for the far North, and for some time. Could it be a surprise attack in the Baltic? Either that, said the wise-heads, or else Archangel. Jimmie had never heard of this latter place, and had to ask about it. It appeared that the Allies had landed enormous masses of stores at this port in far Northern Russia; and now that the Russians had dropped out of the war, the Germans were threatening to take possession.

Jimmie was thrilled to the soles of his new wool-lined boots. He was going to Russia, going to see the revolution! Jimmie had but a vague idea of world-conditions now, for during the past three or four months he had been reading only official papers, which confined their attention to the job, and carefully omitted mention of difficulties and complications. The people with whom he talked insisted that it was necessary for the Allies to do something to counter the Brest-Litovsk treaty; if the Germans were allowed to take possession of helpless Russia and use it for their purposes, they might hold out for another hundred years. The Russian people themselves must realise this, and welcome Allied help! Jimmie wasn't sure on this latter point, but he remembered the Rabin brothers and their enthusiasm for the Allied cause, so he put his doubts to sleep, and helped get his motor-unit stowed on board a transport.

III

There came a passage across the North Sea and up the coast of Norway; a region of fogs and restless winds, and incessant deadly peril of submarine and mine. There were three transports in the expedition, and a couple of war-ships convoying them, and half a dozen destroyers weaving their foam-patterns in and out. Every day the air grew colder, and the period of daylight shorter; they were entering the Land of the Midnight Sun, but at the time of year when midnight noons were approaching. The men had plenty of time for reading and talk; so Jimmie discussed the war from the Socialist point of view, defending the Russian revolutionists; and so, as usual, he made somebody angry, and got himself and his seditious opinions reported.

Lieutenant Gannet was the name of Jimmie's superior officer. He had been a clerk in a cotton-mill before the war, and had never had the exercise of authority. Now he had to learn suddenly to give orders, and his idea of doing it was to be extremely sharp and imperative. He was a deeply conscientious young man, keen on the war, and willing to face any hardship or peril in fulfilment of his duty; but Jimmie could not have been expected to appreciate that—all Jimmie knew was that his superior had a way of glaring from behind his spectacles, as if he was sure that some one was lying to him.

Lieutenant Gannet didn't ask what Jimmie had said; he told Jimmie what he had said, and informed him that that kind of talk wasn't going on in the army while he was in hearing. Jimmie's business was to keep some motor-cycles in repair, and some cyclists on their job; about other matters let him hold his tongue, and not try to run the affairs of the nation. Jimmie ventured the remark that he had said nothing but what President Wilson was saying all along. To which the lieutenant replied that he was not interested in Sergeant Higgins' opinions of President Wilson's opinions—Sergeant Higgins was to keep his opinions to himself, or he would get into serious trouble. So Jimmie went away, seething with indignation, as much of a rebel as he had ever been in Local Leesville.

What were the rights of a soldier anyway? Was he privileged to discuss political issues, and to agree with the utterances of the President of his country? Might he believe, as the President believed, in a just peace and the right of all peoples to freedom and self-determination, even though many of the officers of the army hated and despised such ideas? Jimmie didn't know, and there was nobody to tell him; but Jimmie knew that he hadn't meant to give up his rights as a citizen when he enlisted to fight for democracy, and if these rights were taken away from him, it would not be without a struggle.

IV

The transports came into the region of ice-bergs, and low-hanging mists, and rocky cliffs covered with snow, and flocks of sea-gulls flying over them. For days and nights on end they steamed in those arctic waters, and came at last into the White Sea, and the harbour of Archangel.

The Allies had been here since the beginning of the war, building docks and sheds and railway yards; but they had never been able to build enough, and the transport department of the corrupt Russian government having gone to pieces, here were mountains of supplies of every sort you could think of for an army, piled high on the shores. At least, that was what Jimmie had been told; he had read in the newspapers that the statement was made officially in answer to questions in the British parliament. Jimmie had understood that he was here to save those mountains of supplies from the Germans, and he was surprised when he looked about the harbour and saw no mountains of any sort.

Back in the interior were vast trackless forests of fir-trees, and moss-covered swamps in which in summer-time a man would sink up to his neck. Now, in September, they were already frozen solid, and you travelled over them with a sledge and a team of reindeer, bundled up in furs and looking, except for the whiskers, like the pictures of Santa Claus you had seen when you were a kid. But most of the traffic of the army was upon the rivers which cut the forests and swamps, and the single railroad, which was being put back into commission.

This country had, of course, no roads on which motor-cycles could be used, even in summer. Jimmie found that his job would be confined to the city and the encampments near about. A few streets would be kept clear of snow, and the little band of messengers would scoot about them, now and then taking a slide into a snow-bank and smashing things up. That would have been all right, and Jimmie would have bossed the job and been happy as he knew how to be—had only his mind been at peace.

For the first few days, of course, he had no time to think, he was as busy as an ant, getting himself and his men ashore, and setting up their benches and tools in an iron shed, with a roaring stove at each end, and heaps of fire-wood which the peasants brought on heavy flat sledges dragged by reindeer. Jimmie and his unit worked, not merely during the hours of daylight, but most of the hours of darkness, not stopping for Sundays. There were five thousand men to be got ashore with their supplies—and in a desperate rush, as if the Germans were expected at any hour. It was some while before Jimmie found time to go about the city, to meet the "Tommies," who had been here a month before him, and to hear what they had done, and what they were expecting to do.

Jimmie had understood that this expedition was to fight the Germans; but now he became suspicious; apparently it was to fight the Bolsheviki! The social revolution had accomplished itself in Archangel, and a council of workingmen and peasants had been in full control, when the British troops and sailors had made a surprise attack and seized the port, driving the revolutionists in confusion before them. Now they were sending an expedition up the railroad, and another on steamers up the North Dwina river, pursuing Russian Socialists and driving them back into frozen swamps! And here were American troops, being hurried ashore, and outfitted and made ready to join in what seemed to Jimmie to be warfare upon organised workingmen!

Jimmie was almost beside himself with bewilderment. It was all so new and strange to him—and he had nobody to advise him. At home, if there were a Socialist problem to settle, he would take it to Meissner or Stankewitz, or Comrade Gerrity the organiser, or Comrade Mabel Smith, the chairman of the Literature Committee. But now, in all this expedition Jimmie did not know a single man who had any idea of radicalism; they looked upon the Bolsheviki as mad dogs, as traitors, criminals, lunatics, any word that seemed worst to you. The Bolsheviki had deserted the cause of the Allies, they had gone into league with Germany to betray democracy; so now the Americans had come to teach them the lesson of law and order. The Americans looked upon themselves as an advance guard of a vast expedition which was to march to Petrograd and Moscow, and wipe the idea of Bolshevism off the map. And Jimmie Higgins was to help! Jimmie Higgins, bound and gagged, lashed to the chariot of Militarism, was to take part in destroying the first proletarian government in history!

The more Jimmie thought of it, the more indignant he became; he took it as a personal outrage—a scurvy trick that had been played upon him. He had swallowed their propaganda, he had filled himself up with their patriotism, he had dropped everything to come and fight for Democracy. He had gone into battle, had risked his life, had suffered wounds and agony for them. And now they had broken their bargain with him, they had brought him here and ordered him to fight working men —just as if he had been a militiaman at home! Democracy indeed! Here they were marching in, glorying in their purpose to conquer the Russian revolutionists!

And Jimmie Higgins, under martial law, must obey and hold his tongue! Jimmie thought of all his friends at home who had denounced the military machine; he thought of Comrade Mary Allen, of Comrade Mabel Smith and Comrade Evelyn Baskerville and Comrade Gerrity; he had rejected their advice, and now, if they could see what he was doing, how they would spurn him! Jimmie writhed at the very thought; nor was he consoled when one of the men in his company gave him an "inside" story of what was happening here—that in order to persuade the British to submit their armies to the control of a French general, and thus to save the situation in France, the Americans had been forced to submit their own armies also; and now they found themselves ordered to march in and fight a revolutionary government which had repudiated its debt to France, and so had given offence to a naturally frugal people.

V

Jimmie met a man whom he might almost have taken for Deror Rabin, so much did he resemble the little Jewish tailor. A big, black-whiskered peasant brought a load of wood for the fires; and there was a Jew helping him—a chap with a sharp face and keen black eyes, his cheeks sunken as if he had not had enough to eat for years, and his chest racked by a cough. He had wrapped his feet and his hands in rags, because he had neither boots nor gloves; but he seemed cheerful, and presently, as he dumped down a load, he nodded and said, "Hello!"

"Hello yourself!" replied Jimmie.

"I speak English," said the fellow.

It didn't surprise Jimmie that anybody should speak English; he was only surprised when they didn't. So he smiled and said, "Sure!"

"I been in America," went on the other. "I vork by sveatshop in Grand Street."

You could see that he preferred gossiping to carrying wood; he stood about and questioned, "Vere you vork in America?" When the peasant grumbled at him in Russian, he went back at his job; but as he went away, he said, "I talk vit you sometime about America." To which, of course, Jimmie answered with a friendly assent.

A couple of hours later, when he went out from his work, he found the little Jew waiting for him in the darkness. "I git lonesome sometime for America," he said; and walked down the street with Jimmie, beating his thin arms to keep warm.

"Why did you come back?" Jimmie inquired.

"I read about revolution. I tink maybe I git rich."

"Huh!" said Jimmie, and grinned. "What did you get?"

"You belong to union in America?" countered the other.

"You bet I do!" said Jimmie.

"Vat sort of union?"

"Machinist's."

"You been on strike, maybe?"

"You bet I have!"

"You got licked, maybe?"

"You bet!"

"You don't never scab, hey?"

"Not much!"

"You vat you call class-conscious?"

"You bet! I'm a Socialist!"

The other turned upon him, his voice trembling with sudden excitement. "You got a red card?"

"You bet!" said Jimmie. "Right inside my coat."

"My God!" cried the other. "A comrade!" He stretched out his hands, which were bundled up with old gunny-sacking, to Jimmie. "Tovarish!" cried he. And standing there in the freezing darkness, these two felt their hearts leap into a hot glow. Here, under the Arctic Circle, in this wilderness of ice and desolation, even here the spirit of international fraternity was working its miracles!

But then, shaking with excitement, the little Jew pawed at

Jimmie with his bundled hands. "If you are Socialist, vy you fight de Russian vorkers?"

"I'm not fighting them!"

"You vear de uniform."

"I'm only a motor-cycle man."

"But you help! You kill de Russian people! You destroy de Soviets! Vy?"

"I didn't know about it," pleaded Jimmie. "I wanted to fight the Kaiser, and they brought me here without telling me."

"Ah! So it iss vit militarism, vit capitalism! Ve are slaves! But ve vill be free! And you vill help, you vill not kill de Russian vorkers!"

"I will not!" cried Jimmie, quickly.

And the little stranger put his arm through Jimmie's. "You come vit me, quick! I show you someting, tovarish!"

VI

They threaded the dark streets till they came to a row of workingmen's hovels, made of logs, the cracks stuffed with mud and straw—places in which an American farmer would not have thought it proper to keep his cattle. "So live de vorkers," said the stranger, and he knocked on the door of one of the hovels. It was unbarred by a woman with several children about her skirts, and the men entered a cabin lighted by a feeble, smoky lamp. There was a huge oven at one side, with a kettle in which cabbage was cooking. The man said nothing to the woman, but signed Jimmie to a seat before the oven, and fixed his sharp black eyes on his face.

"You show me de red card?" he said, suddenly.

Jimmie took off his sheep-skin-lined overcoat, and unbuttoned his sweater underneath, and from an inside pocket of his jacket took out the precious card with the due-stamps initialled by the secretaries of Local Leesville and Local Hopeland and Local Ironton. The stranger studied it, then nodded. "Good! I trust you." As he handed back the card he remarked, "My name is Kalenkin. I am Bolshevik."

Jimmie's heart bounded—though he had guessed as much, of course. "We called our local in Ironton Bolshevik," said he.

"Dey drive us out from here," continued the Jew, "but I

stay behind for propaganda. I look for comrades among de Americans, de British. I say, Do not fight de vorkers, fight de masters, de capitalists. You understand?"

"Sure!" said Jimmie.

"If de masters find me, dey kill me. But I trust you."

"I'll not tell!" said Jimmie, quickly.

"You help me," went on the other. "You go to de American soldiers, you say, De Russian people have been slaves so many years; now dey get free, and you come to kill dem and make dem slaves again! Vy iss it? Vat vill dey say, tovarish?"

Jimmie answered: "They say they want to lick the Kaiser."

"But ve help to lick de Kaiser! Ve fight him!"

"They say you've made peace with him."

"Ve fight vit propaganda—de vay de Kaiser fear most of all. Ve spend millions of rubles, ve print papers, leaflets—you know, comrade, vat Socialists do. Ve send dem into Germany, ve drop dem by aeroplanes, ve have printing-presses in—vat you call it, de Suisse, de Nederland—everyvere. De Germans read, dey tink, dey say, Vy do ve fight for de Kaiser, vy do ve not be free like de Russians? I know it, tovarish, I have talked vit many German soldiers. It goes like a fire in Germany. Maybe it take time—a year—two years—but some day people see, de Bolsheviki vere right, dey know de vorkers, de heart of de vorkers—dey have de life, de fire dat cannot be put out in de heart!"

"Sure," said Jimmie. "But you can't tell things like that to the doughboys."

"My God!" said Kalenkin. "Don't I know? I vas in America! Dey tink dey are de people vat de good God made! Dey know ever'ting—you cannot teach dem. Dey are democracy; dey have no classes; vage-slaves—dat iss just foreign—vat you call it—scum, hey? Dey vill shoot us—I have seen how dey beat de vorkers ven dey strike on Grand Street."

"I've been through it all," said Jimmie. "What can we do?"

"Propaganda!" cried Kalenkin. "For de first time ve have plenty money for propaganda—all de money in Russia for propaganda! Ever'vere in de vorld ve reach de vorkers—ever'vere ve cry to dem: Rise! Rise and break your chains! You tink dey vill not hear us, tovarish! De capitalists know dey vill hear us, dey tremble, so dey send armies to beat us. Dey tink de armies vill obey—alvays—is it not so?"

"They think the Russian people will rise against you."

At which the little man laughed, a wild, hilarious laugh. "Ve have got our own government! For de first time in Russia, de first time in de vorld, de vorkers rule; and dey tink ve rise against ourselves! Dey put up—vat you call it—puppets, vat dey call Socialists, dey make a government here in Archangel, vat dey call Russian! Dey fool demselves, but dey don't fool de Russians!"

"They think this government will spread," said Jimmie.

"It vill spread just so far as de armies go—just so far. But in Russia, all de people come together—all are Bolsheviki, ven dey see de foreign armies coming. And vy, tovarish? Because dey know vat it means ven capitalists come to make new governments for Russia. It means bonds—de French, de British debt! You know?"

"Sure, I know," said Jimmie.

"It is billions, fifteen billions of roubles to France alone. De Bolsheviki have said, Ve do not pay dem so quick. And for vy? Vat did dey do vit dat money! Dey loaned it to de Tsar, and for vat? To make slaves out of de Russian people, to put dem in armies and make dem fight de Japanese, to make police-force and send hundert thousand Russian Socialists to Siberia! Is it not so? And Russian Socialists pay such debts? Not so quick! Ve say, Ve had nothing to do vit such money! You loaned it to de Tsar, now you collect it from de Tsar! But dey say, You must pay! And dey send armies, to take de land of Russia, to take de oil and de coal and de gold. So, tovarish! Dey vill put down de Soviets! But if so, dey must take ever' town, ever' village in Russia—and all de time ve make propaganda vit de soldiers, ve make it vit Frenchmen and Englishmen and Americans, just like ve make it vit Germans!"

VII

The little man had made a long speech, and was exhausted; the coughing seized him, and he pressed his hands to his chest, and his white face flushed red in the firelight. The woman brought him water to drink, and stood by him with a hand on his shoulder; her broad peasant's face, deeply lined with care, quivered at every spasm of the man's. Jimmie quivered too, sitting there watching, and facing in his own soul a mighty destiny. He knew the situation now, he knew his own duty. It was perfectly plain, perfectly simple—his whole life had been one long training for it. Something cried out in him, in the words of another proletarian martyr, Let this cup pass from me! But he stifled the voice of his weakness, and after a while he said, "Tell me what to do, comrade."

Kalenkin asked, "You have made propaganda in America?"

"Sure," said Jimmie. "I went to jail once fer makin' a speech on the street."

And the other went to a corner of the cabin, and dug under half a dozen cabbages, and brought out a packet. It contained leaflets, a couple of hundred perhaps, and the Jew handed one to Jimmie, explaining, "Dey ask me, How shall ve make de Americans understand? I say, Dey must know how ve make propaganda vit de Germans. I say, Print de proclamations vat ve give to de German troops, and make English translation, so de Americans and de Englishmen can read. You tink dat help?

Jimmie took the leaflet and moved the lamp a bit nearer and read:

"Proclamation of the Army Committee of the Russian Twelfth Army (Bolshevik), posted throughout the city of Riga during its evacuation by the Russians:

"German Soldiers!

"The Russian soldiers of the Twelfth Army draw your attention to the fact that you are carrying on a war for autocracy against Revolution, freedom and justice. The victory of Wilhelm will be death to democracy and freedom. We withdraw from Riga, but we know that the forces of the Revolution will ultimately prove themselves more powerful than the force of cannons. We know that in the long run your conscience will overcome everything, and that the German soldiers, with the Russian Revolutionary Army, will march to the victory of freedom. You are at present stronger than we are, but yours is only the victory of brute force. The moral force is on our side. History will tell that the German proletarians went against their revolutionary brothers, and that they forgot international working-class solidarity. This crime you can expiate only by one means. You must understand your own and at the same time the universal interests, and strain all your immense power against imperialism, and go hand in hand with us—toward life and liberty!"

Jimmie looked up.

"Vat you tink of it?" cried Kalenkin, eagerly.

"Fine!" cried Jimmie. "The very thing they need! Nobody can object to that. It's a fact, it's what the Bolsheviki are doing."

The other smiled grimly. "Tovarish, if dey find you vit dat paper, dey shoot you like a dog! Dey shoot us all!"

"But why?"

"Because it is Bolshevik."

Jimmie wanted to say, But it's true! However, he realised how naïve that would sound. So he waited, while Kalenkin went on:

"You show it only to men you can trust. You hide de copies, you take vun and make it dirty, so you say, I find it in de street. See, iss it so de Bolsheviki fight de Kaiser? If it iss so, vy do ve need to fight dem? So you give dese; and some day I come vit someting new."

Jimmie agreed that that was the way to set about it. He folded up a score of the leaflets and stowed them in an inside pocket of his jacket, and put on his heavy overcoat and gloves, which he wished he could give to the sick, half-starved and half-frozen Bolshevik. He patted him reassuringly on the back, and said: "You trust me, comrade; I'll hand them out, and they'll bring results too, I'll bet."

"You don't tell about me!" exclaimed Kalenkin with fierce intensity.

To which Jimmie answered, "Not if they boil me alive!"

CHAPTER XXVI

JIMMIE HIGGINS DISCOVERS HIS SOUL

I

JIMMIE went to supper in the mess-hall; but the piles of steaming hot food choked him—he was thinking of the half-starved little Jew. The thirty pieces of silver in the pocket of his army jacket burned each a separate hole. Like the Judas of old, he wanted to hang himself, and he took a quick method of doing it.

Next to him at the table sat a motor-cyclist who had been a union plumber before the war, and had agreed with Jimmie that workingmen were going to get their jobs back or would make the politicians sweat for it. On the way out from the meal, Jimmie edged this fellow off and remarked, "Say, I've got somethin' interestin'."

Now interesting things were rare here under the Arctic Circle. "What's that?" asked the plumber.

"I was walkin' on the street," said Jimmie, "an' I seen a printed paper in the gutter. It's a copy of the proclamation the Bolsheviki have made to the German soldiers, an' that they're givin' out in the German trenches."

"By heck!" said the plumber. "What's in it?"

"Why, it calls on them to rise against the Kaiser—to do what the Russians have done."

"Can you read German?" asked the other.

"Naw," said Jimmie. "This is in English."

"But what's it doin' in English?"

"I'm sure I dunno."

"What's it doin' in Archangel?"

"Dunno that either."

"Holy Christ!" cried the plumber. "I bet them fellers are trying their stunts on us!"

"I hadn't thought of that," said Jimmie, subtly. "Maybe it's so."

"They won't get very far with the Yanks, I bet," predicted the other.

"No, I suppose not, But anyhow, it's interesting, what they say."

"Lemme see it," said the plumber.

"But say," said Jimmie, "don't you tell nobody. I don't want to get into trouble."

"Mum's the word, old man." And the plumber took the dirty scrap of paper and read. "By God!" said he. "That's kind o' funny."

"How do you mean?"

"Why, that don't sound like them fellers were backing the Kaiser, does it?" And the plumber scratched his head. "Say, that sounds all right to me!"

"Me too!" said Jimmie. "Didn't know they had that much sense."

"It's just what the German people ought to have, by God," said the plumber. "Seems to me we ought to hire fellows to give out things like that."

"I think so too," said Jimmie, enraptured.

The plumber reflected again. "I suppose," said he, "the trouble is they wouldn't give it to the Germans only; they'd want to give it to both sides."

"Exactly!" said Jimmie, enraptured still more.

"And of course that wouldn't do," said the plumber; "that would interfere with discipline." So Jimmie's hopes were dashed.

But the upshot of the interview was that the plumber said he would like to keep the paper and show it to a couple of other fellows. He promised again that he wouldn't mention Jimmie, so Jimmie said all right, and went his way, feeling that one seed was lodged in good soil.

II

The "Y" had come to Archangel, along with the rest of the expedition, and had set up a hut, in which the men played checkers and read, and bought chocolate and cigarettes at prices which they considered too high. Jimmie strolled in, and there was a doughboy with whom he had had some chat on the transport. This doughboy had been a printer at home, and he had agreed with Jimmie that maybe a whole lot of politicians and newspaper editors didn't really understand President Wilson's radical thought, and so far as they did understand it, hated and feared it. This printer was reading one of the popular magazines, full of the intellectual pap which a syndicate of big bankers considered safe for the common people. He looked bored, so Jimmie strolled up and lured him away, and repeated his play-acting as with the plumber—and with the same result.

Then he strolled in to see one of the picture-shows which had been brought along to beguile the long arctic nights for the expedition. The picture showed a million-dollar-a-year girl doll-baby in her habitual rôle, a poor little child-waif dressed in the newest fashion and with a row of ringlets just out of a band-box, sharing those terrible fates which the poor take as an every-day affair, and being rewarded at the end by the love of a rich and noble and devoted youth who solves the social problem by setting her up in a palace. This also had met with the approval of a syndicate of bankers before it reached the common people; and in the very midst of it, while the child-waif with the ringlets was being shown in a "close-up" with large drops of water running down her cheeks, the doughboy in the seat next to Jimmie remarked, "Aw, hell! Why do they keep on giving us this bunk?"

So Jimmie suggested that they "cut it," and they went out, and Jimmie played his little game a third time, and again was asked to leave the leaflet he had picked out of the gutter.

So on for two days, until Jimmie had got rid of the last of the manifestoes which Kalenkin had entrusted to him. And on the evening of the last day, as the subtle propagandist was about to turn into his bunk for the night, there suddenly appeared a sergeant with a file of half a dozen men and announced, "Higgins, you are under arrest."

Jimmie stared at him. "What for?"

"Orders—that's all I know."

"Well, wait——" began Jimmie; but the other said there was no wait about it, and he took Jimmie by the arm, and one of the other men took him by the other arm, and marched him away. A third man slung Jimmie's kit-bag onto his shoulder, while the rest began to search the place, ripping open the mattress and looking for loose boards in the floor.

III

It didn't take Jimmie very long to figure out the situation. By the time he had come into the presence of Lieutenant Gannet, he had made up his mind what had happened, and what he would do about it.

The lieutenant sat at a table, erect and stiff, with a terrible frown behind his glasses. He had his sword on the table and also his automatic—as if he intended to execute Jimmie, and had only to decide which method to use.

"Higgins," he thundered, "where did you get that leaflet?"

"I found it in the gutter."

"You lie!" said the lieutenant.

"No, sir," said Jimmie.

"How many did you find?"

Jimmie had imagined this emergency, and decided to play safe. "Three, sir," said he; and added, "I think."

"You lie!" thundered the lieutenant again.

"No, sir," said Jimmie, meekly.

"Whom did you give them to?"

Jimmie hadn't thought of that question. It stumped him. "I—I'd rather not say," said he.

"I command you to say," said the lieutenant.

"I'm sorry, sir, but I couldn't."

"You'll have to say before you get through," said the other. "You might as well understand that now. You say you found three?"

It might have been four," said Jimmie, playing still safer. "I didn't pay any particular attention to them."

"You sympathise with these doctrines," said the lieutenant. "Do you deny it?"

"Why, no, sir—not exactly. I sympathise with part of them."

"And you found these leaflets in the gutter, and you didn't take the trouble to count whether there were three or four?"

"No, sir."

"There couldn't have been five?"

"I don't know, sir—I don't think so."

"Certainly not six?"

"No, sir," said Jimmie, feeling quite safe now. "I'm sure there weren't six."

So the lieutenant opened a drawer in the table before him, and took out a bunch of the leaflets, folded, wrinkled and dirt-stained, and spread them before Jimmie's eyes, one, two, three, four, five, six, seven. "You lie!" said the lieutenant.

"I was mistaken, sir," said Jimmie.

"Have you searched this man?" the officer demanded of the other soldiers.

"Not yet, sir."

"Do it now."

They made certain that Jimmie had no weapons, and then they made him strip to the skin. They searched everything, even prying loose the soles of his boots; and of course one of the first things they found was the red card in the inside jacket-pocket. "Aha!" cried the lieutenant.

"That's a card of the Socialist party," said Jimmie.

"Don't you know that back home men who carry that card are being sent to jail for twenty years?"

"It ain't fer carryin' the card," said Jimmie, sturdily.

There was a pause, while Jimmie got his clothes on again. "Now, Higgins," said the lieutenant, "you have been caught red-handed in treason against your country and its flag. The penalty is death. There is just one way you can escape—by making a clean breast of everything. Do you understand?"

"Yes, sir."

"Then tell me who gave you those leaflets?"

"I'm sorry, sir, I found them in the gutter."

"You intend to stick to that silly tale?"

"It's the truth, sir."

"You will protect your fellow-conspirators with your life?"

"I have told you all I know, sir."

"All right," said the lieutenant. He took a pair of hand-cuffs from the drawer and saw them put on Jimmie. He picked up his sword and his automatic—and Jimmie, who did not understand military procedure, stared with fright. But the lieutenant was merely intending to strap the weapons onto his belt; then he got into his overcoat and his big fur gloves and his fur hat that covered everything but his eyes and nose, and ordered Jimmie brought along. Outside an automobile was waiting, and the officer and the prisoner and two guards rode to the military jail.

IV

There was terror in the soul of the prisoner, but he did not let anyone see it. And in the same way Lieutenant Gannet did not let anyone see the perplexity that was in *his* soul. He was a military officer, he had his stern military duty to do, and he was doing it; but he had never put anybody in hand-cuffs before, and had never taken anybody to jail before, and he was almost as much upset about it as the prisoner.

The lieutenant had seen the terrible spectacle of Russia collapsing, falling into ruin and humiliation, because of what seemed to him a propaganda of treason which had been carried on in her armies; he realized that these "mad dogs" of Bolsheviki were deliberately conspiring to poison the other armies, to bring the rest of the world into their condition. It seemed to him monstrous that such efforts should be under way in the American army. How far had the thing gone? The lieutenant did not know, and he was terrified, as men always are in the presence of the unknown. It was his plain duty, to which he had sworn himself, to stamp his heel upon the head of this snake; but still he was deeply troubled. This Sergeant Higgins had been promoted for valor in France, and had been, in spite of his reckless tongue, a pretty decent subordinate. And behold, here he was, an active conspirator, a propagandist of sedition, a defiant and insolent traitor!

They came to the jail, which had been constructed by the Tsar for the purpose of holding down the people of the region. It loomed, a gigantic stone bulk in the darkness; and Jimmie, who had preached in Local Leesville that America was worse than Russia, now learned that he had been mistaken—Russia was exactly the same.

They entered through a stone gateway, and a steel door opened before them and clanged behind them. At a desk sat a sergeant, and except that he was British, and that his uniform was brown instead of blue, it might have been Leesville, U. S. A. They took down Jimmie's name and address, and then Lieutenant Gannet asked: "Has Perkins come yet?"

"Not yet, sir," was the reply; but at that moment the front door was opened, and there entered a big man, bundled in an overcoat which made him even bigger. From the first moment, Jimmie watched this man as a fascinated rabbit watches a snake.

The little Socialist had had so much to do with policemen and detectives in his hunted life that he knew in a flash what he was "up against."

V

This Perkins before the war had been an "operative" for a private detective agency—what the workers contemptuously referred to as a "sleuth." The government, having found itself in sudden need of much "sleuthing," had been forced to take what help it could get, without too close scrutiny. So now Perkins was a sergeant in the secret service; and just as the carpenters were hammering nails as at home, and the surgeons were cutting flesh as at home, so Perkins was "sleuthing" as at home.

"Well, sergeant?" said the lieutenant. "What have you got?"

"I think I've got the story, sir."

You could see the relief in Gannet's face; and Jimmie's heart went down into his boots.

"There's just one or two details I want to make sure about," continued Perkins. "I suppose you won't mind if I question this prisoner?"

"Oh, not at all," said the other. He was relieved to be able to turn this difficult matter over to a man of decision, a professional man, who was used to such cases and knew how to handle them.

"I'll report to you at once," said Perkins.

"I'll wait," said the lieutenant.

And Perkins took Jimmie's trembling arm in a grip like a vise, and marched him down a long stone corridor and down a flight of steps. On the way he picked up two other men, also in khaki, who followed him; the four passed through a series of underground passages, and entered a stone cell with a solid steel door, which they clanged behind them—a sound that was like the knell of doom to poor Jimmie's terrified soul. And instantly Sergeant Perkins seized him by the shoulder and whirled him about, and glared into his eyes. "Now, you little son-of-a-bitch!" said he.

Having been a detective in an American city, this man was familiar with the "third degree," whereby prisoners are led to tell what they know, and many things which they don't know, but which they know the police want them to tell. Of the other two men, one, Private Connor, had had this inquisition applied to him on more than one occasion. He was a burglar with a prison-record; but his last arrest had been in a middle Western town for taking part in a bar-room fight, and the judge didn't happen to know his record, and accepted his tearful plea, agreeing to suspend sentence provided the prisoner would enlist to fight for his country.

The other man was named Grady, and had left a wife and three children in a tenement in "Hell's Kitchen," New York, to come to fight the Kaiser. He was a kind-hearted and decent Irishman, who had earned a hard living carrying bricks and mortar up a ladder ten hours a day; but he was absolutely convinced that there existed, somewhere under his feet, a hell of brimstone and sulphur in which he would roast forever if he disobeyed the orders of those who were set in authority over him. Grady knew that there were certain wicked men, hating and slandering religion, and luring millions of souls into hell; they were called Socialists, or Anarchists, and must obviously be emissaries of Satan, so it was God's work to root them out and destroy them. Thus the Gradys have reasoned for a thousand years; and thus in black dungeons underground they have turned the thumb-screws and pulled the levers of the rack. They do it still in many of the large cities of America, where superstition runs the police-force, in combination with liquor interests and public service corporations.

VI

"Now, you little son-of-a-bitch," said Perkins, "listen to me. "I been lookin' into this business of yours, and I got the names of most of them Bolsheviks you been dealing with. But I want to know them all, and I'm going to know—see?"

In spite of all his terror, Jimmie's heart leaped with exultation. Perkins was lying! He hadn't found out a thing! He was just trying to bluff his prisoner, and to make his superior officer think he was a real "sleuth". He was doing what the police everywhere do—trying to obtain by brutality what they cannot obtain by skill and intelligence.

"Now, you're goin' to tell," continued the man. "You may think you can hold out, but you'll find it's no go. I'll tear you limb from limb if you make me—I'll do just whatever I have to do to make you come through. You get me?"

Jimmie nodded his head in a sort of spasm, but his effort to make a sound resulted only in a gulp in his throat.

"You'll only make yourself a lot of pain if you delay, so you'd better be sensible. Now—who are they?"

"They ain't anybody. They——"

"So that's it? Well, we'll see." And the sergeant swung Jimmie about, so as to be at his back. "Hold him," he said, to the two men, and they grasped the prisoner's shoulders; the sergeant grasped his two wrists, which were handcuffed together, and began to force them up Jimmie's back.

"Ow!" cried Jimmie. "Stop! Stop!"

"Will you tell?" said the sergeant.

"Stop!" cried Jimmie, wildly; and as the other pushed harder, he began to scream. "You'll break my arm! The one that was wounded."

"Wounded?" said the sergeant.

"It was broken by a bullet!"

"The hell you say!" said the sergeant.

"It's true—ask anybody! The battle of Chatty Terry in France!"

For just a moment the pressure on Jimmie's arms weakened; but then the sergeant remembered that military men who have a career to make do not go to their superior officers with sentimentalities. "If you were wounded in battle," said the sergeant, "what you turnin' traitor for? Give me the names I want!" And he began to push again.

It was the most horrible agony that Jimmie had ever dreamed of. His voice rose to a shriek: "Wait! Wait! Listen!" The torturer would relax the pressure and say: "The names?" And when Jimmie did not give the names, he would press harder yet. Jimmie writhed convulsively, but the other two men held him as in a vise. He pleaded, he sobbed and moaned; but the walls of this dungeon had been made so that the owners of property outside would not be troubled by knowing what was being done in their interest.

We go into museums and look at devilish instruments which men once employed for the torment of their fellows, and we shudder and congratulate ourselves that we live in more humane days; quite overlooking the fact that it does not need elaborate instruments to inflict pain on the human body. Any man can do it to another, if he has him helpless. The thing that is needed is the motive—that is to say, some form of privilege established by law, and protecting itself against rebellion.

"Tell me the names!" said the sergeant. He had Jimmie's two hands forced up the back of his neck, and was lying over on Jimmie, pushing, pushing. Jimmie was blinded with the pain, his whole being convulsed. It was too horrible, it could not be! Anything, anything to stop it! A voice shrieked in his soul: "Tell! Tell!" But then he thought of the little Jew, pitiful, trusting—no, no, he would not tell! He would never tell! But then what was he to do? Endure this horror? He could not endure it—it was monstrous!

He would writhe and scream, babble and plead and sob. Perhaps there have been men who have endured torture with dignity, but Jimmie was not one of these. Jimmie was abject, Jimmie was frantic; he did anything, everything he could think of—save one thing, the thing that Perkins kept telling him to do.

This went on until the sergeant was out of breath: that being one disadvantage of the primitive hand-processes of torture to which American police-officials have been reduced by political sentimentalism. The torturer lost his temper, and began to shake and twist at Jimmie's arms, so that Connor had to warn him—he didn't want to break anything, of course.

So Perkins said, "Put his head down." They bent Jimmie over till his head was on the ground, and Grady tied Jimmie's legs to keep them quiet, and Connor held his neck fast, and Perkins put his foot on the handcuffs and pressed down. By this means he could continue the torture while standing erect and breathing freely, a great relief to him. "Now, damn you!" said he. "I can stay here all night. Come through!"

VII

Jimmie thought that each moment of pain was the worst. He had never had any idea that pain could endure so long, could burn with such a white and searing flame. He ground his teeth together, he chewed his tongue through, he ground his face upon the stones. Anything for a respite—even a new kind of pain, that he might forget the screaming ache in his shoulders and elbows and wrists. But there was no respite; his spirit was whirled and beaten about in bottomless abysses, and from their depths he heard the voice of Perkins, as from a far-off mountain top: "Come through! Come through—or you'll stay like this all night!"

But Jimmie did not stay like that; for Perkins got tired of standing on one foot, and he knew that the Lieutenant was pacing about upstairs, wondering why it took so long to ask a few questions. Jimmie heard the voice from the far-off mountain-top: "This won't do; we'll have to string him up for a bit." And he took from his pocket a strong cord, and tied one end about Jimmie's two thumbs, and ran the other end over an iron ring in the wall of the dungeon—put there by some agent of the Tsar for use in the cause of democracy. The other two men lifted Jimmie till his feet were off the ground, and then made fast the cord, and Jimmie hung with his full weight from his thumbs, still handcuffed behind his back.

So now he was no trouble to the three jailors—except that he was an ugly-looking object, with his face purple and convulsed, and his bloody tongue being chewed up. They turned him about, with his face against the stones, and then they had nothing but the sounds of him, which had become feebler, but were none the less disagreeable, a babbling and gabbling, continuous and yet unrhythmic, as if made by a whole menagerie of tormented animals.

Still the minutes passed, and Perkins' irritation grew. He wouldn't have minded for himself, for his nerves were strong, he had handled a good many of the I. W. W. in the old days back home; but he had promised to get the information, and so his reputation was at stake. He would prod Jimmie and say: "Will you tell?" And when Jimmie still refused, finally he said, "We'll have to try the water-cure. Connor, get me a couple of pitchers of water and a good sized funnel."

"Yes, sir," said the ex-burglar, and went out; and meantime Perkins addressed his victim again. "Listen, you little hell-pup," said he. "I'm going to do something new, something that'll break you sure. I been with the army in the Philippines, and seen it worked there many's the time, and I never yet seen anybody that could stand it. We're going to fill you up with water; and we'll leave you to soak for a couple of hours, and then we'll put in some more, and we'll keep that up day and night till you come through. Now, you better think it over and speak quick, before we get the water in, because it ain't so easy to get out."

Jimmie lay with his face against the wall, and the agony of his tortured thumbs was like knives twisted into him; he listened to these threats, and heard again the cry in his soul for respite at any hazard.

Jimmie was fighting a battle, the sternest ever fought by man—the battle of conscience against the weakness of the flesh. To tell or not to tell? The poor tormented body shrieked, Tell! But conscience, in a feeble voice, gasped, over and over and over, No! No! No! It had to keep on insisting, because the battle was never over, never won. Each moment was a new agony, and therefore a fresh temptation; each argument had to be repeated without end. Why should he not tell? Because Kalenkin had trusted him, and Kalenkin was a comrade. But maybe Kalenkin was gone now, maybe he had died of one of his coughing spells, maybe he had heard of Jimmie's arrest and made his escape. Maybe they would not torture Kalenkin as they had Jimmie, because he was not a soldier; they might just put him in jail and keep him there, and others would do the work. Maybe——

And so on. But the feeble voice whispered in the soul of Jimmie Higgins: You are the revolution. You are social justice, struggling for life in this world. You are humanity, setting its face to the light, striving to reach a new goal, to put behind it an old horror. You are Jesus on the cross; and if you fail, the world goes back, perhaps forever. You must hold out! You must bear this! And this! And this! You must bear everything—forever—as long as needs be! You must not "come through"!

VIII

Connor came back with his pitchers of water and his funnel. They took Jimmie down—oh, the blessed relief to his thumbs!—and laid him on the ground, with his racked and swollen hands still handcuffed under him; and Grady sat on his feet, and Connor sat on his chest, and Perkins forced the funnel down his throat and poured in the water.

Jimmie had to swallow, of course; he had to gulp desperately, to keep from being choked; and pretty soon the water filled him up, and then began the most fearful agony he had yet endured. It was like the pain of the ether-gas, only infinitely worse. He was blown out like a balloon; his insides were about to burst; his whole body was one sore boil—and Connor, sitting on his stomach, sat a little harder now and then, to make sure the water got jostled into place. Jimmie could not scream, but his face turned purple and the cords stood out on his forehead and neck; he began to strangle, and this was worst of all; every convulsion of his body stabbed him with ten thousand knives.

Jimmie had talked with a number of the "wobblies" who had this "water-cure," a regular device of police-authorities in small towns and villages. It is simple and cheap and cleanly; it leaves no blood and no bruises to be exhibited in court; it muzzles the victim, so that his screams cannot be heard through jail-windows—therefore a simple denial covers it completely. "Wild Bill" had had this treatment, "Strawberry" Curran had had it several times. But oh, thought Jimmie, it could not be like this—no human being had ever endured anything like this! Poor Jimmie was not learned in history, and did not realise that men have endured everything that other men can inflict. They will continue to endure it, so long as privilege is written in the law, and allowed to use the law in its unholy cause.

So the battle of the ages went on in the soul of Jimmie Higgins. He was a little runt of a Socialist machinist, with bad teeth and gnarled hands, and he could do nothing sublime or inspiring, nothing even dignified; in fact, it would be hard for any one to do anything dignified, when he lies on the floor with a gallon or two of water in him, and one man sitting on his legs and another on his stomach, and another jamming a funnel into his mouth. All Jimmie could do was to fight the fearful fight in the deeps of him, and not lose it. "Lift your knee if you are ready to tell," Perkins would say; and Grady would raise up, so that Jimmie could lift his knee if he wanted to; but Jimmie's knee did not lift.

Far down in the deeps of Jimmie Higgins' tormented soul, something strange was happening. Lying there bound and helpless, despairing, writhing with agony, half insane with the terror of it, Jimmie called for help—and help came to him; that help which penetrates all dungeon walls, and cheats all jailors and torturers; that Power which breaks all bars of steel and bars of fear—

"Thou has great allies;
Thy friends are exultations, agonies,
And love, and man's unconquerable mind!"

In the soul of Jimmie Higgins was heard that Voice which speaks above the menaces and commands of tyranny; which says: I am Man, and I prevail. I conquer the flesh, I trample upon the body and rise above it. I defy its imprisonments, its prudences and fears. I am Truth, and will be heard in the world. I am Justice, and will be done in the world. I am Freedom, and I break all laws, I defy all repressions, I exult, I proclaim deliverance!—And because, in every age and in every clime, this holy Power had dwelt in the soul of man, because this mystic Voice has spoken there, humanity has moved out of darkness and savagery, into at least the dream of a decent and happy world.

So Jimmie lay, converting his pain into ecstasy, a dizzy and perilous rapture, close to the border-line of madness; and Sergeant Perkins arose and looked down on him and shook his head. "By God!" said he. "What's in that little hell-pup?" He gave Jimmie a kick in the ribs; and Jimmie's soul took a leap, and went whirling through eternities of anguish.

"By Jesus, I'll make you talk!" cried Perkins, and he began to kick with his heavy boots—until Connor stopped him, knowing that this was not ethical—it would leave marks.

So finally the sergeant said abruptly, "Wait here." And he went upstairs to where Gannet was pacing about.

"Lieutenant," he said, "that fellow's a stubborn case."

"What does he say?"

"I can't get a word out of him. He's a Socialist and a crank, you know, and you'd be surprised how ugly some of them fellows can be. As soon as I get the story complete I'll report to you, but meantime there's no use your waiting here."

So the officer went away, and Perkins went back to the dungeon and gave orders that every two hours some one should come and fill Jimmie up with water, and give him another chance to say "Yes." And Jimmie lay and moaned and wept, all by himself, quivering now and then with the perilous ecstasy, which does not last, but has to be renewed by continuous efforts of the will, as a tired horse has to be driven with spur and whip. Never, never could this battle be truly won! Never could the body be wholly forgotten, its clamorous demands wholly stilled! God comes, but doubt follows closely. What is the use of this fearful sacrifice? What good will it accomplish, who will know about it, who will care? Thus Satan in the soul, and thus the eternal duel between the new thing that man dreams, and the old thing that he has made into law.

CHAPTER XXVII

JIMMIE HIGGINS VOTES FOR DEMOCRACY

I

ANOTHER day had come—though Jimmie did not know it in his dungeon. All he knew was that Sergeant Perkins returned, and stood looking at him, picking his teeth with a quill. This little Bolshevik had stood the water-cure longer than any man whom Perkins had ever known, and he wondered vaguely what sort of damned fool he was, what he thought he was accomplishing, anyhow.

But it was necessary to keep after him, for Perkins knew that his career was at stake. He was supposed to have found out something, and he hadn't! So he ordered Jimmie tied up by the thumbs, the poor thumbs that were swollen to three times their normal size, and nearly black in colour. But now Jimmie's good Mother Nature interfered to stop the proceedings; the pain was so exquisite that Jimmie fainted, and when the sergeant saw that he was being cheated, he cut his victim down and left him lying on the damp stones.

So for three days Jimmie's life consisted of alternating swoons and agony—the regular routine of the "third degree" in the more obstinate cases; and always, in his conscious moments, Jimmie called upon the God in himself, and the God responded with his hosts, and trumpets of triumph echoed in Jimmie's soul, and he did not "come through."

So on the fourth day the three torturers entered the cell, and lifted him to his feet, and carried him up the stone stairs, and wrapped him in a blanket and put him in an automobile.

"Listen now," said Perkins, who sat by his side, "they're going to try you by court-martial. Hear me?"

Jimmie made no response.

"And I'll explain this for your health—if you tell any lies

about what we done to you, I'll take you back to that dungeon and tear you limb from limb. You get me?"

Still Jimmie did not answer—the sullen little devil, thought Perkins. But in Jimmie's soul there was a faint flicker of hope. Might he not make appeal to the higher authorities, and be saved from further torture? Jimmie had believed in his country, and in his country's purpose to defend democracy; he had read the wonderful speeches of President Wilson, and could not bring himself to think that the President would permit any man to be tortured in prison. But alas, it was a long way from the White House to Archangel—and still longer if you measured it through the ramifications of the army machine, a route more thoroughly crisscrossed with red tape than any sector of the Hindenburg line with barbed wire.

Jimmie was taken into a room where seven officers sat at a big table, looking very stern and solemn. Perkins supported him under the arm-pits, thus making it look as if he were walking. He was placed in a chair, and took a glance about—but without seeing much hope in the faces which confronted him.

The president of the court-martial was Major Gaddis, who had been a professor of economics in a great university before the war: that is to say, he had been selected by a syndicate of bankers as a man who believed in a ruling class, and could never by any possibility be brought to believe in anything else. He was a man of strict honour, a very gracious and cultivated gentleman if you happened to belong in his social circle; but he was convinced that the duty of the lower classes was to obey, and that the existence of civilised society depended upon their being made to obey.

Next to him sat Colonel Nye, as different a type as could be imagined. Nye had been a soldier of fortune in Mexico and Central America, and had found prosperity as a captain of one of those condottieri bands which were organised by the big corporations of America before the war, for the purpose of crushing strikes. He had commanded a private army of five thousand men, horse, foot and artillery, known to the public as the Smithers Detective Agency. During a great coal-strike he had been placed by a state government in virtual charge of the militia, and had occupied himself in turning loose machine-guns on tent-colonies filled with women and children. He had been tried by a militia court-martial for murder and acquitted—thus making it impossible for any civilian grand-jury ever to indict him and have him hanged. And now he had been automatically taken from the state militia into the national army, where he made a most efficient officer, with a reputation as a strict disciplinarian.

First Lieutenant Olsen had been a drygoods clerk, who had gone into an officer's training camp. As he hoped to rise in the world, he looked to his superiors always before he expressed an opinion. The same was true of Captain Cushing, who was a good-natured young bank-cashier with a pretty wife who spent his salary a couple of months before he got it. The fifth officer, Lieutenant Gannet, did most of the talking, because he was Jimmie's immediate superior, and had conducted the investigations into the case. He had discussed the matter with Major Prentice, the Judge-Advocate of the court, also with Captain Ardner, the young military lawyer who went through the form of defending Jimmie; the three had agreed that the case was a most serious one. The propaganda of Bolshevism in this Archangel expedition must certainly be nipped in the bud. The charge against Jimmie was insubordination and incitement to mutiny, and the penalty was death.

II

Jimmie sat in his chair, only partly aware of what was going on, because of the agony in his swollen thumbs and his twisted arms. His flicker of hope had died, and he had lost interest in the proceedings—all his energy was needed to endure his pain. He would not tell them where he had got the leaflets, and when they badgered him, he just grunted with pain. He would not talk with Captain Ardner, who tried in vain to persuade him that he was acting in his—the prisoner's—interest. Only twice did Jimmie flare up; the first time when Major Gaddis voiced his indignation that any citizen of the great American democracy should ally himself with these Bolshevik vermin, who were carrying on a reign of terror throughout Russia, burning, slaying, torturing——

"Who talks about torturing?" shrieked Jimmie, half starting from his chair. "Ain't you been torturin' me—regular tearin' me to pieces?"

The court was shocked. "Torturing?" said Captain Cushing.

"Torturin' me for days—a week, maybe, I dunno, in that there dungeon!"

Major Gaddis turned to Sergeant Perkins, who stood behind Jimmie's chair, barely able to withhold his hands from the prisoner. "How about that, sergeant?"

"It is utterly false, sir."

"Look at these thumbs!" cried Jimmie. "They strung me up by them!"

"The prisoner was violent," said Perkins. "He nearly killed Private Connor, one of the guards, so we had to use severe measures."

"It's a lie!" shrieked Jimmie. But they shut him up, and the dignified military machine ground on. Anybody could see that discipline would go to pieces if the word of a jailer did not prevail over that of a prisoner, the word of a loyal and tried subordinate over that of a traitor and conspirator, an avowed sympathiser with the enemy.

Presently the presiding officer inquired if the prisoner was aware that he had incurred the death-penalty. Getting no reply, he went on to inform the prisoner that the court would be apt to inflict this extreme penalty, unless he would reconsider and name his accomplices among the Bolsheviki, so that the army could protect itself against the propaganda of these murderers. So Jimmie flared up again—but not so violently, rather with a touch of fierce irony. "Murderers, you say? Ain't you gettin' ready to murder me?"

"We are enforcing the law," said the court.

"You make what you call law, an' they make what they call law. You kill people that disobey, an' so do they. What's the difference?"

"They are killing all the educated and law-abiding people in Russia," declared Major Gaddis, severely.

"All the rich people, you mean," said Jimmie. "They make the rich obey their laws; they give them a chance, the same as everybody else, then if they don't obey they kill them—just as many as they have to kill to make them obey. An' don't you do the same with the poor people? Ain't I seen you do it, every time there was a strike? Ask Colonel Nye there! Didn't he say: 'To hell with habeas corpus—we'll give them post-mortems'?"

Colonel Nye flushed; he did not know that his fame had

followed him all the way from Colorado to the Arctic Circle. The court made haste to protect him: "We are not conducting a Socialist debate here. It is evident that the prisoner is impenitent and defiant, and that there is no reason for leniency." So the court proceeded to find Jimmie Higgins guilty as charged, and to sentence him to twenty years' military confinement—really quite a mild sentence, considering the circumstances. In New York city at this very time they were trying five Russian Jews, all of them mere children, one a girl, for exactly the same offence as Jimmie had committed—distributing a plea that American troops should cease to kill Russian Socialists; these children received twenty years, and one of them died soon after his arrest—his fellows swore as a result of torture inflicted by Federal secret service agents.

III

So Jimmie was taken back to prison. Major Gaddis, who was really a just man, and made law and order his religion, gave the strictest orders that the prisoner should not again be hung up by the thumbs. It was of course desirable to find out who had printed the Bolshevik leaflets, but in the effort to make the prisoner tell he should receive only the punishments formally approved by the army authorities.

So Jimmie went back to the underground dungeon, and for eight hours every day a chain was fastened about his wrists, and the other end run up into the iron ring, so that his feet barely touched the floor; and there Jimmie hung, and tried out his conscience—this being the test then being undergone by many men at the disciplinary barracks at Fort Leavenworth. Jimmie's conscience really was nothing like as strong as it ought to have been. Jimmie had moods of shameless self-pity, moods of desperate and agonising doubt. He did not mean to let his dungeon-keepers know this, but they listened behind the door through a slot which the Tsar had had contrived for that purpose; it could be closed while the prisoner was screaming under torture, and then opened by the jailer without the prisoner's knowledge.

So Perkins heard Jimmie sobbing and wailing, talking to himself and to other people—to some one called "Strawberry," and to some one else called "Wild Bill," asking them if they had ever suffered anything like this, and was it really worth while, would it help the revolution? Perkins thought he had got some important information here, and took it to Lieutenant Gannet, with the result that inquiry was made through all the American forces for men known as "Strawberry" and "Wild Bill." But these men could not be found; as it happened, "Wild Bill" had taken refuge in a place to which not even the army intelligence service can penetrate, and "Strawberry" Curran was just then being tried with a bunch of other "wobblies" in California and subjected to much the same kind of treatment as Jimmie was receiving in Archangel.

It was a big advantage that Sergeant Perkins had in his struggle with Jimmie, that the pitiful weakness of Jimmie's soul was exposed to him, while the soul of Perkins was hidden from Jimmie. For the truth was that Perkins was suffering from rage, mingled with not a little fear. What the hell was this idea that could keep a little runt of a workingman stronger than all in authority? And how was this idea to be kept from spreading and wrecking the comfortable, well-ordered world in which Perkins expected soon to receive an army commission? The very day after the court-martial, which was supposed to be a profound military secret, the army authorities were astounded to discover, posted in several conspicuous places, a placard in English, reading:

"American soldiers, do you know that an army sergeant is being tortured and has been sentenced to twenty years in a dungeon for having tried to tell you how the Bolsheviki are making propaganda against the German Kaiser?

"Do you know the true reason your armies are here? Are you willing to die to compel the Russian people to accept your ideas of government? Are you willing to have your comrades tortured to keep the facts from you?"

And of course the doughboys who read this placard wanted to know if it told the truth. And quickly word spread that it did. Men who still had copies of the leaflet which Jimmie had distributed now found eager readers for it, and soon all the men knew its contents, and were debating the question of the use of American armies to put down social revolution in a foreign country. These same questions were being asked in the halls of Congress back home. Senators were questioning the right of sending troops into a country against which war had never been declared, and other Senators were demanding that they be immediately withdrawn. And this news also reached the men, and increased the danger. Archangel was not a pleasant place to stay, especially with winter coming on fast; men were disposed to grumble—and now they had a pretext!

IV

The authorities who were handling this army laboured under one grievous handicap, probably never before faced by any army in history. The commander-in-chief of the army, who determined its policies and tried to set its moral tone, kept coming now and then before Congress and making speeches full of incendiary and reckless utterances, calculated to set dangerous thoughts to buzzing in the heads of soldiers, to break down discipline and undermine morale. The President wrote a letter to a political convention in which he declared that the workers of America were living in "economic serfdom"; he declared again and again that every people had a right to determine their own destinies and form of government without outside interference. This while the army was trying to put down those Russians who were in revolt against "economic serfdom" in their own country!

An army, you see, is a machine built to fight; a man who goes into it and takes part in its work, very quickly acquires its tone, which is one of abysmal contempt for all politicians, particularly of the talking and letter-writing variety, the "idealists" and "dreamers" and "theorists," who do not understand that the business of men is to fight battles and win them. All the officers of the old army, the West Pointers, had been bred in the tradition of class-rule, they had in their very bones the idea that they were a special breed, that obedience to them was a law of God; while of the new officers, the overwhelming majority came from the well-to-do, and were not favourable to speech-making and letter-writing about the rights of man. They were without enthusiasm for the idea of having a pacifist secretary of war set over them by the "idealist" commander-in-chief. They did not hesitate to vent their indignation; and when this pacifist secretary gave orders about conscientious objectors which were based upon sentimentalism and theory, the army machine took the liberty of interpreting these orders and trimming the nonsense out of them. And the farther away you got from the office of the pacifist secretary, the more thorough the trimming inevitably became; thus producing the phenomenon which poor Jimmie Higgins found so bewildering—that policies laid down by sincere humanitarians and liberals in Washington were carried out in Archangel by an ex-detective trained in a school of corruption and cruelty.

Jimmie Higgins couldn't understand that here in Archangel were Americans, taking their orders from British and French officers, who wasted no breath on pacifism and sentiment, who had no fool ideals about wars for democracy. Was one obscure little runt of a Socialist machinist to be allowed to block their world-plans? Setting himself up as an authority, presuming to accept literally the messages of his President, in defiance of their authority in Archangel! Allying himself with traitorous and criminal scoundrels, trying to poison the minds of American soldiers and light the flame of mutiny among them! Just as once Jimmie Higgins had found himself in a strategic position where he had held up the whole Hun army and won the battle of Château-Thierry, so now he found himself in a position of equal strategic importance—on the line of communication of the Allied armies attacking Russia, and threatening to cut the line and force the armies into retreat!

V

It became more essential than ever to discover these Bolshevik sympathisers and stamp out their propaganda. As hanging Jimmie up by the wrists had not brought forth the desired information, Jimmie was put in solitary confinement on a diet of bread and water, this being another test of sincerity of conscience. For the conscience a diet of white flour and water may be all right, but Jimmie soon found that it is very bad indeed for the intestinal tract and the blood-stream—being, in truth, far worse than a diet of water alone. The man who lives on white flour and water for a few days suffers either from complete stopping of the bowels, or else from dysentery; his blood becomes clogged with starch poisons, his nerves degenerate, he falls a quick victim to tuberculosis, or pernicious anæmia, or some other disease which will prevent his ever being a sound man again.

Also, Jimmie received the water-treatment, as included in the Fort Leavenworth regimen. It was necessary that all prisoners should be bathed; which was interpreted by some guards to mean that they should have a stream of icy water turned on them, and be forced to stand under it. Because Jimmie's arms were too badly injured for him to scrub himself, Connor seized a rough brush and salt, and rubbed off strips of his skin. When Jimmie wriggled away, they followed him with the hose; when he screamed, they turned it into his mouth and nose; when he fell down, they let the cold water run over him for ten or fifteen minutes.

Jimmie had had a good deal of harsh treatment in the course of his outcast life, but never so closely concentrated in point of time. His spirit remained unbroken, but his body gave way, and then his mind began to give also. He fell victim to delusions; the nightmares which haunted his sleep lay siege to his waking hours also, and he thought he was being tortured at times when he was just hanging by his chains. Until at last Perkins, listening through the door, heard strange cries and grunts, beast-like noises, barkings and growlings. He called Connor and Grady, and the three of them stood listening.

"By God!" said Grady. "He's dippy."

"He's nutty," said Connor.

"He's batty," said Perkins.

But the idea occurred to all of them—perhaps he was shamming! What was easier than for one of those emissaries of Satan to pretend to have a devil inside him? So they waited a bit longer; until Connor, coming to chain Jimmie up, found him gnawing off the ends of his fingers. That was really serious, so they sent for the prison-surgeon, who had to make but a brief inspection to convince himself that Jimmie Higgins was a raving madman. Jimmie fancied himself some kind of fur-bearing animal, and he was in a trap, and was trying to gnaw off his foot so as to escape. He snapped his teeth at every one who came near him; he had to be knocked senseless before a strait-jacket could be got on him.

VI

And so it was that Jimmie Higgins at last made his escape from his tormentors. Jimmie doesn't know anything about the

Russian Jew, Kalenkin, any more; he could not tell the secret if he wanted to, so they have given up testing his conscience, and they treat him kindly, and have succeeded in persuading him that he is out of the trap. Therefore he is a good beast—he crawls about on all-fours, and eats his food out of a tin platter without using his gnawed-off fingers. He still has torturing pains in the arm-joints, but he does not mind them so much, because, being a beast, he suffers only the pain of the moment, he does not know that he is going to suffer to-morrow nor worry about it. He is no longer one of those who "look before and after and pine for what is not." He is a "good doggie," and when you pet him on the head he rubs against you and whines affectionately.

Poor, mad Jimmie Higgins will never again trouble his country; but Jimmie's friends and partisans, who know the story of his experiences, cannot be thus lightly dismissed by society. The the industrial troubles which are threatening the great democracy of the West, there will appear men and women animated by a fierce and blazing bitterness; and the great democracy of the West will marvel at their state of mind, unable to conceive what can have caused it. These rebellious ones will be heard quoting to the great democracy the words of its greatest democrat, spoken in solemn warning during the slaughter and destruction of the civil war:

"If God will that it continue until all the wealth piled by the bondman's two hundred and fifty years of unrequited toil shall be sunk, and until every drop of blood drawn with the last shall be paid by another drawn with the sword, as it was said three thousand years ago, so still it must be said, The judgments of the Lord are true and righteous altogether."